BAY OF SECRETS

Sometimes the past is closer than you think.

Best Wishes

Jane

J.A.NEWMAN

'We leave something of ourselves behind when we leave a place. We stay there, even though we go away. And there are things in us that we can find again only by going back there.'

Amadeo de Prado *Night Train to Lisbon.*

BAY OF SECRETS

Prologue

Cornwall 1958

The child sits watching the scene unfold from the back of her father's Ford Zodiac. Below a sky of the brightest blue, the foamy waves spill diamonds onto the wide-sweeping sands. The rugged green-topped cliffs tower above the beach and her imaginative mind plays with the idea that a giant has bitten huge chunks out of them. As the car makes its way up the hill, through the open window the balmy sea breeze brushes her face and invites her to play in the rock pools and shallows.

They have travelled overnight from south east London – the three children in the back with blankets and pillows and their favourite soft toys, their mother in the passenger seat with a rug over her legs, assisting their father with the AA directions.

Their father yanks on the handbrake outside a whitewashed, three-storey house. 'Well,' he says proudly, 'here we are – our new home.'

This house is much bigger than the one they have left behind. It has no front garden but four stone steps that lead up to a porch, with a dark blue front door, where a sun-parched fishing net and a rusty bucket and spade wait for their long-departed owner to claim them. The other houses in the road are also whitewashed, all different shapes and sizes and bathed in the early morning sunlight. Gulls fly overhead acknowledging the family's arrival.

Their father slams the car door, rubs his hands together and barks his orders. 'Right, come on, let's get unpacked. Many hands make light work.'

But from her last visit the child remembers discovering a narrow rugged path at the end of the road which led past a clump of pine trees, through a series of water channels and down to the beach far below. She's impatient to find it again but she knows she will have to wait.

They all struggle up the four granite steps with bags and boxes, suitcases and toys, and pile them up in the hall. Their mother rummages in a box for the kettle and teapot while their father takes out a handmade sign and nails it to the wooden display board. Standing back to admire his handiwork he calls to his wife. 'What d'you think, love?'

She runs down the steps and slips her arm round his waist; a broad smile lighting her face. 'SEAWINDS. Yes, I like it.'

ONE

From the window of the front room, Jayne watched the waves crash and sigh over the rocks and felt the pull of nostalgia – the happy days of her childhood, her parents' cheery greetings, the house bustling with guests running up and down stairs and the clatter of the cutlery in the dining room. But the men from the clearance company had done their worst and Jayne felt as empty as the house. She should never have let it happen but after her mum's passing she wasn't thinking straight. Now she was here to negotiate the sale of *Seawinds* it felt all wrong, to let another family take over this wonderful old house, to possibly change its character and turn it into a second home only to have it stand unloved and abandoned for half the year. So many Cornish resorts had suffered in this way, the rich from the big cities buying up property to turn into second homes, leaving the young local people unable to get onto the housing ladder and the villages resembling ghost towns in the winter months. Luckily Tregenna Bay wasn't one of them. Yet.

Jayne snapped out of her reverie. Time was pressing but she felt compelled to have one last look around, as if *Seawinds* was begging her to reconsider. In years gone by there had been banter from the kitchen, convivial chatter in the dining room and children's laughter echoing from the back parlour but all was now graveyard quiet. As Jayne explored further she realised the once extravagant wallpapers were now faded, damp patches were bleeding through on the ceilings and the whole house smelled musty. She swallowed the pang of regret that rose in her throat and stung her eyes. She should have done more to preserve what her parents had lovingly created but her life in Cambridge had not allowed for many visits.

She poked her head round the door of the bedroom she had once shared with her sister Leyla, the rosy wallpaper replaced by magnolia emulsion some years ago. The bare room looked much smaller than she remembered. She smiled at the memory of waking from her nightmares too fearful to poke her head above the covers and Leyla, although three years younger, trying to reassure her.

The room next door had been her brother Symon's domain where Lego and Airfix models had once littered every surface. With regret, Jayne remembered Symon hadn't been able to come to their mother's funeral. He'd had urgent business to attend to in New York and couldn't get away. Leyla hadn't stayed very long either, eager to get back to the Isle of Wight and her writing. If only there was some way they could keep *Seawinds*, thought Jayne, to bring the family back together, at least for the holidays.

Realising time was short she ran back downstairs to the front room, which had been her father's sanctuary, and was pulled up short by the sun shining on the faded dark red wallpaper. Back when most people's houses were decorated in bland shades of brown, being an artist, her father had wanted colour in every room. Indeed he was a colourful character and she suddenly had a mental image of him sitting in his armchair with a glass of whisky, listening to Beethoven or Mozart on his hi-fi, his gaze fixed on the sea view which was now partly obscured by the overgrown pine trees. She shuddered as she recalled the last time he had sat in here. The faint sound of a waltz began to seep through the silence but she dismissed it as her active imagination playing tricks.

8

She collected her handbag and jacket from the newel post and was just about to leave when she heard a voice.

'That you, Jayne?'

Gladys from next door was mounting the steps, her prying eyes trying to peer into the empty green and white hallway, 'All done, then?'

'I think so, just taking a last look around.'

'Mm, 'tes sad. Do 'ee don't know who's takin' it on?'

Jayne shook her head and feeling the need to preserve the house's dignity, stepped onto the tiled porch and slammed the door behind her.

'I've got kettle on,' said Gladys, 'You'm a long journey, and them motorway services charge the earth for a tay bag in hot water.'

Jayne was anxious to be on her way. If the traffic was anything like yesterday, it would take at least seven hours to get back to Cambridge, but she thought it churlish to refuse. 'Thanks Gladys, but I can't stay long. I've got to drop the keys off to Mr Masterson before I go.' She followed Gladys into her house and through the dimly-lit passage, trying to ignore the stale smell of kippers.

'Come on in,' said Gladys. 'George as just nipped out for a paper. Be back dreckly.'

Sitting at the chenille-covered table, Jayne noticed Gladys's kitchen had changed very little in the past five decades. The kettle whistled on the old range and Gladys warmed the brown teapot, placed two heaped spoonfuls of loose tea in the pot and poured on the boiling water. Jayne couldn't help smiling at this archaic practice – she didn't know anyone who still did this. Taking two Cornish Blue cups and saucers from the dresser, Gladys ceremoniously set them down on the table, accompanied by the brown teapot complete with striped knitted cosy and a milk jug with a beaded cover.

'Still take sugar?'

Jayne nodded. 'Please.' She had given up smoking but however hard she tried she couldn't kick the comfort of a teaspoon of sugar in her tea. As Gladys poured herself a cup Jayne studied her more closely. She was aging well; probably something to do with the sea air and the mild climate.

Gladys looked up at Jayne. 'You seen Paul?'

Jayne frowned. 'Paul's here?'

Gladys slowly nodded and kept her eyes firmly fixed on Jayne. 'He was asking after 'ee.'

Jayne gazed at her cup and fiddled with the teaspoon.

'Oh, dear, 'ave I struck a nerve?'

Jayne wished she was on the motorway – she shouldn't be sitting here. She checked her watch. 'Look, I'm sorry Gladys, I really ought to be going. I must see the estate agent before I leave and the traffic will be building up.'

'Oh, George will be sorry he's missed 'ee. So will Paul. Said he's thinkin o' moving 'ere, dear of 'im. Fancy that.'

'Look, I haven't seen or heard from him for years.' Jayne stood up. 'I'm sorry, I really must go. Catch up some other time, OK?'

'All right, dear, have a safe journey. We'm 'ere if 'ee need us.'

'Thanks. I'll give you a ring when I know what's happening.' Leaving her full cup on the table, Jayne walked the length of Gladys's time-forgotten passage and out into the bright sunshine.

Belting herself into her silver blue Z4, her mobile rang.

'Jayne?'

'Oh hi, Leyla, what is it?'

'Did you find that box of diaries I told you about? In the cellar?'

'No, I'm sorry. I haven't had time. I'll have to come back.'

'But I need them for the book I'm writing.'

Jayne sighed. 'They've probably gone with everything else...'

'...I hope not. Oh bugger, I should've thought about it at the funeral. Please, Jayne, can't you go and have a quick look for me?'

'Sorry, I'm already running late. Gladys collared me and I've still got to see Masterson before I go and you know what the traffic's like. I'll see if I can come back next week.'

Leyla sighed heavily, 'Really? Oh, all right. I'll let you get off then. Let me know how it goes.'

Jayne felt bad but she really needed to get back to Cambridge. Michael had seemed too happy to wave her goodbye, first leaving her to deal with her mum's funeral and now putting *Seawinds* on the market, pleading he was much too busy at work. She just wished her suspicions were unfounded where her husband's infidelity was concerned. Since Jayne had retired from her teaching job, Michael had been given promotion and buried himself in his work, staying later and later at the office, or so he would have her believe. This wasn't how it was meant to be – they should be enjoying life together in the autumn of their years.

11

As she drove down the high street more memories hovered around her: being sent out for the odd item her mum had forgotten, Leyla and Symon pestering for sweets… Mr Pengelly's sweet shop was now a mobile phone outlet and charity shops and discount stores had gradually moved in to replace the other family-run businesses. But like many other seaside resorts, the pasty shops and fish and chip shops were still thriving and the Surf Shack and the beach café were still doing a roaring trade.

Masterson though seemed to be hanging on by his fingernails. Jayne wondered what the estate agent would say about *Seawinds*. When Yvonne's health started to decline, Jayne, Leyla and Symon had wanted her to sell up and move into a retirement home but she wouldn't hear of it; she had preferred to live solely on the ground floor with all her belongings around her, clinging desperately to the reins of independence and the memories of grander times.

Jayne took a deep breath and pushed the door of Mastersons Estate Agents and Valuers. Damn! She'd forgotten they closed on Saturday afternoons. Now what? She thought about posting the key through the letter box but she really needed to speak to Mr Masterson and she didn't want to relinquish her hold on the one and only key to *Seawinds*. And she definitely didn't want to leave it with Gladys, she didn't want her poking around. Then there was the little matter of Leyla's diaries. She should go back and look for them really, but she didn't want to risk another confrontation with Gladys and all the awkward questions she was bound to ask. Not only that but the power had been turned off and it would be getting dark in the cellar. She sighed heavily. There was nothing for it, she would have to stay another two nights at the *Captain Tregenna* and take the key back on Monday.

She sat in her car and took out her mobile to ring Michael. No signal. She cursed again. But she needed to tell him she would be staying in Cornwall until Monday now, although she didn't think he would care one way or the other. If she still had friends in Cornwall she could've stayed with one of them for a couple of nights, but they had all moved away years ago; even Olive, the girl who had helped run the kitchen at *Seawinds* during its heyday.

Jayne drove along the beach road until she came to one of the best views of the bay. She got out and stood gazing at the sparkling sea crashing against the rocks below and gloried in the salty air brushing her hair back from her face. Although the day was overcast this wild and divine bay with its spread of rock pools still tugged at her heart. The original plan was to sell *Seawinds* and split the proceeds between Jayne and her siblings but perhaps she could persuade Symon and Leyla to refurbish it as a holiday home where the family could spend much-needed time together and help keep the memories alive. Or would she be joining the ranks of second home owners whom she despised for turning many a resort into a ghost town in the winter? There was so much to consider, not least the cost of such a project.

She ran her tongue over her teeth, her mouth was dry. She should've drunk the cup of tea Gladys had offered her. Locking her car she walked the length of the sea road to the beach café but that too was closed. Brushing off her despondency she walked briskly back to her car and headed towards the *Captain Tregenna* perched formidably high above the coast road.

The late afternoon light was fading when Jayne pulled into the car park behind the old stone-built inn. A twinkling lantern each side of the low Tudor doorway and a warm glow in the mullioned windows welcomed her. Locking her car with an overloud bleep, her heels clacked on the flagstones as she hurried into the cosy bar where a log fire burned brightly in the granite fireplace.

Jack looked up from the pint he was pulling. 'Oh, back again? I thought you'd be well on you way to Cambridge by now.'

'So did I, Jack, but it seems I have unfinished business. I'll need to stay another two nights, if that's all right?'

Jack nodded, gave the pint to his customer and turned to take a key from the hook behind the bar. 'Here you are. You can have the big room at the front.'

'Thanks.'

'Drink?'

'Mm, gin and tonic, please.'

'Ice and lemon?'

Jayne nodded. She was thankful Jack was a relative newcomer to these parts otherwise there would be too many questions asked and she wasn't in the mood to make conversation tonight.

'Pleasant evening, but still a nip in the air,' said Jack. 'I'd cosy up round that fire if I were you.'

Jayne emptied the whole bottle of tonic into her glass and taking Jack's advice, sank into the deep buttoned burgundy sofa and watched the flames licking and curling up the chimney. Suddenly aware of her rumbling stomach, she studied the specials board next to the bar. Grilled sardines and a salad with crusty bread sounded delicious. She went to the counter to order her meal and sat back on the sofa.

She took out her phone and smiled. She had a signal! She rang Michael's number but it went straight to voicemail.

14

She left a short message and returned the phone to her handbag.

She was grateful the pub was relatively quiet for a Saturday evening. It had been a favourite haunt in her youth and she smiled at the memory of meeting up with her mini-skirted friends in the sixties; panda eye make-up, pale pink lipstick and the juke box belting out The Four Tops and Diana Ross. There was no juke box now. The *Captain Tregenna* had pulled itself smartly into the twenty-first century. What was once the saloon bar had regained the Olde Worlde charm of yesteryear with vintage wall lamps, exposed oak beams and tea lights on the tables. She couldn't remember it having wood panelling before but perhaps it had been boarded up in the 1960s. So many old houses had suffered that fate – beautiful banisters boarded in and painted, fireplaces covered up. Her gaze rose to find swathes of fishing nets draped across the beams. Well, those had certainly never been there in her youth.

She studied the condensation on her glass as she twirled it around to catch the flickering firelight. The sparkling crystal reminded her of the first time she had tasted a gin and tonic.

Jack interrupted her thoughts and placed her meal on the table. 'Here we are, caught fresh this morning. Enjoy!'

'Thanks, Jack.'

The meal was every bit as good as her mum used to cook and as she ate the salty sardines more memories resurfaced: the dining room in *Seawinds* packed with guests all enjoying the delicious seafood which the fishermen landed straight onto the quayside. Going with her mum to select the best fish early in the morning, the family's two cats, Mitzi and Dennis, meowing for the scraps as Yvonne prepared the fish on the kitchen table...

With the help of the alcohol and the warmth from the fire, Jayne sank into a state of cosy reflection. She kicked off her shoes and closed her eyes. She was back in 1967, the wide sun-drenched bay buzzing with holiday-makers, striped deck chairs and windbreaks. Clad in her blue swimsuit, she was running down to the water's edge, eager to jump in. It was her seventeenth birthday.

TWO

The initial freshness of the sea took Jayne's breath away. Bobbing up and down until she became accustomed to the iciness of the water, she began pushing her arms out in front of her, launching herself further into the waves, while the shouts and cries of the children playing on the beach slowly receded.

Suddenly aware of someone swimming alongside her, she realised it was Paul. For the last few years she had looked forward to him coming down with his parents for their customary two weeks' holiday at *Seawinds*. She had watched him turn from a gangly boy into an attractive young man with an athletic body, thick dark brown hair and a ready smile. She was in love! A snatched kiss under the stairs or on the beach when no one was looking was deliciously exciting but that was as far as she was prepared to go. It might be the permissive sixties but Jayne wasn't ready to throw herself into the unknown territory of full-on sex.

Jayne tried to match Paul's seal-like movements, weaving in and out of the water. After a while they scrambled out and ran across the hard wet sand to the mouth of the cave on the east side of the bay they had claimed for their own, only accessible at low tide. She spread out her towel and lay completely still on her front and felt the warmth of the sun drying her body. Paul sat beside her and stroked his fingertips across her upper arm. She knew he wanted to provoke a reaction, but she used all her willpower until finally she gave in and wriggled. He moved her wet honey blonde hair to one side

17

and gently kissed her neck. She turned over and blinked up at him.

'Do you have to get back?' asked Paul.

'I should really. Mum'll need help setting the tables but it's too nice to be indoors. Olive'll be there, though.' Jayne spread out like a starfish and closed her eyes. She felt Paul's closeness and anticipated his kiss. When it didn't happen she opened her eyes to find him gazing down at her. 'What are you looking at?'

'The most beautiful girl in the world.'

'Don't be daft! Come on, I'll race you back to the house.' She stood up but Paul pulled her down on top of him, laughing. They tumbled over and over playfully until their lips met with a clash. She felt his firmness against her but she pushed him away.

'What's up?' he asked.

'I told you, I've gotta go.'

'Huh, go on then! See if I care.'

'Don't be like that.'

'Well, how do you expect me to be after giving me the come-on? You lead me to the door but you won't let me in. It was the same yesterday.'

She winced at the memory – he'd ventured into her bedroom and closed the door, but Leyla had disturbed them by coming in to look for something under her bed and Jayne was secretly relieved.

'You know I can't. Not here, anyway. Someone might see us.' She stood up and scanned the busy beach.

'Where then? Come into the cave.'

She hung her head and dug her toes into the warm sand, tracing patterns in it.

'What's the matter? Frightened of getting pregnant?'

She shrugged.

Paul tried again. He slipped his arm round her waist and pulled her closer. He kissed her lightly on the lips and traced the line of her spine with his fingertips, sending shock waves through her body. It would've been so easy to succumb but she slapped his hand away. 'Paul!'

'I'm beginning to think you're just a tease,' he said, angrily. 'You know what they call girls like you?'

Tears pricking her eyes, she snatched up her towel and ran from him, past the families packing up their belongings, dodging sand castles. She took the short cut, up the wonky concrete steps embedded into the rock, up the steep pebbly track between the grassy banks scattering a group of rabbits. Her lungs felt fit to burst with the effort. She usually enjoyed this climb up from the beach but it was taking too long today; she couldn't wait to be indoors standing in the refreshing shower. She felt weird, confused. She wasn't sure what had just passed between them. Why had Paul made her feel so exquisite one minute but so awful the next?

At *Seawinds* Jayne peeled off her swimsuit and stood in the hot shower washing away her feelings of disquiet and discontent. It was her birthday. She should be happy – the family would be gathering for a little party after the guests' evening meal and she wanted to enjoy it.

She dried her shoulder-length hair and put on her pale blue mini-skirt and a white, short-sleeved blouse, a lick of make-up and went downstairs. Paul met her at the bottom, pulled her into the dark space beneath the stairs and began kissing her neck and running his hands over her breasts.

19

'God, Paul! Not now!' She pushed him away.

'Meet me later then, at the cave?'

'I'll see. But the tide will be in.'

'Where, then?'

Yvonne shouted from the kitchen. 'Jayne? Give us a hand would you? Olive's popped out to the garden for some more parsley.'

Paul stifled a giggle and Jayne forced herself to look composed. She went through to the humid kitchen where Yvonne was sweating over a large pan of watercress soup.

'Had a good swim, love?' she asked without looking round. 'Did you see Paul? He went down just after you.'

'Yeah, I saw him.'

'Oh, that's good. He's a nice boy. I think he likes you.'

Jayne was full of contradictions – she loved Paul but she was frightened of taking that step and she dreaded to think what her parents would say if they found out. She was also frightened of asking the doctor if she could go on the pill for the same reason.

'Can you get the soup bowls down from that top cupboard, love? I can't reach and your dad's not around.'

Jayne stretched up to reach the blue-band crockery and noticed her blouse was undone. She put the bowls on the table, turned her back to her mother and quickly adjusted her clothing.

'Thanks, love. I think I heard your dad go into the front room. Would you go and see?'

Half wishing Paul was still waiting for her, Jayne checked the dark space beneath the stairs, but he had gone.

20

Along the green and white hallway she opened the door to the room on the right. Her father was sitting in his favourite club chair in front of the bay window, gazing out to sea, a glass of whisky in his hand and Beethoven on the hi-fi. Harry had the look of a film star of the pre-war years, his dark hair slicked back from his face and a moustache.

He looked round and smiled when she entered. 'How's my birthday girl, then?'

'Fine thanks, Dad. I had a great swim. It's beautiful in the sea today. You should try it.'

'I prefer to be on it rather than in it. Boats are my thing. Not much time for sailing, though.' He took a drag on his cigarette then stubbed it out in the crystal ash tray. He gave a nod to the window. 'That view's begging me to paint it, too. Not much time for that either.'

'You should make time for the things you enjoy. You'll regret it one day.'

'Mm, you're right.' He drained his glass, moved over to the sideboard and poured another. 'Is your mum OK in the kitchen? Does she need a hand?'

That's my cue to leave, thought Jayne, but she sat resolutely in the chair opposite, watching her father and listening to the beautiful *Pastoral Symphony*. Whatever was troubling him he found a temporary escape in his music and a glass of *Glenfiddich*. She wanted to reach out to him, to tell him everything would be all right, but somehow she knew he needed more than that. Her father had always been a quiet man but he had become more subdued of late. A series of brown envelopes had arrived in the post these past few weeks. Yvonne hadn't asked any questions – all her time was taken up with looking after her guests, preparing and cooking meals and stripping and making beds. Jayne knew it wasn't her place to

21

ask but she wanted to know what had caused this shift in her father's behaviour. She was on the point of asking him, the scrambled words in her head fighting for order, when she retracted them. She didn't want to upset him and especially not this evening. She watched him move over to the window, drink in hand, as if he'd forgotten she was there.

On her way back to the kitchen, Leyla and Symon stood squabbling in the passage.

'Would you like to give them their tea, Jayne?' shouted Yvonne. 'Here, take it into the back parlour. I'll be there in a minute. Olive's keeping an eye on the dining room. I'll just finish up here.'

Jayne did as she was asked and took the tea tray from her mother. 'Come on, you two. Tea-time.'

'Where's the birthday cake, then?' said Symon.

'How do you know there is one?' asked Leyla.

'I saw Mum icing it last night!'

'Symon! It's meant to be a surprise!'

Jayne set the grilled sardines and chips on the table in front of them and glanced at the mantelpiece covered in birthday cards. Her gaze rested on the flowery one from Paul, a run-of-the-mill card, bought no doubt at the corner shop, but it felt special because it was from him. Jayne smiled remembering their exchange this morning after breakfast – she had been walking through from the kitchen, and not expecting to see anyone, had turned round and bumped into Paul in the narrow passage. A dart of surprise had lodged deep in her belly. His eyes told her he wanted to kiss her but at that very moment his little sister, Katie, had tugged him away; they were going out and their mum and dad were waiting in the car.

22

Harry came up behind Jayne and jolted her out of her thoughts. 'Would you like a drink, love? Come on, it's your seventeenth birthday. What d' you fancy? It's time you got to know about alcohol.'

Jayne followed her dad into kitchen. She didn't tell him she'd tasted the dregs from his glass before, or the time she'd been to a friend's house and they'd raided the cocktail cabinet when her parents were out.

Harry took some glasses from the kitchen cabinet and began to go through the bottles of spirits lined up on the side. 'How about a nice gin and tonic? It's a refreshing taste, you'll like it.'

Yvonne took off her apron and joined them. 'Mm, my favourite. Got one for me?' She glanced behind her. 'Olive and I haven't stopped this evening, have we love?'

Olive, herself not much older than Jayne, came forward and nodded.

'Don't complain,' said Harry. 'We need all the money we can get. Pack 'em in, that's what I say.'

Jayne sniffed the drink. It had a clean, refreshing smell, not like the fiery whisky. The ice cube tinkled against the glass as she took a gulp – the cool fizzy liquid slipping down her throat, just a hint of alcohol in the aftertaste.

'Hey, steady on!' said her mum. 'You're supposed to sip it, you know, not slurp it down like lemonade. Don't want you getting drunk.'

'She's all right, Yvonne, it's only a weak one. By the time I was her age...' Harry stopped when he saw his wife's disapproving glare. 'Olive, come and join us. What would you like, love. God knows, you've earned it.'

23

'Thank you Mr Williams. I'll have a glass of Coca-Cola.'

He poured one for her and stood two straws in it. 'There we are. Sure you wouldn't like a tot of whisky in it?' he winked. 'Pep it up a bit?'

'Harry!' scolded his wife, but he ignored her and smiled boyishly at Olive and Jayne.

And so the banter continued into the evening. They all enjoyed the delicious meal of grilled fresh sardines with all the trimmings and drank a toast to Jayne. She would've liked Paul to join them but the guests were kept separate at all times – her father's rule. Her mind wandered back to the beach this afternoon and the cave. Last year Paul had carved a heart in the rock and they had both scratched their initials into it. When Paul had gone home she would often go to the cave and think of him. Part of her was down there now, waiting for him.

Harry placed a pretty parcel in front of Jayne. Excitement building, she unwrapped it to reveal a royal blue satin make-up bag encrusted with coloured beads. She unzipped it to find a gilt powder compact with a sparkly blue lid.

'Wow, thanks, Mum, Dad.'

'They came from Dingles. Something you can keep,' said Harry.

'They're beautiful.'

'Oh!' said Yvonne. 'I nearly forgot.' She left the room and came back with the birthday cake, her face aglow in the light of seventeen candles, Leyla and Symon in tow. Jayne blew out the candles and they all toasted her with a rendition of 'Happy Birthday.'

'Happy birthday!' the outburst woke Jayne with a start. As she regained consciousness she realised she was back in the present, a party of people standing by the bar chinking glasses. She looked at her watch and realised she had been out for the count for over an hour. How embarrassing! She hastily put her shoes back on, gathered her jacket and bag and tip-toed out through the side door and up the red-carpeted stairs to her room.

Jack had done a good job of revamping the old pub and this bedroom was tastefully decorated. Fresh white linen adorned the bed and muted greys and lilacs completed the look. She opened the door to the en-suite – shiny neutral tiles, fluffy white towels and expensive-looking toiletries.

After freshening up, the sea view enticed her to the window and beneath on the table stood a vase of fresh flowers. She sniffed them; the fragrance was divine. How thoughtful! But on further inspection, Jane noticed it was a rather large bouquet and there was a card with swirly handwriting propped up against it.

'It would be great to see you again. Meet me in the bar at 9.30pm. P.'

Paul? Goodness. She toyed with the idea of ignoring his request but in the end, curiosity got the better of her and anyway, what else was she supposed to do to fill her evening? The thought of sitting in her room watching the little flat-screen TV wasn't very attractive and she certainly didn't want to spend her evening with Gladys and George.

She debated what to wear. She didn't want to appear as though she had gone all-out to make an impression but, on the other hand, she didn't want to look too casual. She plumped for her pair of black slim-leg trousers, a boat-necked flowery top and added her turquoise necklace and earrings that complimented her eyes.

With a mixture of feelings, Jayne checked and re-checked her image in the long mirror. Her looks belied her age; her shoulder-length hair, although beginning to lose its honey colour, shone under the light as she turned her head.

Something in the genes.

Her mum had always looked good for her age, even in her eighties. Harry had often joked she could've been a model. She'd pooh-poohed it but secretly Yvonne had liked to think of herself swanning around in couture clothes like the models in the big department stores in London. Jayne had a vague recollection of going with her mum and dad to Selfridges when she was little, in the days when Harry worked in the West End. At lunchtime, the models paraded around the restaurant showing off outfits that could be purchased in the fashion department. Jayne was fascinated by the models who walked very elegantly, showing off the outfits with a flourish as they turned.

She fell to wondering what Paul looked like now, if he still had a thick head of hair albeit streaked with silver. She knew they were both likely very different people from the Jayne and Paul of five decades ago and she hoped he had kept his lean body, not like Michael.

She gave herself one more appraising look and took a deep breath. 'Well, you don't look too bad for sixty-seven, girl. Let's see how the other party has fared.'

Feeling anxious but excited, she trod the red cat-walk landing, down the stairs and into the warmth of the now busy bar. Heads turned as she entered from the side door. Paul's was one of them. The sight of her made his jaw drop. 'Jayne! Over here!'

Her eyes darted around and finally rested on Paul standing by the same sofa she had occupied earlier. She rushed to greet him, a broad smile lighting her face.

He took her hand and tentatively kissed her cheek. 'You look amazing!'

They stood giggling like two teenagers. Time shrank. They were seventeen, eighteen again.

'What brings you down here?' asked Jayne.

He lowered his gaze. 'I dunno. I suppose I had a hankering to see what the north Cornish coast looked like these days. What can I get you, a G and T?'

Jayne smiled. 'You remembered! But I think I'd prefer a glass of red wine tonight.'

'No problem. Any preference?'

'Nope, you choose.' Jayne watched Paul go to the bar and order a bottle of Jack's finest Merlot and realised her heart was racing. He looked as though he'd kept himself fit and he still had a full head of hair streaked with silver as she'd predicted.

Jack asked Paul where he was sitting and he pointed to the table in front of the fireplace.

'I'll bring it over,' said Jack.

Jayne and Paul sat one each side of the deep buttoned burgundy sofa. Paul couldn't take his eyes off her and neither of them could stop grinning. Then his smile dropped.

'I was sorry to hear about your mum. Gladys told me. Was it sudden?'

Jayne chewed her thumbnail.

'Look, if you'd rather not talk about it, that's fine.'

'No, it's OK. It's just...' she took a breath, 'so much to think about at the moment, what with the family all living so far apart and everything.' She fell silent when she saw Jack bringing their wine over. He placed the bottle and two glasses on the table.

'Thanks,' said Paul. He poured a glass for Jayne and handed it to her. 'I'll only drink one glass as I'm driving. You can save the rest for tomorrow, have it with your evening meal.'

'Thank you.'

Paul dispensed with the formalities and got straight down to the nitty-gritty. 'Tell me what happened after we lost touch. Your brother and sister – are they married?'

Jayne nodded and took a sip of the rich velvety wine while Paul poured one for himself.

'Leyla lives on the Isle of Wight. She's divorced; was in psychiatric medicine, now she's writing a book. Got twins, a girl and a boy.' She twirled the stem of her wineglass between her fingers. 'Symon's an architect, splits his time between London and New York. Maggie goes with him whenever she can. Not a bad life, eh?'

Paul digested this information along with a mouthful of wine. Funny, he couldn't imagine them all grown up. He remembered Leyla was about fourteen and Symon twelve when he last saw them. 'Crikey. And what about you?'

'Huh,' she grimaced. She drank deeply and twisted her wedding ring. If she still smoked she would've lit up.

'I'm sorry, I don't mean to pry.'

'You're OK. But I'd rather hear about you. Did you achieve your ambition?'

Paul smiled, showing perfect set of teeth. 'Which one?'

28

'Well, I thought you went to Plymouth University to study marine biology?'

'Yeah.' He subconsciously mirrored Jayne's action, twisting the stem of his glass. 'I had an OK career but not what I originally planned. Had my finger in a lot of pies; I suppose there was always something bigger and better round the corner.'

Now she thought about it, Jayne detected a slight Australian accent. Her curiosity was heightened. 'Don't tell me...you emigrated!'

That broad smile again. '*That* obvious, eh?'

Their eyes met and she felt a flutter deep within her belly. She looked away. All that should stay safely locked in the past. 'Tell me. I'd love to hear about it.'

'Jeez, where do I start?'

'The beginning's a good place.'

'Ha, yeah.' He relaxed back in the sofa and cradled the wine glass while fixing his eyes on her. 'I dunno, after the last time I saw you, I felt I had to do something with my life; something out of the ordinary. I'd heard about the ten-pound-package and thought I'd give it a go.'

'You were a 'ten-pound-pom'? That was brave.'

'Yeah, either that or bloody mindless! But hey, I was young and determined to find my pot of gold at the end of the rainbow.'

'And did you?'

'Not at first. It was tricky settling in a new country – I had nowhere to live, no one to show me the ropes. But I took each day as it was thrown at me, like so many others. I made

29

friends along the way, people I could trust, and gradually found my feet.'

'And what about your mum and dad; how did they feel about it?'

Did she detect a flicker of uncertainty in his eyes?

'They were all for it; I think because they'd been through the war and knew what it was to take risks, take the bull by the horns. After all, you're a long time dead.' But as soon as he'd said it, he regretted not being entirely honest with her.

As she listened, Jayne marvelled at his easy-going philosophy – everything seemed so black and white to him. Her life had never been that simple.

'So, what *are* you doing here in Cornwall?'

'Like I said – having a look around after all these years. What you doing tomorrow?'

She shrugged. 'Nothing much.'

'Well, how would you like to see what Padstow has to offer at this time of year?'

'Ha! Are you asking me out?'

'Yeah, why not?'

'But you know nothing about me, my situation ... '

'...that's cause you didn't wanna to tell me!'

His eyes bore into hers but Jayne couldn't help laughing at his audacity. Her reckless side was shouting at her to go with him and what the hell. 'Where are you staying?'

'At my sister's, in Wadebridge.'

Jayne shook her head, incredulous. 'Your sister lives in Wadebridge?'

'Yep! I'm full of surprises!'

With the help of the wine Jayne began to unwind and to feel more at ease with him. It was as if the intervening years had never happened.

Jayne slipped between the crisp white sheets and turned out the light. As her eyes became accustomed to the darkness she realised the moon was shining through a gap in the curtains. She got out of bed to take a look. The silvery moonlight was highlighting the bay giving it mysterious air. She was tempted to get dressed and go running on the sand. Yes! Why not? There was nothing and no one to stop her. But wait, what was that? It looked like a shadowy figure of a man standing at the edge of the cliff top looking down on the bay. She rubbed her eyes and looked again but he had disappeared.

She thought no more about it, closed the curtains and climbed back into bed. She lay against the cool pillows going over her meeting with Paul. How amazing! After all these years she still felt drawn to him and she suspected he felt the same about her. Her mind was racing. Stop it! she told herself. You're not seventeen any more. Get a grip.

Paul hadn't mentioned if he had a wife or partner – he would say it was because she hadn't asked which was true. Somehow the conversation never strayed to their personal lives. And he only touched on the last time they saw each other. No. She was being silly.

But as she drifted into sleep, Jayne couldn't help but reminisce.

31

THREE

Easter Sunday 1968

It was a bright but blustery morning in April. At *Seawinds* the family was gearing up for the onslaught of a busy Easter Sunday. In the kitchen, Yvonne was putting the final touches to the Simnel cake and trying to keep Symon's hands off the marzipan, while Olive was at the kitchen sink preparing the vegetables for their midday meal. Jayne and Leyla were in their bedroom – Leyla doing her homework, Jayne going through her art portfolio. Harry was in his favourite place, in front of the window with a glass of *Glenfiddich,* immersed in the Johann Strauss waltzes that were vibrating throughout the house. The music was so loud that Yvonne had asked Harry to turn it down several times but he had ignored her.

At first the bouncy music was uplifting; it was enjoyable to dance around the kitchen – it got the jobs done in half the time – but the same music day after day had become very irritating. Jayne, who was working on her portfolio in preparation for her entrance exam to the Cambridge School of Art, was finding it difficult to concentrate. She had tried to ask her dad why he needed to keep listening to the same record over and over again but he had waved her away, poured another drink and lit another cigarette. When lunchtime came he sat eating his meal as if in a trance. Jayne, Leyla and Symon kept their heads down and munched silently through their roast dinners. Yvonne stared at her husband's vacant expression but he didn't pay her any attention. No one broke the silence, not even Leyla who always spoke her mind regardless of the consequences.

After lunch Harry turned off his hi-fi and announced he was going for a walk. The whole house breathed a sigh of welcome relief but no one thought to ask any questions as this was something he did frequently. He loved to walk along the cliff top to his favourite vantage point where he would stand, sometimes for hours, and watch the ever-changing tide.

Paul, Katie and their parents had come down for the Easter holiday – something of a break with tradition, as in previous years they had only ever stayed for a fortnight in the summer. Paul, eager to see Jayne again, had pestered his parents for an early getaway. This afternoon he went looking for Jayne to ask if she could spare a few hours with him. Her bedroom door was ajar and feeling brave, he pushed it open to find her sitting on her bed, alone, pawing over her art work.

'But you'll sail through your entrance exam,' pleaded Paul. 'Surely we can snatch a couple of hours together?'

Jayne shook her head but continued to work. 'No. You don't understand. Dad's been playing such loud music I haven't been able to concentrate. He's gone out now so I want to catch up.' She glanced at him. 'I'm sorry, Paul. Maybe tomorrow?'

'Yeah, that music. What's all that about?'

'I don't know. He's not himself lately; kind of preoccupied. I don't think he knew what he was eating at lunchtime. I'm a bit worried about him to be honest.'

'What does your mum think?'

'I don't know. She won't talk about it.'

Paul wanted to reach out to Jayne, to give her a hug and reassure her that everything would be OK but he knew he

33

didn't stand a chance today. He stood in the doorway hovering from one foot to the other, and noticed a still life resting on her bed. He picked it up to take a closer look. It was drawn in soft pencil, a study of a cup and saucer that looked so real, Paul felt he could reach in and pick it up. Yeah, she was good.

He put the drawing back on the edge of her bed. 'OK. I do like you, you know. I asked mum and dad to come down for Easter especially, just so I can be with you.'

'I know, but it's different for you. You've got your place at university,' she said, her voice rising a semitone. Sitting up straight, she said, 'Anyway, hopefully, I'll be going to the Cambridge Art School.'

'What? When did this happen?'

She shrugged her shoulders. 'Ages ago.'

Paul frowned. 'But... why Cambridge? I thought we were going to Plymouth to study together. We agreed, remember?' His eyes begged her to reconsider.

She couldn't meet his gaze. She retrieved the still life from the edge of her bed and put it in the folder with her other drawings. Hooked a strand of hair behind her ear and picked at a hangnail on her thumb. 'Cambridge offers the course I want – graphic design and illustration. And it's where my dad went. He's all for it. I've got to think of my future, Paul.'

He took her by the shoulders. 'What about *our* future?'

She shrugged him off. She thought she had it all worked out but now she felt awkward with Paul standing over of her. 'It doesn't mean...we can always meet up when I'm home...in the holidays.'

'Big deal.'

His mind was working overtime. Perhaps he *could* meet up with her in the holidays when she came home. Maybe

34

he could come down straight from Plymouth, it wasn't far. But he doubted their paths would ever cross. He was about to discuss it with her when he heard people heading downstairs.

Paul looked round the door, pulled it to and said quietly, 'Look, I want to spend some time with *you,* not hang around with them all the time.'

Jayne kept her head down, eyes on her work.

Katie bounced down the last two stairs, ran along the landing and pushed open Jayne's door and looked at her brother. 'We're going out on a mystery tour. Coming?'

Paul raked a hand through his dark hair. 'Might as well. Nothing to stay here for.'

Feeling the sting of Paul's words, Jayne watched him turn and go. A lot had happened since last year but she couldn't find the words to tell him, to make him understand.

The rest of the afternoon passed calmly. Thankful for some quiet time, Jayne resumed work on her portfolio. Yvonne was ensconced in the kitchen making adjustments to the menus while Olive had gone home until the evening shift. Leyla and Symon were both engrossed in their pastimes – Leyla on her bed, reading, and Symon in his bedroom, building Lego models. In the dreary afternoon the house seemed to be holding its breath until the peace was shattered by a loud knock at the door.

'All right, all right, I'm coming!' shouted Yvonne, taking off her apron as she ran up the hall. 'No need to break the door down.' She quickly smoothed her dress and checked her image in the mirror.

Two police officers, a man and a woman, seemed to fill the porch.

'Mrs Williams?' asked the policeman.

Yvonne nodded. 'That's right.'

' Evenin' ma'am. May we step inside?'

'Yes, of course. What is it?' Yvonne stared at them and stood to one side to let them in. At the sight of the policewoman's dour expression Yvonne felt panic rising within her.

'I'm afraid we've got some bad news, Ma'am. You might want to sit down.'

'Oh, whatever is it?'

The WPC looked at her sergeant, then at Yvonne. 'I'm sorry, but your husband was found collapsed on the rocks in the bay this afternoon. It looked as though he had fallen from the cliff path above.'

Yvonne frowned, 'What? I don't understand. Who found him? Where is he?'

'They've taken him to Newquay hospital, Ma'am.'

'Hospital? But I must go to him.' She went to the hall stand to grab her coat.

The WPC gave her sergeant a sideways look and approached Yvonne. 'I'm sorry Mrs Williams, all in good time.'

Yvonne shook her head. 'But I *must* go...he'll want me there.'

The WPC bit her lip and brought a chair closer to Yvonne. 'Please sit down, Mrs Williams.'

'Tell me. What is it? Why can't I see him?' Yvonne felt herself sinking then everything went dark. The WPC slid the chair beneath her as she staggered backwards.

'A cup of hot sweet tea, I think, Janice,' said the sergeant.

The WPC immediately went to find the kitchen.

'Is there anyone else in the house, Ma'am? Family?'

Yvonne's heart was thumping in her ears. She was struck dumb.

Jayne ran downstairs. 'Who was that at the...' she stopped on the middle stair when she saw the dark uniform. 'What is it? What's happened?'

Yvonne found her voice. 'It's your dad, love. He's had an accident. They've taken him to hospital.'

Jayne frowned. She looked from the sergeant to her mum and back again. 'What sort of accident?'

Leyla and Symon emerged from their bedrooms, ran down the stairs and stopped behind Jayne when they saw the policeman.

Jayne tried to reassure them, 'Don't worry, I'm sure Dad'll be OK.'

'Why? What's happened?' asked Leyla, but nobody answered her.

The WPC came back with the cup of tea for Yvonne. She took hold of the saucer but only stared at the cup. She suddenly stood up. 'Oh dear, what time is it? Olive should be here by now. I've got a houseful of guests to cook for. I shouldn't be sitting down!'

'I'm sure they'll understand, Ma'am,' said the WPC.

'No, no. *You* don't understand. I must look after them. Harry ...' She shook, sending the cup crashing to the floor, the hot tea splashing up the wall. 'Oh, dear, oh dear, whatever will

37

we do?' she slumped back down on the chair, sobbing and shaking.

'Stay with her, Janice,' said the sergeant. He looked at Jayne. 'Is there a telephone, dear?'

Jayne nodded and directed him into the back parlour while Leyla and Symon were left standing on the stairs.

Gladys and George burst in through the front door. Gladys took one look at Leyla and Symon. 'Oh, dear of 'em. Come wi' me,' and she took them into the kitchen, followed by George.

Ignoring the police woman, Jayne knelt down and wrapped her arms round her mother. She was alerted to the click of the telephone receiver and muffled voices in the parlour.

The police sergeant poked his head round the door. 'Janice...a word.'

She nodded and went to him.

At that moment Paul came back with his parents and sister. They stood motionless, shocked at the scene confronting them. On hearing them arrive, Gladys left George with Leyla and Symon in the kitchen and whisked the guests into the dining room, closed the door behind them and lowered her voice. 'Tes Harry. George found him on the rocks this afternoon and rang the coastguard. Looks like he fell from the cliffs. 'Tes awful. The policeman's just rung the hospital but...' she shook her head.

A howl, like an animal in pain, rang out from the hall as Yvonne was told the devastating news that her husband was dead.

Mrs Smythe's hand flew to her mouth. 'Oh, my goodness!'

Mr Smythe stood by his wife's side, unable to utter a word, his face unreadable. 'Poor Yvonne,' continued Mrs Smythe, taking a hanky from her black patent handbag to dab her eyes, 'and those poor children. Whatever will they do?'

Gladys looked at Mr and Mrs Smythe. 'I dunno, but George and me'll do a proper job.'

'Of course,' said Ken Smythe.

Paul went back out to the hall. He wanted so much to comfort Jayne but she was kneeling protectively beside her mother with her arms wrapped around her. He stood there, wishing he could do something, anything, to make Jayne feel better but after a few moments' hesitation he turned his back on the sad scene and reluctantly headed for the stairs. Mr and Mrs Smythe emerged from the dining room, grabbed Katie and followed.

Olive was late. She'd been sailing with her father this morning and they'd got into difficulty when the weather turned, making their outing a lot longer than intended. Olive loved being on the water and although her father was a competent sailor he wasn't as strong as he used to be. Today had been quite a trial and her arms ached with the effort of bringing the old sail boat under control.

Wisps of hair escaping from her ponytail, Olive hurried along the road as fast as she could and noticed a blue and white Morris Minor parked outside *Seawinds*. She wondered briefly what a police car was doing there and ran up the steps to her evening shift. Gladys, who had been watching for her, met her at the door and pulled her into the dining room.

'Listen maid,' began Gladys, closing the door behind her. 'Harry's had a terrible accident. George found him collapsed on the rocks.'

Olive's eyes were huge. 'What? Oh, no!'

'Such a shock for George, dear of 'im. He ran straight to the phone box and dialled 999.'

'Is Mr Williams all right? Have they taken him to hospital?'

Gladys shook her head. 'The police just rung 'em. They tried their best but they couldn't revive him.'

Olive slumped onto one of the dining chairs and shook with sobs. She took out a hanky from her coat pocket, pressed it against her eyes. 'What a terrible thing. I can't believe it. Poor Mr Williams, I was only talking to him this morning.' She sniffed, 'and what about the guests... the evening meal?' She stood up.

'We'll all have to bustle tonight, do best we can.'

'Yes. I'll make a start right away.' Olive hurried into the kitchen, hung up her coat and put on her apron. Luckily, Yvonne had left everything ready. At the thought of Mr Williams having a laugh and a joke with them, Olive couldn't choke back her tears. Gladys came in and put a motherly arm round her shoulders.

'There, there, tes a shock. Sit down a minute, I'll make some tay. Whatever needs doin' we'll together.'

Olive stifled another sob and wiped her eyes. 'Thanks, Mrs Winter.'

'We'll do a proper job, don't you worry.'

Olive nodded, 'But poor Mrs Williams. How is she?'

'She's been taken abed but she's anxious for her guests, of course.'

'Yes, of course.'

Gradually, a blanket of calm settled on the house. Yvonne was gently told she would have to identify her husband's body tomorrow and Dr Graham came to administer some tranquilisers. Jayne, being the eldest, was instructed to give her mother another two tablets at 9 o'clock. Olive kept order and organised the cooking with Jayne and Gladys, the three of them working like automatons. One by one George carried the meals into the sombre dining room, the guests stunned into silence.

Paul had lost his appetite; the gap in his stomach demanded to be filled but he couldn't oblige. He stared at his plate of lamb stew until it congealed and knew the smell would stay with him for the rest of his life. The sound of the cutlery on the plates was deafening. He also knew the sight of Jayne with her arms draped over her mother, the two of them sobbing, would stay imprinted on his mind for all time.

Eager to be anywhere but *Seawinds,* Paul left the table without an apology or a backward glance, ran out of the house, past the pine trees and down to the beach. He lost his footing twice but scrambled down the rest of narrow path until he reached the wonky concrete steps and jumped onto the sand. He took out his sadness and frustration on a pebble, kicking it along the beach until it plopped into a rock pool. He wanted to lash out at everything, anything, even the wind that stung his eyes. He ran, hoping to outrun the feelings welling up inside him. He had never felt so helpless. He was also smarting from Jayne's announcement that she was going to Cambridge instead of Plymouth in September. In the space of one day his whole future had come crashing down. But there was a glimmer of hope on the horizon – he envisaged looking her up when he got some time off. All was not lost, not yet. He wasn't going to give up. He entered the cave and sat cross-legged on the damp sandy seaweed. Huh, their cave. Their initials carved into the rock. It all seemed so sad and pointless now but he felt close to her here, as if her very essence was impregnated in the walls. He prayed she would change her mind and go to Plymouth instead of Cambridge but he knew in his heart that she had left him.

The last of the purple and orange glow was fading from the sky when Paul finally felt able to set foot back inside *Seawinds*. All was quiet save for the ticking grandfather clock in the hall. He crept upstairs to find Katie alone on her bed.

'Where's Mum and Dad?'

Katie looked up from her comic, 'Gone out for a walk, I think they wanted to be alone.'

'Did they say anything about what happened?'

'Not much. Sad, isn't it?'

Much more than sad, thought Paul. It was a bloody catastrophe.

George later told them that he had been walking their dog, Sonny, that afternoon and on his way along the sea front had caught sight of a man sprawled out on the rocks. He ran to the call box next to the café and dialled 999. When the coastguard arrived they drove their Land Rover onto the beach. They assisted the ambulance crew and together they brought the man down from the rocks on a stretcher and George was asked if he knew him. He was horrified to find it was his neighbour, Harry, unconscious. He looked in a bad way when they slid him into the vehicle. A huge bloody gash on his head, his body twisted. A chill had crept over George's own body at the thought of the unsuspecting family; the poor children possibly without a father and their poor mother – would she be able to continue running *Seawinds*? It was all too much to contemplate.

It was the longest evening any of them had ever known. When all the chaos had died down and all the guests had gone up to their respective rooms, Gladys saw a young man hovering in the hallway.

'Hello, dear. What can I get you?' she asked.

He took a while to answer, looked down at the green lino and shuffled his feet. 'I er...is Jayne there?'

'Es, she's out back. Paul, is it?'

He nodded. 'I just want to say how sorry I am about...you know.'

'Of course. I'll see if she'll speak to ee.'

Paul waited in the hall for what felt like an eternity. He began mentally joining up the geometric patterns in the lino until Jayne finally emerged from the parlour, a weak smile on her tear-stained face. He was unsure how to treat her; he couldn't find the right words, or a way to fill the empty space between them. He felt inadequately equipped to deal with such sadness and suddenly wondered why he was standing there. 'I'm really sorry about your dad,' he heard himself say.

'Thanks.' She leaned back against the wall and hung her head, her hair closing like curtains.

Paul tried again. 'We... er...I think we're going home tomorrow.'

She nodded. 'I expect they all will.'

'Yeah, I expect so. I...' he took a deep breath and sucked in his lower lip. 'I just wanted to say... oh, I don't know...I'll see you before we go, OK?'

She nodded again, turned, and left him standing there.

In the morning Jayne woke to the feeling that something was missing. As she regained consciousness the

43

terrible event replayed in her mind. She glanced over at Leyla, still sound asleep, and wondered how she would feel when she woke up. Jayne put on her dressing gown and slippers and went downstairs to her parents' room. She opened the door as quietly as possible to find her mother sleeping soundly on her own side of the bed. The sight of the empty sheets beside her made Jayne choke back more tears. How would they, how could they live without him?

Jayne quietly closed the door and tip-toed along to the kitchen to put the kettles on to boil for the guests' early morning tea. She noticed the tea stain up the wall – someone had cleaned up the mess but she knew that mark would stay there for years to come, a reminder of this tragedy.

Usually it fell to Yvonne to make the tea and take it up to the rooms and Jayne wondered if the guests would still expect it under the circumstances. Olive had laid out the tea trays last night ready for the morning, but it felt so strange to be alone in the kitchen at this hour. Usually by six-thirty her parents were up and doing, preparing the breakfast, boiling kettles. The thought of her dad organising the guests' morning papers at the table brought forth more tears. She wanted to be so brave, to be strong for her mum and help her to continue running *Seawinds* for the rest of the season, but at the thought of them all coping without their father, the sadness he left in his wake... she felt chilled and empty as if part of her soul had gone to join him. She couldn't believe she would never see her father ever again. She could still hear his voice and almost believed he would bounce into the kitchen at any minute.

Her mind was a whirlwind of questions: Why had her father gone out walking in that terrible weather and how did he fall? Although dangerous, he knew that cliff path well. He'd often gone walking along there and stopped to watch the waves slowly rolling in or crashing against the rocks below. It

44

was almost mesmerising. Perhaps that was it — perhaps he had lost his balance? Had it really been so windy that a gust had knocked him over? How long had he been lying on the rocks before George found him?

One of the kettles whistled her out of her thoughts. She poured the water onto the tea in a big white china pot, gave it a stir, and clattered on the lid. Working on automatic pilot she poured a cup and took it along the passage to her mother's room, the silent house waiting for the onslaught of guests coming down to breakfast. Jayne had been instructed to keep her mum in bed this morning but Jayne knew she would want to get up and carry on as usual.

The morning light had not dared to enter the tightly drawn curtains. Jayne switched on the bedside light and put the cup and saucer down. She gently swept the hair off her mum's clammy forehead. 'Mum?' she said softly, 'I've brought you some tea.'

Yvonne looked as though she was unable to focus, lines of trauma etched on her face. 'Thanks, love. What time is it?'

'7 o'clock, but you stay there. Doctor's orders.'

'But there's the breakfast to cook and toast to be made. And the papers...' she flopped a hand over the covers. 'And what about the tea trays? And I've got to go to the hospital...'

'Don't worry,' said Jayne, tucking her mum's hand back in. 'Olive's coming in. We'll do it together.'

'No,' Yvonne shook her head, 'It's not right. I'm getting up.' She threw off the bedclothes and tried to stand but toppled back on the bed.

'There! I told you – you must do what Doctor Graham said. We'll be fine. Everyone will understand.' Jayne tucked her mum back in bed, patted the bedspread and walked to the door. 'I'll pop in later.'

Yvonne looked at her daughter. 'Are *you* all right, love? Did you sleep?'

Jayne nodded and closed the door behind her. She couldn't tell her mother about her nightmare – she had been searching the beach for her father, desperately calling his name into the wind until she finally woke up to the terrible truth in a cold sweat.

As she turned to go into the kitchen, Leyla and Symon came downstairs in their pyjamas and sat at the kitchen table expecting breakfast. Jayne poured them each a bowl of Rice Krispies and put the milk on.

'But we always have boiled eggs,' pouted Symon. When Jayne didn't answer he asked for the sugar.

'Oh, here,' said Jayne, shoving the sugar bowl in front of him. 'You'll have to make do this morning.'

'Why? Where's Mum?'

'In bed, resting. Doctor Graham's orders.'

'But...'

Leyla gave him a kick under the table. 'Do as Jayne says, there's a good lad.'

Olive arrived, threw her coat on the hook on the kitchen door and set to work taking out saucepans and lighting the grill. 'How's your mum?'

'Oh, don't,' sighed Jayne. 'I took her a cup of tea a little while ago but she looks dreadful.'

'Poor lady.' Olive looked around the room. 'And poor you, all of you. What d'you think will happen now?'

'Why?' said Jayne. 'We'll keep the business going of course. I can't see Mum doing anything else.'

'Even when you've gone to art school?'

Jayne nodded but she had the uneasy feeling that nothing would ever be the same again. And being the eldest, would she be expected to help run *Seawinds* instead of going to Cambridge?

Olive began cooking the bacon, sausages and eggs, then the fried bread. The smell of the food turned Jayne's stomach. 'Don't do any for me Olive. I can't face food this morning.'

'All right. Will your mum want any, do you think?' Olive placed more rashers of bacon under the grill and turned the sausages over in the frying pan. 'I'll take it along on a tray if she does.' She popped up the first slices of toast and placed four more in the toaster.

'I shouldn't think so but I'll go and check.'

Thankful to get away from the smell of the food, Jayne uttered a faint 'good morning' to Mr and Mrs Smythe who were heading for the dining room and stood to one side to let them pass. She opened the door a crack and peered into her mum's bedroom. She was fast asleep. Jayne closed the door without a sound and went back to the kitchen.

'Mum's sleeping, Olive. I think it's best we leave her. She'll only want to come and help and the doctor's given me strict instructions to let her rest this morning.'

'OK.' Olive dished up two plates of eggs, bacon, sausages, mushrooms, tomatoes and fried bread and put them

47

on a tray. 'That's Mr and Mrs Smythe's. Do you want to take them in?'

'No.You do it,' said Jayne, 'I'll carry on here.' She couldn't face Paul and his mum and dad after last night; she would never forget their pitiful faces. 'In the meantime Leyla can make some more tea.'

Leyla looked up from her book. 'What's that?'

'I said you can make some more tea, can't you?'

'I 'spose so, but it's my job to feed the hens.'

'You can do that later. We've all got to pull our weight now, you know. All hands on deck,' and as she said this, Jayne had a vision of that first morning in 1958 when they had just arrived and her father barking his orders. She burst into tears and ran upstairs.

'Now you've done it!' said Symon.

'*I* haven't done *anything*, for your information,' Leyla stuck her tongue out at her brother.

Olive burst in through the door. 'Now, now, what's all this? Come on, it's hard enough without you two squabbling. Where's Jayne?'

'Leyla made her cry,' said Symon.

'Didn't.'

'Did!'

'Now, that's enough,' said Olive, 'both of you. You'll have your mum in here, then where will we be? She's meant to be resting.'

Leyla and Symon looked at each other. 'Sorry,' said Leyla.

48

'I'm sorry too,' said Symon. 'Come on, Leyla. Let's get dressed and help Olive.'

They threw back their chairs and clambered upstairs and Olive couldn't help smiling.

After breakfast taxis were summoned to take the guests, who didn't have transport, to Newquay railway station. They gathered together their suitcases and belongings and one by one offered their condolences to Jayne and Olive standing by the open front door. The last ones to leave were Paul, Katie and their parents.

'We're very sorry,' began Ken Smythe standing inches away from Jayne. 'Harry...' he shook his head, unable to utter another word. Jayne searched his face but couldn't read his expression. With bowed head he carried their two suitcases down the steps and out to their Ford Anglia.

'We are very sorry, love,' reinforced Paul's mum. 'Oh dear, I don't know what else to say.' She rummaged in her handbag for her hanky, dabbed her eyes and nose and patted Jayne's shoulder with a gloved hand. 'Bye, bye, love. I hope you'll be all right. We'll be in touch. Give Yvonne my love.' She forced a smile and followed her husband down the steps. Katie gave Jayne and Olive a weak smile and followed on behind.

Paul stood waiting for Jayne to say something, anything. He would've liked Jayne to himself but Olive stood staunchly by her side. They both stared at him. He wanted to say so much, to ask Jayne if he'd ever see her again but he couldn't find the words. He settled for a quick kiss on her cheek and slumped down the steps.

FOUR

In Jayne's bedroom at the *Captain Tregenna,* a slice of sun fell through a gap in the curtains urging her to the window. She padded across the wonky floor and drew back the curtains. Under a cloudless cerulean sky, the sea was calmly lapping the shore, the white cottages that clung to the hillside and the green and purple cliffs were all bathed in golden light. A painter's paradise. Her gaze fell on the vase of flowers and she smiled, remembering the previous evening. Seeing Cornwall on a day like today who would want to live abroad? What had made Paul emigrate to Australia? It was a drastic step. She tried to cast her mind back for clues, to the last time she saw him, but the memory that always fought for attention was the gaping emptiness left by her father's death. But little sparks of memory had surfaced when Paul looked at her last night and her heart had remembered how he'd made her feel when she was seventeen. She recalled the way he'd sat watching her last night, his easy manner and how she'd had to drop her gaze for fear of giving too much away. There was no doubt she still found him attractive, more so now if that was possible. There was a mysterious worldliness about him, something she couldn't quite grasp.

Jayne filled the little kettle and set it to boil on the hospitality tray and placed a tea bag in the white porcelain mug. Remembering the early morning tea trays her mum used to provide – running up and down stairs, collecting the empties, all that washing up – how much easier it would be to run a guest house these days! Perhaps they could resurrect *Seawinds*. It was a very attractive thought.

As she sat drinking her tea and gazing at the familiar view, she imagined spending the day with Paul and hearing more about his life in Australia, walking along with him in the sunshine and maybe sharing a joke. Meeting him again after all these years was unbelievable. If a psychic had predicted they would meet again she would never have believed them. But there were some questions gnawing at the edge of her mind to which she hoped she would find some answers today.

She showered, dressed in white jeans and a navy and white striped sweater and went down to breakfast. The room smelt of the previous evening's revelry with a distant hint of tobacco smoke. In the cold light of morning it looked a little sad as if waiting for a renewed conviviality.

Jack knew she was there and came out from behind the bar with a menu and a cheery smile. 'Mornin'. Sleep all right?'

'Yes, thanks. Beautiful morning.'

'Aye it is. Can I get you a pot of tea or coffee?'

'Tea, please Jack.'

He scurried away and left her with her thoughts. She glanced at the breakfast menu – almost identical to the food her mum and dad used to serve.

Jack came back with a tray bearing a stainless steel pot, a white cup and saucer, milk and sugar. He set it down on the table.

'There we are. Have you decided?'

Feeling suddenly ravenous she decided to forgo her healthy eating for once. 'I'll have the full English, please.'

51

'Toast and marmalade?'

Jayne nodded. 'I know I shouldn't, but hey!'

'That's the spirit!' Jack smiled, wrote it down on his pad and promptly went back behind the bar to the kitchen.

She felt a little odd having the bar to herself and wondered why there were no other guests at breakfast. Maybe it was too early in the day for them or too early in the season. But Cornwall was busy most of the year nowadays, even more popular than when her mum and dad ran *Seawinds*. If only it had continued to get busier, perhaps then her dad wouldn't have worried so much about money.

She poured herself a cup of tea and checked her watch. Paul had said he would come to pick her up at 10 o'clock. She wondered what he was doing right now. Would he be telling Katie all about his evening? What would she think? Would she even remember Jayne? Katie must've been twelve the last time she saw her and she fell to wondering what sort of life Katie had carved out for herself.

Jayne was jogged out of her thoughts by the delicious sight and smell of the fried breakfast coming towards her.

'Here we are, then,' said Jack. 'Anything else you need, just shout.'

The food was every bit as good as she'd expected and Jayne wondered who was ensconced in Jack's kitchen doing all the work. She would pass on her compliments before she left tomorrow morning.

Feeling ready for whatever the day held in store, Jayne gathered her handbag and a pair of sunglasses and ran downstairs. Waiting for Paul in the car park, she felt a buzz of expectation in the air. The vibrant turquoise sea with a strip of purple on the horizon made her remember her father's

52

repeated intentions to paint the scene. But then again, she was guilty of the same procrastination. Even so, it was such a shame Harry never fully made the most of his time here. She shook the thought into the breeze; it spiralled up and away towards the Atlantic. Filling her lungs with the ozone she gloried in the gentle breeze blowing her hair back from her face.

This was the picture that greeted Paul as he drove up. He felt like a teenager again. 'Gently does it,' he told himself.

He greeted her with a smile as she dropped into the passenger seat of his rented silver Honda.

'What a great morning!' said Jayne.

'Yeah,' Paul agreed, 'we must've done something good in our lives to get weather like this today!'

Paul drove smoothly up and down the narrow, winding coast road towards Padstow. Steep grassy banks sprinkled with campion, celandine and valerian lined the roadside. On the hills, cows chewed the cud and in the distance sheep munched at the edges of the moorland. The countryside looked brand new this morning and around every bend little glimpses of sparkling sea came into view.

'Would you like some music?' asked Paul. 'There're some CDs in the glove box.'

'Later, maybe. I want to hear more about your life in Oz. Do you plan on staying there?'

Paul smiled. 'Something tells me you already know the answer to that.'

'So, you want to come back?'

Gladys had been right, then.

'Yeah, I feel I've exhausted all my possibilities down under.'

Jayne's mind was running ahead threatening to trip her up. 'So what *are* your plans?'

'Well, for now, I'm staying with Katie and Martin for a month.'

'I know. Then what?'

Paul didn't want to tell Jayne of his long term plans while he was driving. He wanted to sit face to face, eyeball to eyeball. He wanted to see her reaction, feel the vibes. 'Just a minute,' he swerved round a bend and came upon a lay-by looking out towards Trevose Head where swathes of purple heather stretched far into the distance. He stopped the car and looked at her. 'How would you feel about me putting in a bid for *Seawinds*?'

She blew out a sigh, her eyes wide. 'Gosh! You're right, you are full of surprises! It's a good job I'm sitting down.'

'Well?'

'God, I don't know. Yeah, I suppose so, if that's what you want.'

'I thought you'd be happy.'

'You've just knocked me sideways. What do you plan on doing with it, anyway?'

'Open it as a surf school. That's what I know best and that's what I'm good at. I've had forty years' experience in Oz and now I think the time's right for me to make a difference here.'

'You seem very sure of yourself. Done any research?'

He shook his head. 'No need. There's nothing I don't know about the business and North Cornwall's ripe for the plucking.'

'But don't you think they've got surf schools in Newquay?'

'Yeah, but they're just playing at it. In Australia...'

Paul's words receded into the background as Jayne's thoughts galloped away into the future so fast she couldn't keep up. He wanted to buy *Seawinds*! They could run it together, maybe get Leyla and Symon down here. Daisy and the children could come down in the summer holidays. They could all live together like in the old days, the house was big enough. But then there was Michael – and the memories... Whoa! She put the brakes on.

'You've gone all quiet on me. What's wrong?'

'Nothing. It's just rather a lot to take in at the moment, that's all.'

'Why? You got plans for the old place?'

'I don't know, it's early days, what with Mum not long passed and the memory of Dad...' She picked at her fingernails.

'Aw, Jayne, I'm sorry. I didn't think. That's me all over – I get an idea in my head and just run with it. I shouldn't have said anything.'

'No, it's all right. For what it's worth, I think you might be onto something. But let me think about it, OK?'

'Sure. Like you said, early days.' He reached across her, took out a disc from the glove box and slid it into the slot. The Beach Boys '*I Get Around*' blared out.

It brought a smile to her lips.

'That's better,' said Paul. He shoved the car in gear. 'Come on, let's see what Padstow has to offer.'

They parked down a road overlooking the Camel Estuary and walked along the cycle trail that was once part of the railway that Dr Beeching had terminated in the 1960s. Cyclists sped past eager to get on their way, some with baby carriages strapped to the back of their bikes, dogs running alongside. Jayne and Paul strolled along past the pungent-smelling fisheries with crusty lobster pots stacked in a heap, past the quay with a constant motion of visitors walking by or sitting on the wall. A very expensive-looking fish restaurant and little cottages sat bunched together overlooking the car park where once the railway station had stood, and the Camel Estuary beyond. Further along they came upon some small independent shops displaying an array of goods from beach shoes to seashells, sat amongst Cornish ice cream kiosks and little pavement cafés, all buzzing with activity.

In the little harbour a multi-million pound gin palace was crammed in alongside a few working fishing boats and yachts, their rigging clanking in the breeze and the reflection from their masts rippling on the deep green water.

Jayne stopped and leaned on the iron railings to take in the scene. As always when she was near boats her mind sprang to her father. 'Dad loved boats but the guest house demanded so much of his time. He painted very little too. I used to tell him to *make* time to enjoy the things he loved but he never did.'

Paul nodded. 'Yeah, I remember. I've got a boat back in Sydney harbour.'

Jayne stood upright. There was something she was dying to ask. 'So far, you haven't mentioned having any family over there.'

He smiled. 'I was wondering when you'd get round to that.'

'Well?'

He shook his head. 'Nah, not now. I lived with a girl for twenty years. We had a son.'

Jayne waited for him to continue. She noted he spoke in the past tense.

'He contracted leukaemia when he was three; died when he was ten. He was a great kid, you'd have liked him.'

Jane instinctively squeezed Paul's hand resting on the railing. 'Oh, Paul, how awful for you. I'm so very sorry.'

'Thanks, but it's all in the past now. No good brooding over it.'

'How long ago?'

Paul looked down into the dark water between the boats, as if searching for the right words. 'Five years October just gone. Trish and I...we never had any more. I know what you're thinking – old to be a dad – but she was younger than me. But instead of bringing us closer together it drew us further apart. Things went from bad to worse and we finally split up. I never found anyone else; I didn't want...' he turned his back to the harbour, squinted up at the sky. 'I kept the school going of course; it was a lifeline but I was living like a robot, just going from day to day. Then last year I sold the house. And now I'm here.' He turned back to her. 'Now it's your turn.'

Jane marvelled at the easy way Paul switched off his grief. It had never been that easy for her. 'OK, but do you think we could grab a coffee somewhere first?'

'I don't see why not. Looks like a good place up there,' he said, pointing across the harbour to a café high up above a flight of stone steps. 'Looks like it's got Crazy Golf, too.'

'Ha, count me out. I'm useless at that. Michael...' she shook her head. For a split second she forgot herself. Now wasn't the time to talk about her husband.

Paul smiled. 'Say no more; I get the message.'

They sat at a table on the stone terrace overlooking the harbour, the defunct railway bridge straddling the Camel Estuary in the distance, emerald hills and multi-coloured patchwork fields beyond. Like a scene from an old railway poster, thought Jayne, and she tried to imagine what it must have been like when the steam trains were running. She couldn't remember coming here as a child —with so much going on at *Seawinds* they were prevented from having days out as a family – but she had a few memories of meeting up with her teenage friends in the 60s, popping into different bars in the evenings, listening to live folk music. Good times.

They ordered two cappuccinos and sat back to enjoy the surroundings. Immediately in front of them, sparrows hopped about the low hedge and under the tables, pecking at the crumbs previous customers had left behind. Jayne committed the scene to memory; she couldn't remember a time when she felt so relaxed. She took out her sunglasses, not only was the sun very bright, but she wanted to mask any tell-tale signs of discomfort when she embarked on her story. She wasn't sure how much to tell Paul. If she wasn't careful she'd get carried away, laying her emotional cards on the table and that would never do.

Two foamy cappuccinos sprinkled with chocolate were delivered to their table. Jayne spooned some of the froth to oil her throat and began. She wasn't sure what would come out and hoped she would be able to restrain herself from babbling on.

'Well, here goes... my turn. Michael and I met in Cambridge when I was at the Art School,' she kept her eyes focused on the scene in front of her. 'He was studying economics at university. He was living at home on the outskirts of Cambridge – I used to stay there some weekends.'

Paul took a mouthful of his coffee and nodded for her to continue.

'Anyway, Cambridge became our home town. He got a job with the housing department at Cambridge Council.' Jayne took a breath. There was something she wasn't sure about telling Paul. She didn't know what he'd think of her but they'd come this far and anyway, it wasn't the taboo subject it once was. 'I fell pregnant with Daisy and had to get married.' She glanced at Paul but his expression didn't change. 'I was still at the art school then and Michael moaned bitterly when I told him I was pregnant...'

'...What?' Paul nearly choked on his coffee. 'He complained? What sort of guy is this?'

'Oh, don't. Money is everything to him. He wanted me to give up my course and get a job but I didn't want that. I wanted to finish what I'd started but he said we couldn't manage on his money alone. Anyway, I'm not going into all that now but suffice to say our marriage suffered as a result.'

Paul whistled through his teeth. 'Jeez, I'm not surprised.'

Encouraged by Paul's sentiment she pushed on. 'It was difficult looking after Daisy and going to art school. Michael's mum did what she could but she was a weak woman and I was too far away from my mum. I thank God she never knew the extent of our problems. We used to go down for holidays but Michael, if he went, always put on an act for her. She was running the business as a B&B by then – she'd stopped providing evening meals, it had become too much for her.'

Paul thought about this. There was a memory struggling for air but he smothered it. Instead he said, 'What about Leyla and Symon? Did they used to go down for holidays?'

Jayne nodded. 'And later on, Leyla's kids,' she smiled. 'We all used to have barbeques on the beach...'

'...Ha, yeah, nothing like a barbie on the beach. Sorry. Go on.'

'There's not much more to tell.'

Paul silently berated himself. If he hadn't butted in Jayne might've opened up a bit more. He wanted to ask the ultimate question. He let it whirl around his head to make the words fit together, then he plunged in. 'You still together? You and Michael?'

'Huh, there lies the grey area.' Jayne drained her coffee cup as a full stop.

'I see.' Paul bit his lip to refrain from looking too cheerful. The thought that his plans could finally be realised was like the dawning of a bright new day. *Steady*, a voice in his head told him, *Be careful, or you might send the lady running back to Cambridge. Then where would you be?* 'Would you like to walk on the beach?'

Jayne frowned. 'There's a beach here?'

'Yeah, just up a bit further along that path,' he said, pointing into the distance, 'just past the war memorial.'

'I'd like that. I've been here countless times in my youth but mainly to hang out with friends in the bars. I don't remember seeing a beach. How strange.'

As they walked along the path that led slightly uphill, with a grassy area on both sides, they encountered a trail of people all doing the same – some going, some coming back, parents with babies in lunar-module buggies, children on scooters, dogs wagging their tails, all enjoying the sunshine. Jayne and Paul became more comfortable with each other, a brush of the hand, a knowing smile, a joke exchanged. To Jayne it felt as if the years had concertinaed. Through a gate the view spanning the calm pale blue estuary opened up before them. They trudged down through the grassy sand dunes to the shoreline and took off their shoes, rolled up their jeans and paddled in the cool crystal clear water. They talked and laughed and splashed one another like a couple of kids. They sat overlooking the estuary towards the prosperous resort of Rock in the distance and the playboy yachts of the second home owners from the big city.

Paul nodded to the scene. 'What would you give for a slice of that life?'

Jayne was thoughtful. She'd never needed much to keep her happy. 'It doesn't appeal to me. I'd be happy with sun, sea and sand and just enough money to enjoy it.'

'I'm glad you said that. I think it's a false world they've carved out for themselves over there. They've lost sight of the things that really matter.'

So, thought Jayne, Paul wasn't materialistic like Michael. That was refreshing.

Eventually, they both agreed they were hungry so they walked back into town and bought fish and chips in yellow polystyrene containers as the sun cast long shadows across the pavement. They managed to squeeze onto a bench by the harbour with a family all enjoying their piping hot fish and chips and steaming pasties, their Labrador waiting patiently for and leftovers. The Constantine brass band had assembled close by and people were tapping their feet to the music.

'We used to do this as kids,' said Paul.

Jayne popped a big flake of fish in her mouth and licked her fingers. 'So this is what you used to get up to with your mum and dad when you came down for holidays?'

'Yeah,' said Paul, a nostalgic tone to his voice. 'Good times.'

If only it hadn't turned sour that last year.

The sun was sinking lower over the town, signalling the end to a perfect day. A sudden cool breeze drifted off the water and Paul felt Jayne shiver next to him. He draped his jacket round her shoulders and she gradually leaned into him. It felt as natural as breathing. The band played their last number: *Those Magnificent Men in Their Flying Machines.* The audience clapped and cheered and finally began to disperse back to their B&Bs, holiday cottages or wherever they had come from. Jayne and Paul sauntered past all the shops and outlets now with closed signs on their doors and windows and back along the quay. At the end of the trail the owner of the cycle hire kiosk was taking in the last bicycle and locking up.

Walking back to the car Jayne let her hand drift into Paul's; their palms grazed and Paul's fingers clasped around hers with an affectionate squeeze. She remembered that feeling. It was as if they had awoken from a long sleep, like two people in Sleeping Beauty's castle, and were ready to resume life where they'd left it fifty years ago.

The fading sunlight cast long shadows over the hillsides as they drove back to the *Captain Tregenna*, happy and relaxed in the companionable silence.

In the car park Paul turned off the engine and turned to her. 'Well, have you enjoyed yourself today?'

'Yes. It's been wonderful. Thank you.'

'Good. All part of the plan.'

Jayne thought he seemed very sure of himself. He was free as the wind but it was too soon for her to get romantically involved, and besides, he was a stranger in many ways; someone she had to get to know again. And then there was Michael...

Paul read her mind. 'What do you think you'll do? About your marriage, I mean?'

Jayne wasn't sure how to respond. Paul was running way too fast for her and this needed more than a passing reply, but she felt he needed an answer. 'I don't know. There's a lot to think about.' She fell silent thinking about how she might approach Michael. She wasn't sure how he thought of her these days or how he would react to her wanting to leave him. Although they had grown apart she was frightened to ask him outright. 'Then there's *Seawinds*; I'm not looking forward to negotiating with Masterson over the asking price. But then again...I don't know if we should sell.'

'Sure. You've got a lot on your plate. If you need any help...with legal stuff, I mean...'

'Thanks.'

He nodded to the Tudor doorway. 'Would you like a night-cap?'

'That's very nice but I'm really tired. Do you mind if we call it a day?'

'Not at all. I've enjoyed it.'

He wanted to kiss her, to see if it still had the same effect as he remembered, but he was unsure how she'd respond. She stroked his hand with a feather-light touch sending a sharp wake-up call through his body. A voice in his head told him what the hell, time was running out. He moved closer. Their lips touched, lightly at first then became more urgent, teeth grazing.

Jayne pulled away. 'Oh God, Paul! I'm not ready for this.'

'Of course, I'm sorry.' He put a hand on his heart. 'I'm not *really* that impulsive teenager anymore, honest!'

She smiled, gently kissed him on the cheek and opened the car door.

'What you doing tomorrow?'

'I've got to go to the house to look for something for Leyla, then I've got to take the key back to the estate agent.' She stepped out of the car, eager for escape all of a sudden, and banged the door.

Paul leaned over, wound down the window and smiled up at her. 'I'll come with you, if you like. Be around ten, OK?'

'Sorry, Paul. I need to do this on my own. I'll phone you.'

His face fell. 'Sure. You know best.' He wound the window back up and shoved the car into gear.

Jayne watched him drive away, not knowing if she had upset him or how to take his last remark. She went straight up to her room. She wasn't in the mood to sit in the bar making small talk with Jack.

64

FIVE

The next day Jayne parked well away from *Seawinds* and hoped Gladys hadn't spotted her car. There was no movement in the net curtains next door so Jayne ran up the steps and let herself in.

It had been a long time since Jane had ventured down to the cellar. Memories abounded as she clonked her way down the bare wooden steps: she and Leyla painting the walls of the redundant coal cellar with some green paint they had found, sticking their pictures on the walls and using old cushions to make it cosy. They had renamed it The Den. They'd been so young, so ambitious in their endeavours. But the only snatch of natural light came from the window in the larger room next door. She went in search of a torch and found one in the old desk.

She went back to The Den and flicked on the torch. Yes! It worked, although it wasn't a very strong beam she hoped it would be enough to last until she found what she was looking for. The familiar musty smell rose up as she draped the faded threadbare curtain to one side and pinned it on the hook. Shining the torch around she noticed that the original pictures were long gone, replaced by some that her daughter Daisy and Leyla's twins had drawn, the paper curled at the edges with time. The dusty glass-topped coffee table was still marked by lemonade rings and beside a colouring book lay various coloured biros and felt tips as though the kids had only just left.

65

Leaning against the back wall was the old brown suitcase that Jayne and Leyla used to sit on when they were children. Without thinking, Jayne picked it up and shook it. There was something inside, it sounded like papers or books. She tried the rusty locks but they wouldn't budge. Now she thought about it, that suitcase had always been locked. She wondered if there was a key somewhere and went in search of it.

She turned off the torch to save what little battery life was left. In the larger room below the small window that looked out onto street level, was a wooden bench with old paint cans, the odd roll of brightly coloured wallpaper, jam jars full of rusty nails and some that had once contained turpentine with hardened paintbrushes suspended in them. A few rusty tools hung on the wall. Above and to the right, three stone hot water bottles sat on the shelf, along with other redundant bits and pieces all covered in decades of dust and cobwebs. To the left side of the bench, in the corner, stood the faded leather-topped desk where her father had once kept his business accounts and where she had just found the torch. She began opening the drawers but none of them contained what she was looking for. She rummaged around in the old pens and ink bottles perched on the desk top until she found a tiny brass key at the bottom of a jam jar full of paper clips. She went back and tried one of the locks. To her surprise it sprang open. She unlocked the other.

The suitcase revealed some musty brown envelopes. On further scrutiny Jayne discovered they were tax demands and bills addressed to Mr H. Williams; the most recent dated March 1968. Were these the cause of her father's depression? But she couldn't remember them being mentioned by either of her parents.

66

The family story that Jayne had always assumed to be true, was that Harry had been a freelance artist in the 1950s based at an advertising studio in the West End, and when the work began to dry up Harry decided to leave the rat-race and move the family down to Cornwall. But he must have forgotten to pay his tax demands and let them mount up until years later when the tax office caught up with him and the guest house wasn't doing so well. It was the beginning of package holidays to places like Benidorm and Torremolinos and Cornwall was feeling the pinch. But some faithful guests, including Paul's family, had continued to visit.

She had a vague memory of her father finding it difficult to pay the bills even when they lived in Sidcup, until that win on the horses, and then they were suddenly packing and making arrangements. It all seemed so simple to Jayne as a child. She now felt a deep sadness at the thought of her father keeping all this to himself. Why hadn't he been able to confide in her mother? Or had he? There was no one left to ask now.

Jayne checked her watch – she'd spent too much time down here already but she needed to find Leyla's diaries. She pulled open the cupboard door and there on the bottom shelf was a shoebox decorated with faded pictures of cats that Jayne remembered Leyla cutting out of magazines. She blew off the ancient dust, sat on the old blue floor cushion and removed the cardboard lid to reveal the diaries that ranged from 1964 to 1969. Leyla would've been eleven when she wrote in the first one. Jayne flicked through it; mainly drawings of animals and writing about her friends at her new school – the usual kid's stuff. Riffling through the others, Jayne's gaze fell upon the 1968 volume.

She flicked through the pages until she reached the beginning of April. She sat glued to the writing. It was all there – how their father had become withdrawn, sinking into a deep depression and drinking more and more, and her mum complaining bitterly about the Johann Strauss waltzes reverberating throughout the house and the fact that Harry barely left the front room except for meals. As she read, Jayne thought she heard a faint sound of music coming from somewhere. *The Blue Danube?* But that was ridiculous, the house was empty. Nevertheless, she turned off the torch and went upstairs to investigate.

She entered the front room and stopped. Nothing had changed yet something felt off. A coldness in the room that hadn't been there before and a faint scent of tobacco smoke, but no one had smoked in here for years. She shivered and ran to close the sash window that had been left open a crack. She looked down onto the road and listened. The music wasn't coming from out there. She walked all round the room, listening with her head on one side. It now sounded as if the music was coming from the next floor so she ran up and checked, only to find the waltz faded away when she reached the landing. She shrugged. She must've imagined it. She hurried downstairs. In the hall, her eye was drawn to the place where the tea had splashed up the wall in 1968. The stain was very faint, if it was there at all, but she knew exactly where it happened. She blotted out the memory and ran back down to the cellar.

Two leaves of folded foolscap paper had escaped onto the floor. That was odd – she hadn't noticed those before. She picked them up and read. The content was so adult she could hardly believe it had been written by her fourteen-year-old sister. Leyla must've eavesdropped on a heated argument that had taken place the night before her father died.

Saturday 13th April 1968.

I'm down in The Den to get away from Dad's music. I've got a story to write for English and I can't concentrate upstairs with that racket. There's only a 25 watt bulb in here, but I can just about see enough to write. Jayne never comes down here at night — says it's scary — but I thinks it's quite cosy.

Oh, I think the music's stopped! I can hear voices coming from upstairs. Oh, no! Now they're coming down here!

"We can talk in here, Ken. I know I said you could come down for holidays without paying me a penny but the truth is I can't afford to do it anymore."

"Well, it's just not good enough. How do you think it would look if I told Lottie?"

"I know, but the truth is, the business is on its beam ends. We're not getting the bookings and now the bloody tax office is on my tail. I don't know what I'm going to do. I'm in it up to my neck."

"Come off it, Harry. You're doing all right."

"Huh, it might seem like that to you."

"Look, I'm in dire straits myself and I need that money," shouts Ken. "Lottie's had to take on menial cleaning jobs — it's very degrading."

"Well, I'm sorry about that but I haven't got it. Like I said, the business is in poor shape. Can't you give me more time? "

"More time? You assured me I'd get it back once you were on your feet. That was years ago. Sorry old chum. Enough's enough. If I don't get it soon I won't be answerable for my actions."

"Oh God, Ken! Look, I'm sure we can come to some arrangement. What if I pay you in instalments, five pounds a month? How's that?"

"Huh, you tried that before, remember?"

69

Someone has run back upstairs and banged the door. I hope Dad doesn't start playing Strauss again.

Jayne rubbed her chilled arms. So, Harry had borrowed money at some point, a lot of money by the sound of it, but what on earth was that for? Ken. That was Paul's father, surely? The text on that sheet of paper finished there. The other, headed Sunday 15th April, was too painful for Jayne to read. She wondered if Paul knew about this row. She put the sheets of paper back in the shoebox and closed the lid on the sad story.

Jayne checked her watch. Goodness, she'd been sitting here for over two hours and she had to take the key back to Masterson's and phone Paul before she went home. She still had to make a reservation for the Isle of Wight ferry and she was desperate for a cup of coffee.She stuffed the shoe box into the suitcase and locked it. Tucking the key into her jeans pocket she trudged back up the cellar steps.

Struggling to lock the front door she heard a voice behind her. 'Here, let me.'

She turned to see Paul on the bottom step. 'God, Paul! You made me jump.'

'Ha, you know what they say – guilty conscience! Been doing something you shouldn't?'

She scowled at him.

He held up a hand. 'Hey, only joking.'

He took the suitcase from her. 'Jeez, what's in here? Weighs a ton.'

'Oh, only a few books. Listen, I'm gasping for a coffee. Let's dump this in the car and take the key back and go to the beach café. Then I must go home.'

'Sure.' Paul lifted the case into Jayne's boot. 'I was hoping to get here sooner – have a look around the old place.'

'But you know what it's like – you spent enough time here.' She slammed the boot shut.

'Hasn't it changed, then?'

'Not much. Mum didn't have the money to do it up.'

He thought he detected an off-hand tone in her voice and it looked like she'd been crying. 'What's the matter?'

'Nothing.' she snapped.

'I don't believe you. Come on, I'll buy you a coffee and you can tell me all about it.'

'I haven't got time; I've got to get home.'

'But you just said...'

'...I know what I said!' She hurried down the road ahead of him. People stood and stared but she took no notice.

'Jayne!' he caught up with her and pulled her round to face him. They stood in the middle of the pavement, glaring at one another. 'What *happened* in there?'

'I'll tell you what happened,' she shouted, not caring who heard, 'a family lost a precious father and now it looks like I've lost everything!'

He didn't understand – she wasn't making sense. 'I *know* how upsetting it is to lose a loved one. I *know* about your Dad, I was there, remember?' He touched her arm, 'Jayne!'

She shrugged him off. 'I've gotta go.'

He stood there, dumbfounded.

Without a backward glance she rushed down the road. Tears pricked her eyes, she felt like collapsing in a heap in the middle of the high street.

71

She found herself in the estate agent's facing Masterson's desk.

He looked up. 'Ah, there you are. All done?' On closer inspection a look of concern crossed his face. 'My dear Mrs Green, are you all right?'

Jayne came to her senses. 'Er..Yes...just had a bit of a shock, that's all.'

'Oh dear. I'm sorry to hear that. Can I get you a cup of tea or coffee?'

She nodded, took out a tissue to blot her eyes and nose. 'Coffee, please.'

'Have a seat.'

She sat picking at her hands in her lap. Now the heat of the moment had left her she was embarrassed – she must look such a mess.

Mr Masterson came back with the coffee and put it on the desk in front of her. She stared at it and gave a little laugh. 'Funny, isn't it? You think you know someone but you never *really* know them.'

Mr Masterson had no idea what she was talking about. He assumed it was a personal matter and not something to be discussed with a client – highly unethical. Instead his thoughts turned to the subject of *Seawinds* but from the state of Mrs Green he wondered how to tell her that the old guest house was in need of major refurbishment if it was to be sold as a viable proposition – walls knocked down, en-suites installed and a fitted kitchen – it would amount to tens of thousands. He wondered if she was prepared to spend that kind of money. And if it was to be sold as seen, the asking price would reflect this. His instinct told him it would be another shock for her – being in a prime position, she was probably expecting the

72

house to fetch a good price to be split three ways between herself and her siblings.

He took a breath. 'Mrs Green, I wonder... how would you feel if I told you it would benefit all concerned if *Seawinds* were to be put up for auction?' He let the words percolate and waited.

She swallowed a mouthful of coffee, 'Really? Well, d'you know what? I can't afford to keep coming down here. I'll leave it in your capable hands.'

His eyes widened. 'Are you sure? What about your brother and sister? Don't you want to discuss it with them first?'

'I'm sure they'll agree. I'll have a word with them, of course, but it seems the best way.'

'Very well. I'll get the necessary documents drawn up and be in touch.'

'Thanks. To be honest, it's a weight off my mind. That door should've been closed long ago.'

She ran up the road hoping Paul wasn't hanging around, jumped into her Z4, shoved it in gear and roared up the road. It would be a very long time before she came back, if ever.

SIX

On the west side of the bay, Paul sat at a table on the elevated decking outside the beach cafe warming his hands round a mug of tea. He had a good view of the bay from up here: cumulus clouds bubbling up, waves rolling in. A few couples were walking their dogs, one man throwing a stick for his golden retriever. Gulls cried and circled overhead, kids wrapped up against the chilly wind, digging in the sand. Digging down to Australia it looked like. He remembered doing the same with Katie. How irate she used to get when he wouldn't let her use his special spade! The memory brought a brief smile to his face. He hadn't felt this depressed for years, so baffled was he by Jayne's behaviour this morning.

He didn't know what Jayne really thought of his idea of buying *Seawinds* but her behaviour had not put him off making an offer. Living here in North Cornwall would go some way towards healing his wounded soul. He might even be able to right the wrongs of the past. His dream was to turn old *Seawinds* into a surf school and run it with Jayne, if she agreed, of course. But after that outburst this morning he knew he'd have to tread carefully. He'd sold his beach house in Australia with the terrace that looked out towards Bondai Beach – it had been a good investment back in the day and he thought the return on the sale was more than enough to pull the old guest house into shape.

Yeah, there was a lot he needed to discuss with Jayne. *If* he ever saw her again.

He drained his mug and decided to call into Masterson's.

He hesitated for a second then entered. At the desk in front of him sat a grey-haired man in a pinstripe suit checking his computer screen. Paul had a sense of déjà vu and began searching his data banks but the man tugged him back to the present.

'Can I help you?'

'Hi. Yeah, I'm looking to buy a guest house in this area.'

'Certainly, Sir. Have a seat.'

Paul sat down and took in the surroundings. It was an OK outfit, but a bit old-fashioned by Australian standards. Pale green didn't really cut it these days and in his mind's eye he began changing the colour of the walls and rearranging the reception area.

Mr Masterson came back with a few brochures and handed them to Paul. 'Here we are. That's all we have at present, I'm afraid.'

'Thanks.' Paul thumbed through them but *Seawinds* wasn't there. 'Is this it?'

'Was there something in particular you were looking for, Sir?'

'Er, yeah. I heard there's a place called *Seawinds.*'

Mr Masterson looked over the top of his glasses. 'Ah, I'm afraid I'm awaiting confirmation on that one. The family have yet to decide if they want to go ahead with an auction sale.'

'Auction sale?'

'Yes. That property is in need of major refurbishment.'

'I see. But is there any chance I could take a look?'

Mr Masterson looked at his watch then at his computer screen. 'Not today, I'm afraid.'

'Tomorrow, then?'

'I can do Wednesday?' Mr Masterson thought this man very persistent and if he wasn't much mistaken he had an Australian accent to boot.

Paul nodded.

'Can I take your name, Sir?'

'Sure, Smythe. Paul Smythe.'

Mr Masterson wrote it down. 'Ten o'clock any good?'

'I'll be there.'

'Oh, you *know* the property?'

Paul nodded and set the brochures down on Mr Masterson's desk. 'I've been past it.'

'I see.' Again Mr Masterson studied Paul over the top of his spectacles. Something about the name Smythe was wriggling just out of grasp. 'Tomorrow, then.'

'Yeah, thanks.'

***

The burnt orange sun was sinking low in the sky as the attendant beckoned Jayne onto the Isle of Wight ferry. She counted herself lucky to have gained a place – they'd had a cancellation – otherwise it would've meant staying another night at the *Captain Tregenna*. She had set out in good time to catch the ferry but her journey from Cornwall had been tediously slow until she reached the M27. Had it not been for the rolling countryside and her favourite CDs she would've been chafing against time. But as usual on these long journeys, the driving cleared her head and she was able to think more rationally. However, when it came to Paul, his father and the diaries, she had more questions than answers.

Jayne locked her car, made a note of the deck number and climbed the iron stairs. The viewing lounge was oppressive with people milling around eating pungent food, so she stepped out on deck to breathe in the fresh air and drink in the view. As the ferry set off, the pale buildings of Portsmouth slowly receded and the distant dark blue mass of the Isle of Wight lay ahead. The Solent was calm as a mill pool. On one side of the ferry a couple of yachts with bright red sails drifted past, while on the other a large Brittany ferry had Jayne wondering where all its passengers were going. She felt a tad envious. Michael had never wanted to holiday abroad. It was as much as she could do to persuade him to take a week off to go down to Cornwall.

As the ferry drew nearer to the Isle of Wight, the last of the bright orange sun slipped further into the blue and purple horizon throwing a dazzling glow on the water. Jayne always enjoyed this ferry journey and was sorry when it ended. She looked down into the foaming swell trailing the ferry and a sudden cool breeze had her hunkering into her fleece.

She was looking forward to seeing Leyla again; she was hoping to rectify the regrettable lack of closeness to her sister of late and not just in miles. Their time together at their mother's funeral a week ago had been all too brief – no time for a decent conversation. Jayne would also like to see more of Symon and Maggie, but their lifestyle was so hectic, the demand for his expertise continually being sought on both sides of the Atlantic. Jayne was very proud of her brother but she felt sidelined by his lifestyle.

Jayne began to reflect on her mother's last days. It was one of the carers who found her on the floor – Yvonne had ventured into the kitchen to make herself a cup of tea and tripped over the mat and banged her head on the fridge. The carer rang Jayne to say her mother had been taken to Newquay hospital, complaining bitterly. Jayne had collected Leyla on the way but it had been difficult to contact Symon: he had been in the States on business and finally had to charter a special flight back to England. He arrived the next day but regrettably he couldn't stay – he was needed on a multi-million dollar project; if he wasn't there to oversee the proceedings and something went wrong, there would be hell to pay.

The doctor had informed them that Yvonne had suffered a slight stroke – they were running a series of tests. However, after a week in hospital it became clear that Yvonne's condition was more serious than first thought and she was slipping in and out of consciousness. Jayne and Leyla continued to stay at *Seawinds* during this time, hoping and praying for their mother's recovery. Two weeks after the accident Yvonne seemed to be picking up and the doctor advised she be transferred to a care home. Yvonne was having none of it – she demanded to go home to *Seawinds* so this was arranged. Symon had managed to join them for a couple of days. They watched and waited but none had expected to be orphans within the week. They had watched their mother shrivel a little more with each passing day, her skin paper thin and sallow, until one evening Jayne was alarmed by a further change in her mother and she rang the doctor.

Jayne had listened to what she assumed to be the ramblings of an old woman on the brink of death. None of it made any sense. Yvonne kept saying the same thing over and over. Ken and Lottie Smythe's names were mentioned and Yvonne kept saying, 'I should've helped him.' Could Yvonne have prevented Harry's death? If so, how? Jayne had tried to ask her mother, but she passed away with her dying words, 'I did it all wrong.'

As the ferry came into Fishbourne, Jayne wiped away a tear and ruminated on this unanswered question. She had dismissed it at the time as her dying mother's ramblings, but now, after reading Leyla's diary, she was beginning to wonder if her mother's last words would eventually have some meaning.

The deck rattled loudly as Jayne drove off the ferry and headed up the winding road towards Sandown. Beginning to feel the effects of the journey and eager to be at Leyla's, she put her foot down, the green velvet hills getting darker by the minute. England's green and pleasant land, thought Jane. She couldn't envisage living in hot, dusty Australia and wondered again what had driven Paul to the other side of the world.

Paul. She'd been very short with him. On reflection, she didn't think he would've known anything about the row between his father and hers. But what if he did...She supposed she would have to broach the subject at some point.

As her wheels crunched on the gravel Jayne picked out Leyla's silhouette in the doorway, her halo of unnaturally red hair backlit by the glow from the hall light. Jayne felt a rush of happiness as she locked her car and hurried to greet her sister.

'What took you so long?' asked Leyla.

'Oh, don't. The roads just get worse. Got the kettle on?'

'Of course.' Leyla led the way down the hall to her cosy kitchen drenched in warm light. 'It's lucky you arrived when you did; you've rescued me. I've been slaving over a hot computer all day.'

'How's it going?'

'Not bad. Did you remember those diaries?'

'Yeah, they're in the boot. I'll get them when I've had some tea.'

A meowing Heather, her thick fluffy tail held high, came running up to Jayne. She picked her up, buried her face in her soft blue-grey fur and chucked her under the chin.

'Oh, she can stand any amount of that,' said Leyla, as she stood the kettle on the Aga hotplate. 'I don't give her enough attention, especially when I'm working.'

'What's the project this time?'

'Well, I think I've bitten off more that my quota... I'm writing a book on the changing attitudes towards mental health in the twentieth century.'

'Gosh! That's ambitious, even for you.'

'I know. But I've started so I'll finish – the trouble is there's such a lot to take into account...'

Jayne zoned out; she wasn't interested in all the pros and cons. Her mind settled on what Leyla would think about Paul finding her again after all these years. Being a psychiatric consultant until she retired three years ago, Leyla was always interested in people's characters and what made them tick.

Leyla placed a mug of tea on the granite breakfast bar in front of Jayne then poured one for herself. Jayne smiled – Leyla always used a tea pot, just like Yvonne used to, never a tea bag in a mug. Jayne released the now struggling Heather and the cat ran to curl up in front of the dark green Aga.

Leyla busied herself taking pots and pans out of the cupboard. 'I've got a couple of lemon sole. I thought we could have them with a salad and new potatoes?'

'Mm, lovely. Is it just us tonight, then?'

Leyla nodded and went to the sink to scrub the potatoes. 'The kids are up in the Shetlands, hiking. Sooner them than me! How's Daisy?'

'Battling morning sickness. It's a wonder she was able to make it to Mum's funeral. I told her not to bother but she insisted. I don't think that late flight from Edinburgh did her any favours.'

Leyla stopped scrubbing the potatoes. 'I thought she looked a bit peaky. Ugh, childbirth. I'm glad I never have to go through that again!'

Jayne took a sip of tea and nodded. 'Yeah, I know what you mean, but I'm quite concerned – she's no youngster and with three others to look after... Tim's very good, though. I'm sure he's taking care of her. They both love kids, the trouble is I don't get to see them. I'm missing them growing up. If it wasn't for the house sale, I'd be up there helping out.' Jayne raked a hand through her hair. 'I feel like I'm being pulled in all directions.'

Leyla nodded. 'Yeah, must be hard; a pity they live so far away.'

'Seems to be standard for our family, that's why I'm thinking it might be an idea to hang on to *Seawinds*.' She wasn't going to let on that Masterson had suggested it be put up for auction. Not yet.

'Really? What's the latest?'

Jayne pictured herself sitting in the cellar with the diaries and the suitcase full of tax demands. 'It looked very sad. It *is* very sad.'

'What is?'

'Everything, really.'

81

Leyla put the pan of potatoes on the Aga and looked at Jayne. 'Now, don't start getting all morose on me. Mum wouldn't want us brooding over the past. She wasn't like that.'

It was true; after the shock of Harry's death Yvonne had got on with her busy life and never looked back. Or had she? Jayne often wondered what her mum really thought, deep down. Jayne's thoughts turned to Paul and she wondered when to tell Leyla about him wanting to buy *Seawinds* and the estate agent telling her it should be auctioned off.

'You OK?'

'Sorry. I've had a weird couple of days. I wasn't expecting *Seawinds* to pull me in like it did.'

Leyla studied Jayne's faraway look. There was obviously more to come.

'Don't start analysing me, Leyla. It's just...' Jayne took a deep breath and blew it out.

'OK. We'll leave it there for now. Why don't you make yourself comfy in front of the wood burner while I finish here?'

Leyla sounded as if she was talking to a patient – old habits, thought Jayne. She sauntered into the large square lounge with her mug of tea, stretched out on the squishy grey sofa in front of the wood burner and tried to relax. She looked at her watch. Oh God! She should've rung the adult learning centre to let them know she wouldn't be taking the next art class. They'd be wondering if she was going back after the Easter holidays. She'd do it tomorrow.

Tomorrow. She wasn't relishing the thought of going home, having it out with Michael over his prolonged absences of late. She couldn't help wondering who he was with and what he was doing while she was away, but she had a pretty

82

good idea. Rubie, her old friend from college, had always been hovering on the sidelines but Jayne had refused to believe that Rubie would do that to her. But Jayne had become distanced from Michael, their busy lives, their holidays mostly spent apart. Jayne and Daisy in Cornwall while Michael stayed in Cambridge...

Watching the red and orange flames curling behind the window of the wood burner, Jayne's thoughts turned to a drizzly afternoon in 1970. She was on her way to a seminar, in her second year at Cambridge Art School, struggling with her heavy bag full of books. All of a sudden the handle snapped and she dropped the lot on the wet pavement. She was embarrassed; other students stared as they hurried past but no one offered to help. She quickly bent down and gathered her books and art work and saw two brown moccasins come to rest in front of her.

'Hey, let me give you a hand.'

She looked up into a smiling face framed by floppy blond hair.

'You looked so pathetic there I just had to do something!'

Jayne grinned self-consciously and felt her face colour up.

'Michael Green, at your service!' He wiped two books with his sleeve and handed them back to her. He gazed at a drawing he had picked up. 'Oh, so you're an art student?'

Jayne nodded. 'Jayne. Jayne Williams.' She took the drawing from him and tucked it into the folder with the rest.

He looked at his watch. 'Looks like you could do with a drink. They're still open.'

'Sorry, I can't, I'm late for my seminar.'

'OK, later then? I'll meet you at the main gate. Six o'clock.'

Jayne nodded her thanks and stuffed her books and files into her bag, clamped it under her arm and stared after Michael – his confident swagger, the bounce in his step.

After the seminar, Jayne told her new house-mate Rubie, about the incident.

'Michael Green? You lucky sod! I don't think he knows I exist...'

As Jayne listened to her friend babble on she wondered if she was ready to go out with someone like Michael. She hadn't wanted to go out with anyone since Paul but all her friends had boyfriends and so not wanting to spend another evening alone, she plucked up the courage and went along.

Michael took her to a busy pub in the heart of Cambridge, a favourite haunt for students. Jayne didn't want to get drunk every night like the other girls who went there, flirting with anyone who gave them a second glance and getting into trouble, but for some reason she felt safe with Michael.

The pub was heaving. Michael steered Jayne towards a small table in a secluded corner and went to the bar to order their drinks. She felt conspicuous and vulnerable sitting on her own and was in two minds whether to slip out the door, when he came back and stood a gin and tonic in front of her and pint of beer for himself.

They hadn't been sitting down five minutes when Rubie came up to them. She lived up to her name – dark red lipstick and red hair. 'Hi Jayne,' she said, keeping her eyes fixed on Michael, 'I don't think I've seen you in here before.'

Jayne felt like Miss Goody Two-shoes, took a sip of her drink and smiled.

Michael grinned. 'My idea, I'm afraid.' He leaned back in his chair and drew on his cigarette, studying the two girls; one flaunting herself, the other as pure as the day she was born. He saw Jayne as a challenge; he was looking forward to using his powers of seduction to get under that cool exterior. He hadn't earned the knickname The Fridge Mechanic for nothing.

Rubie realised her charms weren't working on Michael. 'OK. See you around, eh, Michael?' She sauntered off to find someone else to pay her some attention.

Jayne and Michael talked all evening of their likes and aspirations. While he plied her with alcohol she began to gain in confidence and she told him about her home and her family on the Cornish coast. She had wondered if he would be interested in her as he seemed so street-wise and different from anyone else she'd met but to her surprise he listened attentively. After a few hours she'd lost count of how many drinks she'd had. Once outside the cold night air hit her and she threw up on the pavement. She was full of apologies but Michael laughed it off, said it wouldn't be the last time and took her home in a taxi. Her mouth felt dry and even in her drunken state she realised her breath must smell putrid. She rummaged in her bag for a piece of chewing gum and covertly popped it in.

Michael escorted her to the door of her house, steered her into the dark porch, tilted her chin up and went to kiss her. She turned her head away.

'No, Michael. My mouth's disgusting!'

'It won't be that bad. I saw you chewing,' he grinned.

85

She had never been kissed so sensuously and she forgot all about her stale mouth.

'That's just for starters,' he said.

Every nerve in her body was tingling with anticipation as he repeated the kiss, but on that occasion that's where it ended.

They continued dating and one sunny Saturday Michael took her punting on the river Cam. The waterside was bustling with tourists all queuing up to be taken out in punts but Michael was an expert and escorted Jayne onto their own punt, just the two of them. She felt proud to be beside him and basked in the admiring glances he attracted. Jayne decided the other students escorting their companions weren't a patch on Michael – the sun catching his blond hair, his strong arms and expertise as he sank the pole into the water and out again, guiding them smoothly downriver. She felt like royalty as she lay back and let her hand trail in the cool silky water. Looking up at Michael's intent gaze on her, she felt her entire body tingle with anticipation. A few hundred yards further on he found secluded spot, moored the punt under a curtain of willows and lay down beside her. It was as if they were the only two people in the whole world. Slowly and skilfully he seduced her and only when it was too late did she realise what had happened. She was beside herself when she missed two periods. How could she be so unlucky? She kept it to herself at first – she instinctively knew that Michael would not be expecting such news and she couldn't tell her mum. She definitely couldn't tell Rubie and she didn't have anyone else to confide in.

Like most girls, Jayne had aspirations of a white wedding and walking down the aisle but alas, Michael told her he wasn't religious, he didn't believe in church weddings and he wasn't going to be a hypocrite. She pestered him saying her mum would have liked to see her get married in church but he wouldn't relent. However, with no father to give her away and not wanting to cause any arguments, Jayne gave in.

They were married in Shire Hall, Cambridge, in November 1970. She chose her outfit carefully in the fashion of the day – a pale blue jump suit which went some way towards hiding her thickening waist, a white floppy hat and feather boa. It was like a society wedding all paid for by Michael's father. The hall was packed with family and friends, the men in top hat and tails and the women in flamboyant outfits and big hats. But it all went by in a blur for Jayne, wondering how she should break the news of her pregnancy. She felt sick most of the time and ate very little at the reception.

Yvonne, Leyla and Symon travelled up by train from Cornwall and stayed in the University Arms hotel. When Yvonne saw the array of sophistication at the hall she felt like a country bumpkin and unworthy to be the mother of the bride.

'Don't worry, Mum,' said Jayne, planting a kiss on her cheek and looking at Leyla and Symon. 'You all look wonderful. I'm very proud of you and over the moon to have you here.'

'Wild horses couldn't keep us away!' said Yvonne, 'but I would've liked a bit more notice.' She stood Jayne at arm's length to take in her image and Jayne hoped against all odds that her mother wouldn't notice her tight jumpsuit. 'I'm proud of you, love. I just wish your dad could've been here.'

Jayne hugged her mother. 'It's OK Mum. I'm sure he's watching from 'up there."

But Michael wasn't happy when Jayne told him she was pregnant. He had assumed she was on the pill like most

87

girls he knew. Having been forced into an untimely situation, Jayne and Michael were forced to live with his parents until they had saved enough money to put down a deposit on a house. He turned into Jekyll and Hyde; angry one minute then couldn't apologise enough the next. She was distraught; through her tears she told him it took 'two to tango'. He even asked if she'd consider abortion but Jayne stood firm – that went against all her morals – it would be tantamount to murder, she told him. He started staying out late while she stayed in with Michael's parents and she was often in bed asleep when he came home. She gritted her teeth and bore the horrendous morning sickness, some days feeling as though she would die, while Michael acted as if it was nothing to do with him. She couldn't tell her mum, didn't want her to know the extent of her problems. She didn't want to admit to making one of the biggest mistakes of her life.

The birth at the old Cambridge maternity hospital was a terrifying experience. Michael took her to the hospital but wouldn't attend the birth even though he was invited in by the midwives. Jayne was frightened, she didn't know what to expect. The big midwife joked with the little trainee while they went about their business and Jayne felt like a piece of meat on a slab. In the early hours of a dreary February morning, her daughter Daisy was born. Jayne felt a rush of love for the tiny being who screamed in her ear. Above all she was compelled to protect her baby and give her everything she needed; although the only experience of looking after a baby was a distant memory of watching her mother caring for her sister and brother. Jayne had to learn the hard way by trial and error but gradually, day by day, she became a competent mother.

Somewhere far off Jayne heard the tinkling of cutlery and opened her eyes. 'Oh, I must have nodded off.'

'I thought I'd let you sleep,' said Leyla. 'You looked like you could do with it. Here.' Leyla handed her a large gin and tonic and put another log in the wood burner. Heather sauntered in and jumped onto Jayne's lap, padded around and curled up contentedly. Jayne loved stroking the cat's soft thick fur and mourned the fact that Michael would never allow her or Daisy to have any pets.

'I should've phoned Pam at the centre. She'll wonder why I haven't been in touch.'

Leyla looked aghast. 'You're not still teaching?'

Jayne nodded.

'Blimey, Jayne, you should be devoting your time to your own painting.'

'I know, but I haven't had any inspiration for years. I don't seem to be able to settle down to it.'

Leyla stared at her. 'What's that husband of yours doing these days? Still up to his neck in fanny?'

'Leyla!'

'Well...he doesn't deserve you. Never has.'

'Just because you're a feminist and hate all men...'

'That's not strictly true. But after all the years you've given him you should think of yourself and what you want out of life before it's too late.' Leyla went to the kitchen and said over her shoulder, 'Food's about done.'

They both sat in silence at the breakfast bar and tucked in, just the ticking of the school clock for company. 'This is lovely,' said Jayne. 'Do you remember the fish dishes Mum used to cook?'

Leyla nodded and put a forkful of succulent fish in her mouth.

89

'And the herbs...do you remember the little herb garden Olive used to look after? Like the song – parsley, sage, rosemary and thyme.'

Leyla smiled. 'And the new-laid eggs. I used to love collecting them in the morning before I went to school. I can still smell the bran mash I used to feed the hens. Those were the days.'

'They certainly were. Everything tasted so much better back then.'

They finished their meal and Leyla went to put the plates in the dishwasher.

Jayne noticed. 'You use the dishwasher when there's only the two of us? Isn't that a bit extravagant?'

Leyla looked sideways at Jayne and poured her another gin and tonic.

'Sorry. That's not me talking, it's Michael. He's always penny-pinching.'

Leyla stared at her. 'It's about time you ditched him, you know.'

Feeling more relaxed after two G and Ts, Jayne let her guard down. 'I know, and I've got a feeling he's fooling around. With Rubie.'

'What? I rest my case.' Leyla had thought Rubie an unlikely friend for Jayne from the start. 'How long have you suspected there was something going on there?'

Jayne shrugged. 'I don't know, I suppose I shut it out. I didn't like to think she'd do that to me.'

Leyla shook her head. 'You always were too trusting. What about when her marriage went tits-up? That must've made you think?'

'Not really. She seemed genuinely upset and I tried to help her through it.'

Not wanting to cause her sister any more discomfort, Leyla changed the subject. She took their drinks through to the lounge and took out a CD. 'Let's have a bit of Einaudi. That's one guy I could go for in a big way! Anyone who writes music like that, well... I tried to play some once but it's more difficult than you think.'

Jayne looked across at the shiny black upright piano that had belonged to Harry. 'Do you play much?'

'Nah, I'm too lazy. Can't be bothered to practise.'

Jayne remembered how Symon had followed in Harry's footsteps. 'Have you heard from Symon?'

'Not since the funeral. Why?'

Now for the big subject, thought Jayne. 'When I spoke to Mr Masterson about *Seawinds* he suggested all three of us discuss putting it up for auction.'

'Really? *That* bad, eh?'

Jane nodded. 'He seems to think so.'

'Well, in that case I suppose it would make sense. We'd need to get a second opinion though. Why don't you give Symon a ring?'

'What, now?'

'Why not? No time like the present. He had some unfinished business in The States but he should be back by now. Ask him and Maggie down here for a couple of days.'

'OK. But there's something I need to tell you first.'

'What's that?'

Jayne kept her eyes fixed on Heather, 'I bumped into Paul Smythe while I was down at the bay. He's been living in Australia but wants to come back to England.' She looked up at Leyla. 'He's thinking of putting in a bid for *Seawinds*.'

Leyla lifted her chin and narrowed her eyes, 'Is he now.'

Jayne gave her sister a questioning look.

'I don't know, just something about that family.'

Now for the unsaid. 'I've been thinking about what Mum said at the end, you know, about Dad.'

'What about it?'

'Well, maybe there was something we never knew about. Regarding Dad, I mean.'

'Go on.'

Jayne thought very carefully about how to word the next sentence. It seemed all wrong to accuse her long-dead father but after reading Leyla's account of the conversation between her father and Ken Smythe, she was sure there was something he'd done, something he'd regretted. 'Well, after reading your diary I get the feeling he did something that none of us knew about. Something to do with money he borrowed from Ken Smythe'

Leyla was all eyes and ears. 'Surely not! From what I can remember, that family never had two ha'pennies to scratch themselves with. And in any case, he wouldn't have been able to keep it from Mum now, would he?'

'I don't know, but I wish I'd taken her seriously and asked her. She was very distressed at the end but I put it down to delirium.'

92

'People say the strangest things in their final hours, you know. They don't always make sense. I don't think you need worry about it. It would've come out before now in any case.'

Jayne nodded. 'I suppose so. There's no one to ask now, anyway.'

Leyla smiled smugly. 'Now, go and give Symon a ring.'

Symon sat in his study going over the plans for his next project. He hadn't been back long from the States but he'd learned to deal with the jet-lag. Maggie still worried about him though, saying he was 'getting too old for all this'. She thought he should delegate more of his work to the younger members of the company but he wouldn't hear of it. He didn't want people saying he was losing his grip and, in any case, he enjoyed the buzz of meeting deadlines. But he always looked forward to coming home. Maggie was a homemaker in every sense of the word and he was thankful. He was the only one of his siblings in a happy and fulfilled marriage. The only gripe he had was that they'd never been blessed with children. Instead he'd thrown himself into his career in London and New York. Williams Associates was a well-respected firm of architects but it grieved him that he didn't have any children to inherit the business.

Maggie came in with a glass of red wine and put it on his desk. 'Still at it, darling? I thought you wanted to put your feet up and watch *Lewis*.'

'I'll be down in a minute, my sweet.'

She draped her arms round his neck and nuzzled his cheek. 'You work too hard, you know.'

He smiled and took a sip of wine. 'Mm, is this the one from Fortnum's?'

'Yes, the Fortnum and Mason Chateau – if we approve they'll send us a case.'

As he focused on the screen, lost in his work, Maggie knew it was pointless pursuing the wine order any further tonight. She was planning a dinner for one of Symon's clients but he always insisted on selecting the wines. Symon had a good head for business; it had enabled him to rise to the top with a client base envied on both sides of the pond. He had designed and built his own house in Blackheath, but somehow, even though Maggie was an excellent homemaker, it had never really felt like home to him.

Maggie left him and went downstairs and into the kitchen to prepare dinner. In the hall the telephone rang. She picked it up.

'Jayne! How lovely to hear from you. To what do we owe this pleasure?'

Maggie listened as Jayne told her all about *Seawinds* and the anticipated sale and how the estate agent thought it should be auctioned off. 'Just a moment, I'll get Symon. I'm sure he'll be very interested.'

Symon came rushing downstairs and grabbed the phone. 'Jayne! What a lovely surprise. How are you?' He doodled on a note pad while Jayne relayed what she had just told Maggie. 'I'm wondering if it's worth salvaging,' he said, at length, 'give it a makeover. I'd enjoy it and we could get a healthy price for the old girl. I could draw up some plans...maybe spare a couple of days at the end of the month to take a look...any good?'

'I was hoping you'd say that but I was wondering if all three of us should take it on, use it as a holiday home. Mum left it to all of us in her will and I for one would love to see it remain in the family. What d'you think?'

Symon scratched his head. 'Seriously? OK, Jayne, I think we all need to meet up. There's a lot to consider.'

Jayne's thoughts strayed again to Paul. 'I think the sooner the better; there's already someone interested in putting in a bid.'

'Really? Do you know how much?'

'I'm afraid not, early days and all that.'

'What does Leyla think?'

Jayne looked at her sister standing a few feet away. 'Well, I think she'd rather us refurbish it than a certain person get his hands on it!' Jayne put the phone on loud speaker so Leyla could join in the conversation.

'So you know the person in question?' said Symon.

'Yes.' Wait for it, thought Jayne. 'It's Paul Smythe. Remember him?'

'Yeah...hang on,' Symon searched his memory. 'Didn't he used to come down every year with his parents and sister? That was a strange affair as I recall. Why do you think they stopped coming down all of a sudden?'

Jayne looked at Leyla again who took the phone. 'It's because Dad let them stay free of charge every year, and when he died, it all stopped. Dad had a huge bust-up with Mr Smythe the night before he died.'

'Good God! How do you know?'

'I was hiding in the cellar listening to them. It's all in my diary.'

Symon whistled through his teeth. 'Christ, Leyla! And you've sat on it all these years?'

'I'd forgotten about it until Jane brought it up and, in any case, what good would it have done?'

'I can't believe it. So what are you saying? That Smythe was somehow responsible for our father's death?'

'Maybe.'

'Christ. So what about Paul?'

Jayne took the phone. 'I spent the day with him on Sunday and he told me what he had in mind for *Seawinds*. I didn't know about the bust up until Leyla asked me to collect her diaries from the cellar. I sat reading them on Monday morning before I left. Paul was waiting for me when I locked the front door. I was too upset by this time to confront him. I expect he wonders why I left in such a hurry.'

Symon tried to envisage the scene. After all these years Jayne sounded as though she still had a soft spot for the guy. Symon's recollection of Paul Smythe was a cocky little shit who upset Jayne on her seventeenth birthday. 'So what's he been up to all these years?'

'He emigrated to Australia and used to run a surf school. Now he wants to come back and open one here, at *Seawinds.*'

'I see. Well, it all depends on how much the house means to you. You're the eldest, after all.'

'I know, but Symon, we all grew up there and you were *born* there for heaven's sake! It's our spiritual home. It really needs all of us to meet up and discuss it,' she threw her sister a smile, 'and I haven't spent any quality time with my little brother for ages.'

96

Symon chuckled – he wasn't very little anymore. Six foot four and working out in the gym whenever he could. 'All right, I'll see what I can do. Maggie keeps nagging me to take some time off and you're right, it would be really great to meet up.'

June 1956

Yvonne and Harry had decided to take their two little daughters down to Cornwall, to *Bay View* for the summer holiday. It was more expensive in the height of the season but Harry couldn't see how they would manage the train journey with a newborn baby and two young children if they left it to the back end of the year. He was looking forward to the time when he could drive and take his own car down to Cornwall. He was working on it.

Mrs Crago welcomed them as always and showed them upstairs to the family room. She had enjoyed seeing Harry and Yvonne's family grow. Each time they came to stay they were just as enthralled with *Bay View* as the first time. Mrs Crago smiled and hummed to herself as she went about her business. Her guest house was like their second home and Yvonne seemed more like one of her own than a visitor.

This afternoon the sun was beating down on the beach, the dry sand scorching hot. Yvonne shifted uncomfortably on the rug while she watched Jayne and Leyla playing a few feet away in the damp sand at the water's edge. She was thankful she had bought sun hats for the girls and smothered them in sun cream. She had three weeks to go before her baby was due and hoped she would make it home before he put in an appearance, for she hoped the baby would be the longed-for boy this time. Both Jayne and Leyla had arrived ahead of their due date and she hoped for the best.

Harry had insisted they holiday now otherwise they wouldn't manage it at all this year. They would have had to make do with a week in Westgate, staying with his old mum who had moved there to be with her brother, and Yvonne was apprehensive about that because old Mrs Williams had never taken to Yvonne.

Harry looked up from his newspaper. 'Ice cream anyone?'

Jayne and Leyla threw down their spades and began jumping up and down.

'Ooh, yes please, Daddy,' said Jayne. 'Can I come with you?'

'All right.'

'And me,' shouted Leyla, 'don't forget me!'

'Come on then. We'll leave Mummy to have a rest,' said Harry, gazing lovingly at his wife who was positively blooming. He was amazed how pregnancy agreed with her but this time she had found the last trimester rather trying. 'Shall I get you a wafer, love?'

Yvonne nodded and watched them go. She felt so much better here at the bay than she did at home. It truly was a life-giver. Every time they came here she felt the same. As she watched Harry and her daughters walk to the sea front and disappear into the long queue at the ice cream kiosk, her mind began to wander. She imagined living here with the three children growing up, teaching them to swim and taking advantage of the sea air and the wonderful fresh fish. Harry always looked different here at the bay, too. He lost his town pallor and was more relaxed without the deadlines always on his tail. Yvonne enjoyed their prestige but there was a price to pay.

Taking advantage of a few minutes to herself, she lay down and stretched out her legs and gloried in the warmth of the sun penetrating her body. She breathed in deeply of the life-giving sea air and listened to the distant sounds of children playing. The sea was calm today instead of the crashing waves so often experienced here. A few seagulls squawked overhead and a deep contented sigh escaped her. She began to doze.

Harry meanwhile was getting impatient at the amount of time it was taking to buy the ice creams. The queue was slow to reduce with only one assistant in the kiosk. He tried to find Yvonne in the distance and hoped she wasn't getting sunburned – she was all too lax with taking care of her skin – but there were people in the way.

Finally, Harry was at the front of the queue. He asked for two vanilla cornets and handed one each to Jayne and Leyla and bought two ice cream wafers for Yvonne and himself. The ice cream instantly began to drip down his arm and he licked at the wafers whilst seeing the girls back onto the sand. By the time he reached sight of Yvonne, Jayne and Leyla had ice cream all round their mouths and up their arms.

'Look at you two. What will Mummy say?'

They giggled, they didn't care. Harry had finished his wafer and licked most of Yvonne's by the time he reached her. 'Sorry, love. It was melting so I had to lick it up.'

Yvonne opened her eyes and propped herself up on her elbows. Harry thought he detected a pained expression. 'Feeling OK?'

She nodded. 'Maybe a bit too much sun.'

'How often have I told you…?'

Her face crumpled.

'Yvonne!'

She took deep breaths and let them out slowly. 'I think the baby's coming.'

'Oh, God! What shall I do? Call an ambulance?'

She shook her head fiercely.

'All right, let's see if we can get you back to *Bay View*. Can you walk?'

She nodded. She didn't want the girls to see her like this but true to form, her little one wanted to be born early.

Harry stuffed the rest of the ice cream wafer in his mouth and helped his wife to stand up.

'What's wrong with Mummy?' asked Jayne.

'Don't worry, sweetheart. We just need to go back and see Mrs Crago.'

'But what for? We usually stay on the beach all day.'

'I know but we can come back later, OK?' Harry quickly collected their belongings and gave the buckets and spades to the girls to carry.

Leyla looked confused. 'Where are we going?'

Yvonne tried to placate them. 'Just do what Daddy says, my loves. Mummy needs you to be very good girls. Do you think you can do that?'

They both nodded.

They made their way across the bay, up the three steps, across the road and up the hill towards the guesthouse. There was no way Yvonne could manage the shorter obstacle route today, up the steep stony incline. Halfway up the hill she had to stop and cling on to a wall and Harry began to envisage her giving birth right there and then but the contraction subsided and they were on their way again.

Charlie, Mrs Crago's son, was driving back from Newquay when he saw the family struggling up the hill. He stopped the car and got out. 'Is everything all right?'

Harry rubbed a hand over his face. 'It's Yvonne, she's gone into labour.'

'Goodness, get her in the car and I'll drive ee up there, or would ee rather go to hospital?'

'No! Please, not the hospital!' shouted Yvonne.

Harry and Charlie helped Yvonne into the front seat then Harry and the children squashed in at the back. The little Austin Seven groaned and creaked up the hill and Yvonne gritted her teeth hoping her baby would wait until they reached *Bay View*.

When they arrived Yvonne clung to the banisters and sank down onto the bottom stair hunched in pain.

'I'll get Ma!' said Charlie, and rushed down the passage to the kitchen. Jayne and Leyla stood in the hall looking very concerned.

'Is she going to be all right?' asked Leyla.

Harry drew both the children to him and kissed the tops of their heads. 'She'll be fine. Don't worry.'

Charlie ran past them, out of the door and jumped in his car.

Mrs Crago flew out of the kitchen. 'Charlie's gone for the midwife, be back dreckly. Can Yvonne manage the stairs?'

Harry looked at Yvonne still slumped on the stair, his hand to his mouth.

'No matter, help her in 'ere.' Mrs Crago went along the passage and opened another door.

Harry helped Yvonne to stand up. 'Can you make it to the back room, love?'

She clung to him and nodded.

'The cheel can come wi' me,' said Mrs Crago. She took Jayne and Leyla into the kitchen and closed the door. 'Now, you'm gotta be good girls. Mummy's gonna be a bit busy for a while.'

They both nodded although they didn't understand. Mrs Crago found some colouring books and crayons and urged them to sit at the kitchen table. 'There, thass right. Like some lemonade?'

Their faces lit up. 'Yes, please,' said Jayne.

'And me,' said Leyla.

'Good, thass the way.'

And so the afternoon drifted into evening, the children amusing themselves while Mrs Crago hummed to herself as she prepared the evening meal.

Until a baby's cry could be heard coming from the back bedroom. Mrs Crago smiled. 'I think you'm got a little brother or sister. Shall we go see?'

They nodded and jumped down from the table and followed her.

Dr Graham was fastening his doctor's bag and the midwife was wrapping the baby in a clean towel. She placed the little bundle in Yvonne's arms as she lay back on the pillows.

Harry looked round at his daughters. 'Come and meet your new baby brother.'

'What's his name?' asked Leyla.

'We've called him Symon, with a Y.'

'Good weight, is ee?' asked Mrs Crago.

The midwife smiled, 'Yes, a very healthy six pounds four ounces.'

103

'Good. I'll get en a cup o' tay. You'm earnt et!'

Harry gathered his daughters to him. 'Thank you for being good girls. What have you been doing?'

'Mrs Crago gave us colouring books and lemonade,' said Jayne.

'She's a nice lady, isn't she?' said Leyla.

Yvonne and Harry smiled at each other, their faces glowing with love.

Charlie, bearing a tea tray, knocked on the door. 'Can I come in and meet the new arrival?'

'Yes, yes, of course,' said Harry.

Yvonne, enraptured with the new life snuggled in her arms, smiled and beckoned to Charlie who tip-toed in, set the tray down on the chest of drawers and gazed at the tiny baby.' A fitty little chap.'

'He certainly is,' said Harry, 'but I think this has lengthened our stay. I hope that'll be all right?'

'Proper job,' said Charlie. ' You'm more like family, anyhow.'

Harry picked up his wife's hand and kissed it. They exchanged loving glances in the knowledge that their family would always be welcome at *Bay View*.

EIGHT

This evening, Paul was on his own apart from his ailing mother in the annexe. Katie had grabbed a couple of hours to go to her pilates class and her husband Martin, a computer technician who worked from home, had been called upon to sort out a virus problem.

Paul sat in his sister's living room staring at his mobile. He was still brooding over Jayne's behaviour this morning but was frightened to phone or text her. He hadn't told Katie about meeting up with Jayne, mainly because he had nothing concrete to tell her. Jayne had made a big impression on him on Sunday, so much so that he hadn't been able to think straight. He knew what his sister would say, "Why do you want to strike up a relationship with someone you knew fifty years ago? Aren't you past all that?" But Paul had surprised himself; he'd thought he was past any sort of meaningful relationship at his age. He had chastised himself for acting like his teenage self ever since Jayne gave him the brush-off.

He hadn't mentioned Jayne to his mother either in case it sent her into one of her frenzies. Lottie had always been a bit vague but now the old woman hardly knew what day it was. Dementia was a terrible thing; Paul only hoped he'd escape its clutches. When he'd looked in earlier on his mother she was dozing in front of the telly, her small frame curled into the armchair, still dressed in her nightie and dressing gown. She never seemed to get dressed and go out these days, not since Paul had been there anyway.

Paul paced the floor. He needed answers but couldn't think what to say in the text. He didn't want to sound pathetic and whiny but he couldn't let Jayne slip through his fingers again. He hadn't anticipated she would have such an effect on him after all these years and he knew the sight of her walking into the bar that first evening would stay with him whatever happened. No other woman had had this effect on him, apart from Trish, but she was so different from Jayne. Trish was always immaculately made up, her dark glossy hair in a sleek bob. But Jayne had a natural kind of beauty; she didn't seem to know how lovely she was which made her all the more alluring.

He turned the phone over in his hand, contemplating what to say.   'I'm sorry,' he began, but what was he sorry for? He hadn't upset her as far as he knew. No, scrub that. 'I went in to Masterson's when you left.' No that was no good either. Did he want her to know how earnestly he was pursuing the purchase of *Seawinds*? After that outburst of hers yesterday, that house seemed to have a strange effect on her. Hang it all. He'd leave it.

His gaze travelled over his sister's living room. It was comfy and modern, the lounge walls painted in a new shade of grey, but in his mind's eye he began to rearrange the furniture and paint the walls white. He was feeling homesick for his house in Sydney with its bright and airy living room, the French doors flung open onto the sun-baked terrace, palm trees waving in the breeze and a distant view of the white-hot sand and cobalt blue sea. It was a great place but too many sad memories lived there to hold onto it. He had made the rash decision to sell it and come to England, not really knowing why or what he was going to do when he got here. He had got to thinking about doing something with his life before he was too old to enjoy it and the rosy image of Cornwall had grown and blossomed in his mind. Maybe it was a decision he would regret, but hey, nothing ventured, nothing gained. So much had changed in those intervening years – when he'd left England the decimal currency hadn't really kicked off, the cars were streamlined and so were the women's fashions. He remembered the girls of his youth, he'd been spoilt for choice, but there was only ever one he truly loved. But he'd blown it, big time.

He would never forget that dreadful parting when Jayne wouldn't look at him and the journey home the day after Harry Williams died. It had taken the best part of the day to get home – his father's Ford Anglia had a top speed of 70mph and that was pushing it. The weather hadn't helped – rain lashed the windscreen making his father swear at the incompetent wipers while his mother sat in stunned silence. When they finally reached Peckham, Paul ran to his cramped bedroom and closed the door. He threw himself on his bed with his face to the wall and tried to erase the tragic scene that kept rearing up before him: Jayne kneeling in the hall with her arms draped protectively round her mother. His stomach rumbled echoing the thunder outside but he couldn't face food. He finally drifted off to sleep with the rain beating against the windows.

The next morning the atmosphere in the flat was so thick it was stifling. Even though his father was still officially on holiday he had gone to work leaving the rest of the family in a cloud of depression. Paul had tried to ask his mother about his father's black mood but she refused to open up. Sensing the atmosphere, Katie went out to play with a friend.

Feeling at a loss Paul took himself out for the day to Peckham Rye Park. He felt better in the open air, walking usually produced a few answers to the problems he was contemplating, but he couldn't find the reason for his father's attitude.   There was definitely something very unsettling lurking in the background and he wondered if it would ever come to light.

It was a bright sunny day, people lazing about on the grass, children in the swing park, young women in miniskirts and skimpy halter-neck tops. But none were as beautiful as Jayne. Everywhere he looked he saw her face before him. His mind was working overtime – maybe if he bought a rail ticket and returned to Cornwall? He walked to Rye Lane railway station, scanned the timetable and stood facing the ticket office. He searched his pockets but he only had a few shillings. He could just about stretch to it with his meagre savings from his Saturday job but what if, when he got there, Jayne refused to see him? No, even if he scraped up the money he couldn't risk it.

But the worst of it was when his father came home that evening. Paul said he would like to go back to Cornwall in the summer holidays but his father flew at him.

'What?' he shouted, 'after what's happened? What's the matter with you? I thought you had more sense.'

'But surely...'

'...I'll never go back there as long as I live.' He yelled. 'Anyway, we can't afford it.'

Paul frowned. 'But what's changed? We've been there every year for as long as I can remember.'

'I'm not going into all that now, and that's an end to it. I don't want to hear another word about fucking Cornwall!'

Paul winced – he'd never heard his father use the F word. He couldn't begin to imagine why his father felt so strongly. Of course, Mr Williams' death was a dreadful tragedy but there must've been something more to it than that. But

Paul also knew he would never be able to raise the question again.

That September he went to Plymouth to start a marine biology course and mourned Jayne's absence. They'd had such plans – the two of them both studying for a bright future at the same university– but now all that were left were the memories of her golden hair blowing in the sea breeze and her sad little smile the last time they said goodbye.

The following year in the summer holidays, Paul didn't want to go home. One morning he packed a few clothes and his toothbrush in his rucksack and took a train to Newquay to give Jayne a birthday surprise. But when he arrived at *Seawinds* Yvonne looked at him askance as he stood in the porch.

'Hello love.' Yvonne looked past him, up and down the road. 'Are your mum and dad with you?'

'Er..no. I'm on my own.' Paul craned his neck to look past Yvonne into the hall. 'Is Jayne there?'

'I'm afraid not, love. She's in Cambridge.'

'Oh?'

Yvonne shook her head slowly and clicked her tongue. 'Hasn't she told you?'

Paul, wide-eyed, waited for an explanation.

'She's going steady with a boy she met there. His parents live in Cambridge. Nice lad.'

'What?' Paul looked up and down the road, unsure what to do next.

'Have you come down for a little holiday?'

Paul nodded.

'Oh, dear, I'm sorry, love. We're fully booked, I'm afraid but you can try Mrs Bolitho at *The Tides Reach.*'

109

Paul answered in a small voice, 'Thanks. It's not a problem. I just thought...' He thrust an envelope at Yvonne. 'Could you give her this and tell her I called?'

'Of course, love.'

He ran down the stone steps, turned right, past the pine trees and scrambled down the stony track, down the wonky concrete steps at the bottom and finally jumped onto the sand. He didn't know where he wanted to be but he knew he didn't want to go home. He walked all afternoon, along the beautiful rugged beaches and part of the coast path through the purple heather in full bloom towards Bedruthen Steps and beyond. If anyone had asked him where he'd been he wouldn't have been able to tell them. He tried to book into a few guest houses along the way but they were all full. He even tried the big hotel high up on the cliffs but was turned away. Thankfully it was a warm dry night so he returned to Tregenna Bay. He couldn't risk sleeping in the cave in case the tide came in during the night so he made up a bed on a rocky outcrop and slept under a canopy of stars. He dreamt of Jayne. She had come to him in their cave and they'd made love. It was so real he expected her to be lying beside him when he woke up – he could still feel her presence, smell her scent on the breeze. After breakfast in the beach café, he walked down the high street and came across Masterson's estate agents. There were some places to rent advertised in the window. It crossed his mind that he might be able to take a holiday flat for the rest of the summer. He had some money with him and his cheque book. He could hang out, do some surfing. Maybe Jayne would come home at some point...

He found himself standing in front of a desk. A smart young man in a pin-striped suit looked him up and down.

'Yes? Can I help you?'

Paul looked down at his shabby jeans and raked a hand through his hair. 'Er... I was wondering if you have any places to rent, just for the summer?'

The young man screwed up his face. 'Just for the summer? I don't think we do short-term lets. Just a minute, I'll go and ask. Can I take your name?'

'Yeah, Paul Smythe.'

He wrote it down on his notepad and disappeared out the back.

A young woman sat typing at another desk. Paul met her eye but she glared at him. He had half a mind to leave but the young man came back with a large grey-haired man who shot Paul a disparaging look. 'How long do you plan on staying?'

'Oh, probably six weeks. I'm going back to university in September,' he said, proudly.

'I see. Sharing?'

'Sorry?'

'Would you be sharing with others?'

Paul shook his head; he wasn't sure what the man was implying.

'I know your type. We can't afford to have a load of pot-smoking students squatting in our properties!'

Paul felt the heat rise up his neck and flood his face. He wasn't some bum off the street. 'Look, you've got me all wrong. I can pay!' his hand flew to his wallet to prove it.

The man looked at Paul as if he was something nasty on the sole of his shoe. 'I doubt it. Now, if you'll excuse me, I'm very a busy man. Good day to you.'

Paul banged the door and stuck two fingers up.

His mind was made up. There was no point staying in Cornwall a moment longer. By the time he arrived back at the railway station he had walked off his aggression and decided to drop out of university. He was going to get as far away from Cornwall as possible...

His mother was shouting, bringing him back to the present. 'Paul? Paul! You there?' He walked through to the annexe to find his mother trying to stand up with the aid of her walker, her pale face screwed up with the effort.

'Whoa there, Mum! Easy does it.' He hooked his arm under hers and levered her up. 'Upsie-daisy, where do you wanna go?' She nodded to the bathroom. She was skin and bone. A lump rose in his throat remembering how capable she used to be. 'There we are. You sure you can manage now?'

She nodded again and hung onto her Zimmer frame as if her life depended on it , pushing it along at a snail's pace.

He wondered if he'd ever be able to ask her that burning question: what happened between his father and Jayne's? He knew they went back a long way but, for the life of him, he couldn't remember anything being mentioned when he was a youngster.

NINE

Jayne woke up to the sound of a phone ringing and wondered where she was. Then she heard Leyla's voice.

'Oh, fantastic! I'll tell Jayne. She'll be really pleased.'

Jayne got up, threw on her dressing gown and ran out to the hall. 'Was that Symon?'

'Yeah, he's managed to wangle a few days off. He's going down to Cornwall and wants us to meet him in the *Captain Tregenna* this evening, thinks it best if we act on this straight away. He wants to have a good look at *Seawinds* to see if it's bad enough to warrant an auction. And he's asked his buildings surveyor to meet him there tomorrow.'

'Wow! That's great. Is Maggie going too?'

'He didn't say.'

'OK. I'll jump in the shower then we can get going. Oh, I still need to phone Michael. I haven't been able to get hold of him since I left Cambridge,' she said, going back to the bedroom.

'You've got plenty of time,' shouted Leyla. 'It's only 7.30. I hope I can get a ferry ticket. It's always tricky trying to get off the island the same day. I'll be packing a case if you need me.'

'OK.'

'And I need to ask my next door neighbour to cat-sit Heather...'

In their large open-plan kitchen-diner, overlooking Blackheath common, Symon sat at the shiny granite breakfast bar reading his emails on his laptop while Maggie handed him his second cup of coffee.

'I'm looking forward to going to Cornwall.'

Symon half smiled. 'Who said you were coming?'

'Well someone's got to keep an eye on you. You work far too hard. You should be taking some time out, not whizzing off to Cornwall. Tell you what – I'll drive, you can relax.'

Symon ran a hand over his wife's silk-clad bottom, her lilac dressing gown slipping seductively to reveal a smooth thigh. 'Did I ever tell you how wonderful you are?'

'Oh, maybe once or twice.'

'I'm a very lucky man. Pity Leyla and Jayne can't say the same.'

'That's because they're women.'

'Ha!' He tapped her playfully on her rump. 'You know what I mean.'

Jayne rang the adult learning centre and told her supervisor that the past few weeks had taken their toll, what with her mother's passing and having to organize the house sale. She needed some time off.

'Ah, perhaps now would be a good time to think about handing over the reins. I've got a younger woman waiting in the wings. You've been a great asset Jayne, we'll all miss you, but I have noticed recently that you've been coming in late and looking very tired.'

Jayne was taken aback. 'Oh, really? Well, to be honest I was going to ask...'

'...That's settled, then. You know you're welcome to drop by whenever. Cheers.'

Jayne looked at her phone, 'Flipping cheek!' and chucked it on the sofa. But all of a sudden she felt incredibly free. Now she would be able to devote her time and energy to taking control of her life. She rang home. Still no answer so she rang Michael's mobile. After a few rings he grumped, 'Michael Green'.

'Michael, it's me. I wanted to phone before but I couldn't get a signal. You OK?'

'Yeah, why?'

'Look, I'm at Leyla's but I need to go back to Cornwall. Symon's having a survey done on *Seawinds* and we're meeting him down there later.'

'OK. See you, then.'

'Yeah, I don't know when I'll be home, but I'll try and keep you in the...'

He'd hung up. Jayne chewed her thumbnail.

Leyla noticed. 'Everything OK?'

'Michael just hung up on me.'

Leyla gave her a look as if to say 'sounds about right' and went back to the kitchen. Jane felt the snub keenly. Didn't he care at all about what she did? Didn't he care about *her*? She knew they had gone their separate ways these past few years but she would have to sit down with him when she finally returned home and try and sort this out.

115

An hour later Jayne and Leyla bundled their luggage into Jayne's Z4.

'I rang the ferry office in the end,' said Leyla, as she belted up, 'they told me to come down and wait. Could take a couple of hours or more. I might have to throw myself on the mercy of the ferry staff, conjure up some excuse for an emergency. You sure you're OK to drive? You haven't given yourself time to turn round. I could've taken the Range Rover, you know.'

'No, I'm fine. I know what I said on the phone but I'm fine, OK? I hate being a passenger and I know the road so well, the car almost drives itself. Just need petrol then we're off.'

As she drove out of the filling station, Jayne noticed an old Austin 1100 parked at the side. She remembered learning to drive in one of those back in the day. Her instructor was a thin little man who kept lighting up cigarettes, one after the other, and she couldn't help feeling it was a reflection on her driving. There were no health warnings on cigarette packets in those days and Jayne had been among the many smokers at the test centre, all puffing away, trying to calm their nerves whilst waiting to take their driving tests.

Leyla read her mind. 'Do you miss smoking?'

Jayne shook her head. 'You're amazing. How did you know what I was thinking?'

'Well, doesn't take much working out – I remember, not so long ago, you would light up as soon as you sat in the car.'

'I know, but I've seen the error of my ways and after Michael's scare last year....'

'...Really? I didn't know about that.'

'No reason why you should. Anyway, he got over it. Still drinks too much, though. The doctor advised him to cut down but he hasn't taken any notice. He doesn't like being told what to do.'

'Huh, you don't need to tell me. What about Paul?'

'What about him?'

'Does he have any vices? You haven't said very much.'

Jayne drove into the ferry terminal and parked at the designated waiting area. 'I didn't think you'd be interested in Paul Smythe. Not after what happened.'

'You know me – I'm always interested in people and what makes them tick.'

Jayne shrugged. 'No, he doesn't seem to have any bad habits and he's still slim and he's still got his hair.'

'Ah, nothing like Michael, then.'

Jayne shook her head. 'Nope, nothing like Michael.'

'Let's go and get a coffee while we wait,' said Leyla. 'It's a nice day. We can sit outside.'

Jayne chafed against the long queue in the café. It galled her that she'd spent far too much time waiting for things lately, being prevented from going home on Saturday and now kept from returning to Cornwall. It seemed there were forces working against her, delays she couldn't control and it gave her idle mind too much on which to reflect.

Finally, Jayne and Leyla bought their drinks and took them outside and sat at a white plastic table in the sun.

'I'll just go and ask how long we've got to wait,' said Leyla, and disappeared into the booking office.

117

Jayne sat people-watching and tried to stop her impatience from boiling over. Luckily the coffee was acceptable. She sipped it slowly. One of the ferries had docked and she watched the cars driving off and up the road onto their destinations. She wondered where all these people were going. Leyla had chosen the Isle of Wight as a refuge after her divorce; somewhere she could put a sizable amount of water between herself and her ex. It had been a pleasure to come here for holidays when Daisy was little; it was an easier and shorter journey than Cornwall, and as Leyla's bungalow was situated on the east side of the island with access to the beach, they'd had many a day swimming in the sea and picnics on the sand. But again, Michael very rarely came with them saying it was too remote for him. He preferred to be in the middle of the action, meaning the pub culture of Cambridge.

They finally got the all clear to join the ferry queue in one of four lanes.

'I can't believe how long this is taking,' said Jayne. 'I'm glad I don't live here. I'd never leave the island!'

Leyla chuckled, 'Now you know why I'm such a recluse.'

At last Jayne was instructed to drive onto the ferry. She locked the car, made a note of the deck number and together they climbed the narrow iron stairs. Leaving Fishbourne behind, the ferry sailed along on a glass-like sea and Jayne felt instantly calmer. Gulls soared overhead, the sun tipping their wings whilst Jayne and Leyla stood out on deck by the railings watching the distant mainland growing closer.

Leyla turned to take in the view. 'I'm always surprised how beautiful this is.'

Jayne nodded. 'You should've seen it yesterday. The sunset was amazing. I never get tired of watching the sun on

118

the sea, the reflections from the different craft. That's one of the reasons I found it so difficult living in Cambridge. Oh, I know there's the river, but it's not the same.'

'You are getting romantic in your old age! You should definitely get your paints out, you know.'

Jayne shook her head. 'No, I've always felt like that. Michael never understood.'

Her musings took her back to when she met Michael. What if her strap hadn't broken on that fateful day and she hadn't met him...And what did Paul really think of her now? Was there any future in that? What *had* happened all those years ago? Did he know? Although soothing, the ferry journey was taking too long and Jayne felt her impatience getting the better of her again.

Another ferry passed by causing a swell of water. The cacophony of car alarms and dogs barking in the lower decks shook Jayne out of her reverie. 'Gosh! I didn't have that yesterday. I hope my car isn't one of them.'

'Don't worry,' said Leyla, 'it happens. You're supposed to disable your motion sensor but most people forget.'

Suddenly aware their destination was imminent Jayne and Leyla joined the mass exodus down the stairs, sat in their car and waited to disembark.

The gates were dropped with a loud clang and Jayne made her way towards the M27, happy to be on the open road at last. 'Ah, now I feel we're getting somewhere. I don't know about you, but the older I get the more impatient I am. Well, whatever happens, it'll be lovely to catch up with Symon. Like old times. I really miss Cornwall, don't you?'

'I suppose so but I've never really given it much thought; too busy with work and what-not.' Leyla didn't want

119

to voice her thoughts. She had a feeling Jayne's dream of refurbishing *Seawinds* would never be realized, unless Symon was prepared to sink some money into it. She wondered if it was worth all the hassle. Perhaps it would be as well to let Paul Smythe have it after all, if he was that set on it. He must've made a killing in Australia if that was the case. Leyla remembered the Smythes as always being strapped for cash. Mr Smythe was always talking about the price of petrol and about how much things cost when they went out for the day. No wonder they liked their free holidays! Her mind stopped veering off when she noticed the sky growing darker.

'Blimey! I don't like the look of that. It was like a millpond back there, now it's like a bloody monsoon up ahead. Sodding English weather. Wouldn't you like to invest your slice of the legacy in a nice little place in Spain instead?'

Jayne shook her head. 'No thanks, too hot for me. I can't stand the heat. Michael loves it though – he's happy to sit in the sun and roast himself like a well-done turkey on a spit.'

Leyla chuckled. 'Oh, Jayne, you are funny. You wouldn't believe the image I've got in my head!'

They giggled until big spots of rain fell on the windscreen. Jayne turned on her wipers and headlights. The cars in front slowed down, red lights as far as she could see, then they came to a standstill.

Jayne yanked on the handbrake. 'Oh, no. That's all we need. I told you, these journeys just get worse.'

'I expect there's an accident,' said Leyla.

Jayne turned off the engine and slid a *Beach Boys* CD into the slot.

Leyla turned to her, 'God, you are living in the past, aren't you?'

120

'Nothing wrong with that.'

Leyla knew she'd said the wrong thing. Jayne seemed quite depressed when she let her guard down but now wasn't the time to ask her about it – she needed her mind on her driving. Leyla also knew Jayne had sunk into her inner world and wouldn't thank Leyla for trying to pull her out. And how did Jayne really feel about Paul Smythe? Leyla hadn't been terribly interested in their love affair in the sixties. Her memory of Paul was all a bit foggy but she remembered his toned physique and his thick dark hair.

The car in front inched forward. Jayne restarted the engine and drove into the space. The cars further down the queue began to thin out and they were off again. No sign of any accident or road works.

'It must be the sheer volume of traffic,' offered Leyla.

But Jayne remained silent, still deep in her own thoughts.

The rain was now torrential and Jayne turned on her wipers full-blast. The filthy spray from the lorries and juggernauts was blurring her visibility, but she pushed her foot to the floor, ignoring her inner voice.

'Christ, Jayne! Slow down. You should've let me drive!'

'Don't tell me what to do, Leyla!' Jayne flicked off the CD player and they continued in silence.

When they passed the sign for Axminster the rain began to ease and a watery sun poked through a gap in the dark clouds.

Without any warning, Jayne turned off the A30 at Honiton. 'I've had enough. I need a coffee.'

Jayne found a car park, yanked on the handbrake, banged the door and slung her handbag over her shoulder. She arched her back and headed wordlessly for the high street, breathing in the freshness the rain had left in its wake. Bright sun glistened on the puddles as she hurried along in search of a café while Leyla trailed behind.

With relief Jayne almost fell through the door of an attractive tea room, into the warm steamy atmosphere. The place was buzzing with conversation and the tinkling of teaspoons. Wet jackets hung on the backs of chairs and condensation trickled down the windows. At the counter they each ordered a frothy cappuccino and a slice of lemon drizzle cake and found two vacant chairs at a table near the window.

Jayne watched the other customers chatting animatedly and wondered what stories they had to tell. Were they happy? Did they have fulfilling relationships?

'Look,' said Leyla, 'I'm sorry if I spoke out of turn but you were driving a bit fast. Truce?'

Jayne smiled distractedly, rubbed a patch of misty window and peered through.

'You really have got a lot on your mind, haven't you?'

That was all it took. Jayne's face crumpled. She couldn't hold back the tears any longer.

Leyla put her arm round her. 'Oh Jayne, I'm really sorry. I had no idea things were that bad.'

Jayne fished out a tissue from her pocket, blew her nose. 'I'm all right. It's just the whole business of going back and finding your diaries and everything. And on top of all that, Michael doesn't seem to care if I'm alive or dead.'

Leyla drew a breath. 'Yeah, and bloody old Smythe! And you want to pursue a relationship with his son?'

122

'I never said that.'

'Huh, you didn't have to.'

Symon and Maggie were stuck on the M3, cars stretching into infinity, red tail lights blurring into one long stream. The rain was coming down in sheets but Maggie didn't mind, driving the automatic Mercedes was a joy, even in these conditions.

She didn't want to wake Symon. He'd nodded off when they left the M25. Poor darling, she thought, he really could do with a holiday, but his conscientious work ethic had put him above the rest. She felt a smile spread across her face when she thought how hard he'd worked after gaining his degree, working for a firm of architects in London. They jokingly called him the tea boy, but he was prepared to work hard, starting on the bottom rung and climbing all the way to the top. Such a pity his father never got a chance to experience his success. From what Symon had told Maggie, she would've loved to have met Harry. He sounded such a lovely man.

Maggie was looking forward to staying in Cornwall. It had been too long since their last visit but there never seemed to be enough time to fit everything in – jetting off to the States every few weeks, entertaining clients in London – it never stopped, but keeping busy compensated for being childless. She had thrown herself into Symon's whirlwind of business dinners and parties, a more than capable hostess. She felt a warm glow remembering how she met Symon.

She had been a young air hostess on the British Airways 707 flight travelling to America. He'd had a seat on her plane – his first visit to the States to meet a businessman and set up a new enterprise.

There had been some turbulence during the flight. After the remains of the hot meal had been cleared away, the plane lurched and Maggie spilt the whisky she was pouring for Symon. She was embarrassed – she prided herself on her professionalism – this had never happened before. As she tried to sponge his trousers, Symon asked her name and joked, 'Hi, I'm Maggie, fly me!' and made her laugh. When the plane landed he'd asked if she had any free time, invited her to dinner that evening and that was the start of their beautiful relationship.

Symon opened his eyes and rubbed a hand over his face. 'Ah, where are we, my sweet?'

'Stuck on the M3 I'm afraid. Oh, hang on, I think they're moving.' She put the car in 'drive' and they were off again.

As Jayne drove along the bendy rain-washed lanes towards *Tregenna Bay* her body relaxed at the sight in front of her. She never tired of the misty green and purple cliffs that led down to the wide beach. The sun pierced through the last of the cloud, sprinkling stars on the sea in the distance.

Beautiful, I'm home.

Jayne sighed with relief as she parked the car. She got out and stood taking in the splendour of the misty scene.

'I thought you wanted to get inside and relax?' said Leyla, as she slammed the door.

'In a minute.'

While Jayne stood breathing in the sea air Leya grabbed her case from the boot and headed for the bar.

Jack's ready smile greeted her, 'Hi there.'

'Hello. We've booked a room.'

Jayne followed her sister and dropped her case on the floor.

Jack looked up when he saw her. 'Ah, here we are, room three,' he turned to take the key from its hook and handed it to Jayne. 'Twin en-suite, whenever you're ready.'

'Thanks Jack. Is my brother here yet?'

He checked in the book. 'Mr and Mrs Williams?'

Jayne nodded.

'Not yet.'

Jayne turned to Leyla. 'I expect they've got held up on the M25. That road's a nightmare. No wonder they call it Europe's biggest car park!'

'You look like you could do with a drink.' said Jack. 'What can I get you?'

'She'll have a G and T and I'll have a brandy,' said Leyla.

**

'Ah,' said Maggie when they passed the 'Welcome to Cornwall' sign, 'not long now. I'll get us a nice glass of bourbon when we get there, providing they have some, of course.'

'Something tells me I've spoilt you over the years.'

'We spoil each other, nothing wrong with that.'

125

Symon patted his wife's linen-clad knee.

As she drove up and down the wet hilly lanes, Maggie caught sight of the *Captain Tregenna* cloaked in grey perched high up. 'Gosh! Looks formidable, like an old fort.'

'Mm, I don't know about that. I'm beginning to wish we'd booked into *The Metropole!*'

Maggie parked the car and Symon flung open the door, 'Leave the cases – I'll come back for them. Have a recce first.'

'Oh Simon, I'm sure it'll be fine. Jayne wouldn't stay in anywhere shoddy.'

Maggie locked the Mercedes and followed Symon into the bar. She ordered two bourbons on the rocks while Symon cast his critical eye over the bar.

'Right you are,' said Jack. He was very rarely asked for bourbon and hoped they hadn't picked up the surprise in his voice. He began to proudly rattle off a list. 'I've got *Jim Beam, Shoulder Monkey...*'

'...*Jim Beam*'ll be fine,' cut in Symon.

Jack poured two separate measures and added ice from the shiny red bucket on the counter.

'Make those doubles, would you?' asked Symon.

Jack obeyed. 'Still a bit of a nip in the air but you can't expect too much – it is only April.'

'I made a reservation this morning,' said Maggie. 'The name's Williams.'

Jack looked from Maggie to Symon. 'Ah, Jayne's been waiting for you. She's upstairs with her sister.' He stood their drinks on the counter. 'Travelled far?'

Maggie nodded. 'South London.'

126

'Whoa, that's some journey, and I hear the weather's been awful. Well, make yourselves at home. I've just stoked the fire.'

Symon and Maggie plonked themselves on the sofa by the fireplace. Symon was casting his mind back. Now, where had he seen an ice bucket like that before?

Maggie turned her head this way and that and noticed the Olde Worlde charm, the fishing nets draped across the ceiling and the smart monochrome photographs of bygone days.

Symon watched as her auburn hair glinted in the firelight. There were a few white strands he hadn't noticed before. 'You look miles away, my love,' said Symon.

'Hark who's talking. I like the décor. Makes a nice change from tatty horse brasses, don't you think?'

'Yeah, as pubs go. But you forget – I'm used to five-star hotels.'

'Now who's spoilt?'

Symon smiled and took a mouthful of his bourbon, rolled it around his tongue and smacked his lips. 'Still, the man's got a well-stocked bar, I'll give him that.'

TEN

The sharply-dressed, dark-haired Ms Drake ran up the steps to *Seawinds* and turned to Paul. 'Mr Masterson sends his apologies; he's rather busy.'

Entering the green and white hallway, the first thing Paul noticed was the musty old-house smell, and lurking beneath, he thought he detected a stale aroma of cooked breakfasts. He had an odd sensation of stepping back in time and as if the house was reaching out to him in a welcoming hug but, although it looked very familiar, it seemed oddly much smaller than he remembered.

Ms Drake showed him into the front room. 'Here we are. You'll see immediately the potential – the view from the bay window is quite stunning. Needs a bit of TLC of course but feel free to wander.' She took out her mobile and tried to get a signal and gestured to the back lobby. 'I'll be out there if you need me.'

Paul stood in the middle of the room looking around.

So this was where Mr Williams played his classical music.

Paul remembered so clearly the last time he had stayed in the house and the sound of the waltzes pouring out of this room. He hadn't been able to go into much detail with Jayne. Although fifty years had passed, he sensed her father's death was still too painful for her to talk about. He noticed some tell-tale dents in the old Axminster carpet, possibly left behind by an armchair. In his mind's eye, Paul pictured Mr Williams sitting there with a glass of whisky in his hand. The

128

powerful vibes made him shudder. He scanned the sea view briefly and went to find Ms Drake who was hovering between the hall and the back parlour.

She slipped her mobile into her handbag and came to open the door across the hall. 'This was the dining room, I believe. Notice the almost identical view to the previous room. Again, you'll have to use your imagination.'

'Thanks,' said Paul. 'I'm sure I'll manage.'

The empty dining room contained the window seat where Paul remembered sitting as a young boy, hugging his knees and watching the waves rolling in, eagerly waiting for his parents to come down to breakfast and for the day to begin. He couldn't resist sitting on the faded blue cushion to relive the happy memories. Over the years the pine trees at the end of the road had grown and stretched out their branches to partly obscure the view but the scene was still imprinted on his mind: the vast open beach, the dark rocky outcrops, the watery caves, the cliffs...

Clambering over the rocks one day to explore the neighbouring cove, he had twisted his ankle and had to stay there for a good part of the afternoon before he was able to walk again. He smiled at the recollection – his parents worrying about where he'd got to and scolding him when he eventually got back just in time for the evening meal – all part of growing up. Turning from the window he could still hear the echoes of clattering cutlery on china, the hum of conversation and the diners all enjoying Mrs Williams's excellent food.

Feeling like an intruder he tip-toed through to the old kitchen, a room that had always been out of bounds to guests. It was now bereft of any furniture save for a dusty old range, a sink unit and a shabby yellow dresser. It was difficult to imagine all those meals being lovingly prepared and cooked in here. It looked as if no one had lived here for years.

Back in the hall, Paul remembered exactly where he was standing on that last evening when Jayne stood in front of him, head bent, a curtain of hair hiding her tear-stained face. He looked at the spot where he had shuffled his feet on the green lino, now faded and scuffed thinner with time, and where, the year before, he had waited for Jayne to come out of the back parlour, a kiss and a grope under the stairs. He swallowed down the unexpected lump in his throat.

Ms Drake reappeared and shocked him out of his reverie. 'Seen enough? I can take you upstairs if you like?'

He smiled to himself – he wanted to joke with her but he figured Ms Drake would not be amused. 'Yeah, I'd like to see the rest.'

'Sure.'

She showed him briefly into the back parlour she called the breakfast room. He poked his head round the door. The guests had always been excluded from this private part of the house and his poking around felt like a treasonable offence. His eyes skimmed over the empty room with its brick fireplace and the faded richly-patterned blue wallpaper, and he tried to imagine what had gone on in here. The sash window looked onto an overgrown back garden which he assumed had once been lovingly tended.

He turned to the stairs, put his hand on the newel post and felt the vibes of hundreds of hands doing the same. He suddenly had a mental picture of his little sister jumping down the last two stairs in front of him. Was it really all those years ago?

He followed Ms Drake up the bare wooden staircase, where once there had been a burgundy stair carpet secured with brass stair rods, and onto the first floor landing. 'There's a patch of damp coming though on that wall,' she said, pointing to a patch high up above the picture rail, 'and the ceiling needs attention. The roof probably needs replacing and I shouldn't be surprised if there's some dry rot. You'll need a survey.'

Ms Drake left him and clonked her way up the second flight of stairs. Paul flung open the door of the bedroom that had once belonged to Jayne and her sister and instantly an image of his younger self sprang into his mind of the day he daringly ventured in hoping to find Jayne on her own. Then Leyla barging in and finding him on the bed. The whole house seemed to be whispering to him of the poignant secrets it was harbouring.

On the top landing in the family room, he had to turn away and mask his emotion by blowing into a tissue. It caught him unawares.

'Oh, dear,' said Ms Drake, 'I expect it's the dust and the mould spores. Allergic are you?'

Paul nodded, 'I'll see you downstairs.'

'Sure.'

When she'd gone he stood a while to compose himself. This was silly. How old was he, for Christ's sake. When he'd pulled himself together he studied the other rooms for damp patches and dry rot, although he was no expert. He wondered how much it would cost to have it remodelled into the surf school he envisaged. Would it be worth it? Would there be enough punters? Was it close enough to the beach? His sister Katie had been talking about a new spa that had just opened in Wadebridge. Maybe that was the way to go.

According to Ms Drake, only the ground floor had been occupied by Mrs Williams in the last ten years because she could no longer climb the stairs. He couldn't picture

Jayne's mum as an infirm old woman; the last time he saw her she looked just the same as she always had – very smart, hair neatly waved, a spotlessly clean apron over her cotton dress...

He went downstairs to find Ms Drake in the front room, gazing at the bay bathed in sunlight. 'This place does have a certain charm, I suppose.'

Ha, yeah, if you only knew.

Jayne woke up with a big smile on her face. She turned onto her back and stretched, relaxed and happy in the knowledge that she had been right to gather everyone together last night, here at the *Captain Tregenna*. Her cheeks had ached from smiling and laughing so much. She remembered her mum's funeral, a bizarre day, everyone smiling instead of crying, but Yvonne would've understood. She wouldn't have wanted them all to be sad at her passing. She was a cheerful person who loved to see her family happy.

But no matter how hard she tried, Jayne's mind returned to her father's death. It had been ill-timed to say the least – he had only been forty-nine. When she had reached the same age Jayne felt she'd only lived half her life and wondered if her father had ever felt the same. Had it occurred to him, or was he so depressed it hadn't entered his head? There was talk at the time of him having gone for a long walk and being swept off the cliff in the high winds, which was perfectly feasible. But had he intended to end it all? She had a feeling that he wanted her to know the truth after all these years but how was that going to be possible?

There had been one blessing: after the verdict of death by misadventure, all of Harry's debts had died with him, enabling Yvonne to continue running *Seawinds*. Also, she'd had the good sense to take out a life insurance policy on Harry and although she reinforced many times that she would rather have had him alive and destitute, the money was very welcome.

But the really disturbing element for Jayne was the anger between Ken Smythe and her father the night before he died. She had assumed they had always been friends until she read Leyla's hastily written account of that fateful evening. Although she had always wondered why the Smythes never returned to *Seawinds*, Jayne assumed they felt it would never be the same without Harry. And if Paul hadn't known about the row he must've been puzzled by the whole business. She would have to ask him. She felt bad now for leaving the way she had on Monday morning but her emotion had swamped her after being alone in the house for so long. It was as though she really was back in 1968.

Jayne turned over, her thoughts again on last night. Symon had been full of enthusiasm for *Seawinds* which came as a surprise to Jayne after his non-committal attitude on the phone the day before. He'd never been one to dwell on the past or be overly sentimental but after talking about old times and sharing memories, he'd been carried along on a tidal wave of nostalgia, as they all were, helped by a few glasses of wine.

She jumped out of bed and went to the window – the sun was shining, urging her to get a move on. They had a busy day ahead of them. She shook Leyla who was still unconscious. 'Come on, get up! Symon and Maggie will want to get going.'

She moaned and snuggled further down in the bed. 'Can't you do it without me? I'm too cosy.'

'Suit yourself, but you know you don't like being left out.'

Leyla turned over and pulled the duvet over her head whilst Jayne went in the shower, then towel-dried her hair, threw on a pair of jeans and a white cotton top and ran down to the bar to meet Symon and Maggie.

'Where's Leyla?' asked Maggie.

'Still in bed but I expect she'll be down soon – she won't want us to go without her.'

They all took their places at a table and eventually Leyla came sauntering in rubbing her eyes and yawning. 'Gosh, I can't stand the pace anymore. How do you all look so fresh and raring to go?'

Symon smiled and shook his head, 'Still the same old Leyla.'

'Hey! Not so much of it.'

They all began to read the menu. Jack was looking forward to pleasing his customers. Since being newly refurbished a month ago, the pub had not enjoyed such a full booking. He took out his pad and licked his pencil.

'What can I get you lovely people?'

'I'm starving, I'll have a full house,' said Jayne.

Jack lifted his eyebrows.

'It's another name for a Full English,' said Jayne. 'It's what we used to call it at *Seawinds*, remember Leyla?'

Leyla nodded. 'That's right, the full works; sausage, bacon, egg, baked beans, mushrooms, tomatoes – but fresh, never tinned like some guest houses – and fried bread. None of your hash browns. Toast and marmalade to follow. Gosh! I've just made myself very hungry, I think I'll have the same.'

134

Jack made a note on his pad. 'Am I right in thinking you used to own that old place up the hill?'

'*Seawinds,* yes,' said Symon, 'Not us, exactly, our parents. We were just kids. We saw some comings and goings, though, I can tell you.'

'Well I never! Pity. Looks a bit sad now.'

'Yes,' said Jayne, 'but we hope to rectify that.' She looked at the others who all smiled in agreement. It gave her a lovely warm feeling.

Jack's curiosity was heightened. He waited to see if the party spilled out any more information but none was forthcoming so he took the rest of their orders. Maggie said she'd have a mushroom omelette and Symon said he'd like a blueberry pancake but didn't think Jack could oblige.

'Well, you're in luck, my friend! We can do that for you.'

'Really? I *was* joking.'

'No, it's absolutely fine. Your wish is my command!'

Symon was willing to see what sort of a job they'd make of it and sat back waiting with anticipation. The tea and coffee arrived and Maggie poured. She glanced out the window. 'Looks like a perfect day out there.'

'Isn't it just. The bay is a wonderful place to be on a sunny day. Any day, come to that,' said Jayne.

'Here she goes again, waxing lyrical,' said Symon.

Jayne poked her tongue out at him. 'Of course, and you didn't do so bad yourself last night, all those anecdotes...'

'I'm only trying to wind you up – you should know that by now.'

135

'Take no notice of him, darling,' said Maggie, 'he's an old tease.'

Jayne fell silent. In the depths of her mind she remembered Paul using that term for her. But at seventeen she knew she'd been anything but a tease. She was careful not to direct too much attention to her curves. Paul's remark all those years ago still rankled and she secretly wondered what he thought of her now. She hoped she hadn't given him the wrong impression, dropping everything to meet him that first evening in the bar.

Jack served their food and left them in peace to enjoy it. Symon was pleasantly surprised and said his blueberry pancake was every bit as good as he got at the New York *Plaza*.

'That's taking things a bit too far, darling!' said Maggie, 'but my omelette is delicious. More coffee?'

Symon nodded and Maggie, ever the hostess, poured him another cup.

There was a mountain of food on both Jayne and Leyla's plates – Jack and his chef had gone over-the-top to please. Whoever was doing the cooking knew their stuff.

Leyla pushed the last scraps of grilled bacon and sausage to one side of her plate and blew out her cheeks. 'God, I don't think I can move after that!'

'We'll leave you here, then,' said Symon.

'Oh no, you won't!'

'No, this project needs all of us to agree if it's going to go ahead, which I hope it will.'

Jayne was delighted to hear these words; they were together again, all three of them, Maggie too. Jayne hoped they would all come to her conclusion that *Seawinds* would be best remodelled as a holiday home for the family. She pictured Leyla, Symon and Maggie, Daisy and the children and Leyla's twins all together, one big happy family...except her mum and dad wouldn't be there, not in the flesh anyway, but she tried not to let that thought depress her.

'You've got that faraway look again,' said Leyla.

Jayne smiled. 'I can't help it, but now I know I'm not the only one looking forward to revamping *Seawinds*.'

'It'll be wonderful, Jayne. I'm all for it,' said Maggie, looking at Symon, 'and we might actually have some quality time together for a change.'

Symon patted her knee in agreement.

After breakfast, instead of the rugged pathway the other side of the bay, past the pine trees and over boulders, all four made their way down the gentler incline, past the houses and bungalows. They all agreed the stony path was a step too far for them on a full stomach but Jayne fully intended to relive that pretty but hazzardous route in the not too distant future. She just hoped she was up to the task. As a child she loved to take her time to watch the channels of water tumbling over the rocks on their way to the beach. The best time would be when she had it all to herself, to sit on a grassy bank and immerse herself in the sights and sounds and to breathe in the scent of the crystal clear water.

Jayne was suddenly pulled up by the sight of Mastersons green door in front of her. She pushed it open.

Mr Masterson walked up to the desk. 'Ah, Mrs Green, my colleague Ms Drake showed a client round *Seawinds* yesterday morning...' he looked at his notes '...a Mr Smythe. He was very interested, said he'd be making an offer.' He smiled, pleased with himself.

137

She scowled at him. 'But I thought you said you wouldn't let anyone view the property without my knowledge?'

'Yes, I'm sorry, but he was rather persistent and taking into consideration the nature of the sale I thought...'

Jayne felt her face flush and her heart quicken. 'Let me tell you, Mr Masterson, I'm the client here and I expect you to act on my behalf for the best possible outcome!'

His face fell. He'd had two difficult people to deal with in as many days. 'Yes, of course, I'm sorry. It's just...'

Jayne snatched the key from him and banged the door.

Of course! Now he remembered why the name Smythe resonated with him, the two-finger hand gesture all those years ago...

Jayne joined the others waiting outside. 'Huh. Stupid man!'

'What's wrong?' asked Leyla.

'Masterson, God, you'll never guess... he saw fit to show Paul Smythe around *Seawinds* yesterday without telling me! Well, his colleague did.'

Leyla smiled, realising Paul Smythe was still getting under Jayne's skin.

'Don't Leyla. Just don't.'

Leyla turned her head away and pressed her lips together.

They all walked back up the hill and arrived outside *Seawinds* to find a white van parked in the road.

'Ah,' said Symon, 'he's here already.' He walked up to the van where a middle-aged man in jeans and tee shirt was taking out his bag of tools and a clip board from the boot.

'Chaz! Good to see you.' Symon looked round for Jayne. 'Jayne, this is Chaz. He's going to take a look around and give us a run-down.'

Jayne smiled, 'Hello. I hope you don't find too much wrong with it. I...we... have great plans for the old place.'

'Yeah, OK. I'll give it the once-over. What do you hope to do with it? Looks like it's in a prime spot,' said Chaz, looking down on the sun-drenched bay.

'We plan to remodel her into a holiday retreat, isn't that right, Symon?'

Symon nodded, 'Yep, we've got a few ideas.'

They all trooped through the front door and into the hall where the air hung heavy with the smell of damp plaster.

Symon disappeared out the back. Chaz took out his damp meter, dropped his bag of tools on the floor in a cloud of dust and proceeded to check the walls in the front room.

The three women stood in the hall looking at one another.

'Well,' said Maggie, 'looks like we're surplus to requirements. What say we all have a stroll on the beach?'

Leyla agreed, although Jayne was reluctant to leave Symon and Chaz examining old *Seawinds*. She felt like saying, *There, there, these nasty men won't harm you. It's only a check-up.* Instead, she said to Leyla and Maggie, 'I'll see you down there.'

Ignoring Chaz, Jayne walked through to the front room and stood at the bay window. The tide was out exposing a huge expanse of shiny wet sand, rivulets of water running down to the sea. In her mind's eye she was a child again, scrambling all the way down the rocky path, down the wonky concrete steps and onto the beach. Skipping barefoot in and out of the rock pools, Symon and Leyla arguing over who had

139

the biggest crab or shell. But the overriding memory was that of her father sitting in his armchair, in this room, listening to his music. She instinctively turned, as if he was there behind her. She heard the faint sound of Beethoven's Pastoral Symphony and shivered. Chaz, who obviously hadn't heard it, moved wordlessly into the dining room. The music suddenly stopped and she imagined her father lifting the stylus, removing the record from the turntable and turning it over. She could even smell the vinyl and his cigarette smoke. She mentally shook herself; her imagination was getting the better of her again. At times she welcomed it – it was almost like having her father back again – but at others her sadness weighed her down. She supposed it was because she wasn't happy with Michael but she definitely didn't want to dwell on that today.

She turned to see Leyla and Maggie happily striding out down the road. She intended to join them but suddenly found herself knocking on Gladys's door. Somewhere in the back of her mind she thought Gladys might be able to shed some light on that terrible day when her father met his death. She remembered George had found him and called the coastguard. They would surely remember that day, too. How could they not?

She knocked and waited but there were no sounds from inside, no footsteps advancing towards the door. Thinking Gladys was out, Jayne turned to walk away but something pulled her back. She knocked again. Finally a young woman came to the door, wearing paint-splattered jeans and tee shirt, hair scraped up in a knot.

'Oh, hello,' said Jayne, 'is Gladys there?'

The young woman frowned and shook her head, 'Gladys who?'

140

'Gladys and George. They live here?'

'Sorry. This house is empty, has been for years. We've bought it, taken it on as a project,' she smiled. 'We've come down from London, gradually doing it up when we get some free time...'

Jayne was speechless. She shook her head. This wasn't happening...'Are you sure? I know this must sound weird to you but I saw Gladys only last week.'

The young woman shrugged. 'Well, maybe you did but she doesn't live here.' The young woman opened the door wider to reveal the stripped walls and bare floorboards. 'You can come in and look if you like.'

Jayne rubbed her temples, dumbfounded. 'But...I don't understand...'

'You OK? Can I get you a drink or something?'

'No. I'm fine, thanks. Sorry I troubled you.'

Jayne turned and walked down the hill without a backward glance then broke into a run, tears welling up. She couldn't believe what had just happened. Her thoughts sprang to her meeting with Gladys, the tea and their conversation. She couldn't have imagined it, surely? There must be some other explanation.

Jayne watched Maggie and Leyla chatting happily and strolling on ahead. Jayne sat on a wall and tried to gather her thoughts. What was she going to tell the others, if anything? They'd think she was losing the plot. Perhaps it was best kept to herself.

Her thoughts turned to Paul. After leaving her on Monday morning and knowing how upset she was, it was unthinkable that he'd barged into the estate agent's to ask for a viewing. The audacity of him!

Maggie turned to see Jayne sitting on the wall and shouted, 'Hey, you OK?'

Jayne nodded and hurried to meet her. 'I was just sitting down to take in the view,' she lied.

'I know what you mean. It is lovely. I wish I'd brought my cozzie – that sea looks wonderfully inviting.'

'It'll be freezing!' said Leyla, 'people forget it's the Atlantic. It needs to be thirty degrees before I stick a toe in.'

Jayne was still reeling from the revelation that Gladys was probably dead and George too. But when she stopped to think about it, they must have been in their fifties when her father...

Maggie stopped and turned, 'Jayne? What's wrong, sweetheart?'

At Maggie's concern Jayne felt like weeping. She took a deep breath, 'You won't believe this but I just knocked on Gladys's door and a young woman told me the house has been empty for years.'

'And?'

Jayne shook her head in dismay, 'but I went in there and spoke to her only last week. I *know* I did!'

Leyla looked at her. 'You have been under a lot of pressure lately, Jayne. I'm sure that's all it is.'

'What? You think I'm losing my marbles, don't you?'

'Of course not, it's like I said. Now come on, let's enjoy this lovely sunny day.'

Jayne turned to feel the breeze blowing in her hair. 'I've just realised – it's almost fifty years ago to the day when Dad... Don't you ever think about it, Leyla?'

142

'Of course I do. What do you take me for? But what good does it do to keep dwelling on the past?'

Maggie didn't like where this conversation was heading. 'I agree. Come on, let's take advantage of this beautiful day and this glorious beach.' She kicked off her sandals, rolled up her trousers and dug her toes into the warm dry sand. 'Mm, that feels good.'

When Jayne looked back up at *Seawinds,* maybe she was being fanciful, but the house looked happy that they were all back together, here where they belonged. But there were some strange happenings for sure. After finding Leyla's account of the row the night before her father's death and now knowing Gladys was a figment of her imagination, what else would come to light? But Maggie was right – they should all enjoy the gift of this glorious day.

Jayne jumped down onto the soft sand. The sun was warm and the air light and balmy against her face. She spread out her arms and breathed deeply as she padded across the bay.

Back at *Seawinds* Symon was rummaging around the sadly forgotten back garden. The rusted hen house was covered with ivy, the trees and shrubs so dense that they blocked out the light. Brambles and nettles had moved in to replace the herbs that Olive had so lovingly tended, but there, amidst the weeds, was an overgrown rosemary bush, the gnarled stem like a tree trunk. He reached in and picked a piece and crushed it between his fingers. The aroma sent him straight back to his childhood – watching his mother take out the roast lamb from the oven, the rosemary crisp and browned in the pan of meat juices, being handed a hot forkful of meat with salt on. His mouth watered at the thought.

Chaz found Symon standing with his back to him in a patch of weeds.

'Symon? I've finished here, but I haven't been up in the loft. Is there a loft ladder?'

Symon turned and shrugged. 'I can't remember. Have you looked?' He dragged his feet up the cast iron steps to the back porch, bruising the vegetation as he went.

'I can't get up there,' said Chaz, 'I need a stepladder. I thought I had one on the van.'

'Tell you what,' said Symon, 'I'll have a look in the cellar.' He left Chaz and ran down the cellar steps. He began searching in both cellars until he found an old wooden stepladder behind a curtain of cobwebs in the larger of the two rooms. He dusted it off and humped it up the three flights of stairs to the landing where Chaz was standing ready with his torch. Symon opened the stepladder and stood on the first rung.

'You OK with that? You should've let me carry it.'

Symon nodded. 'I'm fine.' In fact he felt more than fine and wondered where this new-found strength had come from.

'I'll get up there if you like,' said Chaz. 'Hold it steady for me.' He carried his heavy-duty torch up the stepladder and pushed the loft hatch to one side. Symon shielded his eyes against the decades of dust that fell like snow and the cold draft that brushed his face. Chaz hoisted himself up into the loft space and Symon saw the beam from the torch flash around.

'Does the roof look dry?' shouted Symon. 'Any woodworm?'

No answer.

144

'Chaz? I'm coming up.'

He was mindful of where he was putting his feet – he didn't want to end up in hospital but he managed to push himself up through the hatch and into the loft. He stood up and noticed the huge church-like roof and the floor expertly boarded. Why had he never ventured up here before? It would've made an excellent den when he was a kid. He could've housed all his Lego models up here instead of filling his bedroom. Even enough room for a train set.

Whilst Chaz shone his torch around Symon spotted boxes of Christmas decorations, an old standard lamp, some books and ornaments on the floor – general bric-a-brac all long forgotten. Then his gaze fell upon an old trunk in one corner. He crept over to it and lifted the lid. At first sight he thought it was full of junk but when he delved further down he realised it was full of objects to do with *Seawinds* from long ago. Only it wasn't called *Seawinds* then – the old wooden sun-bleached sign displayed a different name.

Bay View Guesthouse.

He lifted it out of the box and stood it against the wall. Lying under some heavy musty curtains were some framed black and white photographs. Symon was intrigued. On closer inspection his mum and dad smiled back at him but not as he remembered them. They were much younger and there was a lady with them, someone he'd never seen before. He turned over the picture and there on the cardboard backing was a faint inscription in swirly handwriting. He screwed his eyes up to read. *October 1949.*

So, mum and dad must have stayed here long before we were born.

There were other photos taken outside the guest house – the same lady with a tall young man and a little girl in

145

a summer dress and pigtails, all smiling at the camera. Symon had no idea who these people were but there was something familiar about the child. He tried to think who she could be but he was jolted out of his thoughts by the faint echo of a waltz. He recognised it for the music his father had played just before he died. Symon cocked his head on one side. 'Chaz, can you hear that? Where's it coming from?'

But Chaz had gone back to the far side of the loft still inspecting the roof for dry rot and leaks. 'What's that? Careful, it might be a wasp's nest.'

'No! It's music. Can't you hear it?'

Chaz listened and shook his head. 'Well, I'm finished up here. I'll go back and write up a report. You should have it by Friday.'

Symon didn't answer.

'Symon?'

'Oh, yeah. Right. Did you find anything horrific?'

'No, it's a solid building but a new roof wouldn't go amiss. What did you say you plan on doing with it?'

'Jayne wants to turn it into a holiday retreat for the family. I must admit, I'm warming to the idea.'

Chaz whistled through his teeth. 'Wow! It's in a great spot. Let me know if you need any more advice. '

'Thanks.'

As Chaz made his way down the ladder, collected his tools and made his way out to the van, Symon realised the music had stopped. He dismissed it. Maybe he did need that holiday after all. He stood in the front room and watched Maggie, Leyla and Jayne dancing about on the beach like three sea nymphs. Symon's thoughts strayed once again to the days

146

when both his parents had been alive. Maybe Jayne was right; they should resurrect *Seawinds*. Chaz obviously thought so and Maggie was always telling him to slow down and take things easy. And after what had just happened up in the loft ...

He shut the blue front door on the memories and walked down to the beach to join the girls. Huh, he thought, the girls. They were all well over sixty but to look at them now you wouldn't think it. He realised age was a state of mind – if you thought yourself old, you would be. Time would grab you and trip you up, leaving you infirm and dependant on others. He had an abject fear of old age and tried to keep himself as fit as possible. At least he was spared from seeing his father grow old. It was different with his mother. Even so, she had never looked her age, even on her deathbed. He suddenly felt a pang of guilt for not being the model son and spending more time with her in her final years. She had been a wonderful mother, never complained, and loved them all unconditionally. He ought to take some flowers up to her grave in the little churchyard where she was buried with Harry – it was the least he could do.

He shook the thoughts away and jumped down the last two steps onto dry ankle-deep sand with a whoosh of memories – learning to swim in the sea, the rush of adrenaline the first time he stood up on a surf board, the waves crashing around him, over him. Good times. He'd have to look in the cellar for his old surf board. He hadn't seen it when he was down there but, then again, he hadn't been looking for it.

Jayne came running up to him, anticipation on her face. 'Well, what did Chaz say?'

'He's going to write up a report but he thinks the old house is quite sound.'

'Oh, fantastic!'

147

'Yeah, I thought you'd be pleased.'

'Pleased? I'm over the moon. Don't you see what this means?'

He shook his head but he knew what was coming.

She draped an arm round his waist. 'We can turn *Seawinds* into our very own holiday home. You and I can redesign it and with your expert touch it'll be the best property on the North Cornwall coast.' She kissed his cheek.

He smiled, 'Ha, you know how to get round a guy!' But he *was* beginning to warm to the idea. He'd already envisaged a state-of-the-art open-plan ground floor, a wet room, a gym, decking in the back garden and balconies at the front to take advantage of the view – he would get onto it right away, as soon as they returned home. Maggie would be excited at the prospect of the two of them having some quality time together, eager for him to retire and make the most of the bay.

She came running up to him. 'Oh, darling, isn't this just fabulous? I'd forgotten how much I love Cornw...' the rest of the word sailed away on the breeze. She turned and let her hair blow back from her face and Symon had a sudden rush of love for his wife.

'Coffee would be good,' said Jayne. Symon and Maggie agreed.

Leyla was down by the water's edge, tracing with her toe the sand wrinkles the recent tide had left behind.

Symon cupped his hands and called to her. 'We're going back up.'

148

October 1949

Yvonne scrutinised her reflection in the mirror, smoothed her skirt and secured her little hat with the jewelled hatpin her mother had given her.

Something old, something new, something borrowed and something blue.

For her going away outfit, Yvonne had chosen a smart apple green suit with a peplum jacket and wondered what Harry would say. She would've liked him with her when she bought it but he'd said he was far too busy to get time off and anyway he trusted her judgment.

She didn't think the day could get any better, she was so happy she thought her heart would burst. There was only a small gathering in the little parish church in South London but it didn't matter. Harry had looked so dashing in his double-breasted pin-striped suit when he joined her at the altar a few hours ago. Ken Smythe had been Harry's best man and Lottie Yvonne's maid of honour. As they spoke their vows the surroundings had melted away, their eyes only for each other.

Yvonne wondered how long it would be before she got used to her new name. 'Mrs Yvonne Williams', she said aloud. It made her smile. They had tickets for the *Night Riviera* sleeper train to Cornwall and her heart was racing at the thought of finally having Harry all to herself.

He poked his head round the door of her bedroom. 'All ready?'

'What do you think?' said Yvonne, doing a twirl. 'I wish you could've been with me when...'

149

Harry silenced her with a kiss. 'It's perfect and so are you.'

She flung her arms round his neck. 'Oh, Harry, I'm so happy I can't tell you...'

He put a finger to her lips, 'Come on, taxi's waiting.' He picked up their big brown suitcase and left Yvonne taking one final look in the mirror. She committed her image to memory – the last time she would look on herself as a virgin! It was a bit scary – she didn't really know what to expect – but she loved Harry so much, she was sure their wedding night would be a beautiful experience.

Paddington station was huge. Yvonne decided it was just like a scene from *Brief Encounter* as they took their seats in the empty waiting room. Harry was desperate for a whisky. He looked in the direction of the bar, at his watch, but his mind was made up when the announcement came over the tannoy to board the *Night Riviera*.

They bustled through the narrow corridor to third class and found their berth. There was hardly room to turn round but Harry seemed undeterred. Yvonne wasn't sure if she should undress in front of Harry or if she should make an excuse and go to the bathroom. She felt shy in front of him and she was exhausted from the day's events. All she wanted was to climb into her bunk and sleep away the journey until morning.

Harry pulled her close, taking her by surprise. He began undressing her and running his hands over her body but she stiffened in his arms. Sensing her nervousness and realising the tiny space was not conducive to their wedding night, he said, 'Don't worry, love. We've waited this long, a bit longer won't make any difference. I don't want to cheapen it. We've got all the time in the world.' He tilted her chin and kissed her and he felt her relax. 'I love you and that's all that matters.'

They undressed awkwardly with their backs to each other, put on their night clothes and squeezed into their bunks. Yvonne relaxed and gradually fell asleep lulled by the rhythmic song of the steam train as it trundled along the tracks.

In the morning, after a very sedate breakfast in the restaurant car, they gathered their belongings and waited for the train to pull into Newquay station. They both sat watching the ever-changing scene from the window. At Dawlish the train ran right along the water's edge as if it was actually travelling through the waves.

'Look Harry! Isn't it wonderful?'

Harry was enthralled by his wife's childish excitement. 'Yes, it's amazing.' He looked up at the cloudy sky. 'But I hope the weather cheers up.'

At Newquay, Harry jumped out and helped Yvonne onto the unfamiliar platform. Doors slammed and whistles blew and the *Night Riviera* was off again, a cloud of white steam drifting in its wake.

Suitcase in hand, Harry guided his wife through the ticket office and outside to where a black Austin Seven was waiting. A fresh-faced young man with dark hair got out and came to greet them.

'Mr and Mrs Williams? I'm Charlie.' They shook hands. 'Ma's sent me to fetch 'ee.'

'Thank you,' said Harry.

Charlie opened the passenger door and tilted the seat forward. 'Mrs Williams, if ee do care to sit in the back?'

Yvonne squeezed in and sat on the shiny brown leather seat. She wasn't large by any stretch of the imagination

151

but her knees touched the seat in front. Harry sat in the passenger seat then Charlie went round to the back of the car and strapped their suitcase onto the luggage rack.

Harry turned to Yvonne, 'All right in the back?'

She nodded, eyes filled with childish eagerness.

'Been to Cornwall afore, 'ave 'ee?' asked Charlie, as he slammed his door and jerked the car into gear. He seemed to fill the space.

'No,' said Harry, 'first time, but I hear it's pretty special.'

'Ess, tes.'

Harry turned to Yvonne and lifted his eyebrows. She stifled a giggle.

Although the weather was disappointing and the ride rather bumpy, Yvonne was enjoying the pretty country lanes with the high grassy banks and fields of cows and sheep. She'd hardly set foot outside of London save for the odd day trip and this was a whole new experience. As they drew nearer to the guesthouse the sun pierced through the clouds like a spotlight on the bay. Harry smiled at his wife's wide-eyed excitement as the expansive beach open up before them, framed by cliffs on both sides.

'Look Harry! Isn't it beautiful? I've only ever seen places like this on railway posters,' she said, turning this way and that.

As the car climbed up the hill she twisted round to look down on the scene. Harry's heart was full. Yes, he had made the right choice.

They pulled up outside *Bay View,* the only guest house in the road, set amongst some whitewashed cottages. A plump

152

little woman with iron grey hair in a bun stood on the porch to greet them.

'Muz Crago,' she said, beaming at them. She showed them into a cosy sitting room with its elevated view of *Tregenna Bay,* the waves gently rolling in. Through the open window came the cry of gulls and a balmy sea breeze. 'Make 'eeselves at home. I got the kettle on. 'Spect you'm thirsty?'

'Thank you,' said Harry.

Charlie hovered at the door.

'Charlie? Take Mr and Mrs Williams' suitcase upstairs, will ee? First door on the right.' Mrs Crago looked at Yvonne. 'Given ee the best room as I know you'm newly married,' she said with a broad grin.

Yvonne felt her cheeks turn pink. 'Thank you. That's very kind.'

'Tidn no trouble. I'll look after 'ee.'

'How did she know?' whispered Yvonne, once Mrs Crago had left the room.

'I expect a little bird told her,' said Harry. 'Come here. Look at that view.' He put his arm round Yvonne's waist and she moulded into him. 'Imagine waking up to that every morning.'

'Mm, beautiful.'

They turned to see Mrs Crago place a full tea tray on the mahogany table in front of the window. 'Help eselves to tay, fruit cake, too, if ee's hungry. Dinner's not till six.' She smiled at them. 'Oh, and the bathroom's next door to yours. Right, I'll leave ee to et.'

153

A little girl with dark pigtails and a lemon yellow dress was watching them from the doorway.

'Thass my granddaughter,' said Mrs Crago, proudly. 'Olive, come and say hello to Mr and Mrs Williams.'

But the child bent her head and looked at them from beneath her lashes.

'Aw, how sweet,' said Yvonne. 'How old are you, Olive?'

'Three,' came the faint response.

'Well, we'll leave ee in peace,' said Mrs Crago. 'If ee need anythin' I'm just down the hall.'

Yvonne poured the tea and sat next to Harry on the chunky russet sofa. They ate the rich fruit cake and took their time, all the while gazing at the view from the open window.

Not having slept very well Yvonne's eyelids began to droop but she was too excited to give in. She was itching to go down on the beach and sink her toes into the soft golden sand. Maybe if it was warm enough, a dip in the sea. The closest she'd been to the bay was a day trip to Margate and there was no comparison.

Upstairs in their room they found rosy wallpaper and dark wood furniture, a wash hand basin in the corner and pure white towels on a rack. At the sight of the high double bed Yvonne felt a rush of anticipation.

Harry stood at the open window gazing at the same view as the one downstairs. He heard a rustle of garments and turned to see Yvonne taking off her two-piece, her cotton dress lay on the bed ready to put on. The sight of her lissom body in her ice-blue silk petticoat took his breath away. He couldn't wait any longer. He took her in his arms and kissed her, softly at first then she responded inflaming his passion.

154

They lay on the bed and he began to peel down her shoulder straps, kissing her bare skin. Little flutters of excitement ran through her body and before she knew it, they were naked, skin against skin.

Some time later, Yvonne woke to see Harry standing at the window with his back to her in only his underpants and shirt sleeves, cigarette in hand. She felt warm and lazy and stretched like a contented cat, a smile on her lips and her anxiety long forgotten. She had so much love for Harry she didn't think it was possible. She ached for him.

He instinctively turned to see her watching him. 'Hello, Mrs Williams.' He stubbed out his cigarette in the ashtray and came to lie next to her. He draped her hair back from her face and ran a finger softly down her cheek. 'You're so beautiful I could do that all over again.'

'Oh, Harry, I love you so much.' She entwined her fingers in his and kissed them. Emotion ballooned in her chest and tears trickled down her cheeks.

Harry kissed them away. 'We'll have a fantastic life together, Yvonne. I promise. You're everything I've ever wanted.'

Totally engrossed in each other all thought of time was forgotten.

The sun had slipped lower in the sky by the time they strolled hand in hand down to the beach. It was amazingly warm for October even in the late afternoon. A slight breeze played with Yvonne's hair and she felt truly alive for the first time in her life.

Back at *Bay View*, Mrs Crago was preparing the evening meal. She hummed to herself as she thought of the newlyweds sealing their love upstairs. They seemed such a lovely couple and obviously very much in love. It did her old

155

heart good to think of them now, down in the bay, enjoying their time together. It reminded her of the first time she came here, when she was a young woman in love with her husband...

At dinner, Harry and Yvonne were ravenous and they both cleared their plates of roast sea bream with lemon butter, samphire and spinach.

Harry leaned back in his chair. 'Ah, that was delicious. I've never had fish like that.'

'Yes, wonderful,' agreed Yvonne. 'I wonder if she'll give me the recipe?'

'You'll have to ask her.'

Being the only guests staying at *Bay View* that week, they had the dining room to themselves. They held hands across the table and waited for Mrs Crago to bring in the dessert. Harry turned to see the same view from the dining room window that they enjoyed from their bedroom.

'I can't believe how beautiful it is,' said Harry. 'We certainly made the right choice.'

'We certainly did. Oh Harry, I've never been so happy. I keep expecting to wake up from a dream.'

He picked up her hand and kissed it just as Mrs Crago entered with a tray. Feeling slightly embarrassed, Yvonne pulled her hand away.

'Here we are m' dears, my best apple cake and clotted cream.' She stood smiling at the young couple. 'Enjoy your stroll, did 'ee?'

Harry nodded. 'You certainly live in a beautiful part of the world, Mrs Crago.'

"Ess, bin 'ere longer 'an I care to remember,' she said, 'me an' my Seth, God rest 'en. Anyways, I'll leave to you get on.'

Yvonne suppressed a giggle and whispered, 'I can hardly understand a word she says!'

'Cornish through and through, that one,' said Harry. 'We'll finish this then how do you fancy another walk, up there,' he said, pointing to the cliff top. 'It's still warm and the bay is calling us.'

'Love to. I didn't realize I'd married such a romantic man!'

One day Yvonne and Harry took a bus into Truro and explored the town with its granite pavements and elegant shops. They came across an exclusive ladies fashion shop where he bought Yvonne the best sundress she'd ever seen. She baulked at the price but he confirmed that nothing was too good for his lady.

On another day, Charlie took Harry and Yvonne out in his old wooden sail boat. Not wanting to be left out, Olive came along.

'She knew I was taking the boat out,' said Charlie, 'I hope 'ee don't mind?'

'Gosh, no, not at all,' said Yvonne.

Yvonne was glad she had remembered to pack a pair of slacks and her red rope sandals. Harry wore his newly purchased plimsolls and rolled up his shirt sleeves hoping to look more relaxed. In view of the age of the boat and not

157

being able to swim, he gripped the sides of the craft, but he felt a bit silly when Olive grinned at him. She was obviously used to sailing with her father. Charlie kicked the outboard motor into life and they chugged out to sea. When they were well clear of the coastline, he cut the engine and the large white sail strained against the wind as they picked up speed. Olive giggled with delight. Harry still wasn't sure but as he watched Yvonne revelling in the feel of the salt spray on her face and the wind in her hair his heart turned over. Not only was Charlie an excellent sailor but he was also adept at catching fish. He showed them how to hang the fishing lines over the side to catch mackerel which they took back to his mother to cook for their evening meal.

Everything tasted so much better here at *Tregenna Bay* and Yvonne said she could swear she'd put on half a stone by the time Saturday morning came round.

She stood gazing out the bedroom window. 'Oh, Harry, I don't want to leave. It's been wonderful. Promise we can come back?'

'I promise. Now, have we got everything?'

Yvonne nodded. 'I've checked.'

Mrs Crago met them at the foot of the stairs. 'You'm got a nice day fer your journey. Enjoyed et, av ee?'

'It's been everything we hoped for,' gushed Harry. 'Thank you.'

'Oh, giss on!' she said, shyly. 'Come see en again.'

'Oh, we will! Don't you worry,' said Harry.

Just before Christmas, Yvonne couldn't really put her finger on why her body felt different so she went to see Dr Meredith who told her she was expecting a baby, probably next July. She ran home and could hardly contain her

158

excitement. She pounced on Harry when he came in from work and planted a big kiss on his lips.

'So, what's all this?' asked Harry, smiling.

'We're going to have a baby!'

'Oh, darling, that's wonderful!' He picked her up and swung her round then quickly set her down. 'Gosh, are you OK? I'm sorry, I don't know what came over me.'

Yvonne shook her head, 'I'm fine Harry, honestly. I won't break.'

Harry lifted an eyebrow, 'Must've been our stay at the bay!'

She giggled and felt coy, the first time for ages.

ELEVEN

Back at the *Captain Tregenna* for their evening meal, Jayne, Leyla, Maggie and Symon felt renewed and ravenously hungry after their active day on the beach. Jack suggested they read the specials board. They all plumped for the Catch of the Day - grilled halibut in lemon and dill butter with sweet potato wedges and salad leaves.

'Anything to drink?' asked Jack.

'Yeah,' said Symon, 'I think a bottle of your best Sauvignon Blanc would go down a treat. OK with you girls?'

Jayne, Leyla and Maggie agreed.

Symon remembered the photographs in the loft but he wasn't going to mention the music he'd heard. 'Jayne. I found a photo of mum and dad in the loft, only it must've been taken before any of us were born. They must've had a holiday here. Did Mum ever tell you about that?'

Jayne thought for a moment then nodded. 'Yes, I think they had their honeymoon here. Yes, they did. It would have been October 1949.'

'Hang on,' said Maggie, doing some mental arithmetic, 'your birthday's in July, isn't it? That means you were probably conceived here!'

'Oh, I guess it must. And you Symon were born at *Seawinds* but it had a different name then. Leyla and I were very young.' She turned to Leyla. 'Remember?'

160

'I have a very shady memory of Mum telling us to be good girls and that we had to leave the beach but I didn't know why.'

'Yes, that's right. I think someone gave us a lift back to the guest house and Mum gave birth to Symon in a back room.'

Leyla pulled a face. 'OK, so where does that leave me? Where was I born? I'm always the odd one out.'

'Maybe not,' said Jayne. 'Think about it. Mum and Dad holidayed here out of season most years leading up to when they bought the house. It was cheaper in the spring and autumn. You were born in January 1953. I think they came down here the previous year in April. I would've been coming up for three so I don't remember much about it but there was a photograph album with all the old black and white snaps. I don't know what happened to that.'

'Yeah, maybe,' said Leyla, 'but I can't remember the album.'

'Anyway,' continued Symon, 'up in the loft, there was a framed photo of them with an old lady standing outside what looked like *Seawinds* with a man and a little girl. Do you know who those people would've been?'

Jayne shook her head. 'No. Was there any writing on the back?'

'Only October 1949'

'There we are, then. Must've been their honeymoon but I can't tell you any more than that.'

'OK. Just fascinating, that's all.'

Jack brought their food to the table. 'I'm sorry but I couldn't help overhearing you mention old photos. Have you seen the ones I have on the wall, just round the other side of the bar?'

Symon made to get up to have a look but Jack stopped him.

'Don't get up now, enjoy your meal, but you might be interested.'

'OK, thanks.'

As usual the fish was delicious, so fresh they could taste the sea. They were all tucking in when Jayne's mobile rang.

'Damn, I thought it was turned off. Sorry. I must've left it on when I was trying to get a signal at *Seawinds*.' She put down her knife and fork and rummaged in her bag. As she listened, her frown deepened to one of horror.

'What is it?' asked Leyla. 'Is it Daisy?'

Jayne shook her head, moved away from the table and out to the lobby, leaving the others to speculate.

Rubie was on the other end, sounding very distressed, 'Oh, Jayne, I'm so sorry. I thought he was out of the woods.'

'What?'

Rubie sniffed, stalling for time. 'We were just having a drink this afternoon, nothing much, just a couple of glasses...'

'What are you talking about?' Jayne's heart was pounding in her ears.

Rubie sniffed again. 'It was awful. He suddenly clutched his chest...'

'Is he in hospital? Rubie?' Fear was now threatening to overwhelm her. 'Tell me!'

'Oh, Jayne, I called the ambulance. I tried to revive him, honest. Oh God.' Jayne heard Rubie swallow and blow her nose, 'he was dead by the time they arrived. I'm really sorry...'

Jayne pressed 'end call' and went back to the bar, her legs like jelly. Where did this leave her? She suddenly felt abandoned, like a boat without an anchor.

Symon, Maggie and Leyla looked up expectantly.

'That was Rubie,' said Jayne. It was almost a whisper.

They all looked from one to another, waiting for more.

Jayne sighed and bit her lip. 'It's Michael. He's had another heart attack.'

'Oh Jayne, how awful,' said Maggie. 'Is he OK?'

Jayne shook her head and burst into tears. Her husband was dead and the realisation that Rubie was the last person to see Michael alive was too much. And what the hell had they been doing? Far more than 'having a drink' she was sure.

Maggie got up and put an arm round Jayne, 'If it's any consolation we're all here for you, darling.'

'Yeah, absolutely,' said Symon. 'At least we're all together.'

Leyla put down her knife and fork and nodded. 'I told you – bloody Rubie. You should've known.'

'Not now, Leyla,' said Symon, 'not a good time.' He turned back to Jayne. 'Can I get you anything?'

Jayne shook her head. 'At least I haven't had much to drink. I've got to get back. Tonight.'

163

'Not a good idea,' said Leyla. 'Leave it till tomorrow when you've calmed down and thought this through.'

'No, Leyla! I can't stay here, it's not right.'

'Leyla's got a point,' said Symon. 'Leave it till tomorrow. In the meantime Leyla can work her magic on the ferry staff and I'll drive us all back. You can come back for your car later on. I'm sure Jack won't mind.'

Jayne rubbed her temples – a headache was threatening. She didn't know what she wanted to do. It was all a blur, except for the to-do list that began writing itself in her mind – contact Daisy, arrange another funeral... 'I'm going up to my room.'

'Sure,' said Symon. 'Shout if you need us.'

Jayne dragged herself upstairs leaving Leyla, Maggie and Symon to speculate what had happened.

'I shouldn't be surprised if it *was* Rubie's fault,' said Leyla.

'Yeah, but you of all people should've been more tactful,' said Symon.

'How do you mean?' asked Maggie.

'Oh come on,' said Leyla, 'that piece of trash has always been hanging around.'

'You mean?' Maggie's eyes were wide, looking from one to the other.

'Well,' said Symon, 'the guy was always overdoing it, in more ways than one.'

'Gosh, poor Jayne,' said Maggie.

They finished their meal but none of them had much appetite anymore and all mention of the photographs was forgotten.

Upstairs, Jayne sat on the bed, buried her face in a tissue and let it all out. She should've seen this coming. The absences, the late nights, Michael not showing any interest in anything she wanted to do. She felt betrayed. All the years she'd given him and what did she have in return? The best thing to come out of her marriage was Daisy and she was miles away in Edinburgh suffering with chronic morning sickness. Jayne wasn't looking forward to giving her the news that her father had died while he was shagging his girlfriend, for Jayne had a strong suspicion that's what had happened. Hate rose up within her. Bloody Rubie. If she'd been in front of her right now Jayne would've slapped her face. Hard. All these years and Jayne was willing to turn a blind eye. She began to examine her motives for that: was it because Michael was too demanding in the bedroom? Could their marriage have worked if Jayne had been more attentive? Or was it because Michael resented Daisy? Ah, now that was surely something to do it. But the bottom line was that she would never know, not now. She'd never be able to resolve their differences now he was dead. She pictured his funeral. Leyla smirking, knowing full well that Rubie took anything that was offered, Maggie and Symon bolstering Jayne. And Daisy – if she could physically manage another long journey and a funeral in such a short space of time – what would she be thinking of her father?

Jayne stood up and peered out the window. It was still light. She wanted to go running on the sand, take out her anger, punch the wind. For now that she was over the initial shock, she was angry – angry that she hadn't done more to save her marriage, angry with Rubie and angry with herself for letting it happen. Most of all she was angry with Michael for slipping away so easily, leaving her in a pool of resentment and regret.

165

After Jayne's devastating news, Maggie and Symon had returned to their room. She had told him that even though a shadow had been thrown over the evening, it was still warm and the bay was too beautiful to sit dismally in their room watching the little tv screen and he'd agreed.

Hand in hand they walked the main road down the hill to the beach now bathed in silvery moonlight. The air was perfectly still and Maggie's senses were alerted to an air of expectation, as if the bay was waiting for something to happen. A little way out on the east side of the bay they found a hollowed rock on which to sit. The tide was way out, the distant rumbling of the surf now a whisper. They had the beach to themselves, not even a solitary dog-walker.

'Isn't this just perfect?' said Maggie, gazing out towards the dark velvet sea. 'I wish we'd made more of it when we were younger.'

'We're not exactly ancient now. No reason why we can't come down here more often.'

'Oh, Symon that would be wonderful. Maybe Jayne's got the right idea, turning *Seawinds* into a holiday retreat. It would be lovely to spend more time here. There's no point in slogging yourself to death. You've made an excellent name for yourself, Jason is more than capable and...'

He silenced her with a kiss. She moulded into his embrace while he ran his feather- light touch up her bare leg. He lifted her thin cotton skirt while she unzipped his shorts. Hungry for each other they sank onto the cool damp sand.

'You see? Plenty of life in this old dog yet!'

Maggie giggled, 'Oh, Symon! What if someone's watching?'

'Who cares?'

'But I do feel a bit exposed out here.' She scanned the bay for a more secluded spot. 'Look, over there. I think I can see a cave. Come on, I'll race you!'

As they ran towards it, the cave seemed to be opening up, inviting them to explore its dark inner sanctum. As she grew nearer Maggie soon realised the moon was highlighting an image about halfway up the rock on the right-hand side. 'Darling, look. Can you see it?'

'What am I looking at?'

'It's a love heart! Look. Complete with arrow. And there's something scratched into it.'

Symon stood next to Maggie and ran his fingers over the inscription. 'P S and J W,' he said slowly. 'Are you thinking what I'm thinking?'

'Jayne and Paul? Really? Do you think this was *their* cave?'

Symon nodded. 'It's too much of a coincidence not to be.'

Maggie shivered and ran her hands over her arms. She felt as if she was violating a sacred place and wondered if it had been used recently. 'We shouldn't be here, darling. There's a sad vibe as if it's waiting for them to return.'

'Nonsense, it doesn't belong to anyone. Just because two people carved their initials on it five decades ago...' he pulled her to him, ran his hands over her hips and kissed her warm neck. 'You're so beautiful tonight.' He began to pull her down onto the bed of twigs and seaweed but she stopped him.

'No Symon. You must trust me on this. Come on, we'll find our own place.'

167

March 1952

Yvonne hurried home from the shops, hung up her coat and Jayne's on the hallstand, unstrapped Jayne from her pushchair and took her through to the kitchen. She sat Jayne in her highchair, filled the kettle, put it on the gas stove. While the tea was brewing she fed Jayne some mashed potatoes and gravy. Jayne was a good child but she didn't like waiting for her food. Yvonne's own stomach rumbled. She would've liked a plate of bacon and eggs, but with rationing on that was out of the question. She lit a cigarette, cut some bread and put it in the toaster. She thought briefly of Lyons Corner House and the food she'd enjoyed with the other waitresses but she wouldn't want to go back to that life – living with her widowed mother and cycling into town every day in all weathers. She and Harry were happy, if only they could have another baby. She had wanted another child as soon as Jayne was out of nappies but she had failed to conceive. It seemed to be continually on her mind these days.

When Harry came home Yvonne met him at the door, kissed him and took his briefcase. 'Had a good day, love?'

Harry hung up his coat on the hallstand and rubbed his hands to get some warmth back into them. 'Couldn't be better!'

'That's good. Your dinner's nearly ready.'

Harry walked through to the living room and stood warming himself in front of the glowing coal fire. He turned to Yvonne. 'What have we got tonight, then?'

168

'Only corned beef hash, I'm afraid. I wish this rationing would end. I nearly managed to get some rabbit but it had all gone by the time I reached the front of the queue.'

'Never mind. How's your day been apart from that?'

Yvonne shrugged. 'Oh, all right I suppose.' She looked down at her feet.

'Come here.'

Yvonne moulded into his embrace, breathing in the cold air smell he had brought in with him.

'I think another visit to the bay is in order!'

Yvonne held him at arm's length. 'You haven't?'

Harry nodded. 'I've booked *Bay View* – how does a week in April sound?'

Yvonne was wide-eyed. 'Oh darling that's wonderful, but what about Jayne? Do you think she'll be all right? It's a long journey and have you told Mrs Crago there will be three of us…?'

Harry silenced her with a kiss. 'Don't worry, it's all under control and Jayne will love it. Trust me.'

'I love you, Harry Williams. You never cease to amaze me. So, the studio is doing well?'

'Oh, yeah. I've brought some work home again, though. Mr Smallwood took this one on at the last minute and it's got to be at the printer's by ten-thirty tomorrow morning.'

'Gosh, Harry! Do you think you'll do it?'

He nodded, 'As long as I can get on with it straight after dinner. Where's Jayne?'

'In bed. I think I wore her out today at the swings. Molly was there with little Peter.'

169

'That's nice.'

Yvonne produced two steaming plates of corned beef hash and they sat at the little gate-leg table. They ate in silence. Yvonne knew better than to interrupt her husband while he was reading the evening paper that he'd brought home with him. Her mind returned to *Bay View* – she couldn't wait to go back and she began to daydream about all three of them being greeted by Mrs Crago. Would she put a cot in their room? Would it be the same room as last time? But whatever it was, she was looking forward to Mrs Crago's cooking and not having to put up with boring rations for a week!

Harry looked up from his paper and put his knife and fork down. 'I think we can squeeze a television into that corner,' he said, pointing to the left-hand side of the fireplace. 'Would you like that?'

Yvonne grinned at him, 'Oh, that would be lovely! Just think – we'd be the first ones in our street.'

Harry patted her hand. 'I'll look into it.'

The next day, Harry knocked on Mr Smallwood's office door and handed him the job. He scrutinised the piece of lettering. 'You've excelled yourself, Harry! That's a grand job. A pity the others can't produce work to a deadline and keep to this standard.'

Harry glowed with pride but he couldn't look at Ken. He knew Mr Smallwood was referring to him as one of 'the others'.

At lunchtime, in the studio, Harry made a pot of tea for him and Ken and anyone else that cared for a cup and sat at his desk to eat his spam sandwiches that Yvonne had made him, along with a piece of bread pudding. He marvelled at her imagination – she always managed to make his lunch box special. Although she was a wizard in the kitchen he was looking forward to the day when food rationing came to an end. He was also looking forward to their week at *Tregenna Bay* when they could enjoy some proper food straight from the sea.

All this extra work was paying off. He was feeling very pleased with himself. They would soon be able to afford their own television – he'd seen the ideal model in a shop in Charing Cross Road. One more thing to tick off the long list of items he vowed would be his and Yvonne's by the end of the year. He couldn't see the point in saving his money when he could afford the best of everything. And why wait? All the money he earned he spent on making their lives more comfortable and Yvonne rewarded his efforts by making their home a delight in which to bring up their little family.

He hadn't let on to Yvonne but he harboured a desire to learn to drive and buy his own car, then they might be able to drive down to Cornwall! He would tell her when the time was right. He loved being able to surprise her.

TWELVE

The next day on their journey back to Cambridge via the Isle of Wight, Leyla, sitting in the back of the Mercedes with Jayne, thought long and hard before she asked her why she had never left Michael. She knew about divorce and what you were entitled to – she'd had dealings with solicitors when her own marriage had broken down. But Leyla was silently reprimanding herself for the outburst last night. Symon had been right – she had been less than tactful but on the other hand, Leyla didn't think there was any love lost between Jayne and Michael. However, it was always the other side of the coin that showed itself when a partner died.

'I've told you,' said Jayne, 'it was because of Daisy – I didn't want to be a one-parent-family on benefits. I've seen how those mothers struggle.'

'But you would've been entitled to half his estate, surely?'

Jayne shook her head. 'I couldn't face the court case – I would've come off badly, I'm not as strong as you. Michael knew the law. He said I wasn't entitled to anything as I hadn't contributed much money to the marriage.'

'Bastard! Sorry, Jayne, but you should've looked into it. You're too nice. Never mind the money, you've contributed by providing a home and looking after him and his daughter all these years. Any solicitor will tell you that.'

But Jayne kept quiet, she had never wanted a show-down, she didn't think it was right to take half of Michael's property for which he'd worked so hard, or to rob Daisy of the family unit. She needed a father, however lax. Deep down, Jayne had hoped that one day Michael would mend his ways and become a more attentive husband and father. But Michael grew to love money above all else, always telling Jayne to watch her spending while the cost of living kept rising. She had become an expert at juggling the housekeeping but he had never given her any praise for her efforts. She'd never actually known how much money they had – he'd kept a tight rein on the finances, paid all the bills himself and never told her what savings he had in the bank. He squirreled it all away, well out of her sight and she'd never been brave enough to ask him. Long ago she had harboured a dream that once Daisy left home she'd use her own savings and go to live at *Seawinds*, just her and her mother, Symon and Leyla joining them in the holidays. But even when that time finally came and Daisy got married, her conscience wouldn't let her leave Michael. And now it was all too late. In the space of two weeks both her mother and her husband were dead, leaving her to brush away the sadness and the might-have-beens.

'Bloody old Scrooge!' said Leyla, 'Kept his money close to him all these years and look where it's got him! Has he left a will? You are his next of kin, you know.'

'Leyla!'

Leyla caught sight of Symon's reprimanding scowl in the rear-view mirror and realised she had gone too far. 'Well, that's the practical me speaking. There's no love lost between us. I couldn't stand the man.'

'Come on, you two,' said Symon, 'let's call a truce. Jayne, you should try and relax, get some shut-eye. I bet you didn't get much sleep last night.'

173

Maggie patted his leg and turned round to Jayne. 'Symon's right. Try and have a doze, darling.'

The ferry journey went smoothly. Leyla had telephoned ahead and told them they had to get over to the island today owing to a death in the family. She also told them there would be another outward journey the same day. The ferry staff were doubtful at first – so many people made excuses to get on a ferry at the last minute – but Leyla flung herself on the mercy of the ferry staff and they found them two tickets.

Later that afternoon, the Mercedes crunched on the gravel outside Leyla's bungalow and they all piled out. They stretched their aching backs and limbs and walked through to the welcoming kitchen, Leyla stopping to pick up the post on the way. There was a note on her kitchen table from her neighbour. She picked it up.

'Oh, poor old girl,' said Leyla.

'What is it?' asked Maggie.

'Heather – she's been off her food. I hope she's all right.' She went straight to the Aga where Heather usually lay in her basket but it was empty.

'Shall I put the kettle on?' asked Maggie.

'No, you go and sit down. I'll do it.'

'She probably just missed you. Cats are like that. They pine. She's probably in the garden.'

Leyla nodded. 'I know but she's fourteen. I keep wondering how long she's got left.'

'I'm sure she's fine,' said Symon, knowing how much Jayne loved the cat and not wanting Jayne to worry about that on top of everything else.

'Leyla,' said Jayne, 'can I use your phone? Mine's dead and I need to ring Daisy. I'll give you the money. It won't be cheap.'

'Look, don't worry about it. My name's not Michael.'

Jayne flinched inwardly but held her tongue. She went to the hall and sat staring at the phone trying to compose the words in her head. 'Hello love, your father died yesterday,' wasn't a great opener, especially as Daisy wasn't well, but Jayne couldn't think how best to approach it. She picked up the phone, took a deep breath and hoped for the best.

'Hello, love. How are you? Feeling any better?'

'Not bad thanks, mum. How are you?'

'I'm OK, love,' Jayne blew out her cheeks, 'but I'm afraid I've got some bad news. I don't really know how to tell you. Are you sitting down?'

'Yes, why?'

'It's your father. He had another heart attack yesterday. I'm really sorry love, there's no easy way to say this...'

'You mean... he's dead?'

'Yes. I was in Cornwall, as you know...'

'Oh, Mum. How awful. Are you all right?'

'Don't worry about me, I'm fine. I couldn't ring you before, my mobile needed charging. I'm at Leyla's, I'm on her landline.'

There was a pause. Then Daisy said, 'I can't believe it. I know we've never been close but ...'

'I know, love. I just wish you weren't so far away. Are you OK? Is Tim there?'

175

'Yes, he's got the afternoon off. He's making paper airplanes with Bonnie. Oh Mum... how did it happen?'

'I don't know. Rubie was too upset last night to go into details.'

'Rubie?'

'Yes, apparently they were together when it happened.'

Daisy whistled down the phone.

'You knew?'

'Oh, come on, Mum, don't be so naïve! She was always in the background even when I was a kid. Huh! *Auntie* Rubie.'

'She *is* your godmother. She was also my best friend.'

'Yeah, was. Look how she went behind your back all those years. You must've been blind not to see it. Anyway, what will you do now?'

'Do? God, I don't know. I haven't thought about it apart from sorting out another funeral...'

Somewhere in the background a child was crying. 'Sorry Mum, I've gotta go. Speak soon. OK? Love you lots. And try not to worry.'

'OK. Take care. Love you too.'

After drinking their tea and forcing down a bacon sandwich, Jayne, Symon and Maggie left Leyla and jumped back in the car. Maggie took the wheel and they were soon on board the ferry and then on their way to Cambridge. The traffic was light for a change and the Mercedes purred along the M11.

Hours later Maggie just managed to squeeze into the last parking space in the narrow road. Jayne's house looked abandoned – bits of rubbish had collected by the doorstep, the curtains drawn. Jayne's instinct was to turn tail and run back to Cornwall, but she had to brace herself for what she would find indoors and for what the next few days held in store.

Feeling like an intruder in her own home Jayne let herself, Maggie and Symon into the cold unwelcoming hall. She scanned it for any tell-tale signs of Rubie but all the coats were accounted for and no alien shoes lay about. But Jayne had an uneasy feeling Rubie had stayed more than once while she'd been in Cornwall. The feeling of betrayal engulfed her.

Maggie and Symon followed her through to the kitchen-diner and stood looking out of place. Jayne's first thought was to ask them to stay the night – she couldn't possibly let them drive home at this late hour. 'You can stay the night, you know. In fact, I'd like you to.'

Maggie glanced at Symon. 'What do you want to do, darling?'

Symon was reluctant to answer. He knew whatever he said would upset one or other of the women. He could tell by Maggie's expression that she wasn't too keen on staying. 'I'll let you two fight over it – I'm easy.'

'Well,' began Maggie, looking around at the untidy kitchen, 'I don't mind driving. The traffic shouldn't be too bad at this time of night and I'm not tired.'

'Well, if you're sure?' Jayne went to fill the kettle. 'At least let me make you a drink before you jump back in the car.'

'It's OK, darling, we'll grab a coffee-to-go and I've got a bottle of water.' Maggie draped her arms round Jayne and rubbed her back. 'Try not to worry, sweetheart. We're only a phone call away. '

Symon followed suit and gave Jayne a hug. 'Yeah, look after yourself. I'll give you a ring tomorrow. And try and get some shut-eye.'

Jayne waved them off at the front door, closed it and felt desolate. She hung up her coat, kicked off her shoes and padded back to the kitchen. She could still hear Michael's voice: "*What time d'you call this? Sometimes I swear you forget you've got a husband!*" and "*Think yourself lucky I don't go looking elsewhere.*" But of course, he had.

She was also confused; she didn't know how she should feel about Michael's death. She'd given him the best years of her life and this is how he'd repaid her loyalty, an on-going affair with her best friend while she had remained faithful! Oh, she'd had offers when she was teaching but she didn't want to go behind Michael's back and live a life of duplicity. She'd even felt guilty if one of them invited her out for a coffee in her lunch break. But looking back, she should've gone – it might have made Michael sit up and take notice.

But there was Daisy to think about. Jayne loved being a mum, especially in Daisy's early years when Jayne was finishing her art course. It was difficult to juggle two different aspects of her life but she was determined to finish her course and do the best for her daughter. On the days when she wasn't at art school she threw herself into playgroup activities putting her artistic skills to good use and helped with the finger-painting, cutting and sticking for which the organisers were very grateful. Later on, she had volunteered her services at the

178

primary school until she took a job as an art teacher at the village college. This enabled her to enjoy her own independence whilst having the same holidays as Daisy. It also meant she wasn't reliant on Michael for every penny. They'd had some good times when Daisy was little, but that was because Jayne had made things happen. She'd been clever at finding places and events to entertain them at weekends. Often Michael didn't want to go but that hadn't deterred her.

Most summer holidays were spent at *Seawinds*. Michael sometimes joined them but Jayne sensed there was always somewhere else he'd rather be. He was never very engaged in family activities, would reluctantly kick a ball about the beach until the pub opened.

Yvonne had been a good mother but Jayne felt sure she had also been a good wife. Jayne wondered if she herself had been a good wife. Who would tell her? Certainly not Rubie. Right from the start Rubie would chastise Jayne for not giving Michael enough attention. That should've been enough indication of Rubie's feelings towards Michael, but Jayne had dismissed it, thinking she was imagining things. They all got on so well together when they met up but Rubie's husband had always kept a low profile. They never had any children and thinking about it now, Jayne thought that was probably one of the reasons why Michael, a selfish man, was attracted to Rubie.

Jayne snapped out of her reverie and began scrutinising the kitchen. The farmhouse table displayed an empty red wine bottle and two dirty glasses, one of which held the unmistakable smear of red lipstick. The remains of a Chinese take-away lay congealed in a heap of tin-foil and cardboard. Anger rose within her – Michael would never allow takeaways in the house, always insisted she cook everything from scratch every evening. Maybe Jayne would've gained more respect if she had rebelled.

179

But her beautiful house felt violated. She donned her rubber gloves and gathered together the disgusting mess that had been their last supper, opened the back door and chucked it in the wheelie bin. She feverishly set to work washing the glasses and scrubbing the table and every work surface. Finally, when all signs of Michael and Rubie had been obliterated, then and only then did she allow herself to relax and put the kettle on.

She took her cup of Earl Grey into the lounge and curled up in her blue armchair. Her stomach rumbled but the thought of food made her want to heave. Their black and white wedding photo mocked her from the sideboard. How young and unsuspecting she'd been! When she thought back to that day and the reception in particular, she should've realised what Rubie was up to, only too eager to dance with Michael and laugh at his jokes. She threw the photo across the room, the glass smashing against the skirting board. She collapsed in a heap of tears – tears of frustration, of regret and for being used. She shuddered at the thought; Rubie, her best friend whom she met at art school, how could she have deceived her all these years, the friend she confided in when things got tough, the godmother to her daughter? Her stomach clenched – they must've been laughing at her every time they slipped between the sheets.

Suddenly feeling exhausted, Jayne took herself upstairs to bed. She opened the door to the master bedroom and was confronted with the stale smell of Rubie's musky perfume mixed with the mustiness of the unmade bed. Some of Michael's underwear lay on the floor. She couldn't bring herself to pick it up and put it in the linen basket or to sleep between those same sheets and she was too tired to change the bed. She doubted if she would ever be able to sleep in that bed again. She closed the door on the death stage, ran to the bathroom and retched.

A few hours later in the guest bedroom, instead of the cry of gulls, Jayne awoke to the sound of police sirens and she momentarily wondered where she was. She sighed and dragged her languid body out of bed, put on her slippers and dressing gown and padded downstairs. The kitchen looked even lonelier in the cold light of day; a pair of Michael's shoes lay by the back door waiting for him to put them on and his car keys hung on the hook never to be picked up by him again. She still didn't know how she should feel now Michael was dead. She couldn't quite believe it. He seemed very much alive the last time she saw him. It was as if someone had played a sick joke on her.

She made a pot of tea and mechanically went through the motions of pouring a cup. At the kitchen table, the image of Gladys resurfaced. It had been a shock to know Paul was back in Cornwall but had Jayne actually seen and spoken to Gladys that day or had it all been a figment of her imagination? After finding the young woman in Gladys's house that day, she was seriously questioning her sanity. But the more she thought about it the more she began to wonder if the secrets of the past were reaching out to her in some way. There were a lot of unanswered questions surrounding her father's death. Why had he gone out on that blustery day and what had really happened up there on the cliff top? Did he commit suicide or was it an accident? The inquest had determined 'Death by Misadventure' but there were no witnesses to contradict this theory. What part if any did Ken Smythe play in all of this? Had the row with Ken Smythe been enough to send her father literally over the edge? All this was like coming across signposts but not knowing which way to go. She wondered what else she would unearth when she returned to *Seawind*s.

181

Jayne took her tea out to the secluded patio garden and sat on the bench in the sun. Over the years this little garden had been her salvation but this morning it looked sadly neglected; weeds a foot high, dead leaves choking the fire pit in the centre. Michael was no gardener although he was useful when it came to any heavy work that needed doing, like putting up the pergola for which Jayne had insisted should have a string of fairy lights draped across the top. Something magical about a garden at night, she decided. She had often sat out here in the dark with a glass of wine, on her own, and listened to the creatures in the undergrowth and the occasional owl. Even better if it had been bathed in moonlight. Maybe they could create a night garden at *Seawinds?*

The sun beamed down on her as she slowly sipped her tea and allowed her thoughts to drift back to when Daisy had friends round from college on a Saturday afternoon. The little garden would be filled with animated chatter while they barbequed their food on the fire pit; young people with fresh ideas looking forward to their future. Only on these occasions did the house truly feel like a home.

Even in those days she had wondered about Paul and where he was living. Now an image of the teenage Paul swam before her – his toned young body, his dark hair shining in the sun, his smile. Surfing and swimming with him. She had known him even longer than Rubie or Michael and she wondered if their renewed friendship would ever develop. But after her snub Paul must be in a quandary; she hadn't seen or spoken to him since Monday when she'd stormed off. He wouldn't know she was in Cambridge. He deserved to know. She went back indoors and picked up her mobile. A voice shouted at her to leave a message but she didn't know how to word it. No, she'd try again later when she'd had time to think about what she wanted to say. She yawned. The past few

182

weeks had been like a roller-coaster and there was still a mountain of things to do, places to go and people to see.

THIRTEEN

The call of the bay was too much for Paul to ignore. He'd woken at dawn, had a quick shower and jumped in his rented car and driven to the car park by the beach café. He would've liked some breakfast but the place wasn't open until 9am, so he walked the length of the sea front with only the sea breeze for company. He watched the waves crashing and tumbling over themselves. Herring gulls rode on the wind, their lonely cries mirroring how he felt. It hadn't helped giving *Seawinds* a look over either. He hadn't been prepared for the old place having such an effect on him. It had shocked and saddened him but he couldn't discuss any of this with Katie or Martin; he couldn't burden them with his past, and anyway, he didn't think they would understand. They only knew him for the Australian he'd become – larger than life without a care. But he was a different person since being back in England this time, as though part of the old Paul had resurfaced; the part that fell in love with Jayne all those years ago. He'd been so happy with her in Padstow on Sunday, but in retrospect maybe he was hoping for too much too soon. They were two very different people to the Jayne and Paul of 1967. His mantra in Australia had been, 'Don't think about it, do it,' but since being back in Cornwall he couldn't live up to it. The situation wasn't helped by the fact that the day after the viewing he had gone back to Mastersons eager to put in an offer only to be told that *Seawinds* had been withdrawn from sale.

Now, walking high up along the coast path, he was trying to make sense of what he'd been told. So Jayne wanted

184

to hang on to *Seawinds* did she? For what purpose? Perhaps she wanted to recapture the happy times, *their* happy times. He let out a cynical laugh and told himself to stop being so naïve. There must be a more sensible explanation. Maybe her brother and sister couldn't agree? Perhaps they were going to refurbish it into holiday apartments? So many seaside properties had been upgraded that way, bringing in high returns. But knowing Jayne's attitude towards second home owners he doubted that was the case. He could understand the logic, but if his dream was to be realised he needed to discuss with Jayne the possibility of them running *Seawinds* as a surf school, together, and soon. Old *Seawinds* was ripe for the plucking – three storeys, plenty of bedrooms, in a prime spot...

He pondered these questions as he sat on a bench high up on the cliff path. He looked down on the sun-kissed beach below. The bay had a strange effect on him. It was like coming home except for the memory of the day Jayne's father died. That had been a weird business. There was something lurking beneath the speculation as to how it had happened but there was no one to ask. His father was dead and his mother was less than co-operative. He was sure there was something his father would never tell him – he had died taking the secret with him, if indeed there was one.

Paul stood up and peered down onto the jagged rocks below. It was a steep drop only now there was a wire fence and warning signs to stop people falling to their deaths, not like in 1968 when there had been nothing between Mr Williams and the cliff face. Paul had never been good with heights. His stomach flipped at the thought of slipping and plummeting down. He felt something like a hand pulling him back from the brink but when he grabbed the concrete fencepost and looked round, there was no one there. Jeez, that was weird! A strong wind whipped up suddenly causing him to grab the bench and sit down. What *had* happened on that other April day? It was almost as if there was something on the breeze trying to tell him.

Taking some deep breaths he glanced down at the few families taking advantage of the warm April sun. A few kids in wetsuits surfing, some in the sea, unlike that other April day, which had been cold and blustery and the beach deserted. Why had Mr Williams decided to go out for a walk in that treacherous weather? And did Jayne suspect something sinister? It was highly likely after her reaction on Monday morning. He tried to cast his mind back. He had a vague memory of going with his mum and Katie somewhere that day but was his dad with them? He tried to think. He could remember them all trooping down the stairs but was his father there? And if he wasn't, where was he that afternoon?

He longed to see Jayne. Christ, this was getting ridiculous. He only had two more weeks and he'd be getting back on that plane, organising the rest of his possessions in Sydney, selling his boat and hopefully returning to England for good, but he had to know if he stood a chance with Jayne. He had to know.

He took out his mobile, hoping to get a signal. Jayne answered straight away.

'Hello, Paul. How are you?'

Her voice was like velvet, it sent a shiver through him and made his heart clench.

'I've been thinking...I suppose you wouldn't consider...'

'...Michael's had a heart attack. I'm back in Cambridge.'

'Oh Christ, is he all right?'

186

'No, Paul. He's dead. Look, I've got a lot to sort out, what with the post-mortem and the inquest and everything. I don't know when I'll be back in Cornwall.'

His first thought was that Jayne was free, but he had to stop himself from sounding too excited. 'I'm really sorry, but why a post-mortem and an inquest?'

'He died at home. OK, you might as well know...he was in bed with Rubie, my so-called best friend, when it happened.'

'Christ! Did you know? About the two of them, I mean?'

'I had my suspicions.'

'Oh, God Jayne, I'm really sorry. It must've been a dreadful shock. If there's anything I can do...?'

She sighed. 'Not really. It's just... it couldn't have come at a worse time, what with Mum, the house and everything. Daisy's very upset, of course. I just hope it doesn't affect the baby – she was hospitalised last week but she's out now.'

Paul realised she had a lot on her shoulders. 'Look, if you want some support... ' 'Thanks. I'm sorry, I've gotta go.'

He shoved the mobile back in his pocket. Jayne was free! He felt like yelling it to the four winds and to hell with who heard him. Jayne was free, but he also knew he had to tread very carefully along the path of unpredictability. He couldn't ask what her plans were concerning the house, or where he stood with her right now. Of course he couldn't. That would be very insensitive. One step at a time, he told himself.

187

As he stood up to leave Paul noticed the engraving on the back of the bench.

In Loving Memory of Harry Williams. May his spirit roam free on the breeze.

Paul suddenly wanted to run far away from this place; it had a sad vibe. Watching his step, he trod back down the narrow stony path, down the few steps and ambled along the sea front.

He found himself gazing up at *Seawinds*. Yeah, the old place definitely had potential. He knew there was a cellar – although he'd never ventured down there – he could tell from the window at ground level and, during the viewing, he had hoped, with a bit of refurbishing, it could house all the surfing gear. Upstairs he could picture the old dining room turned into a restaurant with a balcony overlooking the bay, the front room where Mr Williams played his music a comfortable lounge area with a bar. The top floor could be turned into en-suite accommodation...

Something took his eye. Was it his imagination or did the net curtains twitch next door? He didn't want to get caught up with Gladys so he turned and began to walk back down the hill. But on hearing the door open he immediately turned round to see a young woman standing there.

She shouted to him. 'Hey, you looking for someone?'

'No, it's OK.' He frowned and sucked in his bottom lip. 'Er, are you... any relation to Gladys... her granddaughter?'

'You're the second person to mention this Gladys,' she said, hands on hips. 'No, I'm nothing to do with the woman who lived here!'

'Really? '

'Yeah, and there was a woman a few days ago asking questions. From what I was told no one's lived here for years. The place was empty when we viewed it.'

'Oh, right. OK. Thanks.'

Paul scratched his head. He was sure he'd spoken to Gladys only a few days ago.

1958

Harry sat at the dining table studying his latest bank statement. Yvonne was getting the children to bed and he was trying to concentrate through all the shouting and arguing going on upstairs. Leyla had asked him to read her a story and he'd promised he would as soon as she was tucked up in bed.

But something wasn't adding up. He checked and rechecked and rubbed a hand over his weary face. He thought his accounts were healthy but he must've overlooked something. The work at the studio was beginning to thin out of late and that worried him. Being freelance his money was not paid every week but periodically, the last cheque being for a very healthy £70. But because of the irregular payments it was difficult to juggle the finances. Luckily Yvonne had no idea of his anguish – she left him to look after the money and pay all the bills. He gave her a cheque each week for the housekeeping that she cashed at the bank. But if they sold the house and bought *Bay View* he'd worked out that this would solve all his money problems. Not only that, they would all be far better off in Cornwall. They all loved *Tregenna Bay* and Harry knew it would be the best environment for the children in which to grow up.

Charlie had written to him saying his mother was now finding it difficult to run the guest house and they were thinking of selling. Harry had written straight back stating he would love to buy *Bay View* and run it with Yvonne. She was a good cook and she would thoroughly enjoy continuing Mrs Crago's tradition of welcoming their visitors, some of whom returned year after year. Charlie was excited by the prospect

190

but said that his mother had let the business run down in the last couple of years. Nevertheless Harry had big plans for *Bay View*, he knew he and Yvonne could turn it around. He would get onto it immediately and design some adverts to pull in the visitors and get onto the Cornwall Tourist Board.

The next stage was to put their house on the market, the sooner the better. House prices were rising and the country's economy was picking up, so he didn't foresee any problems. The downside was that he shouldn't have bought the newest model of Ford Zodiac. That £950 had been a big drain on his finances, but he loved the freedom it gave him driving the family down to the Kent coast on a Sunday and calling in on his old mother who had recently moved in with her brother. It was a treat to get away from the London grime but it couldn't compare to *Tregenna Bay!*

Yvonne came in and jolted Harry out of his thoughts.

'Leyla's waiting for you to read her a poem. I expect it'll be *The Kings Breakfast* again and you know how it makes her laugh, hardly the right thing to send her to sleep! Perhaps you can persuade her to have a different one?'

'I'll be up directly, tell her. I must just finish this.'

'All right, but she's getting impatient.'

'I know but she's old enough to realise some things are more important. I won't be long.'

Yvonne kissed him on the cheek, left him and went back upstairs to tell Leyla her dad would be up very soon. Jayne was in bed reading *Alice in Wonderland* and telling Leyla to be quiet. Yvonne looked in on Symon who was fast asleep snuggled up with his teddy, turned out his bedside light and went back downstairs.

191

But Harry was still pondering the paperwork spread out on the dining table. Yvonne was becoming concerned – he never took this long over his accounts.

'Is everything all right?'

Harry looked up, 'Eh? Oh, just one or two things I can't quite tally. Nothing to worry about, my love.'

'Oh good, it's just that you seem a bit far away lately.'

'I'm making sure all the loose ends are tied up before we move to the bay, that's all. Looking forward to it?'

Yvonne grinned and nodded excitedly.

'Now, where's the little girl who wants a story?' Harry closed his accounts book, put it away in the desk and ran up the stairs two at a time. Yvonne heard the squeals of laughter as he told Leyla the story of *The King's Breakfast* for the umpteenth time.

FOURTEEN

Leyla fed Heather, poured another cup of tea then set to work. Heather had indeed been pining for her while she'd been in Cornwall. Leyla had found her under the hedge in the back garden, looking thin and bedraggled. A quick going-over at the vet's assured Leyla that all Heather needed was a bit of attention and a good feed.

After reading through her work and what she'd written for her last entry, the old brown suitcase, still in the hall, was beckoning her. Jayne had told her it was full of her father's old tax returns and she now felt compelled to take a look. But where was the key? Now she thought about it she couldn't remember Jayne giving it to her. She tried the rusty catches but they wouldn't budge. Perhaps she should try a hairpin? She went to the bedroom and found one tucked way down in her dressing table drawer.

After some poking about, the first rusty catch flew open but the second one shot open with a vengeance. 'Ow! Bugger!' Blood spurting from her finger she ran to the bathroom, rinsed it under the tap and quickly dried it on some toilet paper, struggled with the wrapper on the sticking plaster and finally stuck it on. But it was no good; the blood was seeping through so she put another one on top and wound some kitchen towel round it. That would have to do for now.

She went back to look in the suitcase. There on top of the letters was her box of diaries, the cat pictures faded with time. She lifted the lid and scanned some of the writing,

193

smiling at the memory of her innocent efforts until she reached the one dated 1968. She remembered writing the extra foolscap sheets, hunched in the cellar, hoping her dad wouldn't discover she'd been eavesdropping. She shivered and put the lid back on and started to paw through the tax demands and old letters addressed to her father.

But what was this? Buried in the silk lining she found some letters from Ken Smythe. As she read, she realised they were blackmail letters. She began to feel a hatred for this so-called friend of the family and found it very difficult to believe Ken's accusation that Harry had robbed him of his savings. As far as she was aware her father had been a good law-abiding citizen; there was never any evidence to suggest otherwise. The original story was that Harry had had a win on the horses, a race at Kempton Park, enabling him to afford the extra money to plonk down on *Seawinds* and do the necessary renovations. No one had ever questioned it. But when she thought about it, Leyla couldn't remember her father gambling at any other time.

Leyla rummaged some more and noticed that, as time went on, the letters were becoming more demanding. She was astounded – she didn't think any of this had come to light before. She read the most recent one again.

10th March 1968

Harry,

This is my last time of asking. When I lent you that £300 for the bridging loan, you assured me that you could pay me back as soon as the guesthouse was up and running, but it hasn't happened. Thanks to you my life has been Hell since the studio went bust and I lost my job. The embarrassing difficulty you placed me in has been trying in the extreme. My job ticket-writing at the supermarket barely pays our rent and Lottie

194

has had to take on menial cleaning jobs to keep our heads above water. I can't tell you what a strain this has put on our marriage. We have had some wonderful holidays at the bay Harry, good memories. I'm reluctant to end our friendship, but unless you find a way to pay me back I will have to take further action.

We will be coming down to stay with you for the Easter holiday (free of charge, I hope) so make sure everything is in order.

Ken.

So this is what it was all about. Not only did her father have tax demands mounting up but also nasty blackmail letters from Ken Smythe. And what would be the 'further action' she wondered. Would Ken Smythe have sent round the heavies to rough up her father? It all sounded so over-the-top, like some gangster movie.

Until now Leyla had thought her father's depression hereditary – he had told them about his mother losing twins years ago and having to go into a mental asylum for a spell. Leyla had used this example as one of the many she'd researched on mental health in the twentieth century for her thesis – but the realisation of the real nature of her father's depression made her insides twist with hatred for Ken Smythe. £300 didn't seem a great deal of money nowadays but it must have been a fortune back in 1968; even more so when he had lent it to him. How on earth had her father got into such a mess? None of them knew Harry had money problems but the more she thought about it, the more Leyla remembered her mother struggling to make sense of the finances after he died. They thought it was just because she wasn't used to handling the money side of the business but now, finding this blackmail letter, all was becoming clear. Leyla wondered if she should phone Jayne and tell her what she'd discovered but what with the trauma of Michael's death and her daughter Daisy's

195

extreme morning sickness, she thought better of it. But Jayne needed to know. She rang her number. No answer just the usual voicemail message.

Leyla's finger was throbbing and the blood had leaked through two plasters and the kitchen towel. She removed them; bound a piece of gauze round her finger and stuck another bigger plaster on top. What with that and the realisation of their father's plight, she wished she had never opened that wretched suitcase.

FIFTEEN

Jayne put the phone down on the pathology technician at the hospital. She didn't know why, but she wasn't expecting to be asked to identify the body of her dead husband. They had told her to come in as soon as possible and she knew she would have to do this alone, today. She felt stranded without her car and wished she hadn't let Symon and Maggie drive her back to Cambridge. She balked at using public transport. She wasn't even sure what to do or how to pay for a bus ticket.

Jayne stepped off the bus at Addenbrookes Hospital and found the directions to the mortuary. Her stomach was in knots and her armpits prickled as she approached the reception desk. The woman asked her to take a seat and someone would be with her shortly, but Jayne was too agitated to sit down – she wanted to get this over with as soon as possible. She stood impatiently looking at her watch, bracing herself for the upsetting sight she knew would confront her. The only dead bodies she'd seen were the ones on television in murder mysteries and on the news, and she wasn't sure how she would react to the sight of Michael's.

After waiting for what seemed like forever, a man in a white bodysuit and a mask slung low on his chin, opened the door.

'Mrs Green? Do come in.'

The first thing she saw was the bluish colour of the top of Michael's shiny bald head. His mound of a body lay facing away from her on a table, covered in a white sheet.

'Take your time Mrs Green,' said the man in the bodysuit.

Jayne's hand flew to her mouth at the sight of the name tag tied to Michael's toe. So this was Michael. But of course it was; she'd know the shape of that foot anywhere. A chill ran through her body and tears threatened to burst forth.

She inched closer, her eyes drawn to the white sheet. But she didn't want to look on the face that had once had every girl in Cambridge swooning at his feet. But she knew she had to. There were the familiar age spots, the shape of his nose...

'Mrs Green?'

She'd been losing him for years, piece by adulterous piece. 'Oh, Michael,' she gasped and dabbed her eyes with a tissue. 'Why?'

The flat voice startled her. 'Thank you. It's never an easy task. If you care to wait outside Jackie will bring you a cup of tea.'

Feeling drained but thankful the ordeal was over she took a seat in the corridor. She closed her eyes and wondered how long that last image of Michael would stay with her. It was unbelievable that overnight she had become a widow and would never see her husband alive again, would never be able to set right the wrongs of the past or to ask why their life together had turned out so colourless.

At the other end of the corridor an immaculately groomed young woman in a business suit advanced through the double doors carrying the much needed cup of tea on a small tray and handed it to Jayne.

'Here we are. Take sugar?'

'Yes, please. One,' Jayne pushed a strand of hair behind her ear and wiped her eyes. The woman placed the tray on the chair next to Jayne and stirred one sugar lump into the tea as though Jayne were a child of three instead of a mature woman of sixty eight. 'There. If you need anything I'll be in the office,' she said, pointing to the double doors.

Left alone in the soulless corridor Jayne stared into her thick white hospital cup and remembered the last time she had drunk tea from one like this – at her mum's bedside. Yvonne had been well-respected; the little church packed to bursting. Michael had said he was too busy to attend the funeral. But now, of course, she knew the truth.

The next few days drifted by in a blur of phone calls and frustration. Having nothing to keep her in Cambridge, Jayne chafed against the delay. She was anxious to move on with her life and return to Cornwall but the funeral had been postponed until after the post-mortem. Rubie was another reason to keep her detained – she'd rung Jayne asking for a meeting. Because Jayne couldn't bring herself to open her front door to Rubie, she had suggested they meet on neutral ground at a café adjacent to Parkers Piece.

Jayne took one last look in the hall mirror, confident she was suitably attired to meet her friend-cum-rival, and walked to the designated meeting place. The rain came from nowhere and matched her mood – dark and cold. She thanked her judgement for taking her umbrella and as she strode across the green expanse of Parker's Piece with rows of bicycles padlocked to the railings and students milling around, Jayne pushed away the happy memories of meeting Michael in their college days and how much in love they'd been. But no, that seemed preposterous now. It had been a one-sided relationship. She fell to wondering if Rubie had played a part in their triangle even then. She wasn't relishing the thought of being in her presence but when she caught sight of her own image in the large windows of the contemporary café – a smart blue raincoat and black high heeled boots – Jayne felt super-confident. As she entered the humid café she spotted Rubie on the far side.

At least she's had the decency to seat herself away from the other customers.

Jayne collapsed her umbrella and approached Rubie who half smiled, looked away and fiddled with the teaspoon in her saucer. Her unwashed, straw-blonde hair was scraped up on top of her head, her grotesque eye make-up smudged. As Jayne neared the table she saw Rubie's ridiculous attempt at dressing like a nineteen-year-old – a black skirt showing a yard of fatty thigh and a skimpy white top showing her bulging midriff. A fuchsia pink rain jacket lay on the chair next to her.

Jayne pulled out a chair and sat opposite Rubie, her false red nails clasped round her empty cup. 'I'm so sorry, Jayne,' she began.

'Save it, Rubie.'

Rubie bit her lip and stood up. 'I'll get us a coffee. Sugar?'

'No, sit down. I can't stay long and I would probably choke on anything you gave me.'

'Oh, please, Jayne, don't be like that,' she pleaded. 'Friends?'

'Huh, I don't know how you've got the gall. Were you fucking him before we got married?'

Rubie's jaw dropped. She scanned the café to see if anyone had reacted to the F word. 'No! Of course not. I would never have done that to you.'

'Really? Even at our wedding you were brazenly flirting with him,' Jayne narrowed her eyes, 'D'you know how that hurt?'

Rubie was immediately on the defensive. 'It takes two, Jayne. If you'd given him what he wanted...'

'How dare you!'

Jayne was aware their raised voices were causing a stir – the people nearest them looking round and talking in hushed tones – but she didn't care. It felt good to blast Rubie while she was feeling vulnerable. She only wished Michael had been there – she would've enjoyed smacking the smirk off his face too.

'When's the funeral?' asked Rubie.

'I don't know.' Jayne let out a sigh, suddenly feeling deflated. 'There's got to be a post-mortem and an inquest. Could take weeks.'

'Why? I didn't kill him!'

Jayne's voice raised an octave. 'Huh! As good as. You knew he had high blood pressure and drank too much but you didn't care... even after his heart attack last year... how could you? D' you know how hard it is to tell your daughter, who incidentally, is pregnant and might lose the baby, that her shit father is dead?'

'Oh, God Jayne, I didn't know.' It was almost a whisper. Rubie rubbed her eyes smearing the mascara further down her cheeks.

'Of course you didn't. All you cared about was him telling you what a good shag you were!'

Rubie looked like a child who had been smacked and sent to her room without any tea. Jayne was satisfied; she'd said enough. Her chest felt tight, her cheeks were hot and the café was closing in on her. 'I'll be in touch about the funeral. Apart from that, I never want to set eyes on you again.'

Jayne left the café with customers staring after her. She didn't care. In fact she felt as if she'd grown another two inches.

Back home Jayne picked up the phone and rang the coroners' liaison officer.

'I'll spare you the details, Mrs Green, apart from his heart... I feel you should know... there were some unexplained marks on his body, large scratches and wheals, particularly on his back. Can you account for those?'

'No, I can't. I wasn't there at the time, I was in Cornwall. I buried my mother two weeks ago and I was dealing with the house sale.'

'Oh, I see. I'm very sorry to hear that. Your husband died at home, I believe?'

'Yes.'

'Well, that'll be all. I have released the body for burial or cremation, whichever you decide. Don't forget, if there's anything you're not sure about or if I can help in any way, please don't hesitate to...'

'...Thank you.' Jayne slammed the phone down. An image of Rubie's legs clasped round Michael's back and her long red nails gouging into his skin made her insides twist with rage.

SIXTEEN

The uncertainty of when Michael's funeral would take place meant that Symon and Maggie were left wondering whether to go back to Cornwall or wait a bit longer, but after a few phone calls their minds were made up. Symon was anxious to get going on the renovation of *Seawinds* and Maggie couldn't wait to get back to the glorious beach where she felt twenty years younger.

They had settled into the routine straight away enjoying Jack's hospitality and the glorious bay. Tonight, Symon fell to wondering if Captain Tregenna had been a real person or just a name given to the pub. He had always been interested in history and the architecture of old houses and this one was no exception. He saw that Jack wasn't busy so after he'd put the bottle of wine on the tab, he asked him.

'Ah,' said Jack, 'I've done a bit of digging on the internet. Turns out Captain Tregenna was in Her Majesty's Navy at the time of the Spanish Armada. After the battle his ship was blown way off course in a horrendous gale and he ended up shipwrecked here, at the bay. He fell in love with it and made it his home. The bay is named after him. He lived to a hundred and ten, so the story goes.

'Really?' said Symon, incredulous. 'Fascinating. And the pub? Was this building here then?'

Jack smiled. 'This was his house – he built it, battlements and all. The oldest part date's from 1589. I'm

203

going to have a plaque made in his honour. What d'you reckon?'

'I think it's a great idea. I've always been into architecture. Would you mind showing me around sometime?'

'My pleasure.'

'Cheers.' Symon took the bottle of wine back to where Maggie was sitting and told her.

'Oh, wow!' said Maggie. 'That's really old. Any ghosts?'

'He didn't say but I wouldn't be at all surprised. Might even be some secret passages.'

'Wow! That's cool.'

Symon looked up from his menu and read from the specials board. 'Pan-fried scallops with chorizo, Thai mussels with coconut, chilli and coriander, or whole sea bream with samphire and baby spinach. What d'you reckon?'

'The scallops sound delicious. What's for pudding?'

'You don't usually eat pudding.'

'No but I fancy something sweet tonight.'

'You're sweet enough,' said Symon and began running his hand up her bare thigh.

She giggled and slapped his hand away. 'Symon! Not here. What am I going to do with you?'

Symon gave her one of his boyish grins. 'I think you know the answer to that.'

Paul strolled along the sea front filling his lungs with invigorating air. Australia had never had this effect on him, although he had enjoyed the beaches and the surf there, the air was always somehow heavier than in Cornwall. He was pleased to see the life guards doing their stuff, white Land Rover parked up and the red and yellow flags indicating the safe place to bathe and surf. In the distance a line of cloud hung high above the crashing breakers, inviting him in. He hadn't brought his surfboard with him on the plane and it suddenly occurred to him that he needed a surfboard and he needed it now.

He strolled into the *Surf-Shack,* next door to the beach café, that hired out surfboards and wetsuits and began examining the gear on the racks. As he did so he saw two people of a certain age looking really happy and glowing with health. They paid the young athletic guy behind the counter and walked out with their belly boards, holding hands.

'I'll take some of what they just hired,' said Paul.

The young guy looked him up and down. 'Must be something in the air; I'm really busy today.'

'Are they local?' asked Paul, watching the couple's receding backs.

The guy shook his head. 'Nah, never seen 'em afore.' He looked at Paul and the surfboard and wet suit he'd chosen. 'You OK with that?'

'Yeah, don't worry mate. Been surfing all m' life.'

'You don't come from around here, either. Aussie?'

'Ha, yeah. How'd you guess?'

'Wow! I bet the surf's great down under?'

'Pretty much.'

'What brings you here?'

'Long story, mate. Some other time OK? Surf's calling.'

The assistant put Paul's money in the till. ' You can change round the back if you want. We've got lockers.' He handed Paul a key.

'Thanks, mate.'

Paul found the changing room and struggled into the wet suit he'd selected. He scrutinized the make – not as good as his own that he'd left at Katie's – but it would do for today.

After securing his clothes and wallet in the locker, Paul strapped the key fob onto his wrist, took the surf board and strode barefoot out of the shop. The sea was way out, exposing a huge expanse of hard wet sand wrinkled by the receding tide. Pairs of footprints ran down to the distant sea, dots of people surfing. Dodging rock pools, splashing through rivulets of water, past the lifeguards' Land Rover, Paul gathered speed and finally arrived at the glistening water's edge. He waded in and pushed the surfboard out in front of him, climbed on and swam out face-down until he reached the biggest wave. Standing up on the board he gloried in the deafening rumble beneath him.

Catch a wave and you're sitting on top of the world.

He couldn't remember who said it but they'd never spoken a truer word. God, he'd missed it! He'd heard on the breakfast news that the surf was three feet high and clean, perfect. As he surfed into shore he imagined the scene with a load of youngsters from his surf school. Yeah, it would be great to do it here. He had to pursue his dream and he knew he had to phone Jayne and tell her of his plans; he couldn't afford to procrastinate any longer.

He coasted into shore and was just about to do it all again when he noticed the two people he'd seen in the shop coasting in on their belly boards. They came to a stop and

206

scrambled out a few feet away from him, laughing with excitement. Paul went up to them.

'Good-day,' he shouted above the rumble of the waves, 'Great isn't it?'

'Sure is,' Symon bellowed back. 'Makes you feel alive.'

Maggie shouted, 'You look like you know what you're doing!'

'Ha, yeah. Old hand you might say.'

'Fantastic. We only dabble, but we enjoy it, don't we darling?'

Symon nodded and put an arm round his wife's shoulders.

'I'm Paul, by the way. Over from Oz for a few weeks.'

Maggie and Symon raised their eyebrows. 'You wouldn't be...'

Paul quickly realised who these people were. 'Jeez, you must be Jayne's brother! I can't believe it! You were just a kid the last time I saw you. And what about that other sister of yours?'

'Leyla. She'll be back here too, at some point.'

'That's great,' he turned to go, 'anyhow, see you later...'

Maggie said, 'Did you hear about Jayne's husband?'

Paul turned back. 'Yeah. I never knew the guy but I was sorry to hear about that.'

'We didn't know him that well either. He was always working – never had time to enjoy this,' said Symon, gesturing to panorama of the bay.

'Well,' said Paul, 'you know what they say...'

'That's what I tell Symon,' said Maggie. 'We should be making the most of it.'

'Absolutely. Well, it's been nice talking to you. See you later...'

Simon watched him go. 'Well, what a turn-up. I wonder where he's staying.'

'I think Jayne said something about him staying with his sister not far from here. He's over for a month.'

'You thinking what I'm thinking?'

Maggie smiled. 'Pretty much!'

Jayne was feeling apprehensive about Michael's funeral. The thought of having to face it without the support of her family was chilling to say the least. She doubted Daisy would be able to make it in her present state and she didn't think Leyla would bother. She didn't feel she could ask Symon and Maggie to come all the way back from Cornwall either.

Jayne hadn't heard from Michael's parents for years owing to a row over something petty and the sudden thought of having to talk to them at their only son's funeral made her want to curl up in a ball in a dark room.

She thought about the day she first met Michael's parents. His mother, Ailsa, was a little down-trodden woman always in the kitchen at her husband's beck and call. David Green was a big bombastic man who demanded his tea on the table as soon as he stepped inside the door. Jayne didn't know how to take him at first, didn't know when he was joking or when he was being serious. She'd never had dealings with anyone like him before but she tried for Michael's sake.

Michael shrugged off his father's remarks. 'Don't worry, you'll soon get used to him. It's just his way.'

But Jayne never did get used to his father's cynical remarks. She just smiled benignly, hoping she wouldn't be asked to take sides.

The story of how Michael's parents got together was a little bizarre. David had moved down from Yorkshire after the war and was looking for somewhere to stay. Ailsa's mother felt sorry for him and took him in as a lodger. Apparently, her mother worked in the pub he frequented and it all started from there. David wasn't interested in Ailsa at first; he had his eye on her sister who was more fun-loving. She wouldn't have anything to do with David but Ailsa fell for him in a big way. A very one-sided relationship developed – she idolised him and he took advantage of her timid character.

Consequently Jayne tolerated Michael's father and pitied his mother and hoped history wasn't repeating itself where she and Michael were concerned. This made for a difficult family relationship, especially when Jayne and Michael first got married. They couldn't afford to buy their own house, had to stay with his parents until such time when Michael was earning a higher wage. Michael, even then, would stay out some evenings with his mates and Jayne became bitter at the thought of the money he spent at the pub instead of saving up for a deposit on their first home.

Night after night she would sit watching the telly with Ailsa, knitting baby clothes and wondering if things would change when they bought their own house. Ailsa's regular outcry was: 'That's what men are like, dear. You'll soon learn. '

But Jayne didn't want to end up like Michael's mother. Ailsa never learned to drive and she relied on her husband for everything. But Jayne was adamant she wasn't going to be a stay-at-home wife and mother. After having Daisy, as soon as she felt able, she took driving lessons and passed her test first time. She bought herself a second-hand mini and began taking Daisy to Cornwall during the holidays where she revelled in her freedom and felt like a different person, the person she used to be before she met Michael.

When Michael got promotion at Cambridge County Council, he came home one day and hugged Jayne taking her by surprise. 'Guess what? We can afford to buy our own house now! I've worked it all out, looks perfectly feasible.'

Jayne felt brighter than she had for years. A fresh start! 'Oh Michael, that's fantastic! We can move to Cornwall!'

But he screwed up his face. 'What? Christ no, we're staying here in Cambridge. It's where the work is.'

Jayne felt crushed but resolved to make the best of staying in Cambridge and hoped to find a house where she would enjoy making a comfortable home for her husband and daughter. Maybe Michael would change his ways and become a proper husband and father, his pub jaunts likely curtailed with a huge chunk of his money going towards the mortgage.

They found a three bedroom terraced house in a back street (Michael having said it was all he could afford) and went to view it. Jayne was hesitant to step inside the dilapidated house at first but as they looked around the empty property she could see its potential. Three good-sized bedrooms, a decent-sized bathroom, the kitchen and lounge were of spacious proportions too. There was a little overgrown garden at the back but the front of the house stood straight onto the pavement.

Jayne hoped things would pick up where their relationship was concerned and threw herself into creating the home she wanted. She loved being able to put her mark on it and was surprised that Michael let her loose on the colour schemes. At this time, the mid 1970s, most people chose brown and beige for their living rooms but Jayne wanted colour in her life; she'd lived too long without it in her in-laws' colourless abode. A beige carpet in the living room was the only compromise. While Daisy was at playgroup she painted the walls brilliant white to reflect the light and to show off her art work. Against Michael's wishes she chose a blue three-piece-suite. He complained it was a cold colour, but she stood firm. This colour scheme reminded her of the colours of the bay – blue, beige and white – a little bit of home in the middle of Cambridge. Michael was reluctant to strip out the old avocado bathroom suite, saying there was nothing wrong with it and they couldn't afford to buy a new one. She backed down on this occasion, she could see the sense in it, but chose pale lemon tiles to enhance the room. Jayne decorated Daisy's bedroom in pinks and purples and framed some of her paintings of wild flowers to hang on the walls. The master bedroom was clean and fresh in navy and white, quite masculine, because of Michael's one stipulation that he didn't want to sleep in a 'tart's boudoir'. Michael's contribution was that he repainted the kitchen cupboards with the intention of eventually refitting the kitchen when they could afford it. Jayne was enjoying herself. Being able to use her artistic flair she felt reborn. But it wasn't to last.

The row that finally split the two families apart blew up when David and Ailsa came to visit Jayne and Michael at their new home. It was a windy day and David decided to clean his car outside their house, going in and out through the front door for buckets of water. Eventually a gust of wind took the front door, tearing a big hole in Jayne's new door curtain. He couldn't see that he'd done anything wrong and refused to apologise. Jayne was livid; she'd bought the curtain with the money Yvonne had given her for her birthday. David slammed a fiver on the table, strode out of the house with

Ailsa trailing meekly behind, jumped in their car and roared up the road. After that Michael remained neutral and took Daisy to visit his parents some weekends, without Jayne. But she never spoke to them or saw them ever again.

Jayne couldn't tell her mum of her troubles; she didn't want to admit she'd made a big mistake in marrying Michael. But there were times when she was on her own when she would look back at the happy memories of *Seawinds* and indulge in the nostalgia. Over the years Paul surfaced more and more in her memory and her dreams. Often, when she was visiting her mum in Cornwall, she would roam the bay half expecting to bump into him. She would sit in their cave on an evening and remember when he carved the love heart out of the rock, how it felt when he touched her hand, her face...

Jayne had often wondered what had happened to Paul after her father died. Now she had her answer. Paul was free as the wind, had no family ties since losing his son and his partner, but it was strange that he never spoke of his parents. It seemed to Jayne that he put it all behind him and got on with life. Had Paul been sent to show her how to live her life from now on? Would they be able to pick up where they left off all those years ago, to live the rest of their lives together? Paul had offered to come up to Cambridge to give her his support and after the last few days, she decided that having Paul with her would be like a balm to her wounded soul.

She was about to phone Paul when her mobile rang. It was her solicitor.

'Mrs Green? Are you available to come into the office sometime today?'

Jayne quickly came back from her daydream. 'Yes, I think so. Why?'

She listened to his cheery voice. 'There's the matter of Michael's estate. I appreciate it's a difficult time for you but I would like to go through some formalities with you, if you don't mind?'

'Why, yes of course. I can come in this afternoon, about two?'

'Perfect. I'll see you then.'

SEVENTEEN

Jayne bounced out of the solicitor's office with her plans fighting for order. Michael had left a will. His estate, which included the house, was to be divided between Jayne and Daisy. It turned out that Michael had stashed much of his money away for a rainy day, but Fate had intervened and the rainy day had happened without him. Jayne's share of the estate was enough to make a huge improvement to *Seawinds* and in her mind's eye she immediately began making the alterations. She began to picture the open plan accommodation, balconies at the front to take advantage of the sea view, once some of the trees had been removed, decking in the back garden and some cane furniture...

So Michael had done the honourable thing for once but there was a codicil – Rubie had been left a complimentary sum which had been added in the last few months. It seemed likely that after Michael had his last heart attack, there had been warning signs that he didn't have long to live. Michael had never mentioned this to Jayne; she felt she never really knew her husband.

After seeing the solicitor she walked to the nearest funeral director and made the arrangements to have Michael's body cremated; this was his wish, also in his will. The assistant at the crematorium had said that one funeral had been postponed owing to some police matter, and they could accommodate Michael next week. After all the waiting and uncertainty Jayne was now feeling rushed and apprehensive about attending the cremation. Her mother had been buried with her father in the little churchyard high up on the hillside at Tregenna Bay. Cremation seemed alien and cold-bloodied to her.

She stopped outside her own house and saw it in a different light. Would Daisy want to live here? She doubted it – Tim's work was in Scotland. That would mean another house sale. She had mixed feelings about that. It meant more money in the bank but all those memories of Daisy growing up; would she be able to leave all that behind? After looking in a few estate agents' windows, she reckoned her house would fetch around £400,000. It was unbelievable. All those years scrimping and scraping and now...

She let herself in, strolled through to the kitchen-diner and studied it from a potential buyer's point of view. She smiled. Although she hadn't redecorated it for the last five years, it still looked fresh and inviting. Putting the kettle on for a much-needed cuppa, her mobile rang.

'Hi, how's it going?' Paul's voice gave her a warm glow. She told him her news and went into all the arrangements. 'Jeez, you have been busy. Listen, my offer still stands...if you need a shoulder...'

'That would be lovely. I feel I've been through the mill these past few weeks. I don't know if I'm coming or going most days. I've had to do it all on my own and it looks like I'll be the only one at Michael's funeral. I don't think Leyla will bother – she couldn't stand him, and I don't know if Symon and Maggie will want to come all the way back again. '

'Heck, what about your daughter?'

Jayne sighed. 'Daisy's got severe morning sickness; she's been advised not to travel. She should be in hospital really but she won't leave the children.'

215

'I'm sorry to hear that. I hope she'll be all right.' There was a pause while they both thought about this. 'It seems to me you're doing everything humanly possible. In my experience, these things have a habit of coming up and biting us when we least expect them.'

'I know, it's just...it feels so wrong that Michael has no one to be there for him apart from me... and the tart,' she spat out.

'Whoa, that could be tricky! What about his parents?'

'I don't even know if they're still alive – I haven't spoken to them for years.'

'Christ... families, eh?'

'Yeah.' She wondered if she should broach the subject of Paul's parents but decided against it – now wasn't the time. She'd wait until she could see him, see his reaction.

'You've gone quiet on me. You still there?'

'Yes, I'm still here. I was just thinking, would it be so wrong for you to come to the funeral with me?'

'What? We're friends, aren't we? Or at least, I hope we are.'

'Yeah, friends,' she chuckled; it was the first time she'd heard that sound since she'd left Cornwall, and Paul.

'OK, I'll let you tell me what you want me to do. I don't want to push you into anything, but I think you ought to know, I haven't got much time before I fly back to Oz.'

Her stomach flipped. 'Oh, when's that? The funeral's next Friday.'

'That's a stroke of luck – my flight's on the Sunday!'

Things were happening fast but she had to grab this chance to ask Paul if he knew about the row between Ken and

Harry in 1968 – she couldn't wait any longer. And what, if anything, did his father have to do with Harry's death? She also had to know why Paul emigrated to Australia but she didn't want to do it over the phone. 'Well, one good thing about all this, if you come up, you'll be nearer to Heathrow.'

Ha, yeah, that's a point. So I take it that's a yes?'

'Yep!'

'Great! I'll pack a few things and leave in the morning.'

'Hang on, you don't know where I live!'

'Oh, yeah. A minor detail!'

Jayne gave Paul directions to Cambridge. 'But remember to keep your wits about you around the M42 and M6, it's quite confusing if you're not used to it.'

'Right, thanks. I've got a sat-nav so it shouldn't be a problem. How long will it take, d'you think?'

'Well, if the traffic's not too heavy you should do it in about six hours.'

'That's nothing; we're used to long journeys in Australia.'

No sooner had she put her phone down when Leyla rang. 'Jayne. How's things?'

'Oh, not bad. I've just had a bit of good news. Michael left a will and most of his estate has passed to me and Daisy.'

'Well, that's something at least. Hang on, you said 'most'. Who else benefits?'

Wait for it, thought Jayne. 'There's a codicil. Rubie's been left a complimentary sum.'

217

'Huh, I bet she has, for services rendered, the bitch.'

'Yeah, look, I know how you feel about that, I do too, but we'll have to try and put it behind us.'

'OK. I really phoned because I found some letters in that suitcase.'

'Yeah, I told you about that.'

'No, I mean other letters, from old Smythe.'

'Go on.'

'Well, it appears he was blackmailing Dad over some money he owed him.'

'Really? How much?'

'Three-hundred quid. It doesn't seem like much now but back then it must've been a small fortune.'

'What was that for?'

'A bridging loan, apparently.'

'Gosh, I can't believe it but that explains a lot.'

April 1958

Harry entered the studio to find Ken sitting at his drawing board, pipe between his teeth, pondering over a piece of work. There were no other artists there and his boss, Mr Smallwood, had nipped out for some ink. Harry saw his chance.

He had been hatching a plan to buy *Bay View,* the guest house on the North Cornwall coast where he and Yvonne had honeymooned in 1949. They had loved it so much they had been back several times. Yvonne suspected Jayne and Leyla had been conceived there, and even more amazingly, Symon had been born there whilst they were on holiday in 1956. The house had come to mean so much to them but after doing the sums Harry realised there was a shortfall. He didn't come from a wealthy family; his mother had never owned any property, had always lived from hand to mouth, and there was no one else in the family to approach. He had asked the bank for a loan assuming it would be easy – he was a good customer – but he was devastated to learn he was overdrawn and they were reluctant to lend him the £300 bridging loan. He needed some room to manoeuvre but all his money was tied up in their house in Sidcup and until he sold it there was nothing he could do.

He was becoming impatient to the point of desperation. Charlie, Mrs Crago's son, had written to him again saying his mother had been admitted into a nursing home and they needed to sell *Bay View* as soon as possible. If Charlie found another buyer Harry knew his life wouldn't be worth living. Yvonne had set her heart on it – he couldn't disappoint her after she had told all her friends and put him on a pedestal, the ideal husband. He couldn't risk the shame and, anyway, he was desperate for the breath of fresh air as much as Yvonne. His mind was working overtime unlike his hands. The work had dried up and there was nothing he could do about that. He had tried to look for another job but all the advertising studios were in a similar position. He knew Ken was careful with his money; he had bragged to Harry often enough that he had 'a nice little nest egg' for when the job came to an end. Yes, Ken, Lottie and the children would be all right.

Harry saw his chance but he had to get on the right side of Ken. He would take him out to lunch, butter him up. It had been too long since they had been able to take time out. Harry knew he could scrape up enough for *Lyons Corner House* and maybe he could ask Ken and Lottie to dinner one evening.

'How goes it, Ken?'

Ken looked up from his drawing board. 'Oh, you know. Plodding on.'

'I thought we could go out for lunch for a change, you know, like we used to.'

'Really? What's brought this on?'

'Oh, I don't know. I suppose it's been a bit fraught of late and we haven't had a chance to catch up properly for ages.'

'All right, I could do with a break. You paying?'

'Yeah, why not?'

'OK. I'll just finish this.'

Harry tried to act nonchalant while he waited for Ken to finish his piece of advertising for *Bird's* custard. He had him by the hook. He just hoped he wouldn't wriggle out when it came to the crunch.

Lyons Corner House was busy, as Harry had expected, and as they waited for a vacant table he was instantly transported back to the day he met Yvonne.

It had been a hectic day at the studio – non-stop telephone calls, not even time to grab himself a cup of tea but the job was shaping up nicely. He was feeling exultant as he entered the noisy restaurant, found a table and beckoned to one of the Nippies. The young woman dressed in black with a white cap and apron hurried to his table with her customary notepad and pen. He ordered a ham salad and a pot of tea and watched her retreat to the kitchens. When she came back with his order, she hesitated a moment, looked at him. Harry gave her a smile; he liked that it made her blush. She hurried away to take another order and Harry found himself watching her, to see if she turned to catch his eye. She did and a coy smile twitched at the corners of her mouth. Before he left the restaurant he asked her name and would she like to go to the pictures? He'd left the restaurant very much looking forward to the Friday night.

Ken brought him back to the present, 'You're quiet, Harry.'

Harry nodded and smiled. 'Yeah sorry, just thinking about the day I met Yvonne. Huh, seems ages ago.'

'Yeah, I know what you mean. A lot's happened since then.'

They were finally seated and one of the Nippies came to take their order. 'What'll it be?'

'Well,' started Ken, glancing at Harry, 'if you're paying I'll have the gammon grill.'

'OK, make that two,' Harry told the waitress.

She jotted it down on her pad. 'Anything to drink?'

221

'Make it two teas,' said Harry, before Ken could ask for anything more exotic.

'Well, this beats a boring egg sandwich,' said Ken, leaning back in his chair.

Harry kept quiet – he wasn't going to volunteer the types of sandwiches that Yvonne made for *him*. She exercised her imagination; she was always surprising him and ringing the changes and he now felt a twinge of guilt at having to dump the ones she'd so lovingly prepared for him this morning.

The Nippie brought the tray of tea and set it on their table. Harry poured himself a cup and one for Ken.

'So tell me,' said Harry, 'what's new with you and Lottie? Got any holidays lined up?'

Ken stirred two sugar lumps into his tea and shook his head. 'I'm reluctant to book anything with the way the job's going. Doesn't look too hopeful, does it?'

'Oh, I don't know. Things can't be that bad or we'd already know about it. Old Smallwood wouldn't keep us in the dark.'

'That's what you think.'

'Why? What have you heard?'

'Well, keep it under your hat, but I think we've seen the last of the jobs for a while. Technology is moving on all the time. I suppose there'll always be jobs for the cartoonists but for lettering artists like us...'

They both fell silent at the thought. The waitress brought their order and set the food in front of them. 'Sauces are on the table,' she said, and nipped off to serve another customer.

While Harry ate his lunch his thoughts returned again to the day he met Yvonne. He had noticed the clientele in *Lyons* that day – fashion models, actors and actresses – and he'd revelled in landing a job in the West End. He felt sure his life was taking a turn for the better and had kitted himself out with clothes suitable for a fashionable gent about town. His old mum had warned him to draw his horns in but he had gaily lived up to his means and ignored her advice.

Ken looked up. 'So, Harry, you taking the family to Cornwall again this year?'

Harry shook his head. 'I had a letter from Mrs Crago's son – she's in a nursing home now. The place has got too much for her.'

Ken lifted his eyebrows. 'Blimey, what will you do now?'

'I don't really know. I was hoping to buy it – Yvonne and I could run it and the kids would love it. It's a wonderful place for them to grow up.'

'And?'

'I'm working on it.' Harry took a gulp of his tea and pressed on. 'The trouble is, until we sell the house, I'll need a bridging loan. I haven't got that sort of money and the bank can't oblige. Yvonne thinks it's all hunky-dory and we'll be moving soon. I can't tell her the truth. It'll break her heart; it'll be the end of the dream if we lose that guesthouse.'

'What's the alternative?'

'There isn't one. I'm going to have to find a way.'

Ken put his knife and fork together and lit his pipe. Took a few puffs and looked thoughtfully at Harry. 'How much do you need?'

'Three-hundred.' Even as he said it, Harry couldn't imagine Ken volunteering to loan him that amount even if he had it. That was what most people earned in a year. He had mentally reckoned up today's bill to £1.10s 6d but if Ken lent him that £300 it would be well worth it.

Ken looked thoughtful. 'Well, I could lend you it.'

'Really? God, Ken, Are you sure?'

'What are friends for? I'll have to do a few sums myself of course, but if it gets you out of a tight spot... as long as I get it back in a few months. Lottie's got her eye on a bigger place now that Paul and Katie have got bigger and want their own rooms.' Ken gave him a hard stare.

'Of course, thanks Ken, you don't know what this means to me. I'll be able to pay you back once we're up and running. I tell you what, as a thank-you, why don't you and Lottie come round for dinner one evening?'

'We'd like that.'

'Good, that's settled then. I'll tell Yvonne – it's been a long time, too long. She'd love to see you.'

That evening, on the train home, Harry began to wonder how he could explain away the lump sum to Yvonne when he got it. Although she was unaware of their financial situation, (he paid all the bills, gave her the housekeeping and kept the bank statements hidden) she would probably want to know how he'd come by such a large sum. He would have to be ready with an explanation. There were various ways he could come into money, one being a win on the horses. Although he wasn't really a gambling man, Harry thought he could tell Yvonne he'd put a bet on the winner at Kempton Park. He devoured the racing pages in the evening paper and came up with a plan.

EIGHTEEN

Paul felt reborn – Jayne wanted to see him! He had to stop himself skipping to the car. He had a distant memory of another journey to Cambridge, one when he had felt in need of direction. He had come back from Australia and stayed with Katie and Martin for a month but hadn't told them the reason for his return. He hadn't contacted Jayne either. He didn't know what he was hoping for but at the back of his mind there was the idea of a new start. It was a long shot but he hoped he would be able to see Jayne. He didn't know if the family still owned the guest house but he went with a hunch and booked a flight to England with the mantra 'nothing ventured, nothing gained'.

During the twenty-four hour flight he had a dream about Jayne. It was so powerful it was as if they were actually together and he began to fantasize about what they would plan when they met up, what they would do, what they would say. He knew she was married but that didn't come into the equation.

When he arrived at his sister's in Cornwall he rented a car and drove down to Tregenna Bay. As he approached the front door of *Seawinds* he felt he'd come home. He tried to put the memory of the last time he'd come here to one side. In any case, a few years living in Sydney had given him more confidence.

On closer inspection the house looked a little sad. There were no buckets and spades or fishing nets in the porch, no vacancy sign in the window and the front door needed a coat of paint.

A balloon of anticipation swelled in his chest as he rang the doorbell. He waited. Looked up and down the road. Nothing had changed. After a few moments the door creaked open and Yvonne stood on the threshold looking smaller than he remembered.

'Hi, have you got any vacancies?' asked Paul, grinning, hoping she would remember him and welcome him like a long lost son.

Yvonne frowned, 'Oh, no dear. I'm sorry. I haven't taken in guests for over five years now. You could try *The Tides Reach*.' She went to close the door but he pushed his hand against it.

'Mrs Williams, it's Paul! Don't you remember me? I know it's been a long time but I thought...'

She shook her head. 'Oh, no, no, I'm sorry, Jayne's not here, lives in Cambridge now.'

'I've come a long way. Surely you can give me her address, for old time's sake?'

Yvonne shook her head again, 'Wouldn't be right,' she said, and closed the door.

All hope drained from him. As he slunk down the steps, Gladys ran out from next door. 'Paul! Tes you! George is indoors. Come and tell en what you'm bin up to all these years.'

He decided to accept Gladys's offer and told her he was back from Australia for a month, staying with his sister, but he didn't go into the details about his personal life or tell her why he was back in Cornwall. During their conversation Gladys must've realised and gave him Jayne's address. He

226

drove up to Cambridge the following day. But when he got there he couldn't bring himself to knock on Jayne's door. What if her husband asked him who he was and why he was there? It was summer and Paul reasoned that Jayne's husband could so easily be on holiday. So he parked some distance away and watched as a little blonde girl rode her bright pink bike up and down the street and ran in and out of the house.

Then he saw her.

He assumed she had come out to tell her daughter it was teatime. His heart filled up at the sight of her and the thought of all the lost years. Jayne looked beautiful, as he knew she would, in a pair of denim dungarees and a check blouse, her honey-gold hair in a pony tail. He couldn't take his eyes off her but he couldn't pluck up the courage to go and talk to her. What would he say? How would he explain his reappearance after all these years? He suddenly felt foolish for even thinking that he could come back and pick up where he'd left off. No, Yvonne had been right. He drove away with the sight of Jayne staring after his car in the rear view mirror.

But this time Jayne knew he was coming.

When Paul arrived in Cambridge he was filled with nervous excitement. He wondered how Jayne would react to him sharing her bed but he didn't want her to think he was only after sex; she meant far more to him than that. He wanted her to make the decision when and if they slept together, but after they had shared a meal and a bottle of wine in her kitchen, it took all of his self-control to finally leave her at midnight and go to the guest room. However, in the early hours she tapped on his door and slipped wordlessly into his bed. They enjoyed every touch, every movement, every sensation. The wonder and beauty of it took Jayne's breath away, their bodies entwined in a sea of pure ecstasy. Never had Jayne felt so complete, her spirit so nourished. Speechless, tears rolled down her cheeks.

'Never leave me again, Paul. I couldn't bear it.'

'Oh, Jayne, you don't know how long I've dreamed of this moment. Nothing and no one will ever part us now. I promise.'

She was astounded at the intensity of her love for Paul. It shook her to the core. They shared their thoughts and dreams and looked to the future. She couldn't remember ever feeling like this. Eventually she fell asleep in his arms. But Paul couldn't sleep. His mind was a whirlpool of plans that could finally come to fruition.

At daybreak Paul made a simple breakfast of tea, toast and honey and took it up to the bedroom. They both ate hungrily, Paul licking the honey off her fingers. It was amazingly erotic and Jayne surprised herself. All these years and she finally realised what it meant to make love with all her body and soul with the person she truly loved. Time was forgotten until eventually Paul reminded her that they should get going.

The crematorium was situated off a slip road to the M11 and Jayne found herself wishing Michael could've had a service at the little church and been buried in their local cemetery. But he wasn't religious; he'd made that perfectly clear from the start.

They drove into the austere grounds and found a parking space. Traffic was whizzing past at seventy miles an hour, not conducive to the sentiments of a funeral. The quick and the dead, thought Jayne.

Also her mood wasn't helped by the weather – it had been a sunny morning until they arrived at the crematorium but as they got out of the car a big grey cloud obscured the sun and Jayne was struck by how empty and unattached she felt, as if she was attending a stranger's funeral instead of her husband's.

Paul held her hand as they walked past the wreaths and bouquets lined up regimentally on the pristine paving, evidence of earlier funerals. As they walked into the stark building Jayne tried to relax and take comfort in the love they shared.

Not long and all this will be over.

They took their seats in the front row on the left hand side of the hall and waited. They were alone. The cavernous space seemed devoid of all warmth; just one white flower arrangement on a pedestal and a modern lectern staring at them. The basic wooden coffin containing Michael's remains already lay in position on a plinth in front of the curtain.

Paul squeezed Jayne's hand as they heard the doors open behind them. She didn't want to look round to see who it was, but from the edge of her vision she saw a wheelchair move into position in the front row on the opposite side. When Jayne plucked up the courage to snatch a look, she saw Rubie offering a hunched, wizened little woman a drinking bottle. Rubie didn't acknowledge Jayne but sat down on the other side of the wheelchair.

The service was as cold as the surroundings with only a handful of mourners whom Jayne had never met. She assumed they were either people who Rubie knew or people from Michael's office, details of whom she had found in his business diary. He had never included her in his work life and Jayne felt as if the funeral was nothing to do with her. She felt sad for Daisy too, not being able to attend her father's funeral,

229

but even if she had, Jayne didn't think it would've made much difference to the way she felt. There were no hymns, only the song *'Morning Has Broken'* that Michael used to like. It wasn't really appropriate; Jayne couldn't think of anything else but the funeral director had insisted she choose at least one piece. Jayne waited to see if anyone stood up to read a eulogy but after a while it was obvious that no one would come forward. She certainly hadn't planned anything, and in any case, what could she say? It had even been difficult to give a few words to the official to read out. As Jayne listened to them she felt sad for Michael, there was only the usual stuff – where he grew up, who his parents were, where he went to school and his work record. No humour to lighten the mood. As the curtains closed on the coffin, Jayne clutched Paul's arm. She dabbed her eyes and mentally said goodbye to Michael and the life they had known.

Paul followed Jayne outside to look at the few wreaths and messages. She hadn't thought to send any herself but when she spotted the ones from Daisy tears stung her eyes as she read the attached message: 'Dear Dad, taken before your time. Love Daisy, Tim and children. ' But the biggest and reddest was obviously Rubie's, it stood out like a beacon. Jayne couldn't bring herself to read the card.

Rubie pushed the wheelchair past Jayne and Paul and stood a few feet away. Other mourners joined them and stood around awkwardly looking at the flowers, not knowing quite what to do next or what to say. Paul thought it would be a good idea if they left.

'I can't go yet,' said Jayne, 'just a minute.' She walked over to where Rubie was standing, having realised the shrunken shape in the wheelchair was Michael's mother. Jayne bent down to her level and took the cold papery hand in hers. But there was no response.

'Hello Ailsa. Remember me? I'm Jayne, Michael's wife.'

It was as if the old woman was looking through Jayne. On seeing Rubie's smirk, Jayne hurried in the direction of the car park without a backward glance with Paul running to keep up. 'Bloody Rubie!' said Jayne, 'I never want to see her again as long as I live!' Then she stopped and stared straight ahead. 'Paul, it's Daisy! She didn't tell me she was coming.' Jayne ran over to meet her then stopped and broke down in tears. She looked in every direction but Daisy wasn't there.

Paul was instantly by her side. 'Come on, let's get you home. '

Jayne sat in the car and turned to Paul. 'I can't believe it. What's happening to me, Paul? I could swear black's white that Daisy was standing there.'

'Look, I'm sure there's a perfectly logical explanation. You have been overdoing it lately. Maybe that's all it is?'

But Jayne was sure she'd seen her daughter – she wasn't a mirage. But then there was that incident at Gladys's house with the stranger...

Paul turned her face to his and gently kissed her. 'I love you. We'll work this out.'

It gave her a lovely warm cared-for feeling and having Paul's full attention, she decided to offload her concerns. 'There's something else I should tell you.'

'Go on.'

'I knocked on Gladys's door a few days ago, when Symon's surveyor came down.'

Paul waited for more.

'You're going to think I'm losing the plot but a young woman came to the door and said Gladys wasn't there; she hasn't lived there for years. She said she's bought the house with her partner and they're in the middle of renovating it.'

Paul whistled through his teeth. 'Well, now I can tell you what happened to me. I was standing outside *Seawinds*, giving it a look-over, when Gladys's door burst open and it must've been the same woman who asked me if I was looking for someone!'

Jayne frowned. 'Really? Gosh, so it's happened to you, too. Maybe I'm not going mad; I was beginning to wonder. So what do you think's going on?'

'I don't know, it's all very strange but I know I spoke to Gladys that first day when I left you the flowers,' he picked up her hand, kissed it. 'And I'm very glad I did.'

'Oh so am I. Thank you for being here today, I don't think I could've done it without you.'

'No worries.'

Jayne smiled, 'That's a very Australian thing to say, you know.'

'Ha, yeah, I'm a bit long in the tooth to change now, though.'

'Oh, I don't want you to change. I love you just the way you are.'

The journey home passed in quiet contemplation on Jayne's part. She felt sorry for Ailsa, no doubt living in an old people's home with no home comforts. It brought back her own mother's plight during her last few weeks and Jayne felt a fresh rush of sadness and regret.

Back home, she kicked off her shoes and went to fill the kettle. 'Well, I'm glad that's over. It all seemed so pathetic and rushed, not like Mum's. Our little village hall at *Tregenna Bay* was full of people afterwards, all enjoying the food and drink and happily reminiscing.'

'Yeah, I can imagine. But don't upset yourself, Jayne, you've done what you had to do.' Paul didn't think it was his place to criticise but he'd never been to a funeral like it. But the most important thing was the fact that Jayne was free and he couldn't wait to start putting his plans into action. Jayne was a big part of them and there was nothing and no one to stop him now.

'Tea, or a glass of wine?'

'I'll have whatever you're having,' said Paul, 'but hey, come here.' He gave her a hug.   She breathed in the warmth of him and something in her snapped. She sobbed.

'That's it. Let it all out. It's been a long time coming.'

'I'm so glad you're here, Paul,' she said, wiping her eyes. 'Do you think we can bury the past and look forward to the future, one with no more regrets?'

'I sincerely hope so. I for one have made my pledge.'

She dried her eyes and went to the wine rack, selected a bottle of red and tried to blot out the image of the smear of lipstick and the empty bottle on the table the day after Michael's death.

'Are your parents still alive?' she asked, whilst pouring the wine. She was hoping to broach the subject of his father's blackmail letters that Leyla had told her about, but wasn't sure how to begin. It didn't seem appropriate right now.

Paul picked up his glass and took a sip. 'Mm, Mum is. She lives in Katie's annexe. She hardly knows what day it is but she's well looked after. A carer comes in twice a day when

Katie's at work. Dad died years ago – I feel bad about that – I never came back for his funeral. We'd grown apart after...'

Jayne looked into his eyes. 'Do you want to talk about it?'

He wasn't sure if he wanted to drag it all up again, not after what they'd just been through. But as Jayne had asked he thought maybe now was the time.

'Come and sit in the lounge,' said Jayne.

He joined her on the chunky blue sofa and glanced around at the décor, large modern canvases on the white walls. 'You've got a nice place, here. Are these yours?'

This brought a smile to her face. 'Thanks for noticing, Michael never did. I felt as if I was doing it all on my own.'

Paul stood up to take a closer look at the paintings. 'He didn't know what he was missing. You're good.' He examined each one then sat next to her again. Put his glass down, looked into her eyes. 'If you really want to know about my parents, I'll tell you.' He tried to get all the facts in order before he told her the reason why he went to Australia.

'Go on, I'm listening.'

He stared into his wineglass. 'After that dreadful day when your dad died I felt terrible and even worse when we got home. Not only was I sad for you but I was devastated by the fact that you were going to Cambridge to study art and not Plymouth. That was in the April and I wanted to go back to Cornwall in the summer, to see you, but he wouldn't, said he'd never ever go back again to bloody Cornwall, not after what happened.' Paul took a sip of wine. 'Well, he used the F word actually. It was a complete shock. He'd never used that swear word before, not in front of us kids anyway. I thought it was because of the traumatic circumstances of your dad's death but

234

I sensed there was more to it than that. When I asked him, he refused to tell me. I thought then, that I'd never see you again.'

Jayne smiled and put a gentle hand on his knee. She wanted to ask about the row between her father and his but she knew she'd have to let him tell it his way, in his own time.

'I nearly got a train but I didn't have enough money. The following September I started the marine biology course at Plymouth and I got to wondering what I was doing there without you. I carried on with it but in the summer the next year, I didn't go home straight away. I managed to scrape up enough money for the train fare from Plymouth to Newquay.'

Jayne shook her head, incredulous. 'What happened?'

'Well, when I got to *Seawinds* your mum said you were living in Cambridge and were going steady with a guy. I left your birthday card with her. But that did it for me, the end of the dream. I couldn't find anywhere to stay so I slept on the beach that night. But then, in the morning, I thought you'd be coming home at some point in the summer and I tried to get a short term let. Huh, Masterson senior was less than helpful; he thought I was some bum off the street and showed me the door. I stuck two fingers up at him and left. It was at that moment that I vowed to get as far away as possible and do something with my life.'

Jayne frowned, her eyes moist again. She'd kept all of Paul's letters and cards but she hadn't received any after April 1968. 'I never got that birthday card. Mum must've kept it from me.'

Paul nodded, 'Naturally I assumed you were happy and had forgotten all about me. But I never forgot *you*. That's why we must make this work, Jayne. Neither of us has got any ties now.'

235

She nodded. 'I assume you were in Australia when your dad died? Who told you?'

'Katie. I kept in touch with her, of course. But I couldn't afford the fare to come back that time. The bad feeling between Dad and me never got resolved in any case, and I decided it wasn't worth getting upset over. I had a life in Sydney by then, doing well for myself. Then that all got blown out of the water when Dayle...'

She stroked his arm. 'Did you ever come back again, or was that the only time?'

He grimaced. 'Yeah, I don't know if you're ready for this.'

Jayne took a gulp of wine and nodded. 'Go on.'

'Well, I thought I'd surprise you – I thought you were probably staying with your mum for the holiday but she looked horrified and wouldn't tell me where you were living. As I was leaving, Gladys shot out of her house and asked me in. At least she and George were pleased to see me. She gave me your address in Cambridge...'

Jayne's jaw dropped. 'I can't believe it. Don't tell me you came up to Cambridge?'

Paul didn't know whether or not to tell her but he'd come this far. 'Yeah, I did, but when I saw you...'

'You *saw* me?'

'Yep, I sat in the car at the end of your road and watched your little girl playing on her bike and you were going in and out of the house telling her to come in for tea.'

'I don't believe you! You're making it up.'

Paul shook his head. 'All right. How about if I tell you what you were wearing? I can still see you quite clearly – you

236

were wearing denim dungarees and a check shirt. White platform shoes, and your hair was in a ponytail.'

Jayne sat wide-eyed – she remembered those clothes – they were her favourites.

'I bottled out – I couldn't barge in and break up that family scene; I assumed you were happily married.'

'This is too incredible for words. If only...'

'Ha, yeah. If only.'

Jayne's burning question was rearing its head again. 'Do you know about the row between your dad and mine, the night before Dad died?'

'Row? What row?'

Brace yourself. 'This might be quite upsetting; I don't know how to tell you...'

'Come on, it can't be any worse than what we know already, surely?'

Jayne smiled cynically. 'I didn't know until I read Leyla's diary, that Monday when I was abrupt with you. She'd left it in the cellar with some others, wanted me to collect them for her. Apparently, you all came down to stay every year, free of charge. But my dad said he couldn't do it any more as he was up to his eyes in debt and the tax man was on his tail. He was worried he'd lose everything. But I didn't know about the blackmail letters until Leyla rang me yesterday. Something about some money my dad had borrowed from yours, a bridging loan to enable him to buy *Seawinds* but he never paid him back. We thought he'd had a win on the horses; that's what he told us.'

'Blimey! That explains a lot. Your dad's death must've weighed heavily on his conscience after that row.'

'I guess so.'

'Fancy, he took all this to the grave with him. Unless...'

'Unless what?'

'Well, Mum must've known. I did try to ask her last week about the last time we stayed there but she said she didn't remember.'

'Maybe she doesn't *want* to remember?'

'That's a fair point. Oh, Jayne. All these years and I never knew any of this.'

They looked at each other. It was a lot to take in.

After a while Jayne said, 'I wish you didn't have to go back to Sydney.'

'So do I but I need to tie up the loose ends, sell my boat and the rest of my stuff, then we can be together. Nothing's going to keep us apart this time. I promise.'

Paul kissed her so sensuously she could see their future stretching ahead. 'Paul, let's go to Cornwall right now, not waste another minute!'

He frowned. 'Are you sure? What about your daughter?'

Jayne thought about how Daisy had been suffering. She was no youngster and things could go badly for her with this pregnancy. Her husband Tim was very caring and capable but at a time like this, surely she needed her mother. 'You're right. I should go to her. But Cornwall is calling me too. I'm torn.'

Paul shrugged. 'It's up to you. I can't decide for you.' He watched her chewing her lips and picking at her fingers.

'What if we go up to Scotland together? Cornwall can wait a bit longer, surely?'

She dropped her hands by her sides and nodded. 'OK.'

'Good, that's settled then. Go and give your daughter a ring.'

She kissed him on the cheek and picked up her phone. Then she put it down again. How would Daisy and Tim feel about another man on the scene so soon after Michael's death? Surely there would be a lot of questions? 'Don't take this the wrong way but I think I ought to do this on my own, Paul. I'll feel awkward us staying at Daisy's.'

He sighed. He thought he was making progress but maybe he was taking too much for granted. It had always been his problem. But on the other hand he had to make her see sense. 'Look, if you want my opinion, time is running out. If you're worried about what Daisy will say, all you have to do is tell her we're old friends.' He gazed into her eyes, 'Unless you don't trust me?'

Jayne rang Daisy.

It was a while before she picked up. She sounded tired. 'Oh, hello, Mum, how was the funeral?'

'Oh, not too bad. Listen, I want to come and see you. I'm worried about you.'

'Don't be. There's nothing you can do here anyway. I'm a big girl now. It's not as if it's my first time. Tim's very good and his mum's close by. Strikes me you've got enough on your plate right now, what with two funerals in the past fortnight and selling *Seawinds*. And what's happening to the house in Cambridge?'

'We...I'll have to sell it. Some of that money can be used to turn *Seawinds* into our holiday retreat. I plan to live there.' She looked at Paul. He smiled.

239

'Sounds a great idea! Lots of family holidays.' There was a pause, then, 'Mum, go do what you have to. Perhaps it's a better idea to come up when the baby's born.'

'Are you sure, love?'

'Honestly. Give yourself a break. You need it. I've gotta go. Love you lots.'

Jayne went back to where Paul was sitting. 'I don't know if you heard any of that but Daisy's told me she doesn't need me up there, told me to give myself a break.'

'There you go, Cornwall it is, then.'

'What about your flight?'

'Stuff the flight!'

'But...won't you lose a lot of money?'

'Possibly, but you let me worry about that. I can do what I have to online, sell my boat and stuff. I've got a good mate over there – Dean – he'll help me.'

Jayne picked up Paul's hand and kissed it. 'Thank you.'

He draped both her arms round his neck, looked deep into her eyes and pressed himself against her.

'I think this is where we left off,' said Paul, his eyes heavy with desire. He began peeling off her clothes while she slid her fingers under his belt. He took her by the hand and led her upstairs.

NINETEEN

When Paul and Jayne arrived at the *Captain Tregenna*, they left their luggage in the room and walked to *Seawinds* to investigate its progress. The scaffolding had been erected and the workmen had started stripping the roof.

Paul shouted up to them, 'Hey, OK if we come in?'

'Sure,' came the answer, 'but watch yourselves – Gary's started knocking one of the walls down. Hard hats on the stairs.'

They walked in to clouds of plaster dust. Paul took out a handkerchief and covered his nose.

'Let's go down the cellar, maybe less dust down there,' said Jayne.

They put on the yellow hard hats and went slowly down the cellar steps. Paul of course, had never been down here. It was a complete revelation. 'Wow! Do you know what I'm thinking?'

Jayne shook her head.

'I can store all the surfing gear down here... boards, wet suits...' he left Jayne and went to have a look around.

Jayne shivered. She'd never felt very comfortable down here, especially at night. She noticed all the old furniture had been taken away – the coffee table, her father's desk, the bench and all the junk in the large room. It looked sadly bare but much bigger now and she could see what Paul was getting at.

She called to Paul who was looking around the smaller of the two rooms. 'Do you think it would work? It's very cold down here and not much light.'

He came to join her, 'No problem. I've got an idea how to sort that out.'

'But...you've never been down here, have you?'

'No, but from that low window at the front ', he said, pointing, 'I knew there was a basement and maybe what I could do with it. Just needs the walls painting white, some decent flooring, maybe polished concrete, and I could rig up some proper lighting in both rooms. A couple of radiators and Bob's your uncle.'

Jayne rubbed her arms. 'I'm going back up.'

'OK. I won't be a minute, see you up there.'

Jayne ran up the steps and back into the noise and warmth of the main house, the builders' radio in competition with their scraping and knocking and banging upstairs. Clouds of dust hung in the air. It didn't look like *Seawinds* anymore. Jayne ventured into the kitchen to find its soul had been ripped out, the old range and sink unit gone. The back parlour was totally bare; the fireplace had been taken out and the wall re-plastered. She knew they had all agreed that the house should be renovated but seeing it like this made her heart ache. As she walked into her father's front room she thought she heard Fats Waller's *'Ain't Misbehavin.'* It put a smile on her face – her father loved to play his record of 'Great Jazz Pianists' in his lighter, happier moods. But why was she hearing this? Where was it coming from?

Paul was suddenly by her side, full of energy and excitement. 'Yeah, I know exactly what I'm going to do with the cellar...'

Jayne stared at him.

'What's the matter?'

'Can't you hear it?'

'Hear what?'

'Listen.'

Paul cocked his head on one side then shook it. 'All I can hear is the builders banging around.'

Jayne frowned, 'Can't you hear the music?'

Paul listened again then took her in his arms. 'Look, it's probably just your imagination getting the better of you. This was your dad's room, wasn't it?'

Her face crumpled as the music faded away. 'But it's not the first time. I heard Beethoven's *Pastoral Symphony* that day I found the diaries... and now this.'

'Has anyone else heard it? Symon or Leyla?'

'Not as far as I know. I'll have to ask them.'

Paul remembered the day he was pulled back from the cliff edge. 'I suppose I should tell you what happened to me.'

Jayne was wide-eyed, 'What? Something else? Tell me.'

'In a minute. Let's go grab a coffee at the beach café, wash the dust out of our throats.'

They left their hard hats on the stairs and walked hand-in-hand down the hill past the houses and the shops, along to the end of the sea front. The café was humid, busy with the hum of conversation and the clattering of cutlery. They joined the queue at the counter where sat a large jar of gingerbread men.

'Dayle's favourite,' said Paul, before he could stop himself.

Jayne' smiled, 'Yeah, Daisy's too.' She squeezed his hand.

They eventually got served. Two piping hot cappuccinos were placed on their tray.

'Sure you don't want one of those?' asked Paul, pointing to the gingerbread men.

Jayne playfully slapped him on the arm. She was eager to hear what Paul had to tell her but she couldn't wait to leave the stifling café and she didn't want anyone overhearing their conversation. 'Let's take this outside.'

They found a vacant table at the far end of the decking with a view of the busy beach. Paul spooned the froth from his coffee and pointed to the wind-ravaged cliff top high above them. 'I was up there when it happened.'

Jayne followed his gaze and knew the place for her father's favourite spot and where he fell to his death. She shuddered. 'What were you doing up there?'

'I fancied a walk. I used to walk for miles along the cliff path when I was a kid. But last week I was standing near the edge when I felt something or someone pulling me back. I've never been good with heights, as you know, and I felt a bit queasy when I looked down on the bay, even though there's a fence now. I didn't know it was your dad's spot until I turned and saw the inscription on the bench.'

'Yeah, it was his favourite place to stand and watch the waves. But what do you think this all means? The music, what happened to you, Gladys's house?'

'I don't know but we can't be the only ones.' Paul stared into Jayne's eyes. 'Have you ever seen a medium?'

Jayne shook her head. 'Don't tell me you're into all that stuff?'

'Well, if it helps...'

Jayne was silent. She desperately needed some answers but this was something else. Paul was right – he was full of surprises. 'Have you?'

Paul took a while to answer. He didn't want to freak her out or look ridiculous in her eyes but he had found it comforting when his son died. 'Yeah, once.'

'What did you find out?'

Paul shook his head and took another sip of coffee. 'It doesn't matter.'

'Don't do that to me. You've got to tell me now.'

'OK. Promise you won't scoff?'

Jayne squeezed his hand. 'I promise.'

Paul took a breath. 'When something so devastating happens that your world caves in, you start looking for answers, signposts. Anywhere you can. When Dayle became seriously ill I didn't know what to do, how to cope. Trish wasn't much help – she just shut it out and pretended it wasn't happening. I couldn't talk to her about it. But Dayle was a brave little boy, I was so proud of him, the way he handled it.' Paul swallowed, rubbed a hand over his mouth.

Jayne was tearing up. 'I'm so sorry. It's bad enough losing a parent, goodness knows what it's like to lose a child.'

'Yeah, absolutely, we've both been there. But I got to thinking...what if there was a way to find out what it's like for them, you know, on the other side?'

Jayne was silent waiting for him to continue.

'I found out there was this spiritual church in a suburb of Sydney. I went along to a couple of meetings...' Paul stopped when he saw Jayne's incredulous expression. 'Yeah, I know what you're thinking – they're all charlatans, right? Wrong. I've seen the evidence, Jayne. They *know* things about a complete stranger. I couldn't believe it at first but it's true. They can *see*.'

'And?'

'Well, the medium was so convincing I just had to believe her. She even gave me a couple of examples of the unique things we shared, pet names for each other and such. Now how would she know that? I didn't know her from Adam and she didn't know anyone else who knew me or what I'd been through. She said something else.'

'What?'

'That our loved ones, even in spirit, are very interested in what's happening to us. They find ways to send us little signs to let us know they're close by. She also said they like us to talk to them.'

She frowned at him and fiddled with her teaspoon. 'Oh, I don't know about that.'

'Think about it. The music, Gladys...'

She blew out her cheeks. 'I suppose.' Jayne drank the last of her coffee and sat back to take in the glorious view. 'So Dad never left the bay and he's still enjoying all this? With Mum?'

'It would seem so.'

'It's a nice thought,' she looked at her watch. The sun had moved round to its setting position. 'Come on, let's get back to the *Captain Tregenna*. Symon and Maggie will be wondering where we are.'

Maggie and Symon had also been to *Seawinds* that day. Symon had been expecting to hear the music again but it didn't happen. They were both full of the plans that were beginning to take shape and they discussed them with Jayne and Paul while they ate their delicious meal. Fish stew made with monkfish, prawns and mussels poured over toasted slices of sourdough all washed down with a bottle of Jack's red.

Symon shoved his plate to one side and took out his lap top. He began showing them the materials he hoped to use, although, eager to start he had begun sourcing some of the materials already without consulting the others.

'I think we've agreed that the dining room and the big front room are crying out for French doors onto a balcony to go the full width of the house?'

They all nodded.

'I suggest a glass balustrade. Here, like this.' He turned his lap top around to show Jayne.

'Oh, so you've gone ahead without me?'

Symon looked sheepish. 'Yeah, sorry, I didn't think you'd mind. But you can change it. It's not set in stone.'

Paul took a sip of his wine and craned his neck to see the picture onscreen. 'Yeah, they use a lot of that in Sydney. You can get it in different colours, too.'

'You're speaking my language!' Symon showed them some more examples in places all around the world.

'Isn't that a bit flash for the old girl?' asked Jayne.

'Nonsense,' said Paul, 'what woman doesn't like new clothes?'

They all laughed at this. Maggie nodded furiously.

247

'Well,' said Jayne, 'if that's the route you're all going down I'm going to paint a mural on the big wall in the front room.'

'Great!' said Symon, 'you'd be using your artistic skills. I like it.'

Paul winked at Jayne, 'And I know what I want to do with the surf school. I've got loads of ideas. We've been along to take a look this afternoon.'

'Oh? We must've missed you.'

Paul went on to tell Symon and Maggie what he had in mind for the basement and they thought it was a great idea.

'And tell them about the dining room,' said Maggie excitedly.

'Ah, yes. Now, how about we redesign it in an Art Deco theme with maybe a shiny black piano, black and white floor tiles and some tables and chairs like this..?' said Symon, showing them more examples. 'What d'you think?'

'Gosh,' said Jayne, 'you sure? It would be unrecognisable.'

'Yeah,' said Paul, 'but we're taking it to a new dimension. I love it.'

'What about Leyla?' asked Jayne.

Symon raised his eyebrows, expecting more.

'She's always complaining we leave her out. She'll be furious if we go ahead with all this and don't tell her.'

'Yeah you're right,' said Symon, still tapping away on his laptop. 'Haven't you heard from her?'

Jayne shook her head and smiled at Paul. 'I've been too busy.' He squeezed her hand.

Symon and Maggie chuckled.

'I'll email her,' said Symon, 'that's the only way we'll get hold of her. No signal here tonight.'

Jayne had been weighing up when to ask Symon if he'd had any weird experiences happen to him but she decided to wait. Suppose he had? She didn't want to worry Maggie if he hadn't told her. It would be a better idea to get Symon on his own.

Jack looked across from the bar. He marvelled at the change in these people since they'd been staying here. Symon had really loosened up and so had his wife. And Jayne was positively glowing since meeting up with Paul. He hoped they would all make the *Captain Tregenna* their local because it sounded as though they were going all out to update the old guesthouse and make it their home. He shouted across to Symon.

'I've got a slot tomorrow morning if you want to take a look around?'

'OK, that's great. What time, Jack?'

'About ten?'

Symon gave him the thumbs up.

'What's all that about?' asked Jayne.

'Jack's told me about the history of this place. Apparently *Captain Tregenna* was a real guy who got shipwrecked here five hundred years ago. This pub was his house.'

'Really? I didn't know anything about that.'

'None of us did. It's quite incredible, really.'

'Blimey,' said Paul, 'sounds like a romantic notion to me.'

'No, his ship was part of a flotilla that fought against the Spanish Armada – Jack's been researching on the internet.'

'Well. I think it's amazing,' said Maggie. 'I'd love to find out more.'

TWENTY

The next day, after breakfast, all four, especially Symon, were ready to see what they would find behind the scenes at the *Captain Tregenna*. Symon was mainly interested in the architecture while Maggie wanted to know if there were any secret passages or ghosts. Jayne and Paul had never known anything about this house or its history but they were willing to find out.

Jack locked the front door before showing them around. He bypassed the kitchen and took them through the hall and opened a hidden door onto another staircase in the wall. Maggie was delighted – one of her wishes had been granted at least. It was a bit of a squash but they all managed to ascend the very narrow and steep spiral stairs. There were tiny doors on different levels and at the top it opened onto the lead roof complete with battlements.

'Wow!' said Maggie, when she emerged from the low doorway, 'look at that view!'

Paul stayed well behind the others with his back to the wall. 'I'll take your word for it.'

Symon and Jayne walked carefully around the lead roof, mindful of where they placed their feet. But Maggie was right – the view was amazing. Inland they could see the hilly green farmland bordered by hedges and trees, stretching into the distance. Pockets of white-washed houses looked like they had been dropped from a great height and the little church where both parents were buried poked its sun-kissed spire majestically up to the heavens.

'So beautiful,' said Jayne.

'Yeah,' said Symon, 'I must take a closer look at that church and put some flowers on the grave. I meant to do it when I first came home.'

That word meant everything to Jayne. 'We'll do it together, tomorrow. There's a little florist in the high street.'

The wind was gusting up there and Paul was tempted to go back downstairs but he didn't want the others to think he was being pathetic. He gripped one of the battlements and remembered again the day he was up on the cliff top and the feeling that someone was pulling him away from the edge.

Jayne turned to him. 'Don't you want to see this view? It's so lovely...'

Paul shook his head, 'No, you're all right. I think I'll head back down,' and he turned to go.

'It's not everyone's cup of tea,' said Jack. 'Scares me rigid, if I'm honest, but I thought I'd show you. You can see why the old captain built his house here, though. He used this tower as a look-out,' he said, pointing out to sea.

Symon was taking it all in and examining the stone masonry, running his hands over parts of it. 'It's great to be able to see medieval architecture up close like this. How old did you say it was?'

'The oldest part dates from 1589, the year after he was shipwrecked,' said Jack.

'Amazing.'

Maggie was pleased for Symon – she knew how much this meant to him. 'Are there any secret passages?'

'Funny you ask. Come with me.'

'Mind if I stay up here a bit longer?' asked Symon. 'I want to check out a few things.'

'Be my guest.'

Jayne saw her chance and stayed behind while Paul was first down the spiral stairs followed by Maggie who was feeling as excited as a child on Christmas Eve.

'Give us a shout when you're done,' said Jack.

Symon nodded.

Jayne approached Symon and thought very carefully how to word her next sentence. She wanted to know if Symon had heard their father's music when he'd been in *Seawinds* on his own, particularly in the front room. She hoped he had – she didn't want to think she was the only one. 'I've been meaning to ask you...when you were in the house on your own, did anything happen, anything weird?'

Symon turned from examining one of the buttresses and stared at her. 'What sort of something?'

'Music, you know, the stuff Dad used to play?'

'Why? Has it happened to you?'

'Oh, thank God for that. I thought I was going mad. So, what do you think is going on?'

Symon shrugged, 'I dunno, I just thought it was me. I haven't told Maggie in case it worried her.'

'Paul thinks we should see a medium. He had a weird experience up on the cliff path, where Dad fell to his death. What do you think?'

Symon blew out his cheeks. 'Not sure about that. Seems a crazy idea and anyway, even if we did, how do you know if they're for real? Most of them are charlatans.'

Jayne thought about her conversation with Paul, 'There could be something in it.'

'I doubt it. Anyway, let's go find the others.'

Jack had taken Maggie and Paul outside round the back of the house and through a weather-bleached oak door set into the wall. This led to a passage with a slate floor and cold damp stone walls where Jack opened yet another door.

'Be careful,' he said, 'the steps can be a bit slippery down here but there is a hand rail.'

Maggie grabbed the cold metal rail. A damp musty smell wafted up as they descended into the dark stair well.

At the bottom, Jack shone his torch and began to lead Maggie and Paul down another passage. These walls were low and rough, as if hastily built. They had to stoop.

Jack stopped. 'Anyway, you can see what this is. I won't bother going any further. It's obvious the old captain was a bit of a pirate on the quiet. A lot of that went on right into the twentieth century.'

'Ha, yeah, I can imagine,' said Paul. 'Customs and excise men lurking round every corner.'

Maggie rubbed her bare arms and turned to go back upstairs.

'Anyway,' said Jack, watching her go, 'you get the general idea.'

Maggie felt apprehensive. She supposed it was because she and Symon hadn't been apart since their arrival at the bay, other than the day when he stayed behind at *Seawinds* with Chaz while she strode down to the beach with Jayne and Leyla. She hurried up the stone steps ahead of Jack, eager to get out in the sunshine. She suddenly felt chilled to the bone.

254

Paul would've liked to explore the tunnel further but he followed the others back up.

Symon and Jayne were already in the bar. Maggie ran to Symon and threw her arms round him.

'Hey! What's all this?'

'Oh, I don't know. I was just feeling a bit cold, that's all.'

Symon rubbed her back. 'Come on, let's get you out in the sun, warm you up.'

The next day, Jayne and Symon left Paul and Maggie surfing and ventured into the florist shop in the high street to select some flowers to put on the grave. Jayne balked at the price but Symon thought nothing of it. Jayne cradled the pink and white lilies like a baby as they strode out of the shop and up the steep cobbled hill, past some higgledy-piggledy white cottages towards the ancient church. This was the oldest part of the village and Jayne saw it with fresh eyes today, like a tourist. Apart from her mum's funeral she couldn't remember the last time she'd ventured up here. Little narrow streets and alleyways leading to dead ends all looked untouched by time. Pots and window boxes full of bright petunias and geraniums sat on weathered stone steps cheering up the bleakness of the dark masonry. A black and white cat sauntered out from an alleyway and surveyed Jayne and Symon as they walked past, but that was the only sign of life. Owing to the orientation the sun could not penetrate the narrow lanes and Jayne was relieved when they finally reached open ground.

They walked through the lych-gate blackened with time and into the churchyard basking in the sunshine. Jayne's heart clenched at the thought of the two funerals that had taken place here fifty years apart, and the even more recent one at the crematorium. She shook the thought away and concentrated on the job at hand.

As Jayne approached their parents' grave she realised someone had been there recently and laid a bunch of flowers.

'Look at that. Who could that be?'

Symon shrugged. 'Beats me, but whoever it was must hold them in their hearts.'

Jayne frowned, 'It's just another weird thing to happen.' She shivered and knelt down on the damp grass to arrange the lilies in the holder, added some water and stood back to admire at them. They were so tall they obscured most of the inscription on the headstone. 'Do you think we'll ever find out what really happened to Dad, the day he died?'

'I don't know but I get the feeling both he and Mum are looking down on us, happy that we're together and making *Seawinds* our forever home.'

'Oh Symon, I do hope so. Have you emailed Leyla?'

'Oops, I'll get onto it when we get back.'

In the days that followed Jayne, Paul, Symon and Maggie swam and surfed and felt healthier and more invigorated with each passing day. Jayne was happier than she'd ever been; she hadn't realised her sex life could be so wonderful in later years. She and Maggie exchanged confidences and they were both amazed at their renewed libido. They felt truly alive, their aches and pains forgotten, put down to the therapeutic effects of the ozone and the sea minerals. No one thought to question why they felt younger or why the weather was always so agreeable. Symon had forgotten about working out in the gym. He didn't need to; the water sports were enough to keep him fit. Paul couldn't believe Cornwall was measuring up to all of his expectations – he had envisaged having to make some compromises, knowing in Australia he'd had it so good – but this couldn't be further from the truth.

The house was gradually taking shape too. Symon and Paul were having a ball with the redesigning and planning and they all agreed on Paul's ideas for his surf school in the basement. Jayne was happy for him; they were making plans together at long last. All in all it was like being on one permanent holiday, until Paul reminded Jayne that he should take her to see his mother.

In their bed at the *Captain Tregenna*, Paul rested on one elbow, gently draped a strand of hair from Jayne's face and looked at her. 'I thought you wanted to get this cleared up?'

'I do, but...I don't know. I'm frightened of what I'll find out, of what we'll both find out, I suppose.'

'I know what you mean, but surely this needs to be put to bed once and for all?'

She took a deep breath, 'Yeah, OK. Shall we go today, then?'

'I think so. I'll ring Katie.' He sat on the edge of the bed and fished out his mobile from his jeans pocket.

Katie was surprised to learn that Paul was still in Cornwall. 'Hey, I thought you were ringing to tell me you were back in Oz?'

'Nah, I cancelled the flight. I'm not going back. I can conduct the rest of my business online.'

'Well, that is good news! I take it you and Jayne are...'

'Yep, everything's great. We'd like to come over today if that's all right? Do you think Mum'll be up for it?'

'Sure, you'll have to take her as you find her, but it'll be great to see you both. I'll sort out a bit of lunch.'

They arrived to see Katie standing at the front door of her detached house which stood on its own down a farm track, the front garden full of colour.

Jayne and Katie hugged each other then stood back to look at one another.

'I can't believe it,' said Jayne, 'after all these years. You look wonderful!'

'Thanks Jayne, you don't look so bad yourself. Come through. Would you like some coffee? I've just brewed a pot.'

'That would be lovely.' Jayne followed Katie through the bright and airy hall into the spacious white kitchen diner with granite worktops, an island in the centre. 'What a lovely house.'

'Thank you. It's a lot to manage, what with Mum and everything. But I like it here. Martin's going to try and get home for lunch. He's dying to meet you.'

'Oh, you shouldn't have gone to all that trouble.'

'It's no trouble and I'd have to do some for Mum in any case.'

Katie took the coffee pot and some homemade scones into the adjoining conservatory with its view of the large well-kept garden. Jayne caught a glimpse of the manicured lawn with a water feature in the centre, some classical statues and urns dotted about. Halfway down the garden there was an archway leading, Jayne assumed, to another part of the garden. Jayne and Paul sat down whilst Katie poured the coffee.

'This is lovely. Who's the gardener?' asked Jayne.

'Oh, that's me. I love pottering about out there, it's very therapeutic.' Katie handed the cups round then there was a shout from the annexe. 'Here we go. I wonder what she wants this time. Never a dull moment, excuse me.' Katie headed towards the kitchen and the annexe beyond.

Jayne looked at Paul. 'Is she really that infirm?'

'Well, I think she plays on it a bit but she can't walk too well.'

Jayne added some milk to her coffee, sat back in the wicker armchair and kept her eyes focused on the garden. She wasn't looking forward to what was waiting for her in the annexe. The last time Jayne saw Lottie Smythe was the day after her father died fifty years ago. Jayne assumed Lottie had been in her forties then, always very smartly dressed and very particular. But she remembered Ken Smythe being rather a stern, controlling husband. Lottie must feel a bit lost now, living in her daughter's annexe.

Katie was soon back. 'She's fine, just a bit agitated this morning. She knew you were coming but I don't think she understands who you are and why you've come to see her. Dementia's a dreadful thing.'

Paul shot Jayne a look that said, it'll be OK, trust me.

'Does she ever talk about the old days?' asked Jayne.

Katie shook her head. 'Not much. She doesn't talk much at all. Makes life difficult. But hey, enough of that.' She passed round the buttered scones and Jayne was thankful to have something to occupy her hands. 'Tell me Jayne, what's it like living in Cambridge?'

Jayne swallowed a mouthful of scone and wiped her fingers on a napkin. 'Not as nice as Cornwall. That's why I plan – sorry – *we* – plan to do the old place up and live there, at *Seawinds* I mean. My brother's an architect; he's helping us to redesign it. These are lovely, by the way,' she said indicating her plate.

Paul nodded in agreement.

'Thanks,' said Katie, 'but that comes as no surprise, about Symon I mean. He was always constructing things in his bedroom, wasn't he? Lego, Airfix...'

Jayne nodded and looked at Paul. 'Paul intends to run part of it as a surf school.'

He returned her smile, 'Yeah, if my plans come together, as I'm sure they will.'

Jayne felt his eyes bore into her soul. She longed to kiss him but she had to restrain herself in front of Katie who looked from one to the other knowingly.

'You've got a daughter, haven't you? Would she want to come and live with you?'

'I doubt it,' said Jayne, 'she's got her own life up in Scotland. I very rarely get up there to see her and the children.'

'Oh, that's a shame. Still, they'll be able to come and visit once *Seawinds* is all done won't they?'

Jayne frowned, 'I hope so.'

Katie decided to drop it. Jayne looked a bit flustered and she didn't want to cause her any more anxiety. Paul had told her about Michael's death, hard on the heels of her mother's, and Katie felt sorry for her. She decided to change the subject.

'Would you like to see the garden?'

Jayne nodded. 'Love to.'

'I'll take you out there when we've finished this.'

Jayne couldn't relate this Katie to the ten-year-old she remembered. She always seemed a bit sulky in those days but now she was full of confidence, her dark hair in a neat style, her trim figure in skinny jeans and a linen blouse. But Jayne wanted to get this episode over and done with and felt that Katie was prolonging the agony. It wasn't her fault – she couldn't have known how Jayne was feeling. She followed Katie into the garden hoping there wouldn't be an unpleasant scene when she finally went in to see Lottie Smythe.

Paul felt left out during all the gardening chatter; he wasn't into gardening. He liked to see a nice garden but he didn't like doing it and he wasn't interested in the names of plants. Not like his sister who was always out there with a fork or trowel in hand. He offered to wash up and went back indoors.

It was a ruse – he wanted to pave the way for when he took Jayne in to meet his mother. He took the crockery through to the kitchen then knocked on the adjacent door. A feeble little, 'Come in', beckoned him. Lottie was sitting by the window in her new upsie-dazie chair as Paul liked to call it, a mechanical chair that tipped her up and forward making it easier for her to stand.

'Hi Mum, how you doing?'

'Is that you, Paul?'

'Don't give me that, you know it's me. I've brought someone to see you. She'll be here in a minute. Katie's showing her round the garden.'

Lottie sank further down in her chair. 'Who is it? What's she want?'

'It's Jayne, Mum. Remember?'

She looked vague so he pressed on, '*Seawinds*? Holidays in Cornwall?'

Lottie looked as if she was trying to recall those long-lost days. She gazed off into the distance and sighed. Finally she said, 'Ooh, that was a long time ago. You liked it there. Wanted to go back but oh dear, your dad...'

Just at that moment, in walked Katie with Jayne in tow.

Lottie scowled at them.

Jayne stepped forward. 'Hello Mrs Smythe. How are you?'

Lottie studied Jayne's face until the light of recognition dawned. She began to relax. 'Well I never! You're all grown up.'

Jayne pulled up a chair and sat next to Lottie and braced herself.

'There's something we want to ask you, Mum,' began Paul, hoping he wasn't jumping in too soon. 'A long time ago, when Dad worked with Mr Williams...'

Lottie's frown deepened, 'Who?'

'Harry. Harry Williams? He worked with Dad, remember?' asked Paul. 'Something happened didn't it, something involving money?'

'Don't know,' her words were clipped. 'What sort of something?'

Paul looked to Jayne for help.

'Way back in the fifties before we moved to Cornwall...' started Jayne. 'Your husband worked with my dad in London, didn't he, in the advertising studio?'

Lottie turned her head slowly from side to side, her lips a hard thin line.

Jayne waited, but she was feeling uncomfortable. She wasn't sure if this was a good idea, dragging up the bones of the past.

Lottie was twisting her wedding ring on her wizened finger. 'Your poor dad,' Lottie's cloudy eyes were now moist. 'He went for a walk and fell off that cliff. Dreadful business, poor man,' she wrung her hands and gave Jayne a hard stare. 'All that money. That was our savings! I went mad when he told me. Harry said he'd pay him back. Free holidays? Huh!'

Jayne felt very uncomfortable but she wanted to know more. This was so out of character for the father she knew. 'Lottie, is there anything else you can tell me?'

Again Lottie turned her head slowly from side to side. 'Ken lost his job and had to work in that awful supermarket,' she spat, 'nowhere to leave his ticket-writing to dry, people treading on it...'

But Jayne ploughed on, 'Do you know what Harry needed that money for? Lottie?'

'Pfft, some loan or other so he could buy that damned guest house,' she said sulkily. 'What about us? We had to live in that grotty flat... My hands and knees were like sandpaper with all those cleaning jobs...'

'It's OK Mum,' said Katie, trying to calm her mother.

But Paul continued, 'Do you know what happened the day Harry died, Mum?'

Lottie's face twisted and her eyes narrowed. 'You *know* what happened! You were there!' she snarled. 'We went on that mystery tour but your father didn't go, said he had a headache.'

Jayne frowned at Paul.

'Oh, yeah, I forgot about that.'

'When we got back,' continued Lottie, in full flow now, 'he met us from the coach, said he'd been for a walk. He looked white as a sheet and his hair was all over the place.'

Jayne realised she'd been holding her breath.

Had Ken had something to do with her father falling from the cliff top? Oh my goodness! Did he push him? Is that what happened?

Jayne and Paul exchanged anxious glances.

'Did he say anything else about where he'd been that afternoon?' asked Paul.

Lottie sucked in her bottom lip and shook her head, getting more and more agitated.

Jayne felt awkward – they shouldn't have come. They should've left the past locked away. 'I'm so sorry, Lottie. We shouldn't have put you through this,' said Jayne.

Lottie began to examine her hands resting in her lap, as if looking for the tell-tale signs of hard scrubbing.

'All right, let's leave her,' said Paul.

Lottie shouted, 'That's right! Leave me, like you did all those years ago...'

Katie came to the rescue. 'It's all right Mum. Here, have one of your tablets.' She poured Lottie a glass of water from the jug on the side table and put a tablet in her papery hand. Katie turned to Jayne and Paul and said softly, 'It's OK. You go. I'm used to her.'

Paul led Jayne back to the sitting room and closed the door behind them. 'Like she said, she's used to her. She'll calm down in a few minutes.'

Jayne took a deep breath, 'But Paul, what if..?'

Paul's eyebrows shot up, 'What? You think my dad pushed Harry off the cliff?'

She shrugged, 'I don't know...'

'I can't believe he'd do such a thing. But there's no way of knowing. Not now. Mum's the only one alive and...'

'I know.' Jayne sank down on the sofa with her head in her hands. 'Why didn't you tell me about that coach tour?'

'Christ Jayne it's fifty years ago. Do you expect me to remember every little thing? And anyway, what's that got to do with anything?'

She thought they were getting on so well but now Paul was angry with her, raising his voice. The day was turning into a nightmare. With tears welling up Jayne snatched up her handbag and headed for the hall. She didn't want to stay in this house a moment longer.

Paul tugged her back.

She shrugged him off.

'Jayne, come on, you can't just walk out.'

The sound of tyres on gravel alerted her to another car pulling up behind Paul's. A man got out and was heading for the front door.

Jayne hastily drabbed her eyes and composed herself.

The man smiled at Jayne and went to shake her hand, 'Hi, I'm Martin. Not leaving already?'

'Well,' began Paul, 'we were, but now you're here...'

Martin chucked his keys on the hall table and went through to the lounge. Paul gave Jayne's hand a squeeze of encouragement.

'Yeah,' said Martin, 'sorry, I wanted to get away before this, but I had a tricky problem that took longer than I thought. Computers, eh?'

Paul and Jayne followed Martin and stood uncomfortably in the middle of the room.

'Everything all right? Where's Katie?' asked Martin, looking around.

'With Mum,' said Paul, 'she was ranting a bit.'

'Ah.'

'Yeah, I'm afraid it was our fault.'

'I shouldn't worry. It happens.'

Katie came back. 'Oh, I see you've met Martin. You are going to stay for some lunch, I hope?'

'Thank you,' said Jayne, 'we'd like that.'

'Martin will entertain you while I get it ready. Salad OK?'

'Look,' said Jayne, 'I don't want to put you to any trouble; you've got enough to deal with.'

'No problem. We'd have ours now anyway.'

Martin nodded. 'Come through to the conservatory and I'll open a bottle. White or red?'

'Ah, not for me,' said Paul, 'I'm driving. Water will be fine.'

266

Jayne said she would like a glass of white wine thinking it might help her to relax.

During lunch, all four of them began to loosen up and enjoy each other's company and Jayne was relieved. All was quiet from the annexe now and she tried to put the whole sorry episode behind her.

Easter Sunday April 1968

Lottie's story.

Katie is sitting on her bed looking bored. We really need to do something today. I'm fed up with the inactivity and Ken doesn't come up with any ideas. If only the weather was better, we could lose ourselves on the beach, but it's blowing a gale. I was hoping it was going to be a bit warmer while we were here.

I heard Paul go downstairs a few minutes ago – he's probably gone to find Jayne. He's been given his own room this time and I'm thankful. At eighteen he's turning into a fine young man, I'm proud of him, but I don't know about his relationship with Jayne, how it can last with 300 miles between them.

Ken hasn't been himself since last night and I'm getting worried about him. Yesterday evening he went to speak to Harry about a little matter that should've been cleared up ages ago apparently, but I didn't ask any questions, I assumed it was nothing to do with me.

I'm just thankful that we can afford to come down here; it's literally a breath of fresh air away from the grime of Peckham. I look forward to the summer holidays. But this year we came down for Easter as Paul had been itching to see Jayne. There hadn't been much communication between them and he wanted to talk to her about their plans.

'Can't we do something?' asks Katie, pulling a face.

'I don't know. What would you like to do, love?' I look across at Ken. He seems on edge and he keeps looking out the window.

'It's Easter Sunday,' says Ken. 'I shouldn't think there's much going on unless you want to go to church.'

'But it's boring staying in,' began Katie, 'there's no one my age here. Well, there's Symon, but I don't want to hang around with him. He's always making Lego models, and anyway, I don't think he's interested in playing with me. It's all right for Paul, he's got Jayne.'

'I know, love.' I picked up a leaflet the other day, something about a mystery tour. I go to the chest of drawers and find it. 'What about this?' I hand it to her.

She reads it and hands it back to me. 'Can we go? It says it's leaving at two-thirty.'

I look at my watch. It's just coming up to 2 o'clock. 'Yes, OK, I think we've got time. Go and see if your brother wants to go.'

Katie bounces off the bed and runs downstairs.

I look at Ken. He's still gazing out the window. 'It'll be something different,' I say, 'what do you think?'

'Oh, leave me out. I've got a headache. You go with the kids. Do you good to get out.'

'You sure?'

'Yeah, I'll have a lie down. I've got some aspirin.'

Katie comes back. 'Paul's going to come but he's not happy.'

I sigh. Teenagers.

'Come on, then. You'll need a coat.'

'Hurry up or you'll miss the coach,' says Ken, looking to see if it's coming along the road.

I grab my coat and handbag, take Katie by the hand and collect Paul on the way downstairs. We only just make it in time. The coach is about to leave but only half full. I pay the driver for three tickets and we take our seats, Paul and Katie behind me. The drive along the coast would've been lovely on a sunny day. As I wipe the condensation off the window, I am wondering if Ken is all right, if he really did have a headache or if it was an excuse not to come with us. It's not something he suffers from. I find it disconcerting that he's had words with Harry – they've been friends for as long as I can remember. We were so happy for Yvonne and Harry when they bought *Seawinds* and I have loved the many holidays we've spent down here. I'd hate for them to come to an end.

The coach swerves into a car park and the driver tells us we have an hour here. It's a pretty cove with a tea room. We rush to get out of the wind and walk up to the counter.

'Oh good!' says Katie, 'they've got chocolate milkshakes. Please, mum?'

I fish in my purse for 1/6d and hand it to her. I turn to Paul, 'What would you like, love?'

He reads the blackboard. 'I'll have a hot chocolate. I'll pay, I've got some money.'

I shake my head, plenty of time for that when he leaves home. 'It's OK, my treat.'

I order the drinks and decide I'll have a cream tea. I can ill afford it but I feel the need for something to cheer me up. Then Katie says she would like a cake. I look at Paul.

'No, it's all right, Mum. I'm fine.'

We take our tray of refreshments to a table by the window. The waves are crashing over the sea wall and soaking the pathways. I shiver and turn my gaze to indoors. The tea room is very pretty with blue and pink tablecloths and pictures of coastal scenes by local artists for sale on the walls. There's a row of tea pots in different patterns, shapes and sizes high up on a shelf. I just wish I felt happier, that I could enjoy it, but there's something Ken's not telling me and I'm worried about him.

I pour myself a cup of tea and spread half a scone with jam and cream. I smile at Paul and Katie enjoying their drinks. They both look sombre, not even the usual bickering. We look like a family at a funeral instead of on holiday.

'How's Jayne?' I ask Paul, mainly to break the silence.

He shrugs his shoulders and mumbles something about her not going to Plymouth after all. They did have plans to go to university together. He looks very upset.

'So what's she going to do now?'

He stares into his hot chocolate, 'Says she wants to go to Cambridge Art School.'

'Oh? Still, she is good at art. Yvonne showed me some of pictures,' but he looks so miserable I want to give him a hug. 'Never mind, love, maybe you'll still be able to see her in the holidays.'

He tries to smile, 'Yeah, maybe.'

Katie has finished her cake and milkshake and Paul drains the last of his hot chocolate. I have only eaten half of my cream tea when the driver announces it's time to get back on the coach. Owing to the strong winds he's reluctant to complete the original tour, says it would be dangerous for the coach on the coast road with the waves thrashing so high. I'm

271

rather relieved – I don't want to stay out any longer – I want to get back and find out what's ailing Ken.

As the driver parks the coach, through the window, I see the pine trees bending in the gale and a clump of dried seaweed bounces down the road. Then I see Ken. He's walking towards the coach, head bowed, collar turned up against the wind and his hair dishevelled. He looks like a man with a thousand troubles on his shoulders.

Katie jumps down from the coach right in front of him. Paul's behind me. I get off the coach and put my arm through Ken's but he's like a block of wood. 'Hello, love. I thought you'd still be lying down. Are you OK?'

He takes a moment to answer. 'I had a walk to clear my head, saw the coach and thought I'd come and meet you. How was it?'

He looks disinterested as if his mind is elsewhere. Katie starts to tell him where we went and about the tea room but I'm sure he's not listening. I look behind at Paul and catch sight of a smear of mud down the back of Ken's overcoat.

Then we turn the corner and see the police car outside *Seawinds*. I don't know why but it sends a chill through me. When we enter the hall I am shocked to see Yvonne slumped on a chair and Jayne kneeling beside her, hugging her. Gladys from next door flies out and steers us into the dining room and shuts the door behind us to tell us the devastating news. I can't believe what I'm hearing. Apparently Harry fell from the cliff top about an hour ago. Gladys's husband saw him sprawled out on some rocks and called 999. I can't believe it. What a dreadful thing to happen.

Then we hear a terrible blood-chilling cry from the hall. Yvonne's obviously been told the worst. Paul leaves the room and as we head out, I catch a glimpse of him trying to

272

console Jayne but she shrugs him off. He drags his feet upstairs. We take Katie and follow.

We're shocked by the news but there's little reaction from Ken and I wonder why. They've always been the best of friends.

Paul's gone to his own room. Katie is sitting on her bed looking at us.

'What a tragedy,' I say, wiping my eyes. 'Poor Yvonne...and the children. I can't believe it.'

Ken is silent. I don't know why but I've got an uneasy feeling about this whole affair.

At dinner, we sit in sombre mood with the other diners. All I can hear is the clatter of cutlery on china and the low voices behind the kitchen door. Yvonne has been put to bed, so Gladys tells us. She and George are helping to serve the meals while Jayne, Leyla and Symon remain out of sight. I dread to think what they're going through.

Paul leaves his untouched lamb stew on the table, crashes his chair back against the wall and bangs the front door on his way out.

Ken still hasn't said anything, didn't even grumble about Paul's behaviour. He sits resolutely eating his meal without looking up. I've lost my appetite – every mouthful is a struggle. The room is airless, stifling. Through the window I catch a glimpse of Paul in the distance angrily walking along with his hands in his pockets kicking a stone until I lose sight of him.

When we go back to our room, Katie lies on her bed, reading. Ken and I look at each other.

'What do you think happened?' I ask him. 'Did you see anything?'

273

He shakes his head. 'No, I told you – I had a doze and when I woke up I went for a walk. Then I met you from the coach.'

'Why on earth did you go out in this wind?'

'I told you,' he snaps, which isn't like him. 'OK, I might've gone to the pub for a couple of brandies, just to warm up. But that's all.'

'Drinking with a headache?'

'What's all this, the third degree? Look, we're all devastated by Harry's accident…'

'…accident, is that what you call it?'

'Why? Do you think I had something to do with it?'

'No, of course not. Don't be absurd,' but I can't seem to quash this uneasy feeling every time he looks at me. There's something he's not telling me, I know.

Later, the wind dies down and we venture out, mainly because the room is closing in on me. Katie stays behind, still engrossed in her book, and I'm relieved – at least we'll be able to talk freely.

As Ken and I walk down the hill, past the cottages with lights in the windows, I keep my eyes peeled for Paul. He still hasn't come back and now I'm worried about him too. As we approach the beach Ken stops and looks over at the rocks where he thinks Harry ended up. The overhanging cliff is very high up and I shiver at the thought of the poor man falling to his death.

'I suppose I should tell you what we talked about last night,' says Ken, turning to face me. I can see it's difficult for him – he looks this way and that, down at his feet. I watch the sun setting, the last glimpse of orange poking through the

274

purple cloud, casting a glow over the waves. It's beautiful and I wonder if we'll ever come back.

'I…' he stops, tries again. 'I lent Harry some money…years ago. A bridging loan… he needed to secure the guest house back in 1958. I was asking him for it back.'

'What? After all this time?' I'm flabbergasted but this explains a lot, why we're struggling to pay our way and why I have to take on the demeaning cleaning jobs. 'How much?'

'Enough.'

'Oh, Ken, how could you!' I am disgusted and angry that he put Harry before his own family. I start to walk away but he catches up with me and pulls me round to face him.

'Look, he assured me he'd pay it back just as soon as they were up and running.'

I shrug him off and head off back to the guest house.

He wrenches me back again. 'Lottie! I was helping a friend. In the meantime, he…'

I stare at him, 'Go on,'

He drags a hand through his hair. 'He said we could come down and stay free of charge for as long as we wanted. But last night he said he couldn't afford to do it any longer, the business is on its knees.'

'How could you? How could you do that?' I shout. I don't care who hears me. I hurry back up the hill, out of breath and seething with anger. When I reach *Seawinds* the hall is deserted, a slow ticking from grandfather clock the only sound.

Upstairs I peer round Paul's bedroom door. I'm thankful he's come back – he's lying on his bed facing the wall. He doesn't look round. I go back to our room and tell Katie to clean her teeth and get to bed. Ken is now lying on the bed staring at the ceiling. My mind is a jumble of what has happened and what will happen to us in the future. This has got to be the worst day of our lives.

TWENTY ONE

Leyla's finger was throbbing. Her feeble attempt at first aid, after her row with the rusty catch on the old suitcase, hadn't worked. She'd had to give in and go to the minor injuries unit to have it dressed properly and was given a course of antibiotics. But the dressing was huge and prevented her from typing. She gave up and took out a biro and notepad hoping to get down the most important points that came to her when she woke up this morning. But the bandage was too cumbersome even to hold the pen. She threw it across the room.

'Bugger! Why did I have to open that bloody suitcase?'

She made a cup of tea one-handed and went back to her study, opened the cupboard and stared at the shelves full of journals that stretched across five decades. Running a hand along the books she stopped at 1970, turned to the dog-eared page the day Jayne and Michael got married and began to read. Suddenly the day opened up before her and she remembered it as if it were yesterday.

The train journey up to London and then on to Cambridge took the best part of the day. Symon and I have never been any further than Exeter and the journey seemed to take forever. We left at the crack of dawn and when we arrived we checked in at the hotel reception and found our bedrooms. I shared one with Mum. We unpacked and hung up our outfits then met Symon downstairs but we all felt out of place in this lobby

277

with its dark, highly polished surfaces and hard chairs. Efficient-looking people dressed in suits kept walking in and out but no one stopped to ask 'can I help you?' or 'would you like to see a menu'.

Mum huffed and went up to a man at reception to ask if she could have a pot of tea for three. She thought him very rude and if she ran Seawinds like that we'd never have any visitors. Symon told her not to upset herself. We were only staying for two nights.

After a while a young woman came to take our order. She took out her pencil and wrote it down on her pad.

Mum smirked. I knew what she was thinking!

While we were waiting I went to have a look at the pictures on the wall painted by students from some of the colleges and the art school. I was delighted to find one of Jayne's. We were all full of pride as we stood and studied the river scene in the impressionist style. People enjoying themselves in boats and punts on the water, willow trees catching the light. Jayne had excelled herself.

We turned to see the tray of tea had materialised on the table and Mum poured. There was a complimentary packet of biscuits, just one, and Symon dived on that, greedy thing. When we finally went into the dining room Mum criticised the food. All in all not a good start to our stay.

The next day dawned cold and grey and I wondered why Jayne and Michael had chosen November for their wedding instead of waiting till the spring or summer. She looked like a film star in a pale blue jump suit, a white feather boa and a floppy hat and her honey-coloured hair in ringlets. But I had my suspicions when I saw that her jump suit was a bit tight round the tummy. Michael actually wore a suit and his blond hair had been cut. Jayne hated it – she loved his hair just the way it was, but he'd had it cut short the day before.

Jayne and Michael spoke their vows and it was over in a flash with the photographer snatching some pictures by the posh car.

278

At the flashy reception, champagne and everything, Michael's parents kept themselves to the top table while we all sat with the other guests. We wished Jayne and Michael a happy married life and sat down to a very welcome cooked meal which, I'm glad to say, was much better than the meal last night! Michael's father made a few lewd jokes and Mum winced as his little wife looked up at him adoringly.

When the disco began, all of a sudden Mum's face crumpled.

'What's up Mum?'

'Oh, nothing. It's just... your dad would've loved to walk her down the aisle, that's all.'

I put my arm round her. 'I know Mum, but I'm sure he's looking down on us right now and wishing Jayne and Michael all the happiness in the world,' but that didn't help.

Symon had his eye on a girl over the on the far side of the hall and went to ask her for a dance. No one ever asked me for a dance.

Leyla closed her diary. The reason Jayne's jump suit was tight was because she was pregnant. Leyla now wondered how many of the guests had come to the same conclusion.

She turned back to her computer. Heather jumped up onto the desk, sat on the keyboard and meowed loudly at her. Leyla ruffled her fur. 'All right, I'll feed you in a minute.' She read through her last paragraph while she stroked the cat. Her book was taking shape and she thanked God that Jayne had brought back her box of old diaries. They were indispensable in the writing of her memoir. She had told Jayne that she was writing a book on psychiatric care in the twentieth century. It was a lie. She wanted to tell the world what it was like for them all growing up in Cornwall and the trauma of their father's death, although some of it would have to be sheer speculation. She only hoped Jayne and Symon would be in agreement with her publishing it but she had changed all their names and made the bay a fictitious place so she didn't think they would hold up any resistance.

She stretched her aching back and went to the kitchen. Heather darted alongside, tail held high, and stared at her empty dish.

'Here you are,' said Leyla, pouring out some dry cat food. Heather ate hungrily. 'You poor old girl, has Mummy been neglecting you?' Leyla refilled the cat's water dish. 'Never mind, I'll make it up to you, promise.' Heather looked up at her as if to say 'about time.'

Leyla had been wading through her writing and her memories for the best part of the day and now she felt very stiff and achy. Her physiotherapist had nagged her to take regular breaks from sitting at her desk and do some stretching exercises but once she got stuck in to her work time had a habit of vanishing. But she was pleased with it all so far.

She got to thinking about *Seawinds* and wondered if the builders had started the renovations. She hadn't heard from Jayne for weeks, nor Symon or Maggie. Leyla had been so engrossed in her writing to the exclusion to all else that she hadn't given *Seawinds* a thought until now. She had welcomed the twins back from the Shetlands two weeks ago and listened to their stories and made notes hoping to use some of them in a novel, but that was the extent of her socialising. She loved having the kids to stay but thankful when they left so she could get back to her work. Huh, she thought, they were hardly kids. She smiled when she thought of Abi and Matt, now in their thirties. Neither was married or in a permanent relationship, instead they had thrown themselves into helping disadvantaged children, taking them to places they would never have experienced but for the charity. Leyla believed Abi and Matt had been put off getting involved with a partner because of

Leyla's own disastrous relationship with their father. They had vowed to live their lives to the full by helping others. She was a little envious if truth be known – she'd never been that adventurous, had preferred to stay within the bounds of what she knew and where she felt safe. She was also auntie to Daisy and great aunt to Daisy's children but, living so far away, she had never really bonded with any of them. She supposed when you got to a certain age life threw up its regrets, especially when you lived alone. But if they were to revive *Seawinds* it might be a different story. Jayne was right about one thing – life had seemed much simpler back then.

She made another cup of tea and thought about putting something together for her evening meal, not really relishing the idea as she couldn't hold a knife properly. It would have to be something simple. She thought grudgingly of the delicious sea food at the *Captain Tregenna*. Now would be a good time to call Jayne.

There was a voicemail message.

You have reached Jayne Green. Please leave a message and I'll get back to you.

Leyla resolved to phone again later. She fried three sausages and four rashers of bacon smothered them in brown sauce and slapped them between two slices of brown bread, ate them in front of the telly and fell asleep.

TWENTY TWO

Having put the uncomfortable meeting with Lottie out of her mind and clearing her conscience where Daisy was concerned, Jayne was determined to enjoy her time at the bay and give her plans her full attention.

Paul was making headway with his plans too – he'd stripped out the cellar and painted the walls white in both rooms. Instead of the polished concrete he'd decided to give the flagstones a good steam-clean and a sealant – less upheaval and much cheaper. He'd installed surf board racks and cupboards for his equipment and he'd ordered the shelves for the wet suits and swimwear. He was just waiting for the carpenter to build two changing rooms then he was done. He stood back to survey his efforts and a little seed of pride began to grow inside him. He didn't know where all this new-found energy had come from but he wasn't complaining. Not so long ago he would've run out of steam by the evening and fallen into bed but not now. His sex-drive was stronger too. His new-found relationship with Jayne was more than he'd dared hoped for; they were both happier than they'd ever been.

Paul had been in touch with Dean in Sydney and arranged to have the rest of his belongings shipped over to England, minus the boat. He was upset about that but Dean had managed to sell it for a good price. Wheeling and dealing was Dean's forte and truth be told, Paul was going to miss his old mate. He'd be a godsend over here with all the transactions he was embarking on, but at least Dean was on the other end of a phone or online if he needed him.

Today, Paul and Jayne took time out to enjoy the bright sunny day. Now that they were truly a couple he was gearing up to ask her more about her life with Michael. He had a need to fill in all the gaps, to paint pictures in his mind. He and Jayne were making up for lost time, a huge chunk of time, as if each of them had been imprisoned for fifty years. They were trying to put their painful pasts behind them and live for today but he knew the only way that this could truly be achieved was if they came to terms with their disappointments. Here at the bay, he felt as if he'd come home to where he was meant to be. Whatever happened, nothing could take that away from him, not now.

As they walked along hand in hand, Paul stopped to take in the scene – the wide bay sheltered by the steep craggy cliffs, the pearly white clouds bubbling up in the piercing blue sky. The tide was way out, sea spray causing the horizon to blur. Surfers were braving the big waves while the lifeguards kept watch from their white vehicle parked between the red and yellow flags fluttering in the constant breeze on the shiny wet sand.

Jayne slipped her arm round Paul's waist. He revelled in her touch; it was like an electric charge every time she brushed his skin.

'I can't get over it,' he began, 'You. Me. This place.'

'I know. I feel the same. We must be the luckiest people alive apart from Symon and Maggie. They look like a couple of kids since they've been here. It's taken years off.'

'Talking of years,' said Paul, 'you still haven't told me much about you and Michael. I think we're comfortable enough with each other now, don't you?'

'Yes, but what difference will it make?'

'Oh, no difference, I just need to fill in the blanks.'

283

'OK, as long as you let me do the same with you.'

'Of course, but me first; it was my idea.'

Jayne thought about her previous life. It was becoming more distant by the day, like a dream, as if it had never happened but, of course, Daisy was proof that it had. Jayne had told Paul how she met Michael but after that it was all becoming a blur. There was one thing, or one person that kept looming up and that was Rubie. Her disloyalty still rankled if Jayne let it but maybe it would be better if she aired her thoughts, got them out in the open and let them blow away on the breeze.

'Where do you want to be?' asked Paul.

'Guess!'

He led her by the hand past families enjoying the beach, kids building sand castles or rock-pooling, just like it had always been.

They made themselves comfortable on the sand floor just inside the mouth of the cave.

Jayne took Paul's hands in hers and kissed them. 'I love you so much. I never dreamed any of this was possible.'

'Oh God, Jayne, it's the same for me. I've never felt like this in my entire life. I don't know where it's coming from but I for one hope it never stops!'

His touch had such an effect on her that everything else was forgotten. She pulled him deeper into the damp cave where they were totally private and lay down on the bed of sandy seaweed. Sex had never been this good for Jayne – she'd always had her inhibitions – but now she was overwhelmed by the sheer magic of the way their spirits entwined every time they made love. They were lost in each other and the afternoon slipped away until Paul propped himself up on one elbow, his sleepy gaze sweeping Jayne's face. 'You're so beautiful, even more now than when you were seventeen, if that's possible.'

She gently brought his face to hers and kissed him. 'It's as if we've been given a new lease of life. You never know, we could go on like this until our nineties.'

'Bring it on!'

'I think it's the same for Symon and Maggie. It's wonderful how fresh and alive they look now he's made his mind up and succumbed to retirement and the bay.'

'What about Leyla? She seems like the odd one out.'

Jayne thought about this. Leyla had never had much luck where men were concerned. 'I feel a bit sorry for her. She had a bad experience with the man she married. She's mentally scarred. She lives on the Isle of Wight for a reason...'

'What's that?'

'...to put that strip of water between her and her ex. She had to take out a court order on him. He was put away in the end. I wish we could find her someone.'

'Yeah, that would be good. Anyway, we were supposed to be talking about *our* previous lives. That's if you're still up for it? It's no big deal.'

Jayne sat up, 'No, I keep putting it off. Let's get it out in the open once and for all. At our wedding, Mum, Leyla and Symon all came up by train to Cambridge and stayed in a big hotel. The reception was held in the hall there. Michael's father paid for the wedding and the hotel rooms. He liked to swank about how much it cost to stay there and everything.'

'Yeah, I get the picture, a real show-off.'

'Rubie was among the friends I invited, my best friend, or so I thought. At the disco in the evening she was wearing a skirt so short that every time she bent over she resembled a duck in a pond.'

Paul laughed.

'It wasn't funny, not when she couldn't get enough drink down her throat and grabbed all the men for a dance, regardless of whether they had partners or not. Michael's father slapped her bottom and called her a cheeky little minx among other things. I went to sit with Mum, Symon and Leyla and when I looked round Rubie was dancing with Michael with her arms draped round his neck, rubbing her body against him and he was enjoying it. You can imagine how I felt. It was my wedding day for God's sake. I went up to Michael and said, "My turn," but he waved me away. "In a minute," he said, "go sit with your family, they've come a long way." Rubie just leered at me.'

'Jeez, what did you do?'

'I ran to the toilets. People were staring, I couldn't face anyone. I haven't told you this before...'

'What?'

Jayne looked at Paul. 'If I hadn't been pregnant, I would never have married Michael.'

'Oh, God Jayne. All those lost years when we could've been living our dream. I'm so sorry. Is that why you stayed with him? For Daisy?'

Jayne nodded. 'When I came out of the toilet Michael and Rubie had disappeared. When the disco ended and we went to our room I confronted Michael...' Jane dropped her head.

'Hey, it's all in the past. It's over and done.' He turned her face to his and lightly brushed her lips with his own.

'No, let me finish. Michael said I was imagining it but I certainly wasn't. Rubie and I patched it up and I stayed friends with her. We used to have a laugh when we got together but she never had any serious boyfriends. It was a long time before she got married; she used to 'love 'em and leave 'em'. The permissive sixties never touched me but it seemed once she'd had a lick at the lollipop she wanted the sweet shop.'

'Ha, so she put it around a bit. Do you think they...'

'Quite possibly but she would never own up to it, nor would he. But when we had parties at home the two of them would go missing.'

'Blimey Jayne, I don't know how you put up with it.'

'She was my friend and godmother to Daisy. I didn't want a divorce and I didn't want to struggle to bring up a child on my own.'

Paul shook his head. 'Well, I for one never want to see her again.'

'You won't, don't worry.' Jayne allowed herself a smile. The outcome of her meeting with Rubie in the busy coffee shop was still very satisfying. 'Your turn.' She rubbed her arms. 'Let's sit in the sun.'

They got dressed and sat at the mouth of the cave watching the gentle activity on the beach. Dots of people were surfing the distant breakers and Paul was thankful the lifeguards were being vigilant.

Paul pointed to them. 'It's the same in Australia; those guys do a fantastic job. But this place has the edge. I don't know what it is but I feel so at home here. I thought I loved

287

Sydney, the beaches and the go-ahead lifestyle but now I never want to go back.'

Jayne glowed. She leaned into him and put her head on his shoulder. 'Tell me, what was it like over there?'

'Well, for a start it's extremely hot in the summer. Forty degrees is nothing but most buildings have air-con now. They have to, wouldn't be able to function otherwise. We're told to stay out of the sun or cover up, plenty of high-factor sunscreen – everyone's very aware of skin cancer.'

'It's the same here, but that's not want I want to know. What was your life like?'

'Busy. The surf school was great fun but I'm thinking I can make it work even better here, and with your help, we'll be riding high. I'm really looking forward to it.'

'Me too. Did you teach Dayle to swim and surf?'

'You bet. He was a great kid. He'd have gone far if...' Paul broke off and turned his face away.

'Look, this was your idea. If it's too painful...'

'No, like you, I need to air it. I've blocked it out for too long. One of the reasons Trish and I fell apart was because we never really confronted it. I wanted another kid but she wouldn't hear of it in case it happened again; couldn't face the heartache. It's devastating losing a child, especially to leukaemia. He used to scream with the bone marrow tests; tore me apart.'

Jayne held his hands and looked into his eyes. 'I'm so sorry you had so much pain. We'll make this work – we can heal each other. There's nothing and no one standing in our way, not anymore.'

288

At the *Captain Tregenna*, Jack was experiencing a slack period in the bar so he took the opportunity to grab a bite of lunch. Olive, dear of her, had left him one of her special pasties to pop in the microwave. Jack never ceased to count his blessings where Olive was concerned. When he first took on the pub a few months ago, his original cook had let him down at the last minute and he was beginning to panic as he was due to open in a fortnight. Olive had answered his advert for a chef. It couldn't have worked out better – she had a lifetime of catering experience and his guests left five star reviews on a regular basis. Olive had told Jack she had connections with *Tregenna Bay* but she hadn't gone into any detail. All he knew was that she'd been working in London hotels for years and now she wanted to come back to Cornwall for an easier life. Jack didn't ask any questions. As long as she kept producing food to tickle his customers' taste buds he wasn't complaining.

He poured himself a pint and sat at one end of the bar with his pasty and kept an eye on the door. His heart swelled with pride at the way his little business had blossomed. The *Captain Tregenna* couldn't be in a better location and now the Aussie was planning to open a surf school, he was sure his business would go from strength to strength. That family seemed to have their hearts and souls set on making *Seawinds* a success. Since they'd been staying with him they'd really got into their stride with plans for the old guest house. Symon in particular had thrown himself into redesigning it and Jack was looking forward to seeing the finished project.

Jack had also come to the bay for a breath of fresh air. His previous business had gone down the tubes – his partner had let him down, personally and professionally – and when he saw the *Captain Tregenna* was up for grabs he knew he had been given a chance to heal his heart and his bank balance. He

289

wasn't young by any stretch of the imagination but he felt he'd been given some extra years since living here and he was going all out to make this business a roaring success. The bay was truly a balm to his wounded soul.

Olive ventured along the road to *Seawinds*. There was a skip in the road and scaffolding all around the property and the noise from inside told her the builders were hard at work. She noticed the front door was ajar and as she stepped inside she was overwhelmed with nostalgia: Granny Crago, her little Cornish grandmother with her dark hair in a neat bun and always a cheery welcome at the door. Olive smiled; she couldn't remember seeing her grandmother without her apron. And her father, long gone, who brought her up without a mother, dear of him. Yes, this guest house had been such a big part of her early life, part of who she was.

Olive was drawn to the kitchen, the one room that resonated with her as she'd spent so much time in there with her grandmother, and later helping Yvonne. But she blocked out the memory of that fateful day when Mr Williams fell to his death and another that was struggling to come to the surface.

Cautiously she picked her way over the dust-covered rubble, trying to keep her balance on her way to the back of the house. Strange – she thought the kitchen would've been stripped out by now but it still looked the same as she remembered. She ran a hand lovingly over the range cooker and remembered the breakfasts she so diligently prepared, the dishes she helped Yvonne cook for the evening meal and the pastry being rolled out on the table for the pasties... she could

290

almost smell them. But that memory struggling for air still made her uncomfortable.

She was jogged out of her thoughts by a voice.

'Olive? That you, dear?'

Gosh! What was Yvonne doing amongst all this chaos? She must be getting on in years, too.

Olive went to find Yvonne. She assumed she was in the back parlour but when she poked her head round the door it was empty, the fireplace stripped out, and fresh plaster on the walls. Olive stood for a moment and listened but all she could hear was the echoing noise of the builders crashing about upstairs. She went to the foot of the stairs and shouted, 'Yvonne? You up there?'

The noise stopped.

One of the workmen bent his head over the banisters. 'Who're you looking for, love?'

Olive mounted the bare wooden stairs and stopped halfway. 'Is Mrs Williams up there?'

'No, love. I haven't seen anyone.'

'Oh. I thought I heard...'

'You're welcome to come up and see for yourself but you'll need a hard hat. There's one on the stairs.'

Olive declined his invitation – she knew all about health and safety and wasn't prepared to risk an accident, not at her age. It was highly unlikely that Yvonne would be up there anyway. Olive went back to the kitchen and froze. Yvonne was sitting on a stool by the table. She didn't look any older than when Olive last saw her. She searched her memory – when would that have been?

'Hello, dear. It's been a long time...'

291

Olive could only nod.

'That's all right, I understand. Cup o' tea?'

Olive found her voice. 'Don't get up, I'll do et.'

Olive suddenly remembered why she felt so uncomfortable in Yvonne's presence. A vague recollection of an argument began to struggle for air. She realised it must've been about 1970.

'Have you seen Jayne?' asked Yvonne, 'She's back you know. For good.'

'Is she?' Olive thought about this. She was always kept so busy in the kitchen at the *Captain Tregenna* and rarely ventured out but surely she would've known if Jayne was here?

As Olive turned to fill the kettle her head began to swim. She gripped the butler sink to steady herself. It must've been the walk up the hill that did it. Her blood pressure must be high again. When she turned round Yvonne had disappeared and the kitchen was empty, no range, no sink and no table. All the cupboards were gone and the lino ripped up from the floor. She dashed to the stairs, sat down and took some deep breaths.

One of the builders ran down from upstairs, squeezed past Olive then looked at her more closely. 'You OK?'

Olive wiped her forehead. 'Juss had a funny turn. Be awright dreckly.'

'Sure? Can I get you anything, glass of water? Oh, hang on. I think it's been turned off.'

'No, I'm fine. I'll just sit here awhile if I may?'

'Sure'.

Olive began to process her thoughts and was transported back in time.

292

Summer 1970

Olive's story

All the guests had gone out for the day. The house was quiet and I was lost in my own thoughts until a knock at the door made me jump, nearly sending the white sauce I was making up the wall. Mrs Williams dried her hands on her apron and went to answer the door while I continued to add the milk to the sauce, bit by bit like she'd shown me. I was curious about the visitor so I kept one ear on the conversation while I stirred, only I nearly forgot to add the bay leaf and that would never do. I could see the back of Mrs Williams but not who was at the door as she'd only opened it a crack.

'Hello love. Are your mum and dad with you?' she asked.

'Er..no. I'm on my own,' a pause. Then, 'Is Jayne there?'

'I'm afraid not, love. She's in Cambridge.'

'Oh?'

I saw Yvonne slowly turn her head from side to side. She clicked her tongue. 'Oh dear, hasn't she told you?'

The person seemed to be waiting for more. I wondered if it was Paul Smythe.

'She's going out with a boy she met there. His parents live in Cambridge. Nice lad.'

'What?'

Yes! It *was* Paul.

293

'Have you come down for a little holiday?'

No reply.

'Oh, dear, I'm sorry, love. We're fully booked, I'm afraid, but you can try Mrs Bolitho at the *The Tides Reach*.'

I had to really listen for his answer. I tried to edge nearer the hall without leaving the pan but curiosity got the better of me.

'Thanks.' I heard him say. 'It's not a problem. I just thought... Could you give her this and tell her I called?'

'Of course, love.'

Yvonne closed the door and I quickly returned to my post and continued stirring the sauce. She came back with an envelope and put it on the table.

'Who was that?' I asked.

Yvonne blew out a sigh. 'Paul Smythe. Bold as brass if you like.'

'But why did you tell him we were fully booked? Rooms five and six are empty!'

'Huh, I don't want anything more to do with that family after what happened.'

'But he must've come all the way down from London...'

'I don't care. Now, how are you getting on with that sauce, Olive?'

'I've finished, just bin keeping et on a low light.' I turned to the table and picked up the envelope. 'Oh, he's left her a birthday card, dear of him.' I turned it over. He'd written S.W.A.L.K. on the back.

'Well, she won't be getting it!'

'But why not?'

'No! I'm *not* sending it. She's in a relationship with a nice young man and that's how it's going to stay.'

'Well, I'm sorry but I think you're wrong.'

Yvonne picked up the pan of white sauce and grimaced. My stomach turned over.   'This sauce is lumpy! What on earth have you been doing, Olive?' She dumped the saucepan in the sink and spat her words, 'Keep your nose out of what doesn't concern you. She's my daughter and I'll do what I think fit!' She swiped the card from the table and threw it in the bin. Without looking at me she snapped, 'Take your break now. I can finish up here.'

I walked home with a lump in my throat. I remembered how much in love Jayne and Paul had been, and not only that, I couldn't believe how brusque Mrs Williams had been with me. She had never spoken to me like that before.

When I came back for my evening shift, I quickly fished out the birthday card from the bin with the intention of sending it to Jayne, but as I turned, Yvonne was standing before me, her hand outstretched.

'Give it to me!'

'Oh, please let me send et. I *know* she'd want to have et. Please Mrs Williams.'

She snatched the card from me and tore it up. 'There, let that be an end to it. And seeing as you *know* so much, maybe you'd like to find yourself another job?'

My jaw dropped. I couldn't believe what I was hearing. Hot tears pricked my eyes as I ran from the house and down the hill so fast I nearly fell headlong into Mrs Winter coming the other way.

''Ere, steady on Olive. Whass matter? Devil after ee?'

By the time I got home I had vowed to apply to catering college, get my qualifications and try for a job in one of the big hotels in London.

In the following days I toyed with the idea of writing to Jayne to tell her what had happened but I knew it would backfire on me – Mrs Williams would know it was me that told Jayne about the birthday card and maybe give me a bad reference. I couldn't take the risk so I decided against it. But I always wondered what became of Jayne and Paul.

TWENTY THREE

Jayne and Paul, Symon and Maggie strolled into the bar at the *Captain Tregenna* for their evening meal. While they were discussing the menu Symon remembered the old photos that Jack had told him about and went to find them on the returning wall. While he was studying them he was alerted by a voice.

'Symon? That you?'

Symon turned and looked the elderly woman up and down. 'Do I know you?'

'Oh, giss on! But it has bin a long time, I'll give ee that.'

Jayne's curiosity was heightened by the Cornish dialect and went to see who was speaking to Symon. She looked from one to the other and slowly the light of recognition lit up her face. 'Olive? Gosh! What are you doing here?'

'I work 'ere, in the kitchen,' she took a step back. 'Jayne! Let me look at ee! Oh my....'

They hugged each other, tears of joy streaming down both their faces.

'I never thought I'd see you again,' said Olive wiping her eyes, 'And Symon! Aw, look at him, all growed up!'

'Blimey,' said Symon, 'the last time I saw you I must've been about twelve. Come and meet Maggie.'

They all went through to the bar. Paul and Maggie looked up expectantly at the newcomer.

'This is the person responsible for all the delicious food we've been eating,' said Jayne, beaming. 'Olive, come and meet everyone.'

They all greeted each other and Jayne explained how she knew Olive, the comings and goings at *Seawinds* in the old days and the last time they saw each other.

Olive said, 'So tell en – what *are* you all doing down 'ere?'

They all smiled, full of excitement. Paul went to speak first but Jayne jumped in. 'I came back for Mum's funeral back in April and I was going to put *Seawinds* on the market...'

'...yeah, but I came back at the same time and scuppered her plans!' said Paul. He picked up Jayne's hand and kissed it. 'We're doing the old place up...'

'...and we're going to use it as a holiday retreat but I'm thinking of living here...'

'...and I've been drafted in to redesign it,' said Symon.

'Whoa!' said Olive, 'One at a time! I can't believe et, after all these years.'

'Yes, I know,' said Jayne, 'I'm still wondering when I'm going to wake up!'

Olive looked at the attractive man, dark hair streaked with silver, holding Jayne's hand. 'And are you..?'

'Yeah. We've finally got together after fifty years!'

'Aw, that's so lovely.' Olive looked around, 'But there's someone missing. Where's Leyla?'

'Still at home on the Isle of Wight,' said Jayne, 'I expect she'll join us when she's ready. She's busy writing a

298

book, something to do with mental health in the twentieth century.'

'Well, she always was the studious one.' Olive stood back and beamed at them all, then at Maggie. 'And you're Maggie?'

Maggie nodded and linked arms with Symon, 'Yes, and I'm married to this wonderful man.'

'Phew, so much to take in but it's so lovely to see you all.' She looked at her watch, 'Anyways, I must bustle or you won't be eating tonight! I'll pop back later.'

Jack, who had been standing behind the bar watching the reunion, came up to them, smiling, pad and pencil poised. 'Well, what a turn up. So you know Olive?'

Jayne and Symon nodded. 'She used to help Mum in the kitchen at *Seawind*s,' said Jayne. 'She was very efficient even in those days. But I thought she'd be retired by now.'

'Yes, I know, but luckily she answered my advert when my previous chef cried off. I don't know what I'd have done without her with only two weeks to opening. She's been a godsend. Anyway, ready to order?'

'Give us a few minutes, will you, Jack?' said Jayne, 'I think we're all still reeling.'

'Sure.'

Jack left them and went to serve another customer. But Jayne's mind wasn't on the food. The words on the specials board swam in front of her eyes and she couldn't concentrate. 'I just can't believe it. Olive. Here! I'll have to find out what she's been doing all these years, where she's been living. I know she left Cornwall, Mum said, but she didn't say why. I don't think Olive would've known about Mum's passing either. We'll have to catch up.'

'Yeah', said Paul, 'we'll have to invite her along to see the old place when it's finished, see what she makes of it.'

'I think we should meet up with her before that.'

Maggie was in the dark about most of this conversation. She hadn't come across Olive before. She'd met Symon long after Olive had left *Seawinds*. 'You'll have to fill me in. Who exactly is Olive?'

'Good question,' said Symon, 'I don't think any of us really knew that much about her, did we?'

'I know she was a local girl, grew up here with her father,' said Jayne, 'but he must've died years ago.'

Simon was thinking about the old photos in the loft and the ones he'd just seen on the returning wall. 'So, do you think...'

'What?'

'Oh, I don't know. I told you about the old photos in the loft when I was up there with Chaz? Well, the ones on the wall round the corner look like they were taken at the same time.'

'Really?' Jayne got up to have a look and Symon followed her. 'This is *Seawinds,* right?' she said pointing, 'But the sign says *Bay View*. Maybe that's what it was called before Mum and Dad took it on?'

'Well, you're the eldest, can't you remember?'

Jayne shook her head and looked at another photo. 'Wait a minute...that looks like Mum and Dad when they were young. How amazing! I've never seen any of these before.'

Jack came up to them. 'You're right, it was called *Bay View*. Olive told me. Her Granny used to run it.'

'So, is that old woman Olive's granny?' said Jayne, turning back to the black and white photograph.

'Yep, and that young man is her father,' said Jack, pointing. 'And that's Olive. She looks very young there.'

Jayne was amazed. 'So this is how the guest house looked when Mum and Dad first laid eyes on it?'

Jack nodded. 'It would seem so.'

Jayne couldn't take her eyes off the photograph. It gave her a strange feeling. 'This is fascinating. I'll have to ask Olive what she knows.'

'Yeah, anyway we ought to go and order our food,' said Symon. 'Maggie and Paul are waiting.'

Paul and Maggie were sitting with their heads together deciding what to eat, having realised that they were the outsiders when it came to the previous conversation. Jayne was happy to see the two of them getting on – she was overjoyed that they all hit it off, like one big happy family.

Paul looked up at Jayne, 'Well, we know what we're having.'

'Oh? What's that?'

'Crab cakes with sweet potato fries and spicy mango puree,' said Maggie.

'Sounds delicious, I'll have the same.'

'Yeah, sounds like a plan,' agreed Symon.

Jack heard and wrote it down on his pad. 'Drinks?'

They all agreed on the Sauvignon Blanc they'd had the previous evening and Jack went through to give Olive the order.

'Maggie and I are going back to Blackheath tomorrow,' said Symon. 'I want to get the business sewn up and sell my share.'

'Gosh!' said Jayne, 'so you're really going for it, retiring and living here?'

'You bet,' he winked at Maggie. She glowed. 'Until we sell the house in Blackheath I expect I'll be up and down. But after that...'

'That's fantastic.'

'Yeah, I want to keep an eye on the builders. They seem a pretty good bunch but you know what Cornish builders are like. It's always 'dreckly'.'

They all laughed.

Jack brought the wine to their table and Symon poured. 'Here's to us and *Seawinds*.'

They all chinked glasses.

Maggie took a mouthful of wine, 'Mm, we feel so much younger and fitter, here, it's amazing, catching up on all the things we missed out on in our younger days.'

'Yeah,' said Symon, 'you don't stop because you get old, you get old because you stop.'

'Yeah, you're a long time dead,' agreed Paul.

'So we're all together on this,' said Jayne. 'That's music to my ears.'

At the mention of music, Symon's thoughts returned to the day when he was up in the loft. He still hadn't mentioned it to Maggie, he didn't want to worry her, but it was good to know that Jayne had heard the music when she'd been alone in the house.

'That just leaves Leyla. I wonder when she's going to grace us with her presence?' said Jayne. 'I haven't heard from her in weeks. I've tried to phone her but I couldn't get through.'

Paul thought Leyla was the odd one out. She didn't exactly fit in with the free and easy ethos of the bay. 'Do you think she'll want to live here? I mean, I might be talking out of turn here, but I don't think she really took it on board, not like the rest of us.'

'I think she'll come round. Give her time. She's been so engrossed in writing her book that I don't suppose she's given it much thought. And it won't stop there. If I know Leyla, she'll be going all out to get it published and then there's the marketing and promotion...taking it to lit fests...'

'Blimey!' said Symon, 'We'll be lucky to see here this side of Christmas, then.'

When they had all enjoyed their meal, Olive came to sit with them. Symon emptied the last of the wine into a clean glass and handed it to her. 'I'll get another bottle.'

Olive held up a hand, 'Oh, no. Not my account. I'll only have one glass. I have to watch my intake but thank you.' She made herself comfortable and began to tell them her story.

Olive took a sip of wine and gave them a potted history – 'When I left *Seawinds* I went to catering college in Truro. When I passed me exams I applied for a job at Claridge's in Mayfair. To my surprise they accepted me – they said I was just the sort of person they were looking fer! I cuddn believe et,' slipping into her old Cornish dialect when she became excited. 'Anyhow the seventies and eighties were a busy time but a very happy time. I met Philip – he was one of the chefs – and married him.' She looked down at her hands in her lap, twisted her wedding ring. 'We had a wonderful life together, working all the London hotels until...' she paused and took a breath, 'Philip died three years ago.'

'Oh, I'm so sorry,' said Jayne.

Olive nodded. 'Thank you. He was a wonderful husband and father. Our son Davey followed us into the catering trade and now he's in France workin' at a fine restaurant in Paris.'

'Gosh. So why did you leave *Seawinds*?' asked Jayne. 'I didn't think you'd ever want to leave Cornwall.'

Olive lowered her gaze, 'I didn originally, but your mum made me mind up fer me.' Olive took another sip of wine.

'So what happened?' asked Jayne.

'It was when you were living in Cambridge, doing your art course. There was a knock at the door one day. I was busy in the kitchen so your mum went to answer it.' Olive composed herself for what she was about to offload. She smiled at Paul, then at Jayne. 'Turned out there was a certain young man asking after ee.'

Paul gasped, remembering that fateful day, and all eyes were on Olive waiting for her to continue. She turned her gaze on Jayne. 'Your mum and I argued over sending you the birthday card that Paul left fer 'ee. I wanted her to send et but she wouldn'.'

'Jeez, that explains it,' said Paul.

Jayne swallowed a big gulp of wine, eyes wide. 'No! Oh my God, I can't believe it. Why?'

Olive shook her head and shrugged, 'I told her she were wrong, that you'd want to 'ave et, but she'd 'ave none of et. I even fished it out the bin but she caught me red 'anded and tore it up in front o' me.'

304

'But why?'

'She said she didn't want any more to do with *that family* after what had happened. Said you were in a relationship with a nice young man and that's how it was going to stay.'

Jayne looked at Paul, 'So she *must've* known something. I wish I'd asked her. She was rambling in her last hours but I put it down to delirium.'

'Oh, Jayne, I wanted so much to write but I knew it'd backfire when I wanted a reference.' Olive's face crumpled. 'I'm really, really, sorry.'

Jayne patted Olive's hand. 'Don't be, it wasn't your fault.' She took hold of Paul's hand and gazed lovingly into his eyes. 'At least we're together now.'

Olive sniffed and smiled through her tears. 'Tes lovely. I'm so pleased for ee.'

They were all lost in their thoughts until Olive said, 'I didn knaw your mum had passed till I went to the churchyard the other day,' she said, looking at them cagily then down at her wine glass. 'I was puttin' some flowers on me dad's grave. Twas a lovely sunny day, so I had a walk round and noticed the new inscription on your dad's headstone.'

'So,' said Jayne, 'was it *you* who left the posy on Mum and Dad's grave?'

Olive nodded, 'I hope 'ee didn mind?'

'No, of course not. It was a lovely thing to do.'

'Well, that's one mystery cleared up,' said Symon.

Maggie looked at him. 'You mean to say there've been others?'

They all looked from one to the other wondering who was going to speak first.

305

'Shall we tell her?' asked Jayne.

'Tell me what?'

They all agreed and Symon held Maggie close in case she freaked out. But she sat entranced while she listened to all their accounts of what had been happening. Jayne and Symon with the music they'd heard in *Seawinds*, Paul with the experience he'd had on the cliff top, Jayne and Paul having seen Gladys, and Olive who'd seen Yvonne in the old kitchen.

'Gosh! Why didn't you tell me?' asked Maggie.

'I didn't want to worry you,' said Symon.

'Oh darling, that's really sweet but I'm fine with it. What do you think we should do now?'

Symon looked at Jayne, Paul and Olive, 'I think we all need to meet up in *Seawinds* one evening when the builders have gone home, see if any of these weird things happen when we're all together. What d'you say?'

'We could go tonight,' said Jayne.

Apart from Olive who pleaded tiredness, they were all in agreement.

Later that evening Jayne and Paul, Symon and Maggie left the *Captain Tregenna* and walked down the hill and along to *Seawinds*. The full moon smiled down on them and the stars shone so bright Jayne felt as if she could reach up and touch them. The only sound came from the waves shushing back and forth with rhythmic regularity. All was still and magical in the moonlight but something was bubbling under the surface, something that made Jayne a little apprehensive. She stopped

306

to take in the scene and remembered the night she saw the shadowy figure of a man on the cliff top after her reunion with Paul that first night. She dismissed it then but now she scanned the cliffs in case the same figure appeared.

Symon came to stand beside her. 'You are OK with doing this? You don't have to.'

'No, it's fine. I'm just looking to see if...'

'What?'

Jayne shook her head, 'Oh, take no notice of me. I don't suppose it means anything.'

'Hey, come on, tell me.'

'All right. I thought I saw a shadow of a man up there on the cliff top...'

Symon followed Jayne's gaze. 'Where?'

'Oh, not now, one night back in April. I was getting ready for bed and I happened to look out the window. I'm sure I saw someone in Dad's favourite spot, where he fell to his death, but when I looked again he'd disappeared.'

'A ghost, you mean? You didn't tell me about that,' said Symon.

'No, I'd forgotten all about it till now.'

Symon looked back across the bay to the same spot. 'Wait a bit longer, see if it happens again.'

'No,' said Jayne, 'come on. The others will wonder why we've stopped.'

They walked on in silence. Jayne was feeling uneasy. What if the music started but she was the only one who heard it? What if only Symon heard it? What if none of them heard anything? What would that mean? If nothing happened where would that leave them? She was desperate to learn the secret

307

behind why her father fell to his death back in 1968 but how was she going to find out? There had been no witnesses at the time. No one saw it happen. George didn't see him fall – he only found him when it had happened and in any case, he would be dead by now.

Ahead of them Paul and Maggie had gained pace and were outside *Seawinds* looking up at the scaffolding that covered the front of the house. The new balcony was taking shape and the wide French windows had been installed.

Symon caught up with them. 'Looking good, eh? But I thought they'd have got a bit further on by now. Still, that's Cornish builders for you. I'll have to have a word with Gary tomorrow.'

Maggie looked at him, 'Not tomorrow, unless you're thinking of postponing our trip back to Blackheath.'

'Oh yeah. I'll email him.'

All four stood in the porch while Symon fiddled with the key. He finally managed to turn it. 'Well, here we go, then.' He turned to Maggie, 'Ready for this?'

She nodded eagerly and rubbed his arm affectionately.

The old door creaked open to reveal dust-laden brick rubble in the hall; the remains of a wall that had been knocked down to make way for an open plan reception area. Jayne swallowed down the lump in her throat, the house felt violated. What would her parents think? This house had been their pride and joy. They had poured so much of themselves and every penny into it.

They all crept in like burglars carefully picking their way over the debris.

'Thank heavens for the full moon,' said Symon. 'I don't suppose anyone's thought to bring a torch?'

'I did,' said Paul, and duly produced a small one from his jeans pocket. He shone it around.

They all stood before the open door to the front room where Harry had listened to his music, whisky in hand, fifty years ago and more.

Jayne was first in, her shadow thrown across the floorboards by the moon shining through the window. The room was completely empty. Nothing of Harry remained. It was as if this lovely old house had had its heart ripped out.

Symon went to inspect the newly opened space in the hall and shouted, 'Paul? Shine your torch in here, would you?'

Maggie stepped into the front room and stood beside Jayne and looked around at all four corners of the room. Although she had visited in the past, Maggie didn't have the same feeling for the house as Jayne who had so much of herself wrapped up in these walls.

'How long d'you think...?' whispered Maggie, 'before we hear...?'

'Why are you whispering?' asked Jayne.

Maggie shrugged.

Jayne closed the door to block out the sound of Paul and Symon rooting around and wished they had left their investigations for later. Jayne and Maggie waited and listened but there were no strains of music, not even faint ones. After another few seconds Maggie went to find Symon.

Now all alone Jayne closed the door again. She concentrated on her father's image and felt a chill pass over her body, like the day when she found Leyla's diaries in the cupboard and the tax demands in the brown suitcase. She'd put it down to the open window on that occasion, but now that window had been replaced by the French doors and they

309

were firmly closed. The atmosphere was eerie but the others came back chattering, full of the plans for the old house and opened the door. They stopped when they saw Jayne standing perfectly still in the moonlight.

'Ssh,' whispered Maggie, pointing to Jayne.

After a few seconds Paul moved slowly towards Jayne and held her hand. The others followed. They all stood together in a ring and instinctively held hands. But after another fifteen minutes Paul said, 'Call me if anything happens. If you hear anything I'll be down the cellar.'

It wasn't long before Maggie was bored and went to join Paul. 'I won't be long.'

Jayne and Symon now stood together but it was still disappointingly quiet.

'Do you think it's because we're all here?' asked Jayne.

'Why should that make any difference? I know what I heard when I was up in the loft.'

'And me, when I was here on my own.'

They looked at each other.

'It's the Ys!' said Jayne.

Symon frowned, 'What the hell are you talking about?'

'Think about it – you, me, Leyla, Mum and Dad all have a Y in our names. Paul and Maggie...' she shook her head.

Symon's eyebrows shot up, 'I think you might be onto something. But what does that prove? '

Jayne didn't want the others to hear what she had just discovered. She whispered, 'I don't know yet, but I think we ought to come back, just you and me.'

At that moment Maggie and Paul came bounding into the room like a couple of children, chattering about Paul's plans for the surf school.

'Paul's been showing me what he's doing with the basement,' said Maggie, 'It's going to be fab...' She suddenly stopped when she saw Jayne and Symon's faces. 'You heard something, didn't you?'

Jayne shook her head, 'No, nothing.'

Maggie looked from one to the other, 'You sure?'

'Nope,' said Symon, 'all very disappointing.'

'Oh never mind. It was worth a try,' said Maggie.

Jayne didn't want to be the one to tell Maggie and Paul of her conclusion. She didn't think they would take too kindly to being excluded. She would have to mention it, of course, but standing here in *Seawinds* tonight it really didn't feel right. Even so, she wondered if her analysis would eventually be proved and if so, what did it mean?

TWENTY FOUR

Symon and Maggie reluctantly said their goodbyes to Jayne and Paul and then to Jack, thanking him for being the perfect host.

'It's been a pleasure. Take care.'

They bundled their luggage into the Mercedes and the car purred up the road. As they drove high along the coast road Maggie looked down on the bay basking in anticipation of another busy day. 'I'll miss all this. Shame we have to leave. It's strange but I don't think of Blackheath as home any more, do you darling?'

'I suppose it's because we've been here so long. I never thought I'd say this but I'm really looking forward to retiring, having the business sewn up, sell my share. Jason or Gordon can fight over it if they like. They're both more than capable.'

'Fantastic! Oh, darling it'll be wonderful. I can't wait. '

'Well, I for one have never felt so alive. I'll certainly miss that when we're back in Blackheath.'

They stopped at motorway services a couple of times and Maggie realised the journey was getting to her more than it used to. Even a strong coffee didn't have the desired effect. Symon took over to give her a break but she didn't complain. She felt curiously bereft. It was as if the bay was a child begging her not to leave him at the school gate on his first morning.

A mountain of mail greeted them as they opened the front door of their house. Maggie scooped it up from the doormat and put it on the hall table. The light on the answerphone was flashing too. She sighed. She'd attend to it all later.

She kicked off her shoes and went through to the kitchen diner. There was a layer of dust over everything and she silently rebuked her cleaner for taking advantage of her absence. Symon went to the wine store and pulled out a bottle of red, came into the kitchen and took two glasses out of the cupboard. 'Here we are, my love. First things first. We can tackle all the mail and messages in the morning.'

But there was a nagging urgency in Maggie's mind. 'I really ought to listen to some of them. They might be important.'

Symon smiled. His wife was nothing but efficient.

Maggie took her glass of wine to the phone. The last message was from Leyla saying she hadn't been able to reach Jayne, and could Maggie ring her? She made a note to ring Leyla and listened to the others. Some were from Symon's office, people who wanted a meeting with him and another one telling him his gym membership had expired.

She padded back to the kitchen and told Symon briefly about the messages.

'Like I said, we can tackle it all tomorrow. Come here.' He pulled Maggie onto his knee and kissed her. But he was feeling too tired to take it any further.

The next day Jayne sat cross-legged on the beach staring up at *Seawind*s. Symon had suggested making the house symmetrical and Jayne was still wondering if it had been the right thing to do. The wide French windows on both sides of the house and the decked area, which ran the full width of the house, had a blue glass balcony reflecting the light. But to Jayne the house looked unhappy with its makeover. She concluded that it would look much better once the scaffolding was removed but there was still a nagging doubt at the back of her mind. She sat a while longer staring at the house. Her eyes grew wide when she saw a human shape pass across the window where the dining room had been. She rubbed her eyes and looked again. It wasn't one of the builders. It looked more like her mother's outline. She continued to stare at the window and saw her mother as she was in her younger days. Jayne turned away and back again but the figure had gone. She dismissed it as being 'another one of those things' and turned back to her work. She was busy making sketches of the mural she intended to paint in her father's old room but after another 'sighting' her heart wasn't in it.

Paul came back invigorated from his swim, his toned body dripping wet, and plonked himself next to Jayne on the beach towel. 'How's it going?'

Jayne snatched her work away. 'Hey! Don't drip water all over it!'

'Oh jeez, I'm sorry.'

'You're OK. I think I've cracked it anyway. I've done so many sketches but I think this one is the best.'

Paul leant across to look, drew her hair to one side and kissed her bare sun-kissed shoulder. 'Yeah, I like it. And I think I know where you got your inspiration from.'

She smiled and waited, 'Go on then, clever clogs!'

'Well, for a start they're all the people we love most in the world and for another, it's like the painting of Henry VIII's family as he would've wanted it: Edward, Mary and Elizabeth with his favourite wife Jane Seymour. But of course, Jane

314

Seymour died shortly after giving birth to her son so she wouldn't have been in the picture.'

'Wow! I didn't know you knew about that.'

'I told you, I'm full of surprises!'

'Yes, they originally thought the painting was by Holbein the Younger but it's actually accredited to the British School. I remembered this from my art history.'

Paul, not relishing the thought of talking about those days, lay down and stretched out his long limbs. 'Ah, this is the life.'

Jayne put down her sketch pad and pencil, leaned over and planted a kiss on his lips. 'I know. It's like those intervening years never happened.'

Paul opened one eye. 'Yeah, but we're so much better together than we ever were. We've learned from the past and we've got experience on our side. That's what life's all about. Look at it this way...it's a reward for all our patience.'

'Do you think we ought to put it to the test?'

Paul squinted and shielded his eyes against the sun. 'What d'you mean?'

'I've been thinking. We never leave the bay. I'm wondering if we'd feel the same anywhere else.'

Paul sat up, a pained look on his face.

'Oh, don't look at me like that. I don't mean how we feel about each other,' she pulled him down beside her and planted a big kiss on his lips, 'I mean, we all feel so much younger and full of vitality here at the bay. I just wondered...'

Paul frowned. 'Not sure what you're getting at.'

'Oh, forget it. Forget I said anything. I'm being silly.'

315

'No, come on, you've gotta tell me now.'

'Well, perhaps we should have a couple of days away from the bay, in Cambridge maybe, and see if we feel just as full of vitality there. It's as if we're getting younger here instead of aging.'

'Nothing wrong with that, is there?'

'No of course not but you're missing the point. Recently when I've been anywhere else I feel old and tired. But immediately I'm back here...'

'Yeah, I know what you mean. But why Cambridge?'

'I need to put the house in the hands of a rental company. I can't be bothered with trying to sell it and all the rigmarole of getting rid of the contents. It'll take ages, but I can't just leave it to rot. Daisy doesn't want it and there's no one else. I certainly don't want Rubie living there!'

Paul lay on his back, looking at the sky, and took a while to think about this. He wasn't looking forward to going back to Cambridge. Truth be known, the effect it had on Jayne, he never wanted to see that city again. 'OK. How about this? If you don't need the money you could give it to the university, lock, stock and barrel, for students to rent. That way, you'll be solving your problem and giving something to the community.'

'Paul! You're a genius! Why hadn't I thought of that?'

He smiled smugly, pulled her back down on the beach towel. 'There you go. Now, where were we...'

Maggie stepped out of the gardenia-scented bath and wrapped herself in a soft white bath sheet. The warm water had relaxed her but she felt a little apprehensive about the dinner tonight. It had been a long time since she'd done any entertaining. Being at the bay and eating whatever was on the menu had been a refreshing change and after only two days she was missing Olive's delicious meals and Jack's wonderful wine. Huh, she'd never thought about it before, life was so hectic that she just got on with it, but now she realised what a difference being at the bay had made to her and Symon's wellbeing. With no work commitments and more time for each other, it had been almost like falling in love and getting to know each other all over again.

She began to reflect upon their last meal and the revelation that Olive had come back into Symon and Jayne's lives. There was something rather wonderful about how it had all come about, like one big homecoming, and it gave her a lovely warm feeling.

Padding back to the bedroom, Symon kissed her bare shoulder on his way to the shower. Maggie wished he'd gone in sooner. Time was pressing – Jason and his partner were due to arrive in an hour and there was still some preparation needed. She smiled as she heard Symon turn on the shower and start singing, 'if you were the only girl in the world...'

Now, what to wear? She had grown so used to living in shorts and tee shirts that her elegant clothes didn't have the same appeal anymore. She searched through her wardrobe, expensive designer dresses she doubted she would ever wear again, and found a little black shift. That would be comfy. And instead of tights she would expose her smooth nut-brown legs and instead of crippling heels wear a little pair of silver thong sandals. She examined her reflection in the cheval mirror. Yes! She brushed her now sun-kissed auburn hair back from her face and applied the minimum of make-up. She looked closer at her reflection and discovered a splash of childish freckles across her nose. She hadn't seen those for years.

Symon materialised from the en-suite. 'Mm, you look ravishing. I could eat you!'

'Well you'll just have to wait for dinner. I hope it's alright. I haven't had time to do anything fancy.'

'It'll be wonderful. Don't worry.'

Symon was feeling apprehensive for a different reason. He knew he'd been seriously remiss where Williams Associates was concerned. He'd neglected to answer most of his emails, so engrossed was he in the excitement of remodelling *Seawinds* and retiring to the bay. He was really getting into it. He'd found even more exciting structures to add to the 'old girl', as he referred to *Seawinds*, the last being a sweeping polished stone staircase, each step curved to reflect the waves. It would mean doing away with part of the reception area but it would be well worth it.

The doorbell rang. Maggie skipped downstairs to answer it but pulled a muscle in her thigh. 'Ow!' She rubbed it and put on a brave face and opened the door. Jason was dressed in a suit and tie and his partner looked fit to go to a wedding. Maggie felt seriously underdressed but smiled at them confidently.

'Hello, Jason,' she looked at the woman with long glossy dark hair, 'do come in.'

'This is Katrina,' said Jason.

'Lovely to meet you,' said Maggie.

They stood in the hall looking around. 'Oh my God!' said Katrina, 'what a house! I want something like this one day.'

'Thank you.' Maggie showed them into the spacious lounge with its wall of windows looking onto Blackheath common. 'Symon will be down shortly. Can I get you a drink?'

Katrina's eyes were everywhere. 'Thanks. What've you got?'

Maggie wasn't expecting such a reaction but she ignored it. 'There's beer, wine or juice.' She couldn't be bothered to go into details.

Jason looked a bit put out at Katrina's uncertainty. 'I'd love a beer, thanks Maggie.'

'No problem,' said Maggie. 'Did you have a good journey?'

'Not bad,' said Jason, 'bit of a hold-up on the M25 as usual, but apart from that...'

Maggie thought he looked a bit on edge and wondered why. She waited for Katrina to turn round.

'Oh, er... I'll have glass o' wine. It is white? Nice and cold?'

Maggie smiled. 'It can be. Make yourselves at home.' They sat on the big white sofa facing the granite fireplace that ran the length of the wall while Maggie went to the kitchen to pour the drinks.

Katrina couldn't stop looking at everything. 'Wow! You didn't tell me it was like this.'

Jason nodded. 'Yep, Symon is a great architect, so many innovations. Keeps us all on our toes.'

Symon came down and went to the kitchen, picked up the beer and the wine. 'I'll take those in for you.'

'Thanks, darling. It's fish for the main course; won't take long. I've prepared the sauté potatoes. Salad's easy.'

319

'OK. I'll leave you to it.'

Symon strode into the lounge and handed Jason and Katrina their drinks. He darted a look at Jason. 'So, what's so urgent that you *had* to see me?'

Jason stared at his glass of beer. He didn't want to be the one to deliver the bad news but he'd taken it upon himself and now he was sitting in front of Symon his stomach churned. He took a deep breath. 'It's the Carmell contract.'

'What about it?'

'Looks like they're pulling out.'

'What?'

'Yeah, I've been trying to contact you for weeks, email, phone, you name it. David Sampson is not a happy man.'

'But this is our biggest contract! How the hell...'

Maggie didn't like the sound of the raised voices radiating from the lounge. Symon very rarely got steamed up over work. She absently took out the leek and potato soup and placed it in the microwave, warmed the bread rolls and placed them in a basket with a serviette to cover them. *Presentation is all,* she remembered her supervisor telling her at British Airways. But after the raised voices she was wondering if they'd get as far as the main course.

She poured herself a glass of red wine, swilled it around and took a gulp. She screwed up her nose. *Mm, not as good as Jack's.*

On her way to the lounge Maggie was pulled up short by the scene that confronted her. Symon was pacing the floor. Jason was staring into his empty glass and Katrina looked as if she would rather be somewhere else. 'Is there something wrong?'

'I'm afraid so,' said Symon. 'Carmell have pulled out!'

Maggies eyes were huge. She knew how much this meant to Symon and Williams Associates. It was their biggest US contract. Symon and his partner Gordon had worked hard to acquire it – it was the main reason Symon and Maggie enjoyed such grandeur. 'Oh, my goodness! What happens now?'

'Well, for the moment, we're going to enjoy our evening,' said Symon.

'But...' Jason frowned, 'I thought you'd be more concerned.'

Maggie went to stand next to her husband. 'I think Symon's right – let's enjoy our evening, try and live in the moment. The first course is served.'

Jason and Katrina exchanged worried glances but followed Symon and Maggie into the dining room. They took their places at the elegant table, all shining silver and glass, and began to eat their soup.

Katrina suddenly put down her spoon. 'I'm sorry, but what's in this? I can't eat onions.'

'It's leek and potato,' said Maggie, 'but I've got some paté if you'd prefer?'

'No it's OK. I'm not that hungry.'

Maggie stole a glance at Symon who kept his head down and ate his soup. Jason did the same. Katrina sat staring into her soup bowl. It seemed everything was reinforcing their decision to leave this life behind. Half of Maggie was still at the bay and she couldn't wait to return.

Wanting to relive their first meal at the *Captain Tregenna,* Maggie served the main course of halibut in lemon butter with sauté potatoes and a green salad. But Katrina stared at her plate. 'Oh dear, I am sorry. I don't really eat fish.'

Maggie shook her head and tried not to look put out. 'Would you prefer a beef burger instead?'

'Please, if it's not too much trouble. I'll do it if you like?'

'No, it's OK. It'll only take a jiffy.' Maggie went back to the kitchen, took out a burger from the freezer and shoved it under the grill. She couldn't remember who she had bought them for – she and Symon never ate beef burgers. She only hoped it was still in date.

Back in the sparkling dining room the atmosphere was not matching up. Symon tried to make small talk but smiled with relief when he saw Maggie bring back the burger on a plate with a salad garnish. Katrina gobbled it up.

Jason looked embarrassed. The conversation was stilted and Maggie was becoming increasingly despondent about the whole evening.

The dessert was crème caramel and Maggie swallowed down a sigh of relief when Katrina ate it without comment.

After the meal they all adjourned to the lounge. Feeling the need to be soothed Symon lifted the lid of the shiny black baby grand and sat down to play one of his own compositions. He suddenly had an image of his father playing the boogie-woogie on a Sunday morning when he was in one of his lighter moods.

Jason loosened up and began to tap his feet to the music. 'That's great. My dad used to play. He wanted me to learn but I never took to it.'

Symon nodded but his thoughts flashed to the music on that fateful day when his father died and the music he'd heard recently in *Seawinds*. He couldn't concentrate on the news that Jason had dropped on him this evening. They'd had such a fantastic time recently, cocooned in a happiness bubble, that he'd overlooked his business. And now he wondered how important it really was in the grand scheme of things. He'd made an excellent name for himself but it all seemed rather pointless when he thought about it now. Money wasn't everything. No, he was looking forward to selling his share and kicking back with Maggie, enjoying their remaining years at the bay.

He stopped playing, stood up and said to Jason, 'OK, how would you like to buy my share of Williams Associates?'

Jason's jaw dropped, 'I'm sorry?'

'The business, you dummy. It's either you or Gordon. You can fight over it, if you like.'

Jason looked blank.

'Buy – my – share. I want to retire!'

'What? But...I always thought you'd go on until you dropped. I'm not saying I don't want it but...'

'Yeah, sorry I've left you with all the crap to clear up,' he looked across at Maggie who was smiling, 'but as my good lady wife is always telling me, it's about time we enjoyed life while we still can.'

Katrina looked questioningly from one to the other but no one enlightened her.

'Well, if you really want to offload it...it's just...you've taken the wind out of my sails to be honest.'

'Come off it, man, I know you've had your eye on the prize for some time. I'm just hastening things up a bit.'

Jason blew out a sigh, 'OK. If that's what you really want. I won't say no. I'll get my solicitor on it tomorrow.'

'Good man.' Symon stood up and strode towards the hall. 'I'll be in touch.'

Jason and Katrina looked at each other, stood up and followed Symon who was now standing at the front door. Maggie slipped her arm round Symon's waist and planted a kiss on his cheek.

While Katrina went to sit in the car Symon pulled Jason to one side. 'I suggest you find a woman who can stand by you, someone who can help you further your career, if you know what I mean?' Thinking he'd over-stepped the mark Symon was waiting for the backlash but Jason agreed with him.

'Yeah, sorry about her. My girlfriend's suffering from a chest infection and Katrina from the office agreed to step in.'

'Thank God for that! Well, I wish you all the best. Keep me in informed. I would like to know how my company is faring. Maybe have a word with Gordon, make me President?'

'Sure.'

They shook hands.

Maggie closed the front door and hugged Symon. 'Well, that's that then. End of an era. How d'you feel?'

'Relieved!' he threw his car keys in the air and caught them. 'Let's go.'

'What, now?'

'Yep, no time like the present.'

TWENTY FIVE

Leyla pressed 'send' on her email to her literary agent. She felt smug. She was looking forward to holding a copy of her memoir in her hands but it was a double-edged sword – life was going to seem a bit dull from now on, now she'd finished writing her *magnum opus*. Perhaps she should start another project –there was certainly enough material after the life she'd led. She viewed her life in three separate sections – childhood at *Seawinds*, university and a career in psychiatric medicine, and now life as an author. She knew she had to organise a book launch and wondered where best to hold it. She was suddenly struck by a brilliant idea – she could hold it at the *Captain Tregenna*! Yes, that would tie in nicely seeing as a large proportion of her memoir was based at *Tregenna Bay*. Or she could hold it at *Seawinds* once all the refurbishments were complete. Yes, even better. She smiled, satisfied with her ideas and her achievements. Although, looking back, the one experience that had always eluded her was a happy married life. She pulled the shutters down on the thought and went to put the kettle on.

She scanned her kitchen. How on earth had it got in such a mess? It looked as if an army had been in here while her back was turned. Well that was the first thing she would tackle but not until she'd had her coffee, if she still had some. She hadn't been outside for she didn't know how long and relied on supermarket drops for her shopping. Now she examined the fridge there was very little food left. She'd drunk the last of the ground coffee so she searched in her cupboards and found

325

a jar of instant. She unscrewed the lid and dipped in the teaspoon but it had gone hard. Oh well, it would have to do. She scraped up enough for a mug and set the kettle to boil. It would have to be black – she'd run out of milk. She looked at Heather who had had to make do with some dried cat food retrieved from the back of the pantry.

'Don't worry, sweetness, Mummy will buy you some lovely juicy melts when her boat comes in.' The cat meowed loudly.

Leyla took her mug of coffee through to the dining room and sat at the table. She couldn't remember the last time she'd sat here. She wrote her name in the dust and glanced out at the garden. Hedges and shrubs she had intended to clip and prune were overgrown and dense, closing in and reducing the garden to half its original size. The grass (she could hardly call it a lawn) needed a herd of sheep to reduce it to anything like presentable. It had all got away from her and now the task of taming it felt monumental. She yawned. She had seriously neglected her home and garden of late and she vowed to do something about it before returning to Cornwall. If she had the energy.

She was looking forward to seeing *Seawinds* in all its refurbished glory, staying in one of the newly-created en-suites that Symon had mentioned. God knows she'd earned it. She drank the last of her coffee and went to put the mug in the dishwasher. On her way through to the kitchen she caught sight of her image in the mirror. Blimey! Her hair looked a sight; a big grey stripe of a re-growth in the red. She'd have to make an appointment at *A Cut Above* and soon. She vowed that by the time she arrived at the bay she would look ten years younger and her bungalow and garden would look good enough to go on the market, which wasn't a bad idea now she thought about it. It seemed as if her life here was done.

326

She picked up her house phone intending to ring Jayne. It was dead. No dialling tone. Ah, now she remembered! She rifled through her mountain of post on the kitchen worktop. Yes, there it was. A big red final notice. How had she overlooked something so important? Living alone she knew her phone was her lifeline. She reprimanded herself and picked up her mobile but the battery was flat so she plugged it in to charge. Next, she checked her email inbox. It was rammed full. There were a string of messages from Symon, the last one saying they were expecting her at the bay and could she get in touch. She felt as though she really had slipped through a time warp but was now miraculously delivered back to 2018. Writing her memoir had been a cathartic exercise, reliving all those days, years, but now she was feeling rather remiss for neglecting her house and communications. The first thing she set her mind to was to make a reservation at the *Captain Tregenna* then she made a reservation for the ferry.

***

Two weeks later, after a five hour journey, Leyla pulled into the car park at the back of the *Captain Tregenna*. Jayne's Z4 looked rather neglected, a smattering of seagull droppings across it as if the car hadn't been driven for ages.

Feeling drained Leyla got out of her Land Rover and arched her back, went through to the bar and rang the bell on the counter.

Jack materialised.

'I made a reservation...' began Leyla.

'Ah, if you'd care to sign in I'll give you a hand with your luggage.'

Leyla could tell Jack didn't recognise her but then again, it had been quite a while since she'd stayed here and then it had only been a fleeting visit. She signed in and

327

wondered if he would recognise her name but he seemed oblivious. She did think there might've been a message from Jayne, though. Perhaps Jayne, Symon and Maggie would be waiting for her in the bar. She'd left another message on Jayne's mobile before she left the Isle of Wight but she still hadn't replied. Leyla left her luggage at the bar and walked through to see if the others were there but the whole place was deserted and all the tables were immaculate. When she went back to the bar she noticed her luggage had gone, so had Jack.

On entering her room, she found that her luggage had been placed by the bed but she couldn't face the thought of unpacking, all she wanted was to relax with a cup of decent coffee. She filled the little kettle, stood it on the courtesy tray in front of the bay window and put a sachet of coffee in the white porcelain mug. A purple-grey mist hung over the bay this evening preventing any sight of the beach, but then it was late autumn. She suddenly had a thought – of course! Jack wouldn't have recognised her with her new hair style and she'd signed in with her married name of Watkins.

Change the name and not the letter marry for worse and not for better.

The coffee was very welcome. She savoured each refreshing mouthful and munched on the chocolate biscuits. Feeling the effects of the journey she slipped off her shoes and relaxed on the crisp white duvet although it instantly brought back the unwelcome memory of her wedding night. No matter how hard she pushed the thought away it kept resurfacing.

Leyla had met Josh while she was studying psychiatric medicine at UCL. Convinced she was the least attractive member of her family Leyla marvelled at anyone taking notice of her and couldn't believe her luck when Josh asked her out. She was instantly attracted to his height and his brown curly hair. He was fun to be with and full of confidence. She'd never met anyone like him but there was something she just couldn't put her finger on at first. She assumed she was worrying for nothing, ignored the danger signs and revelled in the attention he lavished on her.

He wanted to abstain from sex until they were married, which, looking back, Leyla realised should have thrown up danger signals. He'd had other girlfriends and played around but he told Leyla she was different, special. She conceived on her wedding night; she knew because she wouldn't let him near her ever again. She fell for his coaxing at first but then he turned into a hungry animal and pushed her back on the bed demanding more. She begged him to stop, she was getting sore, but he kept going until he was exhausted and she was left bleeding. However in the morning he was full of apologies, remonstrating with himself and swore it would never happen again. But Leyla remained wary of his advances and cooked up excuses as to why they couldn't have sex. Pleading she was on her period became overused and he quickly cottoned on. She suffered no amount of imaginary headaches but he became wise to these too. In the end he would try to take her and it would always turn into a battle. But she drew the line when he became violent during her pregnancy and went to stay with a friend.

As time went on the situation became intolerable. Josh became more violent and Leyla feared for her own and the twins' lives. She knew she would have to take drastic measures. She had doctors from the university on her side. She took out a prohibitory injunction against him but he breached it and was finally imprisoned. But he was clever. They released him and he hounded her relentlessly, vowing to take the twins away. She wouldn't want her worst enemy going through what she'd had to endure. She had the locks changed but he came back with an axe one evening. The twins were screaming. She rang the police and they rescued them all in the nick of time. Josh was again imprisoned, this time with a life sentence. She sold her house in London and bought the bungalow on the Isle of Wight and made it doubly secure but she could never totally relax. Josh was currently in Dartmoor prison and she hoped he would stay there for a very long time.

Whilst working as a psychiatric consultant she focused her attention on bringing up Abi and Matt and never stopped looking over her shoulder. Having a schizophrenic father made the twins distrustful; they could never have a serious relationship or children of their own. Instead they turned their attention to looking after disadvantaged children and making a difference in the world. This had taken them to the four corners of the globe and they welcomed each and every challenge with their positivity, love and kindness. Leyla was a very proud but fiercely protective mother. She rarely sang their praises for fear of someone, anyone, informing Josh of their whereabouts. Instead they were hidden in plain sight, among their fellow co-workers, all with the same altruistic work ethic. They kept their heads down and saved their emotions for the impoverished children in their care.

This then, was the reason why Leyla lived alone on the Isle of Wight and double locked all the doors. She had thrown herself into her psychiatric work and tried to help other people, like Josh, before they placed themselves or others in danger, until a few years ago when she retired and embarked on her writing career, cocooned in her own world.

Leyla now looked at the fresh white bed linen and couldn't blot out the memory of the red and white of her wedding night. Every time she cut herself she was reminded of Josh's brutality, and when the twins were little and either of them came home with a gashed knee, the same memory resurfaced.

Now, here in Cornwall, she hoped she'd be able to let go of her fears and regain some freedom. In the short time she'd been here back in April with Jayne, Symon and Maggie she was beginning to feel relaxed and she now hoped she would feel the same again. She was unsure whether to let go of her bungalow on the Isle of Wight. Living at *Seawinds* again would feel very strange after all these years but perhaps it would give her what she needed – a fresh start while enjoying the protection of her family.

Overcome with tiredness Leyla finally turned over and snuggled into the sumptuous white duvet. She would have a little nap before dinner, soothed by the ever-present sound of the waves and the sea breeze wafting in through the window, after which she would feel refreshed and ready for her very welcome evening meal. A nice piece of fish...

On this Sunday afternoon downstairs in the bar, Olive was putting out fresh menus on the tables and writing the specials on the chalk board for the evening, whilst Jack was busy in and out of the bar checking his stock and setting a few bottles of white wine to cool. So engrossed in their endeavours were they that they didn't notice the tall curly-headed man sneak in and disappear through the door in the corner.

Jayne and Symon were at *Seawinds*. They had left Paul giving Maggie a surfing lesson, making it possible for Jayne and Symon to go to the house without having to tell them why or what they were doing.

After a few initial checks to see how the alterations were progressing, Symon met Jayne in the empty front room. They had come to the conclusion that Sunday would be the best time to put her conclusion to the test as the builders were not there and it was also a Sunday when Harry died. They had discussed their unusual experiences, Jayne realising it was only herself and Symon who had heard Harry's music. The others had had other experiences – Paul on the cliff top and Olive seeing Yvonne in the old kitchen – but Jayne knew she and Symon were the ones singled out to hear the music for a particular reason.

Sitting cross-legged on the bare floorboards, facing each other and holding hands, they take deep breaths and close their eyes.

'What image have you got?' asks Jayne.

'Dad at the piano playing the boogie-woogie on a Sunday morning.'

'Ah, yes I remember. That was fun. Mine is him sitting in his armchair, whisky in hand, listening to Beethoven's *Pastoral Symphony*.'

'OK that's calming. Let's go with that and see what happens.'

It's not long before the room temperature drops but neither Jayne nor Symon acknowledge this. They stay stock still. It's another few minutes before a faint sound can be heard, the beautiful melody of the introduction of the *Pastoral Symphony*.

They open their eyes and look at each other, aware that the music is growing louder. Symon squeezes Jayne's hand but neither dare speak in case they break the spell.

The room begins to spin, slowly at first then picks up speed. At the point when Jayne thinks she's going to throw up the room slows and comes to a stop. Jayne is frightened to look around, scared of what she might see. She looks down at her hands resting on her jeans and realises she hasn't changed.

She is still sixty-eight years old but she is sitting on the Axminster carpet, not the floorboards. She glances at Symon's big knees. He is still in his sixties too. Jayne and Symon slowly turn their heads to find the room back to how it was in 1968. Harry's hi-fi sits on a small table next to the fireplace. His armchair is empty.

A sudden blinding flash of white light fills the room. Jayne and Symon cover their eyes and turn their heads away. After a few seconds Jayne slowly peels her hands away from her eyes to see Harry and Yvonne standing side by side in the glow. They look no different from how they did in the 1960s except the worry has left Harry's face. They both look serene and godlike.

The next sound is a familiar voice, one they both know and love.

'Jayne and Symon. Welcome. Your mother and I are so very happy to see you.'

'But this can't be happening,' says Symon, flustered. 'They must be a mirage or, I don't know, a figment of our imagination or something.' He shuts his eyes tight and opens them again but his parents are still there smiling at him.

'Please, do not worry,' says Harry. 'We come in love. Everything will become clear in a little while.'

Yvonne and Harry look lovingly at each other.

'When your mother and I first came to stay at the bay in 1946, we knew it was our spiritual home. Consequently we were very concerned when you were going to sell our beloved *Seawinds* and we tried all in our power to change your minds.'

Overcome with emotion neither Jayne nor Symon can speak. Tears run unchecked down Jayne's cheeks. She hangs on to Symon's hand.

333

Yvonne turns to Jayne. 'I'm so glad you have decided to keep *Seawinds,* my love. It hasn't been easy for you. Being the eldest you assumed the decision lay with you but you did the right thing in convincing Symon and Leyla not to sell our beloved house, to keep it in the family. I would like to take this opportunity to say how very sorry I am about my actions that led in part to you and Paul Smythe being kept apart for so many years. I'm glad it has all been resolved. Your life hasn't been easy living with Michael, a very self-centred man, but at last you have your reward. Make the most of your time together here at the bay.'

Jayne, still unable to utter a word, sits stock still. Her heart is full.

Symon is stunned. He can't believe what he's witnessing.

Yvonne's smile is radiant as she turns to him. 'And Symon, we're very proud of what you have achieved and we're glad you found happiness with Maggie. We're pleased you have now both fallen in love with *Seawinds* and with the bay. We need all three of you, Jayne Symon and Leyla to be the guardians of our spiritual home.'

'But...' starts Jayne.

'Please do not worry about Leyla,' says Harry, 'she will come home in the end.' He moves to one side. 'Now, let us commence. I have something to show you, something you have been longing to know for a very long time.' He gestures to the blank white wall.

A picture begins to emerge. It's like watching an old film on a big screen. In the first scene Ken Smythe is looking out of the window in the family room at *Seawinds* watching a retreating coach. When it's gone he puts on his coat and hat and runs downstairs, out of the house and makes his way towards the cliff path. The bay is deserted. The wind is gusting and he holds onto his hat as he climbs the uneven steps. His coat flaps violently and his trousers blow flat against his legs as he climbs higher along the narrow pebbly path which winds its way up through the furze and scrub to the top of the cliff. He stops to take a rest, turns round to see *Seawinds* looking grim in the grey light and his hat is taken by the wind. Further up on the cliff he spots Harry standing at his favourite vantage point looking down on the wild waves crashing and rolling into shore. Harry is wearing his cavalry twill trousers, a warm shirt and a cardigan but no coat. His hair is whipping across his eyes unchecked.

Ken calls out to him but his voice is lost on the wind. He battles against the gale as he moves closer. He looks as if he might turn back, his face contorted against the bitter wind but then he sees Harry move closer to the cliff edge.

Ken calls again, 'Harry!' and grabs a branch of furze on the bank. He briefly loses his footing and watches a stone skitter over the edge. But Harry stays in the same position, hands in his pockets, seemingly oblivious.

'Harry! What on earth are you doing up here in this weather? This is madness.'

Harry ignores him and remains looking down on the bay.

'Look, come on. I'm sorry about last night. Come down and we'll go for a drink, talk about it. No one will ever know, just the two of us.'

But Harry inches away from Ken and looks down at the dark jagged cliffs jutting out below. The waves are angry.

'Harry, for God's sake don't do anything silly. It's not worth it.' Ken extends a hand to pull Harry back from the edge but Harry shrugs him off and the crumbly cliff edge he's

335

standing on breaks away from under his feet. Ken makes a grab for Harry but watches in horror as he falls over the edge. Harry's shout is lost on the wind as he plummets below. Ken keeps holding onto the branch and tries to look down to see where Harry has landed, but the wind is too strong and he is beaten back. He leans against the muddy bank and grabs at the scrub and the furze, his coat and trousers still flapping in the wind. He finds a safer, flatter place to stand and rubs a hand over his face. It looks as if he's momentarily frozen to the spot then he stumbles all the way back down the dirt path the way he has come. At the bottom he lurches along the sea front, turns and looks across the bay to where Harry is lying. A hand goes to his mouth as if he's going to be sick.

The camera pans to a man walking his dog. He stops abruptly when he sees Harry sprawled out on the rocks, runs to the telephone box and ties his dog up outside.

In the next scene Ken walks into in an old pub at the opposite end of the sea front, rakes a hand through his hair and orders a double brandy. He downs it in one, orders another. He doesn't talk to anyone but stands looking out the window. When the coach arrives he goes to meet it.

The passengers alight and Katie jumps down in front of her father, followed by Lottie and Paul.

'Hello, love,' says Lottie, 'I thought you'd still be lying down. How's your head?'

'Better,' says Ken. 'I went for a walk then came to meet you. How was it?'

Lottie begins to give Ken a run-down of their afternoon but he isn't listening. He looks across the bay and sees the back of the ambulance retreating up the hill.

The picture slowly fades until there remains only the blank white wall.

336

The room spins again whilst Jayne and Symon hold onto each other. When the room stops it is empty once more and they are back in present time, sitting on the floorboards.

Jayne, unaware that she has been holding her breath blows it out. She looks at Symon. He stares at her. 'I can't believe what just happened.'

'Me neither.'

'Were we dreaming?'

Jayne shakes her head, wipes her eyes and nose, 'I don't think so. It felt too real.'

'Then what was it?' Symon looks thoughtful, 'So, if Ken hadn't gone up there do you think Dad would've survived?'

'Who knows? But at least we now know it was an accident. Poor Ken, he must've lived with that for the rest of his life.'

'Yeah, it'll be good to let Paul know what actually happened.'

'But how are we going to tell Maggie and Paul about our experience? They'll never believe us.'

'I can't quite believe it myself. I think we'll have to play it by ear.'

On their walk back to the *Captain Tregenna* they spot Paul and Maggie walking up from the beach with their surf boards, the sun casting long shadows across the bay.

Jayne is still reeling from both her parents' messages and the love that radiated from them. 'I think it's quite comforting to know Mum and Dad are still at *Seawinds*. Do you think that'll always be the case or do you think they just came to tell us what happened and to put our minds at rest?'

337

'Well, put it this way, I'm not spooked by it. And if their spirits want to dwell in the house with us who are we to argue? Like they said, it's their spiritual home, ours too.'

Jayne beamed and threw her arms round him. 'Oh Symon, I'm so pleased. We've done the right thing.'

Three hours later after a busy evening in the bar, Jack noticed the open visitors' book on the counter. It had been turned round and pushed to one side. Strange, he hadn't noticed before. Maybe Olive had been looking to see how many visitors had booked in. He thought no more about it, put it back in its usual place and wondered when his latest guest would materialise for dinner. Maybe she'd gone into Padstow or Newquay for her evening meal but he doubted it.

TWENTY SIX

Leyla stood at the window in the bedroom of the *Captain Tregenna*. The mist of yesterday had lifted although the grey clouds were still hanging in layers over the bay. As she watched, the sun pierced through highlighting the cliff top where her father had fallen to his death all those years ago. But what was that? It looked like two men, one trying to pull the other away from the edge. She rubbed her eyes and looked again but they had vanished. She was either going mad or she needed to start looking after herself and get some proper food inside her. But she was thankful she'd had an unbroken sleep, for once. Most nights lately she had awoken two or three times with something nagging at her; trying to rewrite a paragraph or phrase or the conclusion to her memoir, or trying to find the right title. But that was all behind her now. Her book was with the publisher and she couldn't wait for her book launch and signing copies of *Life at Seawinds*. It was going to be a great success – all those holidaymakers and visitors would mean plenty of sales. She was planning to display posters all along the sea front and in the pub, there would be champagne and party food enticing people in. She took out her notepad to complete her plans.

She looked at her diary. She needed to write yesterday's entry but her short term memory was failing her. She remembered locking her front door and getting into her Land Rover, stopping at the services and arriving at the bay. After that it was all a blur.

339

Sitting at the dressing table she began to wonder how far they'd got with restoring *Seawinds* or even if it was finished. Symon had had big plans for the old house and knowing him, it would be a state-of-the-art transformation. She also wondered if Maggie had got her way and persuaded him to retire. It would be great if she could be with Jayne, Symon and Maggie for the grand opening and even better if it coincided with her book launch! She was looking forward to showing them her memoir and seeing their surprise. And then there would be Christmas...

And what would her mum and dad have thought of her achievements and all this modernisation of their modest little guest house on the hill? It would look totally different from how she described it in her memoir.

The bar in the *Captain Tregenna* looked somehow sad in the cold light of day, Leyla decided, but Jack kept it immaculately clean, not a bottle or a glass out of place and no sticky rings on the counter or the tables.

Taking a stroll around the bay to work up an appetite before breakfast, she noticed the beach was packed with families all enjoying themselves but no one spoke to her.

Glancing up at *Seawinds* she smiled at the sight of the French doors and the pale blue glass balcony on the first floor that stretched the width of the house. Very posh! *Seawinds* also had a new roof but apart from that it didn't look a whole lot different from the last time she saw it.

When she arrived at *Seawinds* the front door, still dark blue, was ajar. She entered and looked around. She couldn't believe it. Apart from the downstairs being opened up, she assumed, to make way for the reception area nothing had been touched since the last time she set foot in here.

Maybe some of the other rooms have been done.

340

But after examining every room it was obvious the refurbishment had come to a standstill. The kitchen was a blank canvas and so was the back parlour.

She heard a door slam somewhere upstairs and went to investigate. 'Jayne! You up there?' No answer. She searched all the bedrooms, still at the plastering stage, and came down again.

Suddenly a faint echo of *The Blue Danube* began playing. But where was it coming from? The door to the cellar was open. She ventured down the steps but the music faded when she reached the bottom. There was evidence of some improvement down there: all the walls painted white, a new floor and the rooms had been kitted out with shelves.

Standing in the front room a heavy eerie feeling engulfed her. She shuddered and told herself to stop being ridiculous; there must be a perfectly valid explanation for all this. The music had begun again but it was very faint, coming and going in waves as if carried on the wind. It must be her memory, something lodged in her psyche, she told herself. All of a sudden she felt as if she were being pulled by an unknown force through a kind of clear watery screen. Horrified she pulled herself free and shifted to the other side of the room.

She told herself to get a grip, she was imagining it – she just needed more sleep. In the porch she tried to close the door behind her but she couldn't hold or turn the doorknob. What was going on?

TWENTY SEVEN

Daisy cradles the baby in her arms. It has been a difficult delivery; he is very small but perfectly formed. Daisy puts it all behind her and concentrates on getting them both to Cornwall. As she rounds the bay everything looks so familiar but somehow different from how she remembers it. The scene stretches out before her – the wide bay, the sparkling waves lapping the shore, the steep rocky cliffs that seem to go on forever.

Gladys, who has been waiting for this moment, is instantly beside Daisy guiding her and the baby through a watery screen and into the front room at *Seawinds*. Daisy does not resist. Gladys disappears back the way she has come and reappears with Leyla who finally accepts her situation. She shrugs off Gladys's hand and stumbles into the room.

To the sound of the *Blue Danube*, a blinding flash lights up the room and Harry and Yvonne slowly appear as it fades. They come towards Daisy who is standing back.

'Daisy. How lovely to meet you,' says Harry.

Daisy's face glows with happiness. 'Hello Granddad. It's wonderful to meet you too.'

'Dear Daisy,' begins Yvonne, 'this transition has been traumatic for you but now you are in the company of our spiritual family until the time is right for Tim to join you. But this is a long way off in the future. Don't worry about him – he will have a happy life and your surviving children will all be very successful.'

A latecomer, a boy child, steps forward from the clear screen looking very bewildered. He is a younger version of Paul Smythe. Yvonne nods and welcomes him into the fold.

Standing back in the shadows is a short plump figure wearing an apron and her hair in a bun. Satisfied, Myriam Crago nods and smiles as she looks on.

END

Printed in Great Britain
by Amazon

12699703R00202